MW00624880

This Cursed House

This Cursed House

DEL SANDEEN

BERKLEY
NEW YORK

BERKLEY
An imprint of Penguin Random House LLC
penguinrandomhouse.com

Library of Congress Cataloging-in-Publication Data

Names: Sandeen, Del, author.
Title: This cursed house / Del Sandeen.
Description: New York : Berkley, 2024.
Identifiers: LCCN 2024000766 (print) | LCCN 2024000767 (ebook) |
ISBN 9780593639528 (hardback) | ISBN 9780593639535 (ebook)
Subjects: LCGFT: Gothic fiction. | Novels.
Classification: LCC PS3619.A5238 T48 2024 (print) |
LCC PS3619.A5238 (ebook) | DDC 813/.6--dc23/eng/20240112
LC record available at https://lccn.loc.gov/2024000766
LC ebook record available at https://lccn.loc.gov/2024000767

Printed in the United States of America
$PrintCode

Book design by George Towne

Dedicated to the memory of:

Henrietta Louise Grant Roberson, the Angel

and

David Edward Roberson Sr., the Storyteller

This Cursed House

ONE

OUT OF THE corner of Jemma Barker's eye, the woman flickered, a shadow of light shimmering at the edges of her vision.

Don't look at 'em, Jemma. That was Mama's voice.

Ain't nothing but the devil's work if you look. And that was Daddy's.

Taking a slow breath (*five, four, three, two, and one* on the exhale), shakier than usual due to the train's rattling, Jemma stared into her light-wool-skirted lap, where twisting fingers worked wrinkles into a white handkerchief. When she glanced over at the empty seat next to her, the woman was gone.

Jemma smoothed the handkerchief, then her already smooth skirt, then her bobbed hair, the hot-combed bangs fluffing in the Southern heat, humidity intent on disarray. The man who'd sat in that seat, who'd boarded with her when she'd left Chicago two days ago, had gotten off somewhere in southern Missouri, right when one of the white-jacketed porters had hung a COLORED sign in their car. The sign wasn't necessary, as only Black passengers inhabited the car anyway. No white folks would sit in this space, without a luggage rack but with a flattened mouse in one corner.

No one—no living person, anyhow—had sat in the seat since.

The car had steadily emptied as they traveled south. Jemma opened her black patent leather handbag and pulled out an envelope. She'd read the letter inside dozens of times, but she wanted to see it again, to make sure it was real. It was dated less than a week after Marilyn Monroe had died, and even now, the papers were still making much of the actress's death.

The letter read:

August 10, 1962

Dear Miss Jemma Barker,

I am writing to offer you a position with the Duchon family in New Orleans, Louisiana. The Duchons are a prominent family in the city and believe you have the qualities we are seeking. You would have free room and board and be expected to live on the property. The pay is $300 per week. This is nonnegotiable. You must call by August 31 should you wish to accept.

Sincerely,
Honorine Duchon

Of all the details in the letter, Jemma stared at the three-hundred-dollar weekly pay the most. It was more than three times what she'd earned as a teacher in Chicago, before everything had fallen apart. So she had called Honorine Duchon one afternoon in mid-August, a few weeks ago.

"Next stop, New Orleans. New Orleans, next stop!" a porter announced, strolling down the wood-floor aisles. He stopped next to a dozing woman and touched her shoulder, making sure she woke up in time. She, like Jemma, had a single square suitcase between her feet. Jemma put the letter away and smoothed her hair again before slipping white gloves onto her hands and a pillbox hat onto her head.

Half an hour later, she joined a line of passengers who shared her color, disembarking after the white ones had already gotten off. Jemma stood for a minute on the concrete, purse in one hand, suitcase hanging from the other, the clean, modern lines of the Union Passenger Terminal looming ahead of her.

The heat was a womb. She'd thought summers in Chicago were bad, but nothing had prepared her for this.

A white man in stovepipe slacks and a fedora jostled her as he hurried past, and then he turned back, perhaps to excuse himself. The beginnings of a frown set between Jemma's brows, and chiding words formed behind her lips. Before she could say anything, however, his expression upon seeing a lone Black woman in last season's jacket and skirt, the indifference that dulled his eyes, reminded her that she wasn't in Chicago. She remembered the COLORED sign hanging in the train car as she pressed her lips together, watching the man continue to his destination, the encounter probably already seeping from his mind even as it brought a flush to her burning skin. The man's hurriedness was familiar to her, something that, along with his rudeness, reminded her of home. But when she took in the rest of the place, she was reminded of the differentness.

Early September in Chicago was a wave of cool weather, wool jackets and scarves at the ready. It was unpacking heavy sweaters, thermals and mittens. Gray skies and biting winds settled in for a long haul, and the taste of snow was always in the air.

So Jemma's attire was completely out of place. Women of all colors swirled around in silks and linens (linens!), cottons and organdies. The tones were suitable for fall—light gray, sky blue, deep pink, cream—but she was the only one in navy blue anything. And very few of the women she saw were wearing gloves. Moisture sprouted in her armpits, and not only from the heat. She removed her gloves and tucked them into her purse.

"Get you a cab, miss?"

Jemma looked to her right, where a porter smiled at her.

"No, thank you," she said. "But can you tell me where I can get some coffee?"

"Best for you to bypass the French Quarter. They're still boycotting over there on Canal, and you don't want to get mixed up in that. Make your way to this neighborhood called Tremé. You can catch the bus over there."

"Boycotting?"

He cocked his head. "Yeah. They don't want to hire none of us to work on Dryades 'less we're sweeping out the back room or scrubbing the toilets. We can't eat nowhere on Canal. So it's been some sit-ins and little marches and things."

A smile tugged at Jemma's lips. Although not immune to the oftentimes inexplicable whims of white people in Chicago who didn't want Black people to experience full citizenhood, she'd had more freedom there than the folks who lived across the South. And they were fighting back. Good.

"Can you give me directions to Tremé if I'm walking?"

"It'll take you a minute."

"I got time."

He gave her careful directions. Jemma pressed her handkerchief, now bearing blotches of brown powder, to her face and thanked him as she set off, the handle of the suitcase slick in her hand. Rivers of sweat ran freely down her body, and her legs itched in the thick stockings. Cobblestone streets stretched in every direction. There were no skyscrapers or tall housing-project buildings here, only walls of balconied structures and wrought iron railings. Jemma passed yellow, blue and pink stone buildings, with ivy and flowers trailing down from second floors or growing up brick sides like delicate fingers. The smells of soft bread, strong coffee, sweet pastries and thick roux filled the air, a jumble of scents that pulled Jemma's tongue between her lips. She'd eaten nothing since lunch the day before, the last of the roast beef sandwiches she'd packed, as there were no colored dining cars or other places where they were allowed to eat once they'd reached Tennessee. Glancing through the restaurant windows, she saw only white patrons.

As she navigated her way north, the smell of the Mississippi River gradually faded, although not completely. Colorful buildings and storefronts gave way to row houses. On Rampart Street, she turned down an alleyway, her feet in the black heels seeming to grow blisters against the cobblestones with every step. Jemma stopped and leaned against the brick wall between two nondescript buildings, setting her suitcase down and mopping her face again. All her powder had been wiped clean off, the remnants of her carefully made-up face soiling the handkerchief. She glanced around, now sure she was in the wrong alleyway. The porter had told her of a café down a specific backstreet but had also cautioned her, *Stay away from dark alleys where you don't see nobody else.* She'd wanted to remind him that it was morning, but something in his face kept the words inside. As she slipped one foot out of her shoe and rubbed her toes, a door in the building in front of her opened. Jemma tensed at the sight of the light man in a chef's apron until she took in the crinkled hair, the almost imperceptible wideness in his nose.

"You lost?" he asked her after tossing dirty dishwater out of a huge pot into a nearby grate. Hazel eyes appraised her, lingering over her heavy clothing before coming back to her face.

"I'm looking for Lulu's Café."

"Next alleyway over," he said, jerking his chin to the right. "There's no sign, but you'll see a window with some dolls inside."

Jemma had wanted to rest for a few minutes, maybe even cool off before moving on, but she felt like an intruder here, where the man now pulled a rolled cigarette from his apron pocket and lit it with a match. He didn't offer her one. Clouds of smoke obscured his face, but she felt his eyes on her.

She put her shoe back on, hitched up her suitcase and moved on to the next alley, finding the bright blue–painted café by the collection of brown-skinned dolls sitting inside the window, just as the cook had said. Jemma passed two yellow wrought iron table-and-chair sets as she walked inside, the coolness of the dim space so welcoming she shut her eyes, wanting only to breathe it in for a while. Ceiling fans turned overhead, spreading delicious smells around the room, all hot coffee, pralines, beignets and roux.

"Ooh, baby, I know you burning up." A woman's voice brought Jemma back. She found herself looking into the deep brown face and eyes of a middle-aged woman in a light blue dress and with a white apron around her waist. "Come on in here and sit down."

Jemma happily obeyed, taking a spot in a stiff-backed chair by the window. The table was small, made for two, and as Jemma took in her surroundings, she spied nothing but Black patrons at half a dozen tables, hunched over white cups of coffee or plates of bread and sausage.

"You want some chicory, honey?"

"I'm sorry—what?"

The woman smiled down at her. "It's a coffee. I'll get you one."

Before Jemma could protest, the woman walked off and disappeared through a set of swinging doors that led to the kitchen. Jemma opened her handbag and pulled out her coin purse, the peeling red leather petal-soft beneath her fingers. Snapping it open, she made sure she still had five wrinkled singles, along with a small handful of change. A chalkboard hanging on one wall advertised everything from chicory café au lait, pain perdu, beignets, croissants and calas to gumbo, crawfish etouffee, red beans and rice and croque monsieur. Jemma didn't recognize all the words, but the mix of sweet and spicy smells floating through the air reminded her how hungry she was.

"This is on the house." The woman, her head tilted as she looked down at her, slid a cup of coffee in front of Jemma. "Are you visiting?"

"No. I just moved here. I'm working for the Duchon family." Jemma pronounced it *Du-chun*, emphasis on the first syllable, unable to keep the breathy pride out of her voice. The woman stared at her for a moment before a look of recognition washed over her face.

"Oh, the Doo-*chone* family," she enunciated, the soft smile shrinking away. Her back straightened, all the friendly intimacy of their conversation disappearing along with the grandmotherly tone. "You want something to eat?"

Jemma's mouth worked *(What just happened here?)*, but after a moment, she asked for grits and eggs, knowing the breakfast cost just forty cents. She sipped her coffee, and before long, the woman returned, sliding a plate loaded with grits, eggs and toast onto the table. Alongside it, she placed a small plate with a couple of sugary confections.

"Oh, I didn't ask for—" Jemma started.

"It's on me, baby. You're new to New Orleans. You got to try Lulu's beignets." She turned to go but stopped and looked at Jemma again, the softness back in her eyes. "You're working for the Duchons, you say?"

"Yes. I was going to ask how to get to the . . . plantation." That's what Honorine had called the property when Jemma had talked to her a few weeks ago.

"It's not in the parish proper—it's out toward Metairie. You can take the bus, but it's going to let you off before you get there. Cab'll take you straight through, but it'll cost."

"I can take the bus. If I have to walk a ways, that's okay."

Lulu glanced away for a second before turning back, her deep brown eyes full of something disquieting Jemma couldn't quite place.

"Miss, it's not my business, but if I was you, I'd go the other way. Get back on the train or bus or whatever you came here on and go back to where you from."

"I . . . I have a job with the Duchons. They hired me to be a . . . tutor."

"Like I said, it's not my business." She left Jemma to eat in peace.

She had been so hungry, but what Lulu said dampened her appetite. Still, she had a bus ride and a walk ahead of her, so Jemma ate. The food was delicious, especially the sweet and flaky beignets, their powdered-sugar coating drifting down on the plate and her lap.

Afterward, Jemma found the bus she needed and settled herself in the back. White passengers filled the front, and a couple of Black men stood when Jemma and another woman boarded. The woman sat next to her, looking very cool in a striped dress, the skirt full and belted, her hair short and teased high at the crown, bangs swept to one side. Despite the heat, Jemma had put her gloves back on. She tugged the cuff over her right wrist, hiding the scar beneath, the skin raised and riverlike, evidence of an unsure hand. Hot air and dust blew in through the open windows, and with each hard stop Jemma's feet tightened on the sides of the suitcase so that it wouldn't slide away.

Just before noon, she disembarked at the last stop, a two-mile trek ahead of her, according to her seatmate on the bus. Jemma's feet ached, her body felt wrung out and the breakfast she'd eaten had shriveled into a hard knot in her stomach. If she'd had the money, she would've taken a cab then and there. She folded her jacket and placed it inside her suitcase, wiping her forehead with the back of her ungloved hand. Although there was no breeze, just having her arms out in the short-sleeved blouse was a relief.

She'd walked about a quarter mile when she heard someone call behind her. She turned to see a brown-skinned man driving a one-horse wagon, the wooden bed filled with hay.

"You need a lift?" he asked.

Jemma quickly dismissed her disorientation at seeing a horse-drawn wagon in this day and age, reminding herself once again that she'd left a big city far behind.

"I'm going to the Duchon plantation. Is that on your way?"

"It is." Something in the careful way he said it made Jemma think of Lulu back at the café. "Swing that case in the back. I'll help you up."

The man's name was Charlie, he told her, as she nestled on the bench seat next to him. The sleeves of his dress shirt were rolled up his arms, suspenders hanging off, sweat stains bleeding through the T-shirt he wore underneath. His planter's hat was pushed back on his head. Once he'd made sure Jemma was settled, he snapped the reins, and the bay horse moved its slow way down the dirt road.

"What you walking to the Duchons' for?"

"The bus line stopped back there. It's only a couple miles."

"More like almost four." His sidelong glance raked over her in seconds. "You woulda melted out here before you made it."

"I'm extra thankful for the ride, then."

They passed patchy woods and a long stretch of pasture, as well as the occasional towering oak tree, Spanish moss trailing from branches and brushing the ground like spiderwebs, the shade they cast a welcome gift. At Charlie's prompting, Jemma had told him she was from Chicago and was here to work for the family.

"A tutor? For who?"

Jemma almost said she would be a tutor for their child, but no one had actually told her whom she'd be tutoring. In fact, no one had said she was hired to be a tutor.

Ever since she'd gotten the letter, she'd assumed the Duchons knew she'd taught fourth grade, further assuming they must have a child around that age. When she'd called Honorine to accept the position, she hadn't asked many questions. The money had dazzled her. She'd been scared that if she asked too much, the woman with the clipped voice would change her mind about her, renege on the offer.

"Their child," she answered now, frowning.

Charlie looked at her for a brief moment. "Well, maybe something's changed out there."

"Do you know the family well?"

"No. They keep to themselves."

He didn't seem to want to talk much after that. He leaned forward, and something in the way he hitched his shoulders and whistled under his breath shut Jemma out.

A cream-colored Buick Roadmaster swerved around them, white-walled tires spinning up dust that hung in its wake. After a while, she concentrated on the dirt lane and the wooden fence running alongside it. Her world became the dappled light poking through the trees, and the horse in front of her, the soft clop of its hooves and its animal scent pushing the ghost woman on the train out of Jemma's mind.

"This is as far as I go," Charlie said.

They were stopped in front of a wrought iron gate, a huge expanse of lawn behind it. Well behind the gate was a white antebellum house, four pillars standing tall across the front, straight like soldiers. Black shutters framed the large windows, two on either side of the black doors on the first floor, and six spanning the second. A wide porch ran along the first floor, enclosed by a white railing. Oak trees lined the pathway up to the house, and more trees hugged the building, keeping it in shade.

Jemma climbed down and retrieved her suitcase. She opened her handbag, but before she could pull out her coin purse or thank Charlie for the ride, he snapped the reins, sending his horse on a quick trot down the road, dust swirling up in Jemma's face.

She stared after him for a moment, spitting out sand. Picking up her suitcase, she pushed the gate, which opened with a creak. As she drew closer to the house, she noticed details not visible from the road. The white wasn't as pristine as it had appeared from a distance. A light coat of dirt, like settled neglect, tarnished it some, as did the weeds sprouting between porch boards. A large number of tiles on the gabled roof were loosened, their edges not lying flat on their neighbors but curled up like snarling lips. A huge dogwood tree to the left of the lane should have been in bloom in this climate, but pink petals littered the grass below it, leaving most of the branches bare, reaching into the air like crooked and clutching fingers.

Jemma slipped her gloves back on, and at the front door she hesitated before touching the dull knocker in the shape of a grotesque head. She turned to look over her shoulder at the iron gate, still open, as if waiting for her to run back through it.

Instead, she lifted the knocker and banged it against the door.

TWO

IN THE BRIEF second between the door opening a crack and widening further to reveal a woman, an unshaped wisp flitted by, escaping the house and whipping around Jemma before disappearing in the air. She shut her eyes, breathed deeply and then focused on who'd opened the door.

A maid stood there, her black dress and white apron announcing her station. Her slick hair was divided down the center of her scalp with a pin-straight part, a bun sitting at the nape of her neck. Hazel eyes shined out of her bright face.

"Hello," Jemma said. "I'm Jemma Barker, the tutor."

The maid stared at her, neither extending a hand nor opening the door any wider and stepping aside. Her light eyes barely moved, and yet it seemed they took in all of Jemma, from the sweat lines that had disintegrated her carefully applied powder (the little that was left on her face instead of on her handkerchief) to her heat-frizzed hair to the wool suit. Compared to the Duchons' maid, who looked to be in her early forties, Jemma's shabbiness all but crowed.

"Agnes!" came a voice from inside the home. "Are you going to let our visitor in or are you going to stand there all day? Either let her in or shut the door. The last thing we need in here is more flies."

The door opened just enough for Jemma to squeeze inside, her suitcase bumping the frame. In the next moment, another woman approached, swathed in deep pink silk all the way to the floor, heels clicking and right hand out.

"Honorine Duchon. We spoke on the phone," she said, shaking Jemma's hand.

Now Jemma had a face to match the voice. She took the woman to be in her seventies. Her eyes were dark green, and beneath a heavy dusting of white powder, freckles dotted her cheeks. Thinning silver hair was pulled into a French roll. She stood only a couple of inches taller than Jemma's five foot three, but the woman's erect posture suggested much more stature.

"Ah, Miss Barker, you've finally arrived. The heat doesn't seem to have agreed with you." A gentle chuckle at the end did nothing to lessen the sting.

A warmth unconnected with the climate flushed Jemma's cheeks as she wondered how poor she must look. Before she could even think of a reply, the woman continued.

"Not like our ancestors in Africa, hmm?"

Jemma blinked. *Our* ancestors in Africa?

A high voice carried into the room. "Oh, you must excuse Grandmère! She forgets herself sometimes." And a younger woman swept into the foyer, just as pale as Honorine but with black hair trailing in loose waves down her back. "Here you are, only just arrived, and she's already started in on Africa, as if we've forgotten we're all colored. You must be Jemma Barker. I'm Fosette." She clasped one of Jemma's hands in both her own.

Jemma's mind stumbled over the word "colored." These pale

ghosts of women were Black? The three of them stood almost shoulder to shoulder, even Agnes the maid continuing to stare. Fosette's gray eyes danced. Jemma took her to be about her age, but as she studied her face more closely, just beneath the face powder fine lines tried to hide, as if too ashamed to be seen. Like her grandmother, she dressed in a style that hadn't been in fashion in twenty years. Her blue dress draped to midcalf, soft gathers sweeping across the wide shoulders. A double strand of pearls hung to her waist.

Nothing about them suggested that they shared her race. Their skin color served as an unpleasant reminder of even harsher times in the nation, when terms like "octoroon," "quadroon" and "house slave" often hinted at a life that wasn't quite as cruel as it was for people who looked like Jemma.

"Agnes," Honorine said out of the corner of her mouth, "her bag."

Jemma wilted under their direct gaze until Honorine turned to the maid, her stare finally prompting the woman to move. As Jemma started to follow Agnes, to see where she would be staying, Fosette slipped her arm through Jemma's, directing her deeper into the space of the first floor as Agnes carried the suitcase up the wide, grand stairway, red carpet under her feet. Fosette led Jemma past the banister, dark wood showing through chipped white paint, while Jemma thought how desperately she wanted to freshen up, to wipe the moisture from under her arms, to blot her face.

"The trip must have been brutal," Fosette said. "You're sweating like a field hand." A light tinkle of laughter, like a knife tapping crystal, flew from her.

"I . . . I'd like to visit the washroom first, if that's all right."

"We'll get there—don't you worry." Fosette glanced behind them, where Honorine remained in the same spot, watching Agnes, as her and Jemma's shoes clacked on the dusty hardwood floor. "I wanted to apologize for Grandmère. She's used to doing things the old way. She doesn't understand that some of the things she says can be . . . ridiculous. I mean, Africa! And she doesn't mean to say such silly things sometimes. She's just . . . old. Ah, here is the kitchen!"

She allowed Jemma a quick peek inside the expansive space. A slightly burnt odor hung in the air. Jemma had time to see only the white Philco refrigerator, the stove, the sink and the black-and-white tiled floor before Fosette directed her onward, to the parlor, the dining room with its table for ten, the living room and the solarium. Jemma looked longingly at the water closet they passed, and then Fosette threw open the French doors off the solarium to reveal a large back garden.

Squat magnolia shrubs lined both sides of the flat green lawn, the drone of bumblebees an undercurrent to the conversation between a group of three people farther out, a woman and two men. The magnolias drooped, the edges of many of their petals curled and brown. As in the front, dogwood trees crowded together behind the shrubs, and in the far distance, about a hundred yards out, more oaks formed a line in front of wild woods.

"Who are they?" Jemma pointed to the group. From here, they appeared white, but she assumed they were Black, just very light-skinned like everyone else she'd met thus far. The woman held a croquet mallet in her hands, her slim neck bent, the toe of one foot on top of a red-striped ball.

"My uncle, mother and brother. You'll meet them at dinner."

"And the child?"

A blank stare met this question. "Child?"

"Who I'm tutoring." At Fosette's continued confusion, Jemma went on. "What I was hired for."

"Oh!" That tinkling laugh again, all champagne bubbles and sparkling gems, contrasting with the hot press of her hands. Jemma wanted to shake her off. "Of course, your job here. We'll get this all sorted out at dinner. Come on. I'll show you your room."

As the two of them walked up the stairs, their footsteps muted by the thick rug while they passed tall portraits of Duchon ancestors in gilded frames, Fosette apologized. "Forgive me for saying what I said back there, about you being a field hand. Sometimes I'm as bad as Grandmère! We don't get a lot of visitors and I'm afraid we've forgotten how to talk to people. It's so wonderful having someone younger here. Besides Laurence, I mean. You're twenty—?"

"Twenty-seven."

"Right." She stopped Jemma with a light touch on her arm at the top of the stairs. "Please don't think the worst of us."

"It's all right," Jemma said. "I've said things out of turn plenty of times."

Perhaps it had been a taxing day for Fosette, too. To have a stranger in the house could upset all sorts of things. Jemma looked into Fosette's eyes and offered a small smile. Yes, let this first day at least be a drip of honey and the brush of soft fingertips. Maybe things could stay that way.

"It would be wonderful if we could be friends." Fosette gave her hand a quick squeeze and led Jemma to the left, passing several closed doors, until they reached the end of the hallway. To the right was a small bathroom. "You can have this washroom all to yourself. And this is your room. It's right next to mine."

When they entered, Agnes straightened up from smoothing the covers, placing her hands together in front of her. The maid's gaze moved across Jemma's face, her eyes eager and quick, making Jemma think of little insects crawling over her skin.

"Agnes, if you're done here, it's time to get back to the kitchen," Fosette said in a tight voice completely unlike the light one Jemma had heard for the past fifteen minutes. The maid gave a brief nod and left the room, Fosette's narrowed eyes watching her go before she turned to Jemma, her smile reappearing in fits and starts. "She doesn't talk. You'll get used to it. Well, this is it, where you'll be staying." She swept a slim arm in the air. "Dinner is at six. Sharp. So you have time to freshen up and rest a bit. We're so happy to have you here."

Fosette shut the door on her way out, leaving Jemma in blessed silence. She sank onto the soft white chenille bedspread, under the mournful eyes of Jesus hanging on a small silver cross. Agnes had placed her suitcase in front of the green chifforobe in the corner. A small desk and a high-backed chair faced the open window, where no breeze disturbed the gauzy curtains or the yellow brocade drapes.

Jemma slipped her hat, shoes and gloves off, wishing the languid spinning of the ceiling fan would do more than move the heat around. She placed her watch on the nightstand, under a milk glass hurricane lamp, yellow flowers dancing across its surface. She stood and grabbed the towel and washcloth from the bench at the foot of the bed and went to the bathroom.

When Jemma returned to her room, her face and underarms wiped clean, she removed her clothes and hung them in the chifforobe, enjoying the cooler sensation now that she was just in her slip. Movement outside caught her attention and she went to the window, wondering if the rest of the family was still out there, playing croquet. She hoped to get a better look at them, but the lawn was empty.

No. It wasn't.

A ghostly figure walked out of a shrub and crossed the short expanse to another shrub, disappearing inside it before emerging again and continuing on her way. Jemma swallowed, her eyes following the form, unable to tell the age or color, simply recognizing that it was a woman, her long skirts trailing over the grass without disturbing it. Sweat beaded along Jemma's forehead and bloomed under her arms, the tangy musk of fright rising in the air. She backed away, her hands over her chest.

Ever since she'd boarded the train in Chicago, she'd been seeing them. She'd tried to ignore them, had practiced the breathing Mama had taught her, had averted her eyes . . . but they were still here.

This was her chance at a fresh start, her opportunity to leave the ghosts of Chicago behind—the real ones and the ones that haunted only her mind—and they'd followed her. Jemma rubbed the scar on her wrist, trying to calm her ragged breathing. She wouldn't let them ruin this chance for her. The only chance she had.

The idea of a nap had slipped away, much like the way that lost soul had slipped through the shrubs.

Jemma sat on the edge of the bed, facing the chifforobe in the corner but not seeing it.

What she did see was Marvin in the pool hall back in Chicago, smoke so thick she could taste it. He was leaning on the bar and talking to a woman in a tight red dress. Jemma saw Marvin's fingers on the woman's thigh, rubbing in small circles. She saw the wide eyes of two other men around the pool table as Jemma grabbed a cue and swung it with all her might across Marvin's back. The damn thing hadn't broken, but she'd thought it might if she could only get another crack at it, but by then someone had wrestled the stick out of her hands, while Marvin stood up straight and backhanded Jemma so hard she was afraid she'd lose a tooth.

Her tongue moved to that spot now, the tooth in place although still a little wobbly.

The chifforobe came back into view, pushing aside brick row houses, housing projects reaching for nothing, broken concrete and the green tiled floor of an elementary school.

Checking her watch, she had half an hour before dinner. On her way back from the bathroom, she'd found no one in the hall, heard no voices. Jemma washed up again, patting her hair, which had completely given up in the face of the humidity. Unlike the Duchons', at least the ones she'd met so far, her hair didn't lie in gentle waves. She doubted any of them even owned a hot comb, let alone used one. There was no time to do anything more than get ready for dinner, so she slipped into the lightest cotton dress she owned and hurried downstairs, getting turned around and walking into the empty parlor before she remembered where the dining room was.

Six pairs of eyes met hers when she walked in, all varying shades of gray or green or hazel. Like Honorine and Fosette, the remaining members of the family were all incredibly light, their hair either straight or barely waved.

Jemma wasn't late—she had a good five minutes left—but with everyone else already seated, she felt uncomfortably like she wasn't on time.

"This is Jemma Barker," Honorine said from her place at the head of the table. "Jemma, do come in and sit down."

There were five empty seats at the gleaming table, wood shined to a bright glare. A lacy runner extended down the center, and six places were set, silverware and crystal shimmering. The sticky gazes of the Duchons and Agnes pressed against Jemma's skin as she settled next to Fosette, at the opposite end from Honorine. A rich smell hung in the air, reminding Jemma of Lulu's, but underneath, she detected that same old burnt odor.

Across from her, a young man stared, his dark hair slicked back, curiosity widening his hazel eyes for a brief moment as Honorine introduced him as her grandson, Laurence. He gave a quick nod. He was about Jemma's age, so not the child she'd come here to tutor. Next to Laurence sat a green-eyed older man with salt-and-pepper hair.

"My eldest, Russell Duchon," Honorine said before finally gesturing to the woman sitting closest to her, a woman whose dark hair was swept into an unfashionable updo. "And this is Simone Duchon Lemont, my daughter, and Fosette and Laurence's mother."

Jemma tried not to stare at these people, who wore their beauty like comfortable designer coats. It took an effort to pull her gaze away, to resist the enchanting pull of them.

"Pleased to meet you all," Jemma said, nodding to the others in turn. She unfolded her napkin and laid it across her lap, more to direct her attention down and still her shaky fingers than anything else. The family members' gazes scuttled over her. And although they were Black, she felt as out of place in their company as she would in a roomful of whites.

Childish voices sounded in her head:

If you're light, you're all right.
If you're brown, stick around.
If you're Black, stay back!

How many times had she heard that on playgrounds and row house stoops? And how many times had she felt relief to be brown enough to be able to stick around?

"I was hoping to meet my student. Is he here? Or she?" she asked, looking toward Honorine. On their phone call a few weeks ago, the woman hadn't mentioned anything about a student. Jemma had been so stunned by the pay, and now it was too late to ask for details like a name or sex. She should have been paying more attention.

But who noticed the color of the life preserver when one was drowning?

"Who, my dear?" Simone asked, leaning forward, the thick blue lace on her ill-fitting gown bunched around her neck and shoulders. Next to Jemma, Fosette's hands twisted the napkin in her lap.

"My . . . my student? I'm sorry—I've forgotten the name." Jemma's gaze darted over to Agnes, standing in the corner, her eyes downcast. The maid suddenly disappeared through the doorway to the kitchen.

"Ah, that," Honorine said, folding her hands in front of her empty plate. "What made you think you were hired to be a tutor exactly?"

"I thought . . . you said there was a . . ." Her voice trailed off, the word "child" slipping back. Because Honorine hadn't said there was a child. Jemma thought of the letter. The phone call. At no time had a child been mentioned. Or the title of tutor. How presumptuous she had been.

"We will get to your duties in due time, Miss Barker. For your first dinner with us, why don't you get comfortable and settled? We have ample time to discuss what you're here to do."

Before Jemma could reply, Agnes returned, rolling a cart in front of her. She placed covered silver tureens and platters on the table, and once she left, the family blessed themselves in the Catholic fashion and said grace.

Amid the heady aromas filling the room, Jemma's hunger pushed any questions out of her mind. Bowls and platters of steaming red beans and rice, gumbo, fried shrimp, stewed okra and tomatoes, crawfish etouffee and French bread covered the table. But from the first bite, the difference between Agnes's cooking and Lulu's at the café was distastefully evident. The curious undercurrent of smokiness that hung in the air came across in the gumbo, the etouffee, even the bread. And yet opposite Jemma, Russell and Laurence ate as if this were their last meal. Although Simone took only tiny bites of everything, she did eventually clear her plate, as did Honorine. Fosette had only a small amount of food, and despite her spending much of the meal pushing it around, she managed to eat most of it.

"Do tell us about Chicago," Honorine invited, patting the corners of her mouth with her napkin.

At that, everyone turned to Jemma, Russell's mouth half open, a crumb hanging off his bottom lip. Laurence and Fosette appeared unnaturally interested.

Jemma didn't know what to say at first, as the family stared at her like she was a specimen on a microscope slide, but a quick glance at Fosette's open face warmed her.

"It's nothing like here, especially the weather." A short laugh escaped Jemma's lips, too loud in the quiet room. "Not a lot of big houses like this, at least not where I grew up."

"What are they wearing up there?" Simone asked.

"What kind of foods do you eat?" That was Russell.

They lobbed questions at her, some of them odd (like Honorine's "What type of jobs do colored people do up there?") and some intrusive (Fosette: "How many boyfriends have you had?").

And then, without warning, as if Jemma had provided them all the answers they needed, the Duchons talked among themselves, shutting her out with a simple, subtle turn of their faces toward one another. She listened as they discussed Thurgood Marshall's finally being confirmed as a judge in a US appellate court and President Kennedy's promise to get a man on the moon. They talked about croquet and the weather, and argued over whether the priests should speak English at Mass.

"They've spoken Latin since the beginning," Simone said, pulling a cigarette from a slim silver case. "It's scandalous that the council is even thinking of changing things."

"Maman," Laurence said, the first time Jemma heard him speak, "you know that things are changing, not just with the church, with everything."

"And you want to be one of those radicals, do you?" she asked with a small smile, and blew a stream of smoke out the side of her mouth. "You want to go to those sit-ins and demonstrations and marches? And how would you take part in any of that?"

"Those demonstrations and marches work," Jemma said, tearing her eyes away from Laurence to address his mother. "You see what they did in Montgomery."

"Why am I not surprised that you'd say such a thing?" Simone turned to her.

"What does that mean?"

"I've never ridden a bus, so I damn sure wouldn't know how it feels to ride in the back."

Jemma's hands tightened around her napkin. "Reverend King isn't just fighting for people who look like me, if that's what you mean. We're all Negroes here, whether you like it or not."

"We're very proud to be colored," Fosette chimed in, the words skipping out in an irregular beat.

"'Colored'? Why do you keep saying that?" Jemma asked.

"There's nothing wrong with the word," Simone said. "Are you not colored?"

Jemma looked at the woman's frumpy dress, her hair. She then took in Honorine's gown, a deep blue number with style details from the thirties. Fosette, the youngest of them, seemed afflicted by the same old-fashioned dress sense, as were the two men at the table. None of them, it seemed, embraced what was happening now, so of course they'd still refer to themselves as colored.

"I'm a Negro. That's the term I prefer," Jemma said.

Russell, whose second helping was now eaten, sucked his teeth before jabbing at them with a toothpick. "What difference does it make, huh? 'Negro,' 'colored,' 'Black'—they're all words that mean the same thing."

"But words matter, Mr. Duchon. Not that long ago, white people were calling us 'nigger' like it was our names. Even now, especially here, they still do. Surely you all know that."

He waved a hand at her. "As long as you know who you are, does it matter what anyone else calls you?"

"To me, it does." And it seemed she was alone in this, as Russell continued his tooth picking, Simone her smoking, Laurence his studying an empty plate and Fosette her napkin twisting. Only Honorine seemed engaged with Jemma, her cool green eyes locked on her.

"We are a proud family, Miss Barker, colored or Negro. The Duchons were free people of color in this city when Africans were still setting foot on this land, chains around their ankles. We may have a slave ancestor somewhere, but his name certainly wasn't Duchon. All this debate has been most interesting. As this is your first day here, I've granted you a little leeway. Beginning tomorrow, however, you'll be expected to behave as an employee, with the exception of dinner. You'll dine in here with us and I'll expect you to be on time."

Jemma opened her mouth to ask for details on her employment, but the five Duchons pushed their chairs back as one, rose from the table and filed out of the dining room, leaving her alone.

She stayed in place for several moments, her mind working to process the meal and the conversation. The family was certainly backward, but it wasn't her first time dealing with different types of people. Maybe, if they liked her enough, she would influence them to come into the present and stop using terms like "colored." Perhaps even help them update their style.

As Jemma tossed her napkin on the table and rose out of her seat, an amorphous form flashed in front of her. She worked to still her trembling, following the spirit's movements as it meandered along the wall, until she remembered to shut her eyes and count.

Five, four, three, two, one.

Go away. Please.

When she opened her eyes, it was gone. On a wave of relief, Jemma raced upstairs and shut herself in her room, peeling herself from the door only when her breathing slowed to normal.

Later, settled in bed but unable to sleep, Jemma listened to the quiet sounds of Fosette's humming through the wall. She pretended the lullaby was for her.

THREE

JEMMA WAS BACK in the one-bedroom walk-up in Chicago, the dingy space she'd shared with Marvin.

She'd been wrestling her key in the front door, a bag of groceries balanced in one arm, the sound of ringing from inside rushing her. She'd made it in, set the bag on the small kitchen table and snatched the phone up.

"Hello?"

"Is Marvin there?" a woman's voice asked.

"Who is this?"

"You tell him that I couldn't go through with it, okay? I'm gonna have this baby. He can either be a man about it or not. Either way, me and this baby gonna be just fine. You tell him that."

A loud click ended the call.

Jemma didn't know the woman's name, but she knew it was the same one from the pool hall, the one in the red dress, with the red lipstick and the long neck, head thrown back in laughter at something Marvin said.

No one had been arrested that night, not him for splitting her lip or her for whacking him across the back with a cue. People in the neighborhood knew when to get gone. He'd run in one direction and she'd run in another, but they'd both circled back to their apartment, where Jemma's mind broke and bled, same as that one wrist. If Marvin hadn't come in when he did, she would've finished the job. Her anger at his interruption was worse than her fury at his deception.

Afterward, her friend Betty had been there. And now, Jemma reasoned that had she listened to Betty, she'd still be there and not here, surrounded by an eerily beautiful group of people who, despite their charms—with the exception of that rude Simone—struck her as more than a little odd. She'd probably still be in Chicago, never mind the nervous breakdown, the suicide attempt and the firing from her teaching job.

If she could have forgiven Marvin.

"A man's going to do what a man's going to do," Betty had said after Jemma told her about the other woman. "Ain't no changing that, and the sooner you realize it, the sooner you can go about your life. Take what happiness you can, but don't depend on a man to give it to you."

Jemma had been in bed, her wrist heavily bandaged, her bottom lip swollen. Betty had just come back into the bedroom with a fresh, cool washcloth, trying to press it to Jemma's mouth, but she put her hand up.

"He promised me a family, that we'd make a family together. He knows my daddy just died. Why would he . . ." Unable to find the words to complete her mixed-up thoughts, Jemma took the washcloth and put it to her aching lips.

"Why do they do anything? You'll go crazy for real trying to figure that out. Half the time, they don't know why they do the shit they do. Marvin loves you, right? I know, I know, it don't seem that way all the time, but you're here, ain't you? And where's that chick? It's some men would've kicked you out, so think about that. What you can live with and what you can't. If you can forgive him . . . yes, find it in yourself to forgive him. It's freedom in that."

And while Jemma had taken the first chance she'd been given to run, to break free, she hadn't done it by forgiving.

Betty, Chicago and the mess she'd left behind faded. Her current surroundings included sea green floral wallpaper, creamy wainscoting and gilded mirrors. If she didn't inspect things too closely, she didn't see the peeling corners or the cracks.

ON JEMMA'S SECOND day in the house, she'd been disappointed to learn that she hadn't been hired as a tutor at all. Instead, she was an assistant of sorts to Honorine.

"You'll keep track of my calendar, be on call should I require anything further and eventually organize the shelves in the library," the matriarch said after breakfast. "Other times, please keep Fosette occupied. She loves having a young lady her own age here."

It didn't take Jemma long to see that Honorine's calendar had very little on it. No visits from acquaintances, no trips into town. Instead, many of her days consisted of morning and afternoon tea, croquet with the family and short siestas before dinner. Jemma couldn't imagine why Honorine couldn't set these appointments herself.

Chicago had been a bustle—of work, transportation and people. Jemma had often felt like she had no spare time for herself, no quiet.

Here, she was kept busy but in different ways.

When Jemma wasn't assisting Honorine, she played card games

or assembled puzzles or helped Fosette decide what to wear for dinner. It was nothing like preparing lesson plans and taking two buses in the morning and two more in the afternoon to go to and from work. Once, after Fosette pulled a frumpy light green gown from her armoire and pressed it against herself while she admired her reflection in the long mirror, Jemma caught herself staring at the young woman's hair, hanging in a thick sheet down her back. Not fashionable at all, but still beautiful, the type of hair that could turn a plain girl into a pretty one in Jemma's neighborhood. She studied Fosette's pale arm, wondering why she wasn't married and why no men her age came around to ask after her.

Jemma thought about her first day in New Orleans, about Lulu at the café and Charlie who'd driven her here. She couldn't imagine why they'd reacted so strangely when she'd told them she was working for the Duchons. They might be a little odd, and yes, they did keep to themselves—not one visitor had come to the door since Jemma had been there, and none of the Duchons left the property—but they seemed harmless.

Each morning was the same. Ever since Fosette had invited Jemma to sit with her at breakfast the day after she arrived, she'd been taking all her meals—not just dinner—with the family, marveling at how they greedily pored over the *Times-Picayune* in the morning and the *States-Item* in the afternoon. Each read a section of the newspaper from front to back before silently exchanging it with the person next to them. And while the family didn't treat her as they did Agnes—as if she were almost invisible—the only Duchon who made her feel truly welcome was Fosette, with the endless chatter about nothing and the laugh bubbling up at things both amusing and serious. She kept Jemma occupied with games of cribbage or rummy. Sometimes Laurence joined them.

This afternoon was the first she'd had to herself, begging off

Fosette's request for yet another game of cribbage. As soon as Jemma heard the woman go into her bedroom and shut the door, she'd raced downstairs, relief spreading over her at not running into anyone. The older family members often napped before dinner; maybe Fosette would do the same, or whatever she did when she hummed that song in her room. Jemma usually heard the humming through the wall that separated their rooms late at night, when quiet settled over the rest of the house.

But now, all that mattered was that Jemma finally had the chance to explore the grounds on her own.

She made her way outside, the heat sticking to her skin like suckling lips despite the lightness of her cotton dress, one of the few items of clothing she had suitable for the climate. She hoped to run into the gardener, a brown-skinned man she'd spied from upstairs a couple of days ago. By the time she'd rushed downstairs, with no idea what her intentions were besides to talk to someone different, someone who looked like her, he'd disappeared.

Several buildings dotted the huge expanse, including what Fosette had explained were the carriage house, chapel and old washhouse. She'd briefly mentioned a family burial vault, and Jemma recalled the way Fosette's gaze had shifted then. At the time, Jemma assumed it was a painful subject; maybe she'd lost a beloved family member recently. Jemma approached the one-story structure, behind the croquet pitch and set off against a jumble of bushes that appeared ready to overtake it.

Over the door was the family name DUCHON etched in stone. Bronze plaques dotted the exterior in neat columns.

LUCIE DUCHON LEMONT

OUR LITTLE ANGEL

JANUARY 4, 1932–MARCH 12, 1935

Lemont, Jemma thought. Simone's surname. This must be her daughter, gone so young. Jemma frowned at the date of death, which so happened to be her exact birth date.

She scanned nearby plaques.

RAYMOND FRANCIS DUCHON
BELOVED FATHER AND HUSBAND
AUGUST 3, 1890–MARCH 12, 1942

ANDRÉ RAYMOND DUCHON
BELOVED SON AND BROTHER
APRIL 8, 1913–MARCH 12, 1949

They'd all died on March 12, Jemma's birthday. Just as her mind tried to work its way around the bizarre coincidence, as her gaze began to move to the next plaque, someone grabbed her from behind. A short scream erupted from her as she twisted around to find Fosette smiling at her, too many teeth gleaming between stiff lips.

"What are you doing in this gloomy old place?" she asked, tugging Jemma's hand even as Jemma stood rooted to the spot.

Jemma pointed behind her. "Those dates. They all died . . . on my birthday."

Fosette turned back to the house, Jemma's hand tightly held in her own. She wouldn't even look at the vault.

"Fosette, that Lucie—she was your sister? She died the same day I was born."

"I was a little girl. I don't even remember her. Come on. I want to play a game of rummy and I can't find Laurence anywhere."

Jemma turned back to the vault, unsure of what she wanted, and in light of Fosette's strange behavior, she didn't move. She wanted answers.

Before she could demand any, however, Honorine stepped out through the French doors, looking imposing even from a distance.

"Come on," Fosette said, pulling Jemma's hand. This time, Jemma walked with her, trying to tamp down the sense of unease that wormed its way around her. Again, she thought of Lulu.

Get back on the train or bus or whatever you came here on and go back to where you from.

Of Charlie.

Well, maybe something's changed out there.

Of how he wouldn't look at the house when he brought her, the way he'd moved on the moment she'd stepped down from his wagon, as if he'd been in a hurry to get away.

Of the ghosts she'd already seen.

As the two women approached Honorine, Jemma made up her mind to ask about her job, but being polite was key. She didn't want to antagonize her employer, not when she so desperately needed this chance.

"Mrs. Duchon, I wanted to talk about my duties here and helping you with your calendar."

"It's hot as Hades out here," the woman said, slipping back inside. Fosette followed, looking back at Jemma, her face full of curiosity.

Jemma's lips pressed together at the deflection, but she stepped inside, moving to block Honorine's path. Afraid that her voice would betray her annoyance, she worked to control it. "Mrs. Duchon, you're paying me an awful lot of money to be a glorified girl Friday. I was a teacher back home and I assumed I'd be teaching here. I'm wasting everyone's time planning a nearly empty social calendar and playing games. Three hundred dollars a week is a . . . sizable sum. I want to earn it."

"Three hundred dollars?" Honorine echoed.

Jemma stared at her, any words she thought she'd wanted to say melting away as if the heat affected them, too. And maybe that's why Honorine answered so strangely—the heat. Had it addled the old woman's brain? Was she unwell?

"Why are you trying to be more busy?" Fosette asked. "Aren't you enjoying an easier time of it?"

It seemed Honorine had broken out of whatever spell she'd been under. "Don't worry. We'll have more for you to do soon enough."

She began to turn away, but Jemma put a hand on her arm to stop her, not missing Fosette's tiny gasp.

"It's just that I feel like I'm taking advantage. I wasn't raised that way."

Honorine removed Jemma's hand with deliberate slowness, and the look in her eyes made it clear that she'd entertain Jemma no more.

Jemma watched Honorine's retreating back in silence, her mouth open, her ears closed to whatever nonsense Fosette was uttering. She was just thinking how rude the old woman was when Laurence emerged from the library, his gaze following his grandmother up the stairs until it landed on Jemma and his sister.

"I've been looking everywhere for you," Fosette breathed, rushing toward him and slipping an arm in the crook of his elbow. She rested her head against his shoulder, beaming, as if completely aware of the charming picture they made for their newcomer's benefit.

"What's going on?" Laurence asked, lifting his chin toward the staircase.

"Oh, you know Grandmère." Fosette rolled her eyes and then turned him toward the parlor, looking back over her shoulder at

Jemma before beckoning her to follow. Jemma looked to the French doors before catching up to Fosette and Laurence, tuning out the constant prattle. Relief fell over her as they sat around the coffee table, a half-finished puzzle surrounded by random pieces almost covering the entire surface. Jemma feigned quiet concentration as her mind swam with questions, her eyes trained on the puzzle even as the brother and sister across from her rested their heads against each other on occasion. One of Laurence's fingers danced circles on Fosette's knee, but Jemma was too focused on her own thoughts to register their behavior.

She'd rushed to accept the job offer from the Duchons because of everything that had happened back home, events that had fallen like tragic dominoes.

Her father's death had been domino one.

Marvin's other woman, number two.

Her suicide attempt followed.

And the last one, the domino that wiped out a viable future for Jemma in Chicago, was the loss of her teaching job.

A part of Jemma's mind was vaguely aware of Fosette planting a kiss on Laurence's cheek, her lips lingering a second too long, but most of it recalled her last day at Carver Elementary School.

The principal's secretary had been waiting outside the office before the first bell rang. The bespectacled woman, whose salt-and-pepper curls always appeared fresh off a roller set, had asked Jemma to step inside.

"I'm not going to be on time, Mrs. Oliver," Jemma said, glancing at her watch, grateful she wore it on her left wrist, the undamaged one.

"Principal Evans needs to talk to you. We'll have someone cover your class."

Had Jemma been less distracted, little details would have caught her attention. The way Mrs. Oliver's eyes wouldn't meet her own. How Mr. Evans shut the door behind her, when that door was nearly always open.

"Glad you made it back, Jemma," he said, settling into his chair, a squeaky sigh escaping the leather.

"Thank you. I'm feeling much better." She took the hard seat across from him, years of disobedient students having worn it smooth.

Her gaze fell on the large box on the corner of his desk and the familiar umbrella handle sticking out of it.

"Is that my—?" she started, the rest of her question fading away at his quick nods.

"Jemma, I'm afraid that in light of your recent troubles, we're going to have to ask that you take some time off."

"Is this about my daddy?"

"No. But there's been . . . talk . . . about other troubles."

The principal's deep brown eyes met hers for a moment before moving to her lap, where she unconsciously pulled her right sweater cuff down. She held her breath, waiting for him to say that he knew. Because until he did, she didn't have to admit to anything.

"We know about the hospital stay."

"I was sick, Mr.—"

"Like I said, Jemma, there's been talk. You might have to look for a job in another school system."

Just like that, she knew that the "talk" wasn't only about the suicide attempt, which was enough on its own. Parents didn't want crazy people teaching their children, after all. But someone must have told that she was living with Marvin.

Jemma snatched up the box and marched out the door toward the bus stop, tears blurring the wire fences and brick facades. Before Marvin came home, she'd packed her few belongings and headed to Betty's, wondering how long she'd be able to stay before her welcome wore out.

After several days of sleeping on her friend's couch and circling want ads in the newspaper, she'd received the letter from the Duchons. With no job, no money and nowhere to go, it had seemed like a miracle.

She'd been too grateful for the opportunity the letter presented to consider that it had Betty's address on it, as if the sender knew exactly where she was.

FOUR

JEMMA'S ATTENTION HAD been on Laurence when the spirit from the other night (at least, she thought it was the same, mostly unformed as it was) floated into the room. Her eyes drifted away from his handsomeness to the form hovering behind Russell. The rest of the family were engrossed in their breakfast of shrimp omelets, grits and rice fritters. Jemma gripped her fork, her teeth biting into her bottom lip.

"You look like you've seen a ghost, my dear." Russell chuckled, joined by Simone's low titter.

It was only then that Jemma realized she'd stopped breathing. Exhaling heavily, she tried to catch her fork before it fell from her shaky fingers, but it clattered to the floor.

"Agnes!" Honorine shouted at once.

"I can get another—" Jemma started, rising from her chair, glad for any excuse to escape.

"Nonsense. Sit down."

She didn't know why she complied, but Jemma resumed her

seat. Honorine yelled for Agnes again, and the maid entered after a few minutes.

"What the hell took you so long?" the older woman demanded. "Get another fork for Jemma."

It pained Jemma to see Agnes duck her head and immediately obey orders. The maid soon returned with a clean utensil.

"Thank you," Jemma said in a clear voice, something she'd never heard any of the Duchons say to Agnes, who held her gaze for a moment.

"Get back to the kitchen, imbecile," Simone drawled.

Jemma's mouth dropped open at the explicit rudeness, but what was she but another employee? What could she do?

She needed this job, so she closed her mouth and focused on her plate, pushing the food around.

"Eat," whispered Fosette next to her, patting Jemma's lap.

Although Jemma had no appetite, she took a small bite of rice fritter. The golden color of the soft pastry belied the slight burnt aftertaste. She glanced across the table, feeling eyes on her, only to find Laurence looking at her. Her face flushed, growing hotter once he gave her a small smile.

They were all so beautiful, even if their behavior wasn't.

After two weeks at the Duchons', Jemma was six hundred dollars richer, in theory. Following breakfast, she trailed Honorine to the large secretary in the parlor and waited while her employer made out a check for three hundred dollars. Jemma thanked her before folding it and slipping it into her pants pocket.

"I'd love to go into town and cash my checks."

What she didn't say was how much she could do with the money: visit a beautician for a hard press that might (heavy emphasis on "might") resist the humidity; buy some clothes that were more suited to the climate, even if her old fashions fit in with the

Duchons' frumpiness; buy a train ticket to get her anywhere else but here.

While life in the house and with the family was mostly agreeable, she hadn't been able to escape her cursed ability to see spirits.

Jemma had considered that she was having another nervous breakdown, something the Duchons couldn't know, not if she wanted to keep this job.

Now, as she wondered what else she could do besides count down from five to push the spirits away, a tactic that didn't seem to be working much, Honorine interrupted her thoughts. "I'm sorry, but you won't be able to go into town today. I have some work for you in the library. As for your checks, since we live so out of the way, I thought it would be easier if I simply paid you once a month—say, on the first? You could then go to a bank and open an account, but I'd prefer that you allow me to open one for you at my family's bank. We could even arrange to have your funds directly deposited from our account into yours. It would be much more convenient all around."

It wasn't what Jemma wanted, but before she could protest, Honorine continued. "You're saving money by not paying for room and board or utilities. You don't even have to buy your own food. We really have tried to make things as comfortable for you as possible. Surely you can humor an old woman."

She looked down at her lap, picking at an invisible thread, while Jemma stood next to her, intrusive guilt preventing any objections.

Honorine looked up. "You're young, so of course you want to be out there, doing things, living life. I forget sometimes that I don't have much need of that anymore, that desire to constantly move, go from one place to another. My granddaughter, Fosette—she still has it."

"But Fosette doesn't even go anywhere." The words were out before Jemma could stop them. "No one does."

The older woman studied her for a moment, rising out of her chair. Jemma instinctively stepped back. Honorine laced her fingers together and walked out of the parlor, toward the library, a graceful move of her head indicating that Jemma should follow. "Maybe our isolation puzzles you, the fact that no one here goes to work. My grandfather invested in the railroad business, but even more heavily in shipping. Since we live in a port town, his investments paid off generously." Here, a peculiar smile smoothed out the wrinkles on the woman's lips before evaporating, thin lines settling into their usual places. "We don't have to work, dear."

"But doesn't anyone"—Jemma thought of Laurence especially, and Russell to a lesser extent—"get bored just being at home all the time? I'd think you all would love to go into the city and see what's new. Stores, restaurants . . ."

Anything, her mind shrilled as her lips closed. *Anything outside of this monotonous existence.*

"You'll get used to the way we do things, Miss Barker, the way we *must* do things." Honorine flung open the glass doors to the library, similar to the dining room in size, although it looked smaller with the walls lined in bookcases. Each shelf was completely full. While many of the books stood tall, their spines visible, others had been stacked horizontally on top of them, because there was no other place to put them. Messy piles of books rested on top of the bookcases.

Both women stood in the doorway as Jemma's spirits fell; she was afraid of what was coming.

"It's been ages since these shelves have been organized," Honorine said, confirming Jemma's worst suspicions. "I'll need you to put this all in order."

"Is there any particular order you'd like?" Jemma couldn't tell what types of books the room held. "Classics in one area? History in another?"

The other woman's lips disappeared in a tight smile. "I trust your judgment in figuring out what will work best." She backed out of the library in one step, shutting the doors in Jemma's face.

"Well, shit," Jemma muttered.

"I'd start there if I were you."

Laurence looked around the side of a big armchair that faced a wall of shelving. His feet rested on a short footstool in front of him, a fat book on his lap. Jemma's back pressed against the glass doors; she was startled by his presence.

He cocked his head toward a spot to her left.

Her eyes drifted over before returning to his face, which drew them like a magnet. Forcing her gaze to the shelf he'd indicated, Jemma moved on clumsy legs.

Every one of the books in the whole bookcase concerned the occult. Jemma didn't even want to put a finger on them, most of which were dusty or faintly cracked.

Mysteries of the Occult: On Witchcraft and Voodoo. The Philosophy of Curses: Throwing, Binding, and Breaking. Secret Societies of the Occult. Gods, Demons, Angels, and the Devil: A Fairy Tale. Damning for Eternity: Black Magic and Witchcraft.

And on they went, with some titles written in foreign languages and a few without words at all, just a collection of symbols.

She glanced over to find Laurence studying her; she was bewildered that her sudden attention didn't drive his open gaze back down.

"Why should I start here?" she asked, working to keep her voice light.

"It's the messiest, isn't it?"

Looking back at the shelves in front of her, she wasn't sure about that. Most of the books grouped here were on similar subject matter, creepy as it was.

A hot puff of air on the back of her neck elicited a squeal, and as she twirled around, expecting to find Laurence there, she was alarmed to see him still seated and no one behind her at all.

"Are you all right?" he asked, only the mildest curiosity evident in his voice.

"Yes." Jemma touched the back of her neck with trembling fingers. Not wanting him to see how frightened she was, she squeezed, hoping the pressure would calm the tremors. Only when the shaking stopped did she bring her hand down, but his attention had returned to his book moments ago. Her gaze roamed the room, finding nothing that could have *breathed* on her.

Clap.

At the soft sound, Jemma turned back to the shelf, finding a slim book on the floor. *How did it get there?* She hadn't been close enough to knock it with her shoulder.

No, it had fallen on its own. Or some *thing* had pushed it off.

She picked up the gray volume and stuffed it between two others.

She had to get some air.

Five, four, three, two, one, she counted in her head as she scrabbled at the doorknob, ignoring Laurence's questions, until she was out of the library and away from whatever was in there. Not wanting to run into Honorine and endure the inevitable probing that would follow about why she wasn't doing her assigned duties, Jemma rushed into the solarium, only to see through the wide window the usual family members playing croquet on the back lawn, Honorine included.

Jemma dashed out the front door instead, aware that she had two three-hundred-dollar checks in her pocket, enough to get her far away from this place. All she had to do was go into town and find the nearest bank that catered to Black clientele.

But could she really escape the ghosts that way?

She stopped at the bottom of the porch steps, her breaths evening out as her mind raced, the late September air wet enough to drink.

How far could she go on six hundred dollars?

Better yet, where could she go? Not back home, where she had nothing. No place to live, no job (and no hope of getting one as a teacher), no man.

She'd find a job in New Orleans for now, maybe even convince a school to hire her. She had enough money to rent a room for a while, until she began working. Jemma glanced back at the door, which she'd left ajar. All she had to do was creep upstairs, quickly pack and slip out.

And yet, although she could sneak clear across the country, she couldn't outrun the entities that danced just beyond the corner of her eye.

Wasn't that why Mama and Daddy had tried so hard to teach her to ignore what was plain to see?

Don't look at 'em, Jemma.

Ain't nothing but the devil's work if you look.

"Hey, are you all right?"

Laurence's voice snatched Jemma into the present. He stood just outside the door, his gaze flicking to the wrought iron gate that bordered the front lawn. Something uneasy shifted across his striking features before moving on, knowing it didn't belong there.

"Yes," Jemma said through tight lips, wishing he'd stayed in the library.

Once he told his grandmother how erratic she was behaving, she probably wouldn't have to sneak off. She'd fire her.

His hazel eyes searched her face for a few moments. When he held out a hand, Jemma only stared at first.

"Come on," he said in a soft voice similar to the one he used with Fosette. It thrummed with a strange intimacy, and a part of Jemma delighted at it, at what it promised beneath the surface: lazy mornings in bed, locked gazes that shut everyone else out.

Stop it. You work for this man's family.

She climbed the steps and took his offered hand, which tightened on hers before she could pull back.

"You're shaking like a leaf," he murmured. "What happened back there?"

He flipped her hand over before she could stop him. She worked her fingers free, but he'd already seen the scar. Meeting his eyes for a moment, she found she wanted to confide in him, wanted to be close to *someone.* But if she told him what she'd felt, what she'd been seeing, it would only add to what he'd just noticed.

"Please don't tell your grandmother," she whispered. "Don't tell anyone."

"That you tried to kill yourself? Then tell me what happened in the library."

Jemma's fingers twisted around one another. "I can't."

"No, I think you can."

Although he blocked the doorway, neither his voice nor his stance presented a threat. All Jemma sensed was interest, deep enough to flatter her.

The decision to hold back or confess was ripped from her as Agnes appeared, seemingly out of nowhere, her hand on Laurence's shoulder pulling him inside while her steady gaze rooted Jemma in place. He shook himself free and sauntered toward the solarium and out the back door, but not before throwing a menacing glare at the maid. Before Jemma had time to wonder what that was about, Agnes pointed to the library.

"I wanted to take a walk," Jemma said, turning to the front lawn. But the other woman gently touched her arm, beckoning her inside and shutting the door. Jemma wondered why the maid didn't talk. If the family asked for something, Agnes only nodded before obeying commands.

Now, just as on Jemma's arrival, the woman's eyes moved over her face, the gaze full of something she couldn't identify. It was as if she was looking for something in Jemma's features.

"Surely you can't be finished already!" Honorine boomed as she came in the back door.

Agnes promptly rushed off to the kitchen. Guilt nibbled at Jemma as she recalled how close she'd been to leaving the house—and the job—without a word to anyone.

"I just needed some air." The weakness in the excuse was uncomfortably plain. Jemma moved to the library, disturbed by Honorine's close presence. She turned to the older woman just outside of the room's doors. "Mrs. Duchon, I wondered if it would be possible for me to get a room in town and come in every day to do my job." The words rushed out before she had a chance to stop and think. "We can negotiate the pay, if you want. I'm willing to take a cut since—"

Honorine's interruption was unexpectedly welcome, as Jemma had no idea how she would sweeten the deal. "No, Miss Barker, you may not rent a room in town. Our conditions were explicitly clear. You are to live and work on the property. Should you choose not to accept the conditions we agreed upon, you forfeit your position."

Images of the amorphous body and the ghostly woman floating across the back lawn swirled in Jemma's mind. She'd seen spirits before. But here . . . some *thing* breathing on the back of her neck. A book's falling off the shelf, which she knew she hadn't caused.

The house was haunted.

Was three hundred dollars a week really worth staying for?

"Is there some reason you'd like to live in town?" Honorine asked.

"I'm just used to being busier." A shaky chuckle escaped Jemma, one she hoped didn't sound as unhinged to the other woman as it did to her. "Being so isolated out here has caused me to feel a bit of cabin fever, I'm afraid."

The sudden smile that lit Honorine's face bloomed out of nothing. "It happens to the best of us, you know. I'm sorry. I'm sure this has been an adjustment for you. The weather, the remoteness, even our family. But I am afraid that I must insist that you live on the property. What can I do to make your stay more comfortable?"

In an instant, the woman transformed from a strict battle-ax into a sweet lady of the manor. Jemma imagined her fifty years ago, when she probably looked very much like her granddaughter. Beauty wasn't the only thing the family was awash in. Their charisma was unmatched.

Shame swept over Jemma at her ingratitude.

"Nothing, really. I'm sorry to be such trouble."

"Of course not. Here, why don't you tackle the library later? For now, entertain my granddaughter. She's dying to play gin rummy with someone, and she gets tired of her brother being her sole playmate much of the time."

Before Jemma could protest, Honorine steered her toward the parlor, where Fosette played solitaire, her face brightening at her arrival.

As her opponent shuffled cards, she asked Jemma, "Did you get started on the library?"

Jemma frowned. Fosette so often chattered in a breathy voice, but there was no warmth in the question. It was almost as if she were talking to her mother.

"Not really." Jemma accepted her hand and fanned the cards out.

"Lots of interesting books in there. Grandmère has probably read every single one." Her gray eyes didn't move from the cards in her fine-fingered hand. "She's very familiar with everything on those shelves."

Jemma found herself staring at the woman across from her until Fosette prompted, "Your go," in her usual bright tone, the deep smile opening her face into a pretty canvas that just begged to be admired.

JEMMA KNOCKED THE red ball through the wicket, her first time making it through.

"Brava!" Fosette called from across the lawn.

Next to his sister, Laurence applauded, grinning. When Fosette had first invited Jemma into a family game of croquet, she'd resisted.

"I don't know how to play," she'd said, thinking that her childhood double Dutch and hopscotch were miles away from the types of games the Duchons played.

"I'll teach you," Fosette had insisted. And she had, although Jemma had played several games without ever making one point until this afternoon.

Laurence bent over his mallet, concentrating on his ball, sweat dotting his forehead.

"Good job," Russell said from his place beside Jemma, his eyes on his nephew before following the movement of the yellow ball through a wicket.

"Thank you," she replied, unable to hold back a smile. She watched Laurence, too, for different reasons.

"You'll get the hang of things soon enough, fit right in."

Her gaze moved back to Russell then, as if for confirmation. Being here with the family, except Honorine, who was resting, was curiously comfortable for her. With the sunlight washing over the back lawn and the sounds of lively chatter competing with the lazy drone of honeybees, things felt normal.

They'd invited her into their conversation, their game and, to some extent, their lives. Sometimes she felt more like a guest than like an employee. And she loved those times, more than she cared to admit. She loved the feeling of fitting into the family, even if they weren't hers. It was a new thing, and she marveled at the difference between how she felt with her parents, Carl and Mabel, and how Fosette and Laurence were treated by Simone. The warmth the older woman displayed to her children, if not to Jemma. Maybe if Mama and Daddy had been the same, her life would have been different. If she'd been their natural child, perhaps Carl would have embraced her instead of pushed her away. Or if she'd been able to grow up with her real parents, especially her real father, she would have had a place and therefore wouldn't have been so quick to turn to Marvin for acceptance.

The game ended, with Russell the victor. They headed indoors for a brief rest before dinner, the sunlight glimmering on the Duchons' pale skin. Instead of giving in to envy, Jemma sank into the midst of their togetherness, with Fosette's arms loosely entwined in hers and Laurence's, and Simone teasing Russell that he'd cheated.

Jemma's laughs rose into the air, joined by all the others.

AFTER A FEW weeks at the Duchons', Jemma was finally feeling settled. She arranged books in the library before dinner, quietly humming Ray Charles's "I Can't Stop Loving You." In the parlor there was a television that was never turned on. Having heard the low sounds of music through the door, she knew Fosette had a radio in her bedroom. After asking if there were any extra radios around, Fosette had brought one to Jemma's room. "You have to leave it here. Grandmère doesn't want any noise in the library." So she worked in silence, surrounded by dusty piles of books, the soft flapping of pages the only sound.

No more strange incidents had occurred. She was beginning to think she'd been stressed by so many things happening in quick succession: leaving home, moving into a new environment. With these heaped on top of the other recent events, it was no wonder she was feeling uneasy. But no spirits had bothered her since the first time she'd been in this room. She'd settled into a rhythm, and working every day (including Saturday and Sunday) left her very little free time to venture into town. Honorine had assured her that her money was being deposited every week, but Jemma had nothing to spend it on and not even a chance to spend it anywhere. Except for seeing the same sights and the same people every day, she enjoyed her new environment, the easy camaraderie with Fosette and the way the young woman welcomed her. What would her childhood have been like if she'd had a sister like her?

Despite Laurence's suggesting that Jemma start by organizing the weirder books, she'd begun with a shelf devoted mostly to classics. *The Great Gatsby. Jane Eyre. Frankenstein.*

She thought of what Fosette had said: *Grandmère has probably read every single one.* But Jemma couldn't remember ever seeing Honorine with a book. The woman pored over the morning and afternoon newspapers, but the only person Jemma regularly saw reading books—in or out of the library—was Laurence.

A swirl of dust tickled Jemma's nose, bringing about two quick sneezes. She stepped away from the shelf.

Clap.

Jemma didn't want to look toward the source of the familiar sound, but her eyes moved of their own accord.

The gray book had fallen off the shelf again.

She'd been able to fool herself that nothing strange had happened since her first day in the library, but this was the third time the same book had fallen on its own.

For several moments she simply looked at it, as if it would do anything more than lie there like the inanimate object it was.

Finally, with trembling fingers, she snatched it up, ready to shove it back on the shelf like she'd done twice before. But something stirred in her. Maybe just the urge to stop it from happening again. She opened the book and wondered what she was reading until she realized the words were written in a foreign language. Flipping through the pages, she could make no sense of it. Some pages were full of cramped cursive, while others contained spaced columns of numbers.

"There," she murmured. "I opened you. Is that what you wanted?"

Don't talk to them!

She pushed the book in so far that it touched the back of the shelf. No way it could fall off on its own now. It didn't matter that she was only halfway done for the day. She had to get out of there.

Jemma glanced at her watch as she left the library. Only one minute until dinnertime, so no time to run upstairs and freshen up. Laurence had strolled into the dining room a few minutes late just a few evenings ago, and Jemma didn't want the look his grandmother had directed his way shining on her. She rushed into the small water closet around the corner from the library and quickly washed her hands. Before she exited the space, the sound of footsteps and Simone's voice—the last person Jemma wanted to run into—stopped her, made her shrink back.

"How long are you going to wait? She's been here nearly a month. One of us is going to die if she doesn't fix this!"

"She has to trust us. If she finds out why we really brought her here, what do you think she's going to do? Do you think she's going to believe us right away?" That was Honorine. "Besides, we don't even know if she's affected the same way we are. She was able to leave before, after all—"

"She's affected—she has to be!"

The footsteps receded.

Jemma exited the water closet, catching sight of a skirt tail swishing into the dining room. They'd been talking about her.

One of us is going to die if she doesn't fix this!

What did that mean?

And getting her to trust them, which was exactly what they had done. They were strange but surely not dangerous. Weren't they?

Lulu's words echoed in her mind, the way she and Charlie had reacted on hearing the Duchon name. Lulu had tried to warn her away: *If I was you, I'd go the other way. Get back on the train or bus or whatever you came here on and go back to where you from.*

And Jemma had ignored all of that, had convinced herself that Lulu and Charlie were mistaken about this beautiful group of people, because she *had* to. She needed this. So she pushed aside the rational thoughts that rose up at night, right before she dropped off to sleep, the sensible voices that asked why anyone should pay Jemma so much money for such a simple job. It was easy to do when she realized how much she wanted to be a part of them, their beauty, their togetherness as a family.

But now uneasiness arose, smacked Jemma lightly across the cheek.

Get moving. You're going to be late.

And get answers from Honorine. Tonight.

JEMMA EXPECTED THE worst when she entered the dining room a full ten minutes late, but Honorine said nothing. The family had already said grace and were passing platters around. As she took her seat, she didn't miss the meaningful look Simone directed to her mother.

Dinner dragged on, and while everyone ate and talked (always about the same topics), Jemma picked at her food, her mind churning. Fosette chattered in her ear or across the table to her brother. Finally, Simone pulled out her after-dinner cigarette and Russell plowed through his second helping. Agnes began clearing away dishes, and before the family could all stand up and go their separate ways, Jemma turned to Honorine.

"Mrs. Duchon? I'm sorry, but I overheard a conversation between you and your daughter. It's about my being down here."

The weight of five sets of staring eyes seemed to press Jemma down in her seat. If she expected Honorine to react in anger or with pretend ignorance over her eavesdropping, she was surprised when the woman reacted with neither.

"Ah, that. I had to get you down here somehow, Miss Barker. If I'd told you that we hired you to break a curse, would you have come?"

FIVE

WHAT DID YOU say?" Jemma asked, although the question seemed stupid. She'd heard the woman perfectly.

"Our family, although proud and distinguished, has a curse on it. Every seven years, on March twelfth, one of us dies. In a most unpleasant way, I might add. We've hired you in hopes that you can break the curse before that date next year."

The plaques on the family burial vault loomed in Jemma's mind.

One of us is going to die if she doesn't fix this!

Jemma glanced at Simone, whose face registered no shock. Looking around, she saw that none of their faces did. They all believed this.

"What makes you think I can break a curse? I'm a teacher, not a . . . a . . ."

"You have more talents than you think. Don't be so sure you can't save this family. We looked into your background. We know about you. A couple of mediums we've consulted in the past have told us what you might be capable of. And we know you need this position. We know about your old job, the one you lost after you tried to kill yourself. We know that your father, Carl Barker, died just a couple of months ago and that you spent nearly your last penny giving him a proper burial. You were living with a man you're not married to and he put you out—"

"He didn't put me out," Jemma spit, her face hot. "I left."

"Rather than raise another woman's bastard, of course you did."

Jemma sat, the stillness of her body in contrast with the many questions running through her head, each clamoring for first place in line.

How did they know all these things?

Who were these people?

Would they hurt her?

How crazy were they?

And something else, a surprising thing beneath her fright. She'd grown to like it here. She'd put Lulu's and Charlie's warnings aside, had convinced herself that *they* were the crazy ones. She had a place here, even if it wasn't her home, even if the Duchons weren't her family. She'd ignored the whisperings of her intuition, shut her eyes to the ghosts, because she wanted so much to stay.

Even now, as a part of her shouted for her to stand up and run, another part glanced at Fosette's open and inviting face. That part also glossed over the anxiety shining out of the woman's eyes.

"I don't know how you know all these things about me," Jemma started, faced with the futility of denying any of the truths. "But I think there's been a mistake. I'll pack my things and head to the train station." She pushed her chair back and stood.

"And go where? And with what money?" Honorine asked mildly. "You accepted the job I offered you because you're all but penniless. Are you going to go back to that man? Why, he probably has his whore moved in already. Your parents are dead and they left you with nothing." She leaned forward, her eyes fixed on Jemma. "Where will you go?"

Jemma looked across the table at Russell, with his slight paunch pushing against an oxford shirt, the boxy shoulders of his blazer well out of fashion. At Simone, her gray eyes studying an amber liquid in her goblet. At Laurence, in a dowdy tie and blazer. At Honorine, who spoke in tones that suggested nothing more unusual than the day's menu.

"Please, Miss Barker, sit down, and I will explain why we hired you."

"No, I don't think I will. I'm leaving."

She pushed herself out of the room and up the stairs, a mix of fear, sadness and confusion weighing down her steps. As much as she liked it here, she had no idea what intentions the Duchons had for her. Since they knew she was from Chicago, they should also know that she wasn't some naïf. She'd seen plenty growing up, and one thing she learned early on: leave crazy people to be crazy.

Jemma squashed the pile of wrinkled clothes flat before slamming her suitcase shut. She couldn't believe her new life was ending before it had really begun. She'd grown to like the ease and the budding acceptance this chapter had offered.

After she packed, pushing aside the fact that she had a four-mile trek ahead of her (perhaps longer if the buses had stopped running for the evening), she turned to find Fosette leaning against the bedroom doorframe.

"You can't leave."

"You're wrong. Please move out of my way."

She was afraid that Fosette would do no such thing, but she allowed Jemma to pass. She ignored the questions rising in her mind, each one a wave with a bigger one behind it, as she scurried downstairs, quick footsteps behind her. Jemma turned to the woman when they were halfway down.

"You knew. You treated me nice, and all the time you knew why I was hired. Why didn't you say anything?"

"Jemma, I'm so sorry, but please, listen to Grandmère. We had good reason for bringing you here, and you never would have come if we'd told you the truth. You'd have thought we were mad and never even responded to us."

Jemma's lips tightened, holding back a retort, which Fosette seemed to sense.

"All right, it sounds crazy. I know that. But you're safe here. No one's going to hurt you! Can you just come back in and sit down and listen? After that, you can decide. But we do need you."

She didn't want to be pulled in by Fosette, but curiosity tugged at her. They needed her. And as much as she didn't want to admit it to herself, she needed the job.

At the very least, it couldn't hurt to hear them out.

She returned the suitcase to her bedroom and followed Fosette to the dining room. As they took their seats, Fosette said, "There's nothing for you back in Chicago. Your place is here now. With us."

"Do you know about this, too?" Jemma asked Agnes, who pushed a rolling cart toward the doorway that led to the kitchen. Surely someone around here had to be sane! But the maid only stopped for a brief moment before she disappeared into the next room.

"You're wasting your time expecting any answers from her," Honorine said. "She's dumb."

Jemma faced the family matriarch, her mouth open.

"That's right. She cannot speak. Miss Barker, as I've told you, we believe you have the power to break the curse that's been set on our family. It's vital that you do this before next March twelfth, before another of us dies."

"Is that what you're paying me for?"

Honorine gave a brief nod.

"Then you're wasting your money. I don't know the first thing about curses, let alone breaking them. And yes, you're right. I need the money. That's why I accepted this job. I don't know how you know all these things about me, but since you did all that digging, you should've known that I don't know how to do what you're asking."

Jemma sat back, puffing out a quick breath.

"I trust that you'll figure things out."

"How, Mrs. Duchon? I don't see how I could possibly do anything to help you." She looked at the others' faces, searching for any hint of reason among them. Turning back to Honorine, she insisted, "I don't even think I believe in curses. None of this makes sense."

"Whether you believe or not, this is real. And if you do not break the curse, Miss Barker, you face the same possible fate as the rest of us."

"What?"

"The curse affects all of the Duchon line. And you are a part of that line. You are our family, our prodigal daughter returned. If the curse remains unbroken, you also risk a most horrible death."

Simone cackled, her head thrown back, her fingers gripping the edge of the table. Jemma paid that only cursory attention as Honorine's words echoed in her head. The woman was telling her she was related to them. That she could die, just like them.

"You're wrong," Jemma whispered to Honorine, shaking her head at the absurdity. "That can't be."

"You know you were adopted, right?"

"Yes . . . but I can't—" The words "be part of this family" rested behind Jemma's lips, only for her to bite down on them. Whether she believed it or not, that she belonged with these people, she *wanted* to, wanted to be part of their beautifulness, as if it were a thing that rubbed off. Jemma knew she was no ugly duckling, but she was as drab as one when compared with this family of swans. Her certainty had little to do with the shape of her eyes or the way her nose stopped in a rounded point. It had nothing to do with her figure, which was willowy and fine. But her skin and kinky hair, which set her firmly in the *brown* camp, made her second tier in a world where "if you're light, you're all right" was the place many of them aspired to be. A flush warmed her face. Had any of the Duchons seen her shame at being adopted but never feeling wanted?

"Be part of this family?" Honorine finished for her. "How do you think we know so much about you? Why do you think we offered you this position, out of all the people we could have hired? It's not a job for just anyone. The curse has to be broken by family."

Jemma looked at each of the others, her mind a chaotic minefield. Honorine was lying; she had to be. Yes, she knew Carl and Mabel Barker had adopted her as a baby. They'd told her as much when she turned fourteen. Apparently her mother hadn't wanted to, but Daddy had insisted.

"We owe you the truth," he'd said, a self-satisfied gleam in his eye.

Jemma hadn't asked for the truth, though, had been fine believing that the adults who raised her were her biological parents. She'd never once noticed a lack of a resemblance, because like her, Carl and Mabel were brown-skinned people, and she looked like she belonged to them.

And yet . . .

Something had bothered her from the time she was very young, when she'd first seen a ghostly woman sitting at the foot of her bed. When Jemma had told Mama about it, her mother had looked frightened but had tried to explain it away. While Daddy, for some reason she didn't understand then and had only a wisp of understanding dancing just beyond her grasp now, had seemed furious.

But to be one of the Duchons?

"I don't believe you," Jemma said, crossing her arms. "If I'm actually part of this family, who are my mother and father? How am I related to you, to each one of you?"

"Your mother's name was Inès Lily Duchon—"

"Was?" Jemma interrupted.

"She died, tragically, right after you were born."

"Who was she to you?"

"My youngest daughter."

Jemma caught Simone's gaze. If that was true, it made Simone her aunt, Fosette and Laurence her cousins, Russell her uncle.

"That makes you my . . ."

"Grandmother," Honorine finished, giving Jemma a brief nod.

The horror and pride this elicited in Jemma shocked her, brought about a self-loathing that she should want so badly to be one of them. She covered her face with her hands, shaking her head.

"No, no, no, no, this can't be. I am not related to you people."

"Your birthday is March 12, 1935. You were born upstairs, in the room you occupy now."

"Who's my father?" The question seemed to come on its own.

"A man your mother fancied but wasn't married to."

Another blow.

"But . . . if I was born here and I'm related to you, why did you give me away?"

"That was your mother's wish."

Jemma pushed back from the table, rising to her feet without being fully aware of it. None of this made sense.

She needed proof, and yet she didn't want it. Because if it was proved to her that she was Honorine's granddaughter, that her mother had wanted her to go away *(Why? Why?)*, Jemma didn't think she was ready for whatever answers she'd get to the questions that would arise.

"I don't believe you."

"I told you this ungrateful brat would react this way," Simone said to Honorine. "We were right to get rid of her."

"Maman!" Fosette cried.

Jemma stumbled backward, turned and was across the foyer, almost at the front door, when she remembered her suitcase. Three hundred dollars a week or not, she couldn't stay here. Before she could run upstairs, Honorine approached.

"Miss Barker, you cannot leave the property. No, we have no intention of stopping you. But part of the curse binds you to this house, to this property. You're bound, like all the Duchons who were here when your mother placed the curse."

"My—my mother?"

"Yes. Inès cursed our family with her dying breath. None of us has been able to leave the grounds since the day you were born."

"But why . . . why would she do that?"

Honorine held out her hands, palms up. Jemma rushed toward her, stopping short of grabbing the woman and shaking her.

"Why would my mother curse you? Her own family? Me? Don't you see that what you're saying makes no sense?" A hard laugh erupted from Jemma. Why was she asking questions like this, as if what Honorine had said could possibly be true?

"And yet a part of you does believe." Honorine's eyes held Jemma's gaze. "I see it. You'd do well to believe what I'm saying if you want to live beyond your next birthday. You saw the plaques on our vault. You know I'm telling the truth."

The rest of the family hovered in the archway to the dining room, Laurence standing behind his sister, his hands resting on her shoulders. Menace shone out of Simone's eyes, while Russell dug a pinkie nail between his teeth.

Jemma's eyes darted to the front door, just steps away. She could be out of here in seconds, suitcase be damned. She'd steal money to get on a train if she had to. Anything to get away from here.

And then Fosette was there, slipping her hand in Jemma's, whispering in her ear.

"It really is a matter of life and death. If you help us, you help yourself. We're family now."

SIX

JEMMA OPENED HER eyes the next morning, the sight of medallions on the ceiling pulling forth tears. So it wasn't all a nightmare. Except it was, if any of it was true. As she lay there, she tried to recognize anything of any of the Duchons in herself.

Physically, there was nothing, from the color of her skin, to the texture of her hair, to the shape of her nose. Wouldn't she know if she were related to them? Wouldn't she feel a connection? Noting the quiet, from outside and in, she checked her watch. Six twenty. She swung her legs out of bed and looked for a telephone in the room, already knowing there wasn't one. In the light of a new day, the fright that had gripped her the night before receded. She dressed, checked that she'd packed everything and carried her shoes in her hands as she tiptoed downstairs.

She was breaking the promise she'd made to Fosette the night before, but she couldn't stay with these unhinged people. Just as she turned the crystal knob on the front door, she spied a telephone table to the side of it. Was there *anyone* she could call?

Glancing around and seeing no one, Jemma picked up the phone receiver and, with trembling fingers, dialed the operator.

"I need to make a person-to-person call," Jemma said, and recited Marvin's number in a whisper, the shame of wanting to talk to him instead of her friend Betty driving down her voice.

"Hold, please," the voice on the other end said.

When Jemma heard the phone ringing, she wanted to weep.

"Hello?" her ex-boyfriend's sleep-slurred voice answered.

"Marvin, it's me. You gotta help me."

"Who is this?"

"It's Jemma. Remember me?" When he didn't respond, she went on. "I'm in New Orleans and I need your help getting home."

"You must be out your mind, girl. You left on your own account."

"And why was that? Was it because I didn't want to play mammy to your baby?"

Behind Marvin's wall of silence, her ears picked up a woman's voice, similarly sleepy and asking what sounded like "Who you talking to?" Jemma's hand tightened on the phone, but she maintained a level tone.

"I'm in real trouble here. Are you going to help me or not?"

"You in jail or something?"

"No, but—"

An uneasy breeze sliced up Jemma's back and she turned to see Agnes in the dining room archway, watching her. Feeling caught but also not feeling like she'd done anything wrong, Jemma twitched her lips in a semi-smile. Would the maid get one of the Duchons? Jemma almost shuddered at the thought of Simone being the next one to come downstairs.

"I'm not in jail—"

"Look, you left. You never even thanked me for saving your life, and now you call first thing in the morning with some mess? If you're in New Orleans, stay in New Orleans. Don't call here again."

Click.

Jemma almost dialed the operator again, but the heavy press of Agnes's stare pushed her out the door. She'd call Betty from the nearest phone booth.

She had five dollars in cash, not enough for a bus ticket across state, let alone back to Chicago. But she also had six hundred dollars in checks. All she had to do was go to the bank. She had a walk ahead of her, and Jemma would use that time to think of her next move. Did she want to go back to Chicago, with its increasingly painful memories? There was clearly no future with Marvin—and there hadn't been, not after everything that had happened. The bastard wouldn't even help her when she called and told him she was in trouble.

As she descended the porch steps, she saw a man sawing a downed tree limb. His short-sleeved shirt was soaked through, his booted foot resting on one end of the branch as he made smaller pieces of it. Even from this distance, it was obvious she hadn't met him, as his skin was a dark brown, making it highly unlikely that he was a Duchon.

The gardener.

Her steps slowed, but she had no plans to stick around any longer than necessary. Jemma just wanted out. As she drew closer he paused his sawing, tipping back his planter's hat to wipe his forehead and standing up straight.

"Good morning," she said in a low voice.

"Morning. You must be Jemma." He smiled at her, giving her a light appraisal. Only the most subtle bit of slackness in his jawline and a few gray hairs along his temples signaled his middle age.

Jemma gave a short nod and stared at his offered hand for a moment before deciding it would be rude if she didn't take it. "Nice to meet you."

"You going somewhere?" He pointed to her suitcase. "How you getting where you going?"

Jemma hitched the case closer to her. "I'm just going to walk until I reach the bus line."

His eyes narrowed. "You're part of the family."

She didn't know how to answer that, although it hadn't been a question, and when she tried to shake her head, she succeeded only in half shaking, half nodding. He nodded back, his increased interest evident.

"You can try and go, I guess, but you ain't gonna get far."

Jemma took a step toward the gate before stopping and facing the man again. "Are you related to them?"

"Oh, no." He chuckled. "I'm Dennis, the gardener, handyman, runner. No, I ain't family. Can't you tell? But you are. And that's how I know you might be able to walk out them gates, but you won't get fifty yards up the road, where the property line ends. You'll be back sure as the sun rises in the east." He wiped his face with a wrinkled rag.

Jemma told herself this was some elaborate joke and now the Duchons had the gardener in on it.

"And what'll happen to me if I walk past the property line? I fall down dead?"

"No, nothing like that, but you won't get past it. It's like it's an invisible wall or something right there. It'll turn you around."

"But . . . but I didn't grow up here. If . . . if it's true that I was born here—"

"You was. I was here the day you was born. Right up there." He pointed to the second floor of the house.

"But obviously I left. Someone took me away, so I'm not bound to this place."

"You was just a baby then, Miss Jemma. And maybe you being carried away made a difference. I don't know how these things work. But you came back on your own and you're here now. And like the rest of your family, you can't leave."

She'd prove them wrong. Once she escaped, and she got far enough away, they'd realize how silly their stories had been, how wrong they'd been for trying to trick her.

"I'm going to try, though. Goodbye," she told Dennis.

Fear tingled its way up her body as she approached the gate, but she pushed it open, a heavy creak slicing the morning quiet.

As she looked down the empty road, the only sounds that reached Jemma's ears were blue jay and mockingbird calls. The heat settled on her shoulders like a wool shawl, drawing itself down her body.

Once she exited, Jemma released a thick breath. She wouldn't even chance a glance backward.

She hitched her suitcase once and walked, not going fifty feet before a black Studebaker nearly sideswiped her, sending her sprawling onto the grass, her suitcase flying away and snapping open. With shaking hands, she stuffed everything back inside. Despite what those lunatics at that house had told her—*Your family; they're your family*—she was not bound there. She'd make it into New Orleans, and the first chance she got to leave the city, she'd grab it with two desperate hands.

"Jemma!" a man called from behind her.

She pushed herself up, brushing the dirt from her palms, inspecting the runs at the knees in her stockings. A light drizzle had started, but she didn't open her case again to find her rain bonnet. She willed herself not to turn around, swinging her suitcase up.

Just take a step. Put one foot in front of the other. Just go.

"Jemma, come back!"

She turned to see Laurence standing just outside of the gate, one hand tight around a picket, as if he couldn't go any farther. Dennis stood to one side, his face a mask of horror at her near accident.

It couldn't be true. She couldn't be trapped here.

Fosette rushed down the porch steps, her lacy white dressing gown trailing behind her. She skidded to a stop behind Laurence, refusing to take one step out of the gates. The light rain threatened to expose her underneath her nightclothes, but she seemed not to care.

"Jemma, please. We're your family," she called out. "We can help each other!"

Jemma looked down the road, so still and quiet at this time of morning. All she had to do was walk. Against her will, she turned back to the house, to the three people staring at her as if she were about to step on a mine.

I'll stay and help, she'd told Fosette just last night. *I promise.*

She would have said anything last night, however, to bring a semblance of sanity to things. Inside the gates, Fosette made her careful way toward Jemma, grabbing each picket like it was a lifeline. She pressed her face between two of them, pleading with Jemma to return to the house.

"We need you. I don't want to die. I don't want anyone else in our family to die. Now that you're back, we can be a real family again, *cousine.*" Her trembling hand reached out.

Jemma looked down the road, empty and eerily quiet, before turning back to her cousins hanging on to the gate, clearly afraid to take another step. Maybe they'd tested the so-called curse before, tried to escape just as she was doing now. Whatever had stopped them had cowed them.

"Please. You promised me."

There it was. Fosette's brief reminder, thick as a rope around Jemma's waist, ready to snatch her back.

Jemma looked at the road once more before returning to the Duchon property, the rain falling steadily, Laurence closing the gates behind them.

LATE THAT AFTERNOON, Jemma dressed for dinner.

No one had seemed surprised by her return. Everyone had simply watched as she tracked rainwater across the foyer and up the stairs to her room. She'd been in there all day, and hadn't let Fosette in when she came knocking. She didn't feel like dealing with the guilt of trying to escape. Agnes had left a covered tray of food, which Jemma ignored. But now that it was almost dinnertime, she was extremely hungry.

She still didn't believe that she was trapped there, not really, but it was clear that the Duchons believed they were. They wouldn't even set a foot outside of the gates.

She looked in the mirror above the dresser. The rain had completely ruined her hair. As she'd suspected, there were no hot combs to be found. When she'd asked the maid about one earlier, the woman had given a brief shake of her head, making Jemma feel stupid for asking, as if these people with their good hair had need of such primitive contraptions. All Jemma could do was rag curl her hair, and now, as she unraveled each scrap of cotton—torn from an old shirt she'd found in the chifforobe—dismay washed over her at the sight. A frizzy, uneven shape haloed her head, neither kinky nor straight, just a mixed-up wasteland of hair. She almost tied a scarf around her head, but she discarded the idea because it would make her look like she worked here. But she did, didn't she? Even Agnes didn't wear a head rag, Jemma thought, as she tossed the scarf aside and squared her shoulders before opening the door.

Dinner was much the same as it always was, with the conversation revolving around newspaper headlines. Jemma tried to shut the family out, much as she shut out the spirits she didn't want to see. She lost herself in her bowl of gumbo, the same slightly burnt taste there as always, as a realization washed over her.

The Duchons hadn't left this property in years. That explained the dowdy, old-fashioned clothes.

Simone was outfitted in a pale pink collared dress, wooden buttons trailing down the center, a string of pearls matching the globes in her ears. Before Russell had sat down, Jemma had seen his wide-legged trousers, cuffed at the bottoms, completely unlike the fitted slacks men wore nowadays. Laurence, in his slightly newer but still hopelessly outdated plaid blazer and linen pants. It all made sense. They hadn't been to the shop in years.

Instead of simply viewing them as her employer's family, now she couldn't help but think of them as *her* family. Fosette and Laurence, her cousins. Russell, her uncle. That nasty piece of work Simone, her aunt.

Jemma thought she'd feel more of a tie to them, but skepticism and bewilderment seemed to override any emotions. She didn't want to ask anything of them, wanted simply to eat and return to her room, but one thing bothered her enough to force the question out of her.

"Who does the grocery shopping if none of you can leave?"

"Dennis does it," Honorine answered.

"What about Agnes?"

"Agnes is busy enough with her duties here. Besides, Dennis likes doing it. Agnes hates going into town. People have . . . teased her in the past."

"About . . . ?"

"About her being dumb, of course."

"And church?"

"We have an understanding with Father Louis. He comes out at the beginning of the month and holds Mass for us in our chapel."

By "understanding," Jemma assumed Honorine meant the family paid him. Those questions answered, she resumed her focus on her meal, doing her best to tune out the low buzz of their conversation.

After Honorine excused everyone, Jemma retreated upstairs, with Russell close on her heels. She stopped on the landing, looking at the framed family portraits on the wall. "Are any of these of my mother?" she asked Russell.

"No."

"Why?"

This was the first time she'd really studied him. She imagined his good looks twenty, thirty years ago, which even now held on with a steely grip. If Honorine was to be believed, he, like the rest of them, hadn't left the property in nearly three decades. Since Jemma had arrived, none of them had gone anywhere off the grounds. Not once. But holding on to a healthy dose of skepticism about what her employer had told her allowed her to imagine a way out of this mess.

"My mother was very angry with my sister for what she did."

"For the curse," Jemma whispered. "But why did she curse you?"

"Apparently she hated us."

"Why?"

He rocked back on his heels, hands in his pockets. "You're asking about ancient history. It's been years since I thought about why Inès did any of what she did. What matters now is that it's done."

Something about his offhand reply convinced Jemma that he had actually given a great deal of thought to why his sister had cursed them.

"But someone has to know. Your mother, maybe."

"*Your* grandmother, you mean?"

"So there are no pictures of my mother here at all? Not even a small one?"

He shook his head.

"But you knew her. What did she look like?"

An uncomfortable stretch of silence passed, and Jemma looked away from Russell's unblinking stare. "My sister . . . was very beautiful. She looked a little like Lena Horne. We've seen her in the magazines, you know, and on the television once or twice." A faraway look glazed his eyes for a moment before he cleared his throat. "Even so, Inès was very troubled."

Judging by this family, Jemma wasn't at all surprised to hear that.

"My sister saw things, could feel things."

"Saw things?"

"Ghosts," Russell whispered.

JEMMA STOOD AT the window, looking out over the grounds. The half-moon gave off just enough light to make out the croquet pitch. A narrow path led from there to a small building a dozen yards away. Maybe that was the chapel.

The house was quiet at one in the morning. Jemma had been in her room since after dinner. Someone had knocked around ten o'clock, but she'd pretended to be asleep.

According to Russell, her mother had seen ghosts, just like Jemma. The tiny kernel of doubt that she actually was a Duchon seemed to shrink further with each scrap of information she gathered. Was it passed down, then, seeing ghosts? She'd asked him if he'd ever seen them, and her uncle had shaken his head, his voice rising from its usual low rumble into a harsh denial.

What she wanted more than anything else right now was to know what her mother had looked like. Was she even prettier than that horrid Simone? There had to be a picture here somewhere. Jemma found it hard to believe that even Honorine could be as heartless as to remove all evidence of Inès's existence.

Movement outside of the window caught Jemma's eye. Two people had emerged from the back of the house. At first, her breath caught; she was afraid ghosts were walking the grounds. But even in the dimness, she recognized their movements. Fosette and Laurence. When Fosette turned back, Jemma moved aside, her heartbeat quick and erratic. Surely her cousin had seen the drapes twitch. When Jemma chanced another look, the two of them continued across the lawn, disappearing off the path opposite the chapel into thick shrubbery.

Where were they going at such a late hour?

This house was full of mysteries.

Jemma had no idea where they'd gone or for what purpose. The only thing she knew for sure was that they couldn't have gone far.

Tomorrow, she'd walk the property, find out just how much leash she had.

SEVEN

THE NEXT MORNING, after breakfast, instead of heading outside, Jemma accepted Honorine's invitation to the parlor "for a brief chat about your actual duties."

"I'm sure this has been a shock to you. I forget sometimes that we've had decades to get used to this," the woman said, settling in her wingback armchair with a cup of café au lait balanced on a saucer. The heat had lessened some, and what Jemma assumed was fall weather had begun, although it reminded her of high summer in Chicago.

"Since I was born?" she asked.

"Yes. The day you were born, your cousin died."

"My cousin? And my mother, on the same day?"

"Yes. Soon after your mother set her terrible curse on us, she died. There was a lot going on, you see, between that and your birth. We lost sight of Lucie, Simone's other daughter. She was just three. By the time we missed her, it was too late. She'd gotten into the carriage house. Somehow a saddle fell from the wall on top of her. The weight of it snapped her little neck and she died."

A chill gripped Jemma's hands, despite their being wrapped around her own cup of café au lait.

"But we didn't know the whole of it then, not at first. Inès had cursed us, but we thought Lucie's death was just an accident. It didn't take long for us to discover that it was no accident. Each one of us tried to get off the property at different times. We had a car back then, and my husband, Raymond, took off in it, only to have it break down just outside the gate. A brand-new car. Your uncle Russell tried to escape through the backwoods, only to run into such a tangle of branches that he could go no farther. Each of us was stopped in our own way, some of us more than once."

"I don't understand why my mother supposedly cursed you."

Honorine's right brow lifted as she studied Jemma over the rim of her coffee cup. "You still don't quite believe."

"Why should I? I don't know you people. You've lied to me about things that you shouldn't have lied about. Leading me on that I was hired to be a tutor—"

"You made that assumption, Miss Barker."

Jemma brushed that aside. "I want to know why Inès cursed you. Until then, I don't want to hear anything more you have to say."

The older woman set her cup down on the saucer, the small clink barely louder than a cat's paws across a rug. "Your mother was, for lack of a better term, the black sheep of this family. We had an impeccable reputation and she wanted for nothing, but she seemed determined to throw it all away. Instead of looking forward to her debut in society, she was interested in frequenting dance halls and surrounding herself with the very dregs of this city. She met your father, but she knew we wouldn't approve of a marriage between them. When she turned up with child, she thought that would persuade her father to approve. And when he didn't, she turned on us completely."

"Why didn't you approve of my father?"

"He was dark," Honorine said without any hesitation or shame.

Jemma didn't know if it was the matter-of-factness of the statement or what it implied that hurt more.

Her grandmother continued. "By the time we realized how cursed we were, we'd already sent you away. How could we keep you when your mother had damned us? And although our orbit had grown so small as to be claustrophobic, we were still caught by surprise when, on your seventh birthday, another one of us died. That time, it was my husband."

A stillness washed over Jemma, her coffee lukewarm by then. She wanted to ask how he'd died, but a part of her shook its head, covered its ears, not wanting to hear what it knew was horrific.

"March 12, 1942, not too long after we were pulled into the Second World War, my husband, Raymond, choked on a chicken bone at dinner. It caught in his throat, and one end of it was so sharp that it cut him from inside. He choked and bled to death at the same time."

"Please," Jemma said, but her grandmother steamrolled on. Although Honorine's voice was flat, her face expressionless, there was some type of light dancing in her eyes, a flare of seeming delight at Jemma's discomfort.

"March 12, 1949. You were fourteen and in junior high school up there in Chicago. That bastard Truman was president. Our family had not set foot in a church in nearly fourteen years. All day, we were terrified, just waiting for something to happen, for someone to die. We all gathered in the living room. We thought that, perhaps, if we were all in one place, where we could see one another, we'd be all right. We'd survive. We took all our meals in there, and you'd better believe there was no chicken served that day. No, all we had was seafood gumbo, with the tiniest bits of crab and sausage. After dinner, we were all still alive. My family thought, foolishly, we'd beaten it somehow. We'd beaten her. But I knew better. And I was right.

"I told them we should sleep downstairs, but my youngest son, André, insisted on going up to bed. It was very late by then; he thought the danger had passed. I was so worried that I followed him to the stairs. I wanted to make sure he reached the top safely, that he didn't tumble down and break his neck. I watched him go into the bathroom and a little bit of relief washed over me. But within minutes, all of the lights flickered out. When we had candles lit and could see, we found André in the tub, along with the radio he always listened to. It had fallen in when he reached for a washcloth and knocked it off the sink. It was eleven thirty at night. My son was thirty-five."

"Mrs. Duchon," Jemma started, her trembling hand threatening to spill coffee all over the floor.

"March 12, 1956. You were celebrating your twenty-first birthday. I wonder—did you have cake? A party? Were you out trying to integrate lunch counters or universities? Whatever you were doing, you were not, like us, trapped here, as we'd been for twenty years by then, nearly frightened of our own shadows. I don't think any of us ate. We were too scared even to sip water. Luckily—or maybe not so luckily, I should say—it happened early. Russell's wife, Lenore, tried to open a bedroom window to let in some air. She struggled with it, and when she finally got it open, she rested her hands on the sill like a dimwit, and it came crashing down on her fingers, breaking at least two of them. I'll never forget her screams."

"But . . . she didn't die, then?"

"I wasn't finished. While we all came running from down here to see what had happened, she got one hand free. The glass was broken but still intact. Until she somehow managed to push against it, catching her arm in the process. It sliced her wrist into ragged ribbons before we made it to the room. She bled to death within minutes."

As gruesome as Honorine's story was, something else had nagged at Jemma from the moment she'd heard the victim was Russell's wife.

"Lenore wasn't a Duchon, though, since she'd only married into the family. She couldn't have been affected by the curse."

"Lenore was indeed a Duchon, a second cousin on my father's side."

"A cousin?"

"Don't look so shocked. Royal families do it all the time. How else do you think they maintain those bloodlines?"

"And what's the prize in that? It's . . ." Jemma bit down on the word "disgusting."

"It's what? Sick? No more sick than me marrying Raymond, who was a second cousin to me. You find it shameful? What's really shameful is how we felt about you every year your birthday rolled around. With each March twelfth every seven years, we hoped, prayed, that none of us here would die. How was it fair that I should lose a husband, a son, a granddaughter, a daughter-in-law, while you, Inès's offspring, should be allowed to live, unknowing, unharmed?

"After Lenore, we had to do something. We began looking for you. We hired a private detective. It took him a while since we didn't know where in this country you might be, but he finally found you. We had him watch you. That's how we knew about your adoptive father's death, which couldn't have come at a better time. That's how we knew about the man with whom you were living in sin, his other woman, your failed suicide attempt, your moving in with your friend. We were fortunate that you didn't succeed in killing yourself, because the only person besides your mother who could break the curse was you.

"'I curse all the Duchon blood,' your mother said. 'From this day forth, I bind the family to this house. I bind them forever.'"

Jemma realized she'd been gripping the cup in trembling fingers only when a bit of coffee sloshed onto her skirt. All this time, Honorine's voice had remained as level as if she were reading a passage from the *Iliad* to students in a literature class. Her long fingers alternately folded together or rested—seemingly innocent, harmless—in her lap. And yet the coolness of the words contrasted with the words themselves, the way the woman hurled them in clipped precision, with edges hard and sharp enough to cut.

So why Jemma continued to open her mouth and ask questions was beyond her understanding. What would make the most sense would be to flee this place. Yes, she'd tried that already and failed, but she refused to accept that she was as trapped here as the Duchons believed themselves to be.

"Why would I be able to break the curse?"

"When Inès said those words, you were still part of her body. The cord connecting the two of you hadn't yet been severed, so your blood and her blood still mixed."

Jemma shook her head, unsure why she'd expected Honorine's story to become less horrible instead of more.

"She cursed you as I was being born?"

"Yes. Her mouth spit out the curse the same way her body spit out a bastard. And because she cursed us while you were still connected, you may as well have said the curse yourself. We've consulted with a few mediums, and they've all told us the same thing.

The person who cast the curse can break it, but since Inès can't, you're the next best thing. So you see, Miss Barker, we need each other. We need you to undo your mother's curse, and if you ever want to know who you truly are, you need us."

How did Honorine know that one of Jemma's greatest desires was to know where she was from, *who* she was from? To fit as seamlessly into her real family as a baby chick fits beneath its mother.

Try as she might, Jemma hadn't forgiven Carl Barker for shattering her sense of belonging, even before delivering the news of her adoption. She'd fooled herself that she had, with the expensive funeral that had drained her savings, with the loud accolades that slipped across her tongue, slick and false. But with every day of his holding her at arm's length, even as Mabel, her mother, tried—and failed—to reel Jemma in, the resentment grew until it was a high wall between her and her parents.

She'd told herself that she loved her father, repeated it over and over until she convinced herself of it.

"Even if you don't truly believe," Honorine said now, "we are your family. We are all you have."

AS JEMMA VENTURED onto the back lawn an hour later, her mind churned. She walked across the croquet pitch, kicking a wooden ball into the bushes as she passed. Beyond that, she found a dilapidated carriage house, which must have been the place where little Lucie had died. Jemma gave it a wide berth.

Deep down, despite Honorine's duplicity in bringing her here, Jemma's suspicion that the woman was actually telling the truth about them being family was rooting. How could the idea both thrill and horrify her at the same time?

Before she realized it, the family vault loomed ahead. She

approached it, gripped by the emotion rising at the sight of her mother's name on one of the plaques.

INÈS LILY DUCHON

SEPTEMBER 29, 1915–MARCH 12, 1935

Nothing else. No *beloved daughter and sister.* No engraved images of angels. Just this stark and simple memorial.

Jemma traced the outline of her mother's name. She then searched for Lenore Duchon, Russell's wife, and found the plaque, March 12, 1956, her date of death, just as Honorine had said. Before she could peruse the rest of the plaques, a cool breeze pulled goose bumps from her skin.

Jemma spun around to find a spirit behind her. The ghost's eyes were the only opaque part of her, bottomless black orbs dull with hatred.

The only sound was that of Jemma's chattering teeth, even as sweat sprouted beneath her arms.

"No," she said. "Five . . . four . . ."

The spirit raised an arm, one finger outstretched.

If it touched her, Jemma would go insane.

She turned and ran toward the woods, her skirt flapping around her thighs. Right before she hit the wall of trees, she wondered just how far she'd be able to go in, how far before her mother's curse would stop her. Once she made it past the edge of the woods and the coolness of the shade began to lick the sweat from her brow, Jemma slowed, too afraid to peek behind her, in case the ghost had followed her, had floated while she'd stampeded.

Jemma stopped and pulled in gulps of air, her hands on her knees. She'd made it this far without being turned back to the house.

How much farther could she go?

She looked over her shoulder, a breath full of relief escaping her. The spirit hadn't followed. Jemma took several tentative steps deeper into the woods, a soft bed of leaves and pine needles sinking beneath her feet, the air thick with a marshy odor. With each step, she told herself that she had to be past the property line. Once the trees were dense enough to blot out much of the sunlight, Jemma quickened her pace.

I'm free! I'm not bound.

It turned into a run, this time without the fear of being chased. This time, Jemma ran toward freedom, away from the Duchons and their strangeness, away from their trap and everything she owned in this world.

When she was sure that she was far past the property line, she slowed again. Nearly invisible through the foliage was a rundown wooden shack that looked like it had been deserted for a hundred years. Jemma didn't approach it. Taking in her surroundings, she was sure she was lost. She turned around and around, trying to get her bearings, looking for a trail. The beige of her flats was hidden under a thick layer of dark mud, leaves and twigs stuck to the soles. Her stockings were ruined between the runs up the legs and the burs dotting them. The hem of her skirt was splattered with soil.

As she worked to slow her breath, she wondered if the Duchons had lied about yet another thing—being bound to the property. If she truly was related to them, how was she able to break free? Unless . . . she wasn't really related to them. Or . . . the property line ran much farther than she thought. Or . . . there was no curse at all.

Yet she believed the Duchons were bound, and not only because Dennis had confirmed it. None of them had left the property since she'd arrived. Jemma thought of Fosette seeming too scared even to venture out of the front gates. She saw the woman's face pressed between two pickets, remembered the sense of desperation humming off her and Laurence as they begged her to return.

She also believed, inexplicably, that she was part of their family.

Too afraid to go any deeper into the woods, Jemma returned to the abandoned shack. Once she was on the side she'd first approached it from, she retraced her steps, finding a narrow overgrown path and walking carefully until the trees began to thin and the Duchon back lawn gradually came into view.

Despite everything, she wanted answers. She deserved them.

Dennis was pruning a shrub on the far end of the croquet pitch.

"Afternoon, Jemma," he greeted her as she approached, his eyes widening at her disheveled appearance.

"Hello, Dennis." Jemma took in his brown arms, the sweat running freely down. He and Agnes were probably the only sane ones on this property. She pointed over her shoulder. "How deep do those woods run?"

"Pretty deep. Why? I don't think you're going hunting—I don't see no rifle in your hands," he said with a small smile.

Jemma wiped her forehead with the back of her arm. "Is there a trail in there?"

"Not that I know of, but I don't go in there, either." He stopped pruning, and pushed his hat back as if to get a better look at her. "All sorts of critters be back there. 'Shiners, too."

She decided to be direct. "How far does the property line run back there?"

Dennis looked down for a moment, his lips tight. When his eyes lifted again, what looked like pity shone in them. Jemma didn't want his pity.

"You already know you can't leave."

Jemma didn't reply, simply held his steady gaze.

"Property line stops right at them woods and go all around in a big square. It doesn't matter which way you try to go—it's going to stop you eventually." He pointed with the clippers in one hand.

She tamped down a smirk. She'd gone much farther than that.

"How long have you worked for them? How much do you know?"

"I've been here going on thirty years. I know enough."

"Why don't you leave? You're not family. You can go anytime you want, right?"

A sad smile touched his lips. "My place is here."

It made no sense.

"I can't be part of them," she whispered, crossing her arms. "All those lies. I don't know what to believe, so why should I believe anything they tell me?"

"But you are part of them," Dennis said, his voice gentle. "People did die here, lots of them, in bad ways. From the baby back when you were born to Miss Honorine's husband to Mr. Russell's wife. And it happens every seven years, March twelfth. That part's no lie. They had a good reason to bring you here. I know they can lie, but who doesn't in this life? They need you."

"They hate me. Because of who my father was, because of my color."

"Even so, they need you." They both stood silently for a few moments until Dennis went on. "Think about this. If you free them so that they can finally leave this place, it frees you, too."

Jemma thought about the Barkers, the man and woman who'd raised her, and how they'd taught her to fear the one thing Jemma now knew she had in common with her mother. The one thing she'd suppressed her entire life was a link to who she really was. But except for Fosette, her actual family was barely more welcoming to her than her adoptive father had been.

Where did she belong?

"Think on how mad you'd be if you'd been trapped here all

these years," Dennis said. "You don't think it'd make you crazy not being able to even go into town, to have to give a list to the gardener every time you want something?" His voice lowered. "Women things, too. Yeah, I have to get all of that, 'cause Agnes . . . she don't leave either on account of . . . Well, how sane do you think they can be, considering that?"

Jemma shivered at the thought of it, at the idea of her sanity loosening, the anchors of it lifting from stability. She thought of Fosette, whom she'd grown so fond of. Of Laurence, whom she'd been attracted to. The thought sickened her now. But it all fit, didn't it?

Her cousins were bound like the rest of their family, which meant one of them could be the next to die on her birthday.

"It's tempting to just think about yourself in this," Dennis said, as if he'd read her mind. "Especially because I know how the Duchons are. Running is easy, until it ain't. How many times have you run from something?"

A flicker of anger rose in Jemma at the man's uncanny ability to sense her thoughts. Yes, she'd run from things. Vaporous ghosts. Cheating boyfriends. Hard truths about people she loved. As long as she kept running, she didn't have to face the past.

Dennis went on. "But if you can forgive them for what they did, if you can help them, things might turn out different."

"I don't have the first idea of what to do, and even if I did, what? You think they'll accept me with open arms?" Jemma scoffed.

She hated the small part of her, the hurt childlike part hiding its face behind little hands, that wanted exactly that, wanted nothing more than to have Honorine accept her as one of her own, introduce her as her granddaughter, look at her with love instead of indifference at best. Perhaps it *was* the house and being tethered to the property that fed the family's peculiarity. Like Dennis said, who wouldn't go mad? Even Simone, with her haughty meanness, and Russell, with his detached disinterest in anything that wasn't food.

Jemma covered her face for a moment before looking toward the woods and then back at the house. She took in its clean lines, the clinging dirt, the ivy creeping along the walls. At first glance, everything appeared perfect—even the structure that looked out of place jutting from one side, perhaps an old walled-up fireplace—but the more she looked, the more decay she found. It had probably been a grand place once, before Inès's curse had destroyed everything.

Absently, she rubbed her wrist, remembering that she'd wanted to die not so long ago. But if she lived now, if she undid the damage her mother had done, the family might embrace her as one of their own.

Dennis opened his mouth as if he was about to say something, but then his expression transformed into a stony mask. He lowered his head and resumed his pruning.

"There you are." It was Honorine. She waved a hand toward Dennis, and he gathered his gardening supplies and headed toward the old washhouse.

A hot hatred swirled inside Jemma as she faced the woman.

We are all you have, her grandmother had said.

Jemma despised the truth in that, but also felt a small slice of satisfaction at having her own secret.

Unlike them, she was free to leave.

"We need you to get started on figuring out how to break the curse."

"I don't have to do anything for you," Jemma said.

"You're right. You don't have to. Simply sit around, do nothing, and maybe you'll die next March twelfth instead of turn twenty-eight."

But I won't die, Jemma thought. *Because I'm not cursed like the rest of you.*

"Or perhaps it will be Fosette next time," the older woman continued.

"I barely know her."

"But you're getting to know her, just as you're getting to know Laurence." Honorine reached toward a bush, snapped a brown magnolia flower off, and dropped it onto the grass. "You might hate us, but you still want to be a part of us, part of something. I can give you that something."

"What do you mean?"

Despite everything, Jemma wanted to hear Honorine out. And her grandmother must have sensed it, the way her coyness drifted up like an invisible snake. On a woman her age, it was unpleasant. And yet Jemma listened.

"You want to know more about your mother than how she cursed us. You want to know what she was like as a girl. Did she like the same things you like? What things do you have in common with her? What about your father? You want to know who he really was, don't you? You barely know your cousin, you say, but you want to know more about all of us. Your aunt, your uncle. We are all the closest thing you have to your mother right now. So you can sit and do nothing, Miss Barker, or you can help us and learn more about your family and where you come from. You'll never know your history if you let us die."

Jemma met Honorine's eyes. For the first time, she believed everything the woman said. The words were too cold and calculated to be lies.

Her grandmother tilted her head and held out a hand. "Do we have an agreement, then?"

Jemma studied the offered hand, an old phrase ringing through her head.

Like making a deal with the devil.

She looked behind her at the woods. That way lay freedom.

She turned back to Honorine. This way lay family.

Although Jemma didn't know how she could possibly help the Duchons, Honorine was absolutely right about what Jemma wanted.

A place to belong.

A family to love her.

To know who she was.

To have an identity.

As Inès's daughter, maybe she was the only one who could fix this mess.

Jemma reached out and shook Honorine's hand.

EIGHT

FOR JEMMA, OCTOBER in New Orleans still felt like summer. She, like the rest of the Duchons, walked about in inappropriate attire—they out of fashion for the year, she out of season. Sure, the heat didn't have the same intensity in the fall, but it made itself known in everything from the constant marshy odor in the woods (which had become her occasional escape now that she'd found a walking trail) to her damp mattress after a restless night. Although she was now certain that no leash tethered her to the Duchon property, Jemma never stayed away for long. She guarded her little secret like a priceless gem, too precious to share.

The day after Jemma and Honorine cemented their agreement with a handshake, Jemma had started her research in the only place she could think of, the library, but her efforts among the dusty books so far hadn't yielded any results.

"It's time for your homework," Laurence said now, looking around the side of what must be his favorite chair.

She recalled the last time they'd been alone in here, how he'd indicated the wall of occult books as a place to begin organizing.

She also remembered the blistering heat she'd felt on her neck, which had sent her running, and how he'd grabbed her wrist and seen evidence of her past.

At that time, she'd had no idea they were related.

A sudden thought occurred to her.

"Have you ever seen anything . . . strange around here?" she asked him, moving farther into the room and faking casualness by leaning against a shelf and crossing her arms.

A slight smirk lifted one side of his mouth. He reclined on an arm of the chair, one gabardine-trousered leg thrown over the other in a careless way that other men could practice for years and never master. Brown leather suspenders contrasted with his crisp white shirt. "You'll have to be more specific."

Jemma inhaled, as if just saying the word would conjure forth something she didn't want to see. "Ghosts."

"Ghosts?" he repeated, his eyes wide. "You mean specters and spirits, haints and other things that go bump in the night?"

It wasn't until his lips quivered and then opened to emit a full-throated laugh that she realized he was mocking her. But right before that taunting roar, something flickered in his eyes.

"All right, if you haven't ever seen ghosts, have you seen something else?"

His laugh ended at once. "Do you mean besides the nasty deaths that take place every seven years on your birthday? Because I can tell you, when that date rolls around, it's not exactly a picnic around here. But no, I've never seen any ghosts."

"You don't seem to take the curse seriously."

"Oh, I most certainly do. I don't want to be the one to die next in some freak accident. But I think Grandmère is wasting her time on believing you'll be the one to save us."

"Why's that?"

"Our grandmother has hired many mediums over the years. She started with the priests, and when they didn't help, she moved on to the psychics. They've held séances, circles, done all kinds of things. They've tried to summon spirits, and yes, they succeeded in calling up some long-dead ancestor here and there, but they're not going to figure it out. Inès is going to get what she wanted. She's going to continue picking us off, one by one, until there's not a single Duchon left in this house. And now that you're here, which I'm sure makes Grandmère and Maman incredibly happy, since you're as trapped as we are, you're just as liable as the rest of us to be next."

Here, Laurence drew a long finger across his neck while baring his teeth at the same time, shocking Jemma into momentary silence. He tossed his book on the footstool in front of him and leaned forward, elbows on his knees.

"But are you really as trapped as we are, Jemma? You grew up far away from here. You actually saw some of the world. You left once; maybe you can leave again."

She turned to the shelf behind her, afraid that if he continued to stare at her the way he did she'd slip up and admit everything.

"Just because I don't know the first thing about curses doesn't mean I can't try to fix things, especially because I'm just as trapped as you are." The lie swam up her throat. "You think I don't want to get out of here?"

She grabbed *Simple Rules of Cursebreaking* off the shelf and took a cursory flip through it before settling in the chair farthest from Laurence. She scanned the chapter titles and turned to the chapter detailing curses and how they worked. Gruesome illustrations of people looking tortured, without any devices or tormentors near them, dotted the pages.

"That day you tried to leave, you didn't really go far."

Jemma glanced up to find Laurence standing in front of her. She forced her gaze back to her book as he went on.

"If you tried, how far could you go?"

"If I'm really related to you, I can't go anywhere."

Now she met his gaze, searching for the slightest wobble, the merest hint that she wasn't actually family.

He gave her no such clue before heading to the door. As he reached for the knob, Agnes walked in with a tray. When the maid saw Laurence, she stopped in her tracks. Jemma's eyes moved between the two, the briefest note of something familiar hanging in the air and dispersing before she could catch it.

"I don't want your tea," he hissed, striding past Agnes, his shoulder bumping her roughly enough to send the tray and its contents flying. A teapot, cups, saucers and dessert plates shattered, pieces scattering, along with a couple of slices of coffee cake.

Jemma jumped up.

"Fucking imbecile," Laurence muttered, his eyes on Agnes, now sweeping up the mess with her hands, before he walked out.

Jemma stood rooted in place for several seconds, trying to decide whether she was going to run after him and ask what in the hell his problem was or if she'd help the maid. It seemed easier to stay, so she squatted next to Agnes and tried to place broken china pieces on the tray. But the woman shook her head, not meeting Jemma's gaze, and pushed her hands away.

"Let me help you," Jemma insisted.

Now Agnes did look at her, her eyes moving across her face the same way they had when Jemma had knocked on the door that first day, as if there were contained inside her an answer to a desperate question.

The maid leaned forward and pressed her lips against Jemma's before Jemma had a chance to react. By the time she realized the woman was kissing her, Agnes had moved back, tears shining in her eyes.

Then she pushed Jemma's hands back toward her and gestured for her to go.

As she walked out, Jemma put a hand to her mouth in shock, her mind churning with the bizarreness of what had just happened. She not only wondered why the woman had kissed her but also felt deeply disappointed in Laurence. It was his fault the maid had dropped the tray. Jemma assumed his reaction was just another affectation of these people, but to be so hostile to a woman who was already at a disadvantage didn't make sense to her. Neither did the way Laurence could be kind to Jemma at times and at other times be eccentric bordering on frightening (like today). She wasn't rich, never had been, but she'd heard stories her whole life about how the other half was, the strange ways they behaved under the protection of their money, as if wealth made manners and good sense unnecessary.

Jemma stopped in the foyer, seeing no trace of Laurence or anyone else. She'd left her book in the library, but she would wait until Agnes was finished in there before retrieving it. She needed time to think, and she wanted to be alone. Taking a quick look around to make sure no one saw her, Jemma slipped out the back doors and headed toward the woods.

Fireflies flitted in scattered patterns among the bushes, and as the thick line of trees loomed closer, a flash of light shone through the branches and leaves. Jemma paused, remembering Dennis's words: *All sorts of critters be back there. 'Shiners, too.* She'd seen and heard all kinds of animals and they didn't frighten her. But moonshiners? Jemma decided that she'd be quiet and careful, but she knew she'd seen a light. She needed to know where it came from.

She took a tentative step into the thickness of the trees, instantly enveloped by the noise of frogs and crickets. The sun had only just begun to set, but in here it was twilight. As she made her way along the now familiar route she took when she wanted to be alone, she drew closer to the abandoned wooden shack. She counted on the diminishing sunlight to hide her but took careful steps, avoiding the crunch of pine needles and dried leaves the best she could.

"You trying to get shot, girl?" a woman barked from behind Jemma.

She twirled around, a scream pushing up her throat, but all that escaped her was a wheezing breath.

It was a ghost, dressed in white.

No, it was a woman. A live, brown-skinned woman with thick braids trailing down either side of her body, the loose ends brushing a low-slung leather belt in which she'd placed a gun, the butt of it in front of her hip. The ragged hem of her white cotton dress brushed her ankles, not quite reaching her bare feet.

"I thought I saw . . . a light," Jemma said, the words separated by harsh breaths.

"You look like you saw a ghost," the woman said, moving her hand from the butt of the pistol.

"That's what I thought you were . . . at first."

A deep laugh rolled out of the woman's mouth, the white of her teeth catching the last of the sun's rays. "A spirit, huh? No, not me. Although there's plenty of them around, but ole Magdalene ain't part of that yet. Not yet." She cocked her head. "Who are you?"

"Jemma Barker. I work for the Duchons."

"The Duchons." As Magdalene said the name, Jemma didn't

miss the way her eyes narrowed. Her right hand moved back to the butt of the gun and her grin disappeared behind a curled lip.

"So you know them?"

"Everyone round here knows them, girl. Your name's Barker, you said?"

"Yes." She peered at the woman more carefully. Something in the way she said her name hinted at familiarity.

"Is your mama's name Mabel? Mabel Barker?"

One of my mamas, Jemma began to think before it struck her. How did this woman know her adoptive mother's name? Before she could ask, Magdalene frowned, and her eyes widened as they studied Jemma's face closely.

"What is it? What's the matter?"

"Oh God. Oh God, no. Why are you here?"

Jemma didn't know why she should be so afraid, but Magdalene's reaction scared her more than when she'd thought the woman was a ghost.

"What do you mean? How do you know Mabel?" she asked.

"We took you away from here, Emmaline. Why are you back?"

"We? We who? You took me away? Who's Emmaline?" Jemma stepped closer, her hands raised. If the woman tried to run, to snatch any answers out of Jemma's hands, she'd grab onto her. But Magdalene shook her head, a low wail escaping her.

"You're damned now, damned! Why would you come back?"

Jemma grabbed the woman's arms, only now realizing that Magdalene was older, threads of gray hairs standing out starkly against the black. Shaking her, heedless of the clacking of Magdalene's teeth, Jemma demanded, "How do you know me?"

"I was the midwife. I delivered you."

Jemma stepped back as if Magdalene had shoved her. "You were there?"

The woman's gaze moved over Jemma's shoulder, toward the direction of the Duchon property. Seizing Jemma's hand, she led her inside the cabin. The interior looked nothing like the outside. A lit candle sat in a shallow bowl filled with water on top of a square table, which took up most of the single room. In one corner was a potbelly stove, and in the other a tattered quilt covered a sagging mattress, pine needles strewn along the edges. Bundled herbs hung from the ceiling, giving the space a woodsy smell nothing like the stuffy air in the Duchon house. Magdalene brought out a few more candles and lit them, placing them around the bowl on the table. She dragged a wooden chair from the wall and pushed it up to the table, looking around absently. It was clear she lived here alone and didn't have guests often, if ever.

"Sit down. Jemma, you said your name was? How did you . . . ? No, never mind that for now—we'll get to all that later. The family, they can't come out this far, which is good for me. I don't have to see them, the snakes. But you! Why are you here?"

Jemma had what she was sure were more questions than Magdalene, but she'd answer first. Taking the seat while the other woman paced, she said, "They hired me. I thought they wanted a tutor. Only, once I got here, I found out there was no tutoring job. They wanted me to break the curse that's over the family."

Magdalene nodded, as if the Duchons' duplicity was exactly what she expected.

"But if you delivered me, you knew my mother."

The woman bowed her head, her brows knitted, her eyes fixed on the floor. "I knew Inès. And I was there when you slipped out of her body, when she delivered you along with a curse that she couldn't take back. I tried to stop her, but once words are out, you can't unspeak them. It was too late for her, for them, for you, the minute she said them."

"But you got me away after I was born. I'm not bound like they are."

Magdalene stopped, staring at Jemma from the other side of the table.

"How did you get me away if I'm really one of the Duchons?"

The woman shrugged. "You are a Duchon—don't doubt that. I don't have the answer for how you're not trapped there like the rest of them. But before you were an hour old, Honorine told me she was going to kill you, and your mama begged me to get you away. Maybe it's 'cause I took you away so soon. Or maybe 'cause I carried you and I ain't a part of them. I don't know how that worked, but I was just happy it did."

"You said 'We took you away.' Who was with you?"

"Dennis."

Jemma's shoulders dropped; a short breath rushed out of her. "You know him?"

"Knew him. I ain't seen or talked to that man in years. We took you into the parish proper. He said he knew some people who wanted a baby, a couple who was moving up north, where there were better jobs, better money. We thought that was best, giving you to people who'd take you far away from here, where nobody knew where you came from, where nobody would tell you about your real family." Magdalene slapped her palms on the table. "We did all that and now here you are."

"What happened to my mother?"

"She died. They told me when I came back to check on her, and I saw them burying her later that day. I stayed back here, but I got close enough to see that. It's not like they invited me to the funeral."

Jemma's gaze wandered over the small space. Finally, someone who'd known her mother and didn't hate her. And if she didn't hate Inès, maybe she didn't hate Jemma, either.

"Do I look like her?" The words, low, escaped Jemma's mouth before she had a chance to stop them.

Magdalene cocked her head, shadows dancing merrily across her face. "You must look more like your pa. I never met him, but Inès told me about him, about how handsome he was, about how the family would never accept him 'cause he was dark. He wanted to marry her, but that wasn't going to happen."

"I still can't believe I'm related to them. I don't look anything like them."

"I guess not, not with that pretty brown skin. There ain't nothing in this world that family hates more than being reminded of what they are."

Fosette's words echoed in Jemma's head: *We're very proud to be colored.*

Looking around, wanting to talk about, think about, anything else, Jemma asked, "You live here alone?"

Magdalene nodded.

"What do you do? You still midwife?" A list of questions sprang up in Jemma's mind for this new person, unrelated to the Duchons, to her. She hadn't realized until now how much she craved something different. Just the sound of Magdalene's voice, an even hum, was like a balm on Jemma's skin.

"Not so much anymore. The older I get, the less I want to be dealing with folks. That's why I stay out here, where it's quiet and deep enough in the trees to not see that family."

"You don't have electricity or running water, though. That doesn't bother you?"

"No, child. I got everything a person needs. All that other stuff is extra."

"You called me Emmaline out there."

The older woman waved a hand. "Just a mistake. But forget

about me, 'cause Magdalene ain't the important person in this story. We're going to talk about you. Where'd you come here from? Was Mabel good to you? How about her husband?"

Jemma took a deep breath, unsure of how much to tell. "I grew up in Chicago. My parents, Carl and Mabel—they're dead now."

"I'm sorry."

"It's okay. They were good people."

Magdalene gave her a sharp look, as if the simple statement hid something behind it. Jemma's gaze rested on her hands in her lap; she wondered at her desire to say more to this stranger.

"Mama tried to make me feel wanted. Daddy . . . It seemed like I couldn't do anything right to please him. After she died, it wasn't much there to hold us together. So I moved out as soon as I could. I had a boyfriend, but we split up before I came down here." Jemma stopped there, leaving out the more salacious bits, although something in Magdalene's face told her she knew all about them, about the trouble swimming underneath Jemma's carefully chosen words, about how with one misstep Jemma would fall into the real story, where a pregnant woman and sliced wrist and split lip waited.

"How are *they* treating you?" Magdalene lifted a chin toward the door, indicating the Duchons.

"Honorine, my grandmother—she's kind of cold. Simone, my aunt—she's probably worse. But Laurence and Fosette aren't too bad. Neither is my uncle Russell. They can be a little odd sometimes, but I think it's because of the curse." Jemma looked into Magdalene's face. It was now fully dark outside, and in here, with the weak candlelight, shadows cast eerie shapes in every corner. "I don't know anything about curses, other than what I've read. And when I saw you, I thought you were a ghost, like a couple others I've seen on the property—"

"You see haints?" Magdalene cut in, her body quite still.

"Yes."

"You talk to them?"

"No! No." A pause. "Why would I do that?"

"They scare you?"

"Of course."

Magdalene shook her head. "What you got to be scared of? They can't hurt you."

Jemma took that in for a moment. "Who's not scared of ghosts?"

"Inès wasn't. She just got tired of hearing them."

"What do you mean?"

"Sometimes, when people can't move on to what's next, they stick around. Most of the living can't see or hear them, but some, like you and your mama, can. When a spirit realizes that, they're drawn to you like moths to light. Some want to tell you something or maybe need you to do something for them." Magdalene grew quiet for several moments, as if unsure how to proceed. "Inès told me they bothered her all the time. She couldn't get no rest at the house. That's why she spent so much time in the city. She said when she was dancing or talking or making love she didn't have time to pay attention to all the voices going on around her."

"How well did you know her?" Jemma had assumed from what Magdalene had said that she'd only been her mother's midwife. But it seemed the woman had known Inès quite well.

"I wasn't all that close to her, if that's what you're thinking. The Duchons got no friends or family darker than a china plate, except for you. When I'd check on her every now and again while she was pregnant with you, she'd talk to me sometimes. I think she wanted to talk to somebody so bad who wasn't going to judge her, so I'd just sit there and listen. She told me there was a mess of haints all around the house, on the grounds. She knew they were troubled, but she couldn't figure out how to help them. They don't talk clear most of the time, and I think she couldn't understand what they were trying to say. After a while, she learned to ignore them."

Like me, Jemma thought.

"I don't want to talk to them. Even if I knew how, I wouldn't want to."

Magdalene looked at Jemma as if she were just remembering she had company. "I don't talk to them 'cause I don't see them. But if I did, if I met some poor haint who seemed lost and confused about why she was here instead of in heaven, why not help her get to where she needs to be? Seems like the decent thing to do."

"Maybe that's easy for you to say since you don't see them," Jemma said with more venom in her voice than she'd intended.

"Okay, girl, I'm sorry. Magdalene said the wrong thing. Ain't the first time and won't be the last. But it looks like you got something in common with your mama that can maybe help you. Instead of running scared, why not look at it as some kind of gift? Not everybody has that, you know. And maybe one of them got an answer for you."

"An answer?"

"I'm sure that house and all that land got a whole mess of secrets. Who better to ask about them than the haints who live there? Even . . . even Inès might be there." Magdalene said this last bit just above a whisper.

Yes, Jemma thought, her mother might be among the ghosts walking around the property. The thought frightened her more than a little, but at the same time, it awakened a desire in her to meet her mother, the woman who'd birthed her along with a terrible curse, perhaps not realizing how she'd damned her daughter along with the rest of her family. If Jemma could talk to her mother, then perhaps she'd find out how to break the curse, free them all.

NINE

SINCE JEMMA HAD made the decision to stay, it seemed something had shifted, just slightly. That harridan Simone didn't seem quite so awful, although she couldn't see herself referring to the woman as Aunt Simone. At dinner, Jemma joined in the conversation a little, still too intimidated to do more than contribute her opinion about the latest headlines, from James Meredith integrating the University of Mississippi (Jemma had been alone in considering him a hero) to debate over whether Billy Eckstine or Jackie Wilson was the better singer. Jemma was completely lost over their discussion of Vatican II.

After breakfast, she often visited the library with a yellow legal pad, rapidly filling with notes, tucked under her arm. The books helped in her research into curses, but she needed more. She wished she knew someone who was an expert in occult topics, someone who could guide her toward the solution.

Between the research and finding a rhythm that fit with the rest of the family, she'd suppressed any thought of ghosts.

Until a week after meeting Magdalene.

As Jemma placed a few leftover calas from breakfast in a napkin, intending to take the soft rice fritters to her new friend, Simone strolled into the dining room. Jemma ignored her, although it was unusual for her aunt to come back into the room after their meals. But not sensing any movement or hearing Simone speak, Jemma looked over to where the woman leaned back against the sideboard, her hands gripping the edge of it, her eyes locked on her niece.

"Are you getting close to figuring things out?" Simone asked. "We only have a few more months before your next birthday."

Jemma tied the cloth napkin into a loose knot and hugged the small bundle to herself. "A little."

"I would love for my daughter to get out of this place." Simone's eyes took in the room, but Jemma knew she was talking about the house, the entire property. It was the first time her aunt had talked to her without venom dripping off every word. Yet Simone was the last person Jemma trusted. She imagined her aunt was like a mad dog—it might only look at you while you reach a hand out, but you shouldn't be shocked when it turns around and snaps at you. "She might still have time to find a husband. He'd have to be okay with her age, though, the fact that she can't have children. She was fixed but good, you know. No idea where such a man exists. But she didn't deserve this. None of us did." Simone leveled Jemma with a look that let her know exactly who was to blame. "Where do you go when you walk out back?"

The sudden question caught Jemma off guard. She'd stopped listening at "She was fixed but good." What did that mean for Fosette? Had someone *fixed* her so that she couldn't have children?

An image of Fosette fussing in Jemma's hair, helping her with rag curls, rose in her mind. The delicate way her cousin patted her handiwork and, beaming, held out a mirror for her. And her cousin slipping her arm through Jemma's as they climbed the stairs before bed, Fosette kissing her on the cheek and whispering, "Sweet dreams, cousin."

Oh God, what had they done to her?

Simone was waiting for an answer. Jemma had wondered if anyone would notice her absences, and if so, when they'd question her about them. Of course they'd pick up on any little action that deviated from the monotony of their days. She hadn't hidden that she was visiting Magdalene, but she hadn't told anyone about it, either, simply would walk across the back lawn into the cool of the woods and spend half a day, sometimes until dinnertime, with the only nonfamily she knew here.

Did they even remember that the midwife lived back there?

"I just like spending time along the edge of the woods. It's cooler there."

"Russell thinks you're back there rutting with some moonshiner just inside the trees. The property line ends right there, so you can't go far. Maybe. Is that what you're doing? Fucking some dirty old man?" Simone pushed herself off the sideboard to make her slow way around the perimeter of the room. Jemma clutched the napkin tighter, her head down. She didn't care what they thought, but she also didn't want to tell her aunt anything. None of them deserved the truth. Jemma wanted to hold Magdalene, and the time she spent with her, close, in secret. Something of her own.

Simone stopped behind Jemma, the warmth of her body pressing against her niece's shoulder. "I told him you weren't doing anything of the sort. Not our little Jemma, Inès's little mistake—"

Jemma whirled and faced the woman. "Don't say that about me."

"Or what? What are you going to do? Curse me like my sister cursed us? You don't have it in you. I've told Maman that you also don't have it in you to undo what was done. Come March next year, one of us will be dead, just like every other time. But probably not you, because you're not really one of us. I've watched you cross that back lawn and go into the trees and not come out for hours. What are you really doing back there?"

"Why do you hate me so much?" Jemma deflected, Simone's proximity to uncovering her secret too great for her liking. "This isn't my fault. And believe it or not, I'm trying to help. All these years later you're still angry with a woman who's been dead all this time. What good is it doing you?"

Simone only looked at Jemma for several moments, an odd smile fleeting across her lips, before she strutted out of the room, heavy perfume snapping under Jemma's nose before dispersing in the air. When Jemma's breathing returned to normal, she looked down to find the bundle of calas crushed beneath her fingers. Placing it on the table—not wanting to throw it away in the kitchen, where Agnes surely was, Agnes with her uncomfortable stares, Agnes who'd pressed her lips against hers—Jemma headed out, and as she passed through the foyer, her eyes fell on the black telephone by the door.

She hadn't been in touch with anyone back in Chicago, not after that disastrous phone call with Marvin. She hadn't even called Betty, although she'd told her friend that she'd call and write. Jemma picked up the receiver; she thought of the expense of the call, but she dialed anyway.

The operator connected the call, and Jemma asked the person who answered the common phone on the second floor to get Betty in apartment 11.

"Hello?" came Betty's voice over the scratchy connection. Even though the call wasn't clear, Jemma relished the sound of her friend's voice.

"Betty. It's Jemma."

"Girl! So you are all right! I was worried about you. But I said they must be keeping you mighty busy down there for you not to call or write. How is the job? Are the people rich as you thought?"

Jemma looked around before answering, choosing her words carefully. "The job is fine. Yes, they've been keeping me busy."

When Betty didn't respond right away, Jemma wondered if the call had been disconnected, but after a moment, her friend asked, "You okay? You sound funny. It could be this connection, but—"

"I'm all right."

"Okay, if you say so. And, um, maybe I shouldn't say anything, but, shit, I've already said something, haven't I? I saw Marvin at Dominick's, him and that woman." Even through the distant connection, Betty's anger was clear. "She's showing." Another pause, which Jemma didn't fill. "You talked to him?"

The memory of that one phone call Jemma had made, her plea for help, flitted through her mind. She chased it away. "No."

"You thought about coming back?"

Jemma wanted to laugh. Of course she'd thought about going back, of going anywhere. "For what, Betty?"

"I don't know. To work things out."

Jemma's hand tightened on the phone, her face lifted to the ceiling. She took several deep breaths before returning to the conversation. "I have a job here." Such as it was.

"What about a man?"

"I don't have time for that right now." Even as she said it, she knew it wasn't something her friend would understand. Betty was one of those women who believed that having part of a man's attention was better than having none at all. She never would have attacked her husband, Jimmy, with a pool cue if she'd found him in a billiards hall with another woman. Or in her own bed, for that matter. "Even if I did, if I'd stayed with Marvin, I would've had to forgive him for what he did."

"Forgive and forget, they say. You could still do that."

"Girl, it's not always that easy."

Jemma was about to tell Betty that forgiveness wasn't always the balm her friend seemed to think it was, when something fluttered in the corner of her eye.

A woman drifted out of the kitchen, her long dress rough-hewn under an apron. Jemma could make out those details, as well as the kerchief wrapped around the woman's head. When she turned and looked at Jemma, despite her near transparency her features were apparent: full lips, wide nose, high cheekbones.

Five . . . four . . . three . . .

Vaguely, Jemma was aware of Betty's voice reaching over the line, her name coming at increasing decibels.

The ghost turned toward the back French doors, looked over her shoulder at Jemma once and then floated through them before stopping right outside.

"Betty," Jemma whispered, the phone receiver inches from her mouth, "I have to go. Here's my number, if you need to reach me." She read the digits written on a small card taped to the phone.

"Jemma? Jemma!"

Click.

Jemma shut her eyes and began counting again. *Five . . . four . . .*

"You all right?"

Barely suppressing a shriek, she opened her eyes to find Russell in front of her, one hand in his vest pocket, a cigarette dangling from the other.

"I'm fine."

"You don't look like it. Come on. Let's sit."

When he started toward the parlor, she reluctantly followed, averting her gaze from the back doors.

Was it her imagination, or had he glanced at the doors before leading her away?

Magdalene's words came back to her: *If I met some poor haint who seemed lost and confused about why she was here instead of in heaven, why not help her get to where she needs to be?*

Maybe one of them got an answer for you.

The only answers Jemma wanted now were about her mother, which Honorine had promised her. She flopped into an armchair while Russell took the settee across from her, carefully smoothing his pant legs before fixing her with a stare.

"It's rude to stare at people," she said, realizing only at that moment how often the Duchons made her feel like a sideshow freak with the way they studied her, sometimes covertly but other times out in the open.

Russell chuckled, smashing his cigarette out in the crystal ashtray on the side table. "You're right, of course. I'm sorry. I guess I'm still getting used to your presence. It's been so long since we've seen a new face." With what appeared to be some effort, he looked toward the doorway before studying the room. Jemma knew he had to be intimately familiar with all four corners, just like the rest of the family who'd been trapped here. She wondered how soon she could leave without appearing impolite. Right now, she wanted nothing more than to shut herself in her room, forget about seeing Magdalene today if she had to go out the back, where that spirit might be waiting.

"My mother tried to break the curse, you know," he said, leaning back.

"She did?" Jemma's attention snapped to him.

"Yes. She thought because she's Inès's mother, that blood link was enough. That's what some medium told her, anyway. But it didn't work. My sister made sure that each of us would be punished."

"'Each of us'?"

"All the Duchons who were here when she cursed us. But you . . . How were you able to get away?"

"How should I know? I was just born when it happened."

"I didn't think they should've sent you away. It wasn't like Inès was the only woman in history to have a child out of wedlock. Maman and Papa were so worried about the scandal, but worse things have happened, no?"

"I suppose they have."

He leaned forward, animation lighting up his face. "Of course they have! If they'd let her marry who she wanted to marry, none of this would have happened. It's all so ridiculous, trying to arrange things that way."

"Was your marriage arranged?"

Russell's smile shrank, and with it his light, an expression that reminded Jemma of Honorine sliding into its place. "I loved Lenore very much."

Which wasn't at all an answer to what Jemma had asked.

"What else did the mediums tell your mother? And what did she do to try and break the curse?"

"I'm really not sure. All of that was years ago, when people were still willing to visit us." He waited a beat, and his voice dropped. "I am glad you're here, despite the circumstances. All these years, we wondered about you."

Jemma wanted to believe him. Unlike Simone, her uncle had never said or done anything hostile to her. If she could have another friend in this house, someone like Fosette, she'd feel more like she belonged.

"What was my mother like? Besides being beautiful, I mean."

Instead of his demeanor softening further, Russell's face closed, his lips pursing, the change shocking Jemma into silence. Hadn't he just implied that Inès wasn't the monster Honorine made her out to be? So why did he look like he'd just tasted something nasty?

He rose abruptly, looking out of the window, his back to Jemma. "She . . . was friendly. Never met a stranger, as they say."

When he grew quiet, Jemma reminded him, "But you said she was troubled. Because of the ghosts. Did you all think she was . . . crazy?" She rubbed her wrist.

"No more crazy than the rest of us," he murmured.

Unsure of what he meant but desperate to grab onto something that would help her, Jemma asked him, "Do you see them, too?"

She expected him to turn around and act ignorant, as if he had no idea what she was talking about. But he only continued staring out, his body unmoving.

"If it's ghosts you mean, no," he said in a flat voice.

"But . . . earlier . . . I thought I saw you looking at . . . I thought you saw something . . ."

He turned back to the room, his usual pleasant expression in place, and Jemma imagined the effort he expended to hold it there. He wasn't going to answer her, which was all the answer she needed. Maybe he couldn't see them as well as she could, as well as her mother had, but he seemed aware of their presence.

"If you just tell me, you could help me. That would help all of us."

"Jemma, I have no idea what you're talking about." Suddenly her uncle clapped his hands and headed to the doorway. "I could use another cup of coffee. Care to join me?"

A person could grow dizzy with the sudden turns conversation took around this place. Jemma shook her head. Russell shrugged, digging a box of Camels out of his vest as he exited. She waited a few moments before leaving the parlor, her eyes seeming to move of their own accord to the back doors.

No ghostly woman stood there.

Jemma exhaled slowly and then made her way out, toward Magdalene's. She knocked, although the door was never locked. Coming from Chicago, Jemma couldn't imagine such a thing. Getting no answer, she went around the back of the cabin, finding no sign of her friend, who was probably traipsing through the woods.

"Magdalene!" Jemma called, cupping her hands around her mouth, sending a flock of crows cawing into the air from a nearby tree, the sudden rustle of feathers surprising her as much as she'd startled them. "Magdalene!"

From a short distance away, Jemma heard, "Yah! Go on in."

She let herself into the shack through the open back door, inhaling the mixed scents of herbs and the remnants of a gamy meal. Probably rabbit, or maybe squirrel, as Magdalene hunted local animals for food. She'd offered a bit of squirrel to Jemma the last time she'd visited, which she'd turned down, her nose scrunched.

Jemma grabbed an empty pot and filled it with well water from outside before placing it on the woodstove and lighting a fire. Magdalene loved hot tea, no matter the season, but her pine needle tea and nettle tea were an acquired taste, so Jemma had declined after the first unpalatable cup. Magdalene liked reading tea leaves, although she admitted she wasn't that good at it.

Her friend came stomping in the back doors ten minutes later, a skinned animal slung over one shoulder.

"What the hell is that?" Jemma asked, her eyes following the woman with the bloody carcass draped over her shoulder the way other women wore fox stoles.

"It's a coon. You ever had coon meat?" At the look on Jemma's face, Magdalene let out a howl of laughter. "I can tell you ain't ever had it. I'll make up a stew. You might like it."

"No, thank you. I have to be back at the house for dinner anyway—you know that."

Magdalene humphed, moving to the counter and slapping the dead animal on it. She took a cleaver to it and, with the skill of a trained butcher, chopped it into pieces. Pointing with the cleaver to a basket in the corner, she told Jemma, "Chop up some of them taters for me, Emmaline."

Jemma was halfway out of her seat. "That's the second time you've called me that."

Magdalene ceased chopping, her head dropped and her shoulders slumped. "Damn," she whispered.

Jemma was fully prepared to badger the woman about why she'd called her by another name when Magdalene said, "It's your crib name. The name your mama gave you."

Jemma fell back in the chair. "Why didn't you tell me this before?"

"I don't try to think about all that. It happened a long time ago. Your mama is dead now. Ain't no point in trying to bring her back by talking about that old stuff."

"But how did you know that?"

"Inès told it to me, right after I handed you to her. She said that's the name she wanted you to have. That's the name we gave the Barkers, but I guess they wanted to change it."

Forgetting about the potatoes, Jemma wondered exactly why her parents had changed her name to Jemma. Would her life have been different if she'd been Emmaline? She knew the Duchons still wouldn't have kept her. Or maybe they would have, with that French-sounding name that eased its way into her ears. When she mouthed it, it tasted sweet, like a little pastry. She imagined being more beautiful if only the Barkers hadn't thrown that name away like the Duchons had tossed her out.

"Does the family know this?" Jemma asked.

Magdalene finished cutting up the animal and moved to grab a few potatoes, but Jemma took them from her and began cutting. As the older woman slid the meat into a pot and chopped up a sprouting onion, she continued. "Of course they know. They were there. Honorine and Simone were, anyway. They probably have your name written down in one of their Bibles or something."

"Written down?"

"Like a record of who's who. They're mighty proud of that family name. I'm sure they've got a list of their people going back all the way to slavery times."

Jemma could only imagine how that family tree would look, with cousins marrying cousins. She also wondered if the Duchons had actually kept her name in their records, or her mother's, for that matter.

"I wish I could've met her," Jemma said as she placed the potatoes in the bubbling pot and stood next to Magdalene at the counter.

"Your mama?"

Jemma nodded.

"Well, with all them ghosts walking around the place, she might be one of them. You ever tried to look for her?"

"No. They still scare me a little."

"Huh. It's the living you need to be scared of. Haints can't hurt you, but maybe they can tell you some things you want to know."

"I still don't know how to talk to them. Or where to even look for my mother."

Magdalene dumped the last of the onion and carrots into the pot and placed the cast-iron lid on it after checking on the fire in the belly of the stove. She wiped her bloody hands on a dishrag before tossing it into a pail in the corner. "Maybe you need to call her."

"How?"

"Hell, I don't know exactly, but I bet that family does. Word was, they used to have séances back in the day. I'd ask them if I was you."

A bitter laugh escaped Jemma. "You really think they're going to tell me how to contact my mother, who they can't stand?"

Magdalene put a hand on her hip and faced Jemma squarely. "Who said you gotta tell them who you're trying to talk to?"

TEN

MAGDALENE HAD GIVEN Jemma a lot to think about, but as much as Jemma wanted to hear her mother's voice, she didn't know if she could call her up in a séance. She'd done the exact opposite of reaching out to spirits her whole life.

Sitting on the floor of her bedroom, Jemma flipped through one of the library books, stopping on a page she'd found a few days ago, the corner folded flat. She scanned the ritual—simply titled "cursebreaking"—for what felt like the hundredth time.

She'd made sure to lock her door when she turned in for the night, not wanting anyone to disturb her.

A circle of white candles, which she'd collected from various kitchen drawers, surrounded her. Several were tea candles and the rest were tapers. In front of her sat a bowl of water and a saltshaker.

Jemma had no idea if this would work, but if it did, she wouldn't have to hold a séance. She wouldn't have to do the thing that scared her the most.

A vision arose behind her closed eyes: the Duchons at the front gates of their property, gazing with longing at what lay outside before taking a few slow steps out. They were walking more quickly now, their strides confident, their smiling faces turned up to the sky. They were free, like she was. Once they realized it, they embraced her. Even Simone smiled at her. And for the first time in Jemma's life, she felt completely accepted by family.

The main thing was believing it would work. If she didn't convince herself of it, the book said, she wouldn't see any results.

I believe I can do this. I believe I can break this curse.

She opened her eyes and set the book aside, the cursebreaking page showing, and began, the words of her mother's curse ringing through her mind:

I curse all the Duchon blood. From this day forth, I bind the family to this house. I bind them forever.

Jemma poured the salt into the water. She shut her eyes again and spent several minutes picturing the house and the family bathed in a white light.

A long exhale escaped her.

Did it work?

She didn't feel any different, but then, she wasn't the one trapped, she thought as she blew out the candles. Were all of the Duchons now in their beds, turning slightly at some unperceived shift in the atmosphere? Would they fling open the front gates in the morning and run out through them?

Jemma held the vision of them doing just that in her mind when she climbed into bed. As her consciousness slipped away, a whisper breathed against her ear. Sleepiness hung heavy on her, but a part of her mind shrank back at what she heard.

Not like this.

ON HER WAY into the dining room the next morning, Jemma had decided she'd tell the family over breakfast what she'd done. She ignored the nagging doubt that she hadn't broken the curse. After all, she'd followed the directions of the ritual and, more importantly, she'd believed in her ability to succeed.

Just as she entered the room, Agnes came in from the kitchen, a silver coffeepot in her hand.

They both saw it at the same time.

A loud clatter broke the silence, the coffeepot now spilling hot liquid all over the floor. Before Jemma could speak, the rest of the family entered, their voices dying down when they saw it, too.

Fosette screamed.

"What is it?" she cried, pointing at one wall.

But there was something on each of the four walls.

Thick black streaks, as if smeared soot, reached from the top of the wainscoting to the ceiling.

At first, Jemma had seen only the marks. But as they all turned their heads to take in the whole room, they realized the dark streaks formed letters.

B

O

N

E and **S** together.

BONES

The five Duchons, plus Jemma and Agnes, could only stare.

The idea slammed Jemma suddenly, so fiercely that she grabbed onto the back of a chair to keep from falling.

This was her fault somehow. The ritual hadn't worked.

Honorine's eagle-eyed stare hadn't missed Jemma's near faint.

"What did you do?" the woman asked, each word clipped and clear.

All eyes moved to Jemma, just as they had on her first dinner here. The strangeness of that evening was nothing compared with what felt like growing malice now. They blamed her for this. And she knew they should.

Not like this.

It hadn't been a dream. Something had whispered to her as she was falling asleep last night. She'd dismissed it, of course, not knowing what the words meant and not wanting to face their source. It was much easier to ignore it all.

But there was no ignoring the scorch marks marring the dining room.

Honorine grabbed Jemma's upper arm now, shaking her. "What did you do?"

"I . . . I did a ritual. To break the curse."

Gasps rose from the others.

"When?"

Tears sprang into Jemma's eyes, turning the other woman into a blurry mass.

"Last night," came out on a sob.

"Bones," Honorine whispered, shoving Jemma away and turning her attention back to the walls.

"What does it mean, Maman?" Simone asked in a low voice, her eyes wide.

Honorine didn't answer. Instead, she approached the nearest

wall, the one with the letter "B" on it. She reached a hand forward as if she meant to touch it. A cry rested just behind Jemma's lips. *Don't,* she wanted to yell, but the word wouldn't come, as if she had no breath to release it.

Honorine touched the wall briefly and studied her hand, slightly dirtied but unharmed.

"Agnes," she said, still staring at the letters. "We'll eat in the parlor this morning, while you get this cleaned up."

Before Jemma could do much more than begin to wonder how her grandmother expected the maid to accomplish that task, with the ceilings being twelve feet high, she looked around. Each family member wore a different expression, none of them welcoming. Fosette was clearly terrified and ran to another room. Simone's face was a blank stone now that she'd overcome the worst of her fear. Laurence's eyes moved from the walls to Jemma and back again several times, his features unreadable but hard. And Russell appeared more strangely curious than anything else.

Jemma had no intention of joining them for breakfast, and when Honorine finally turned away, Jemma slipped out the back doors, running for Magdalene's.

WHAT DO YOU think it means? And what did that? The ghosts?" Jemma asked her friend after telling her about the ritual and the aftermath.

Magdalene had listened without interruption, and now she was slow to find words. They sat on a shaded log outside of the cabin, the fall air cool on their skin.

"'Not like this,'" the older woman said. "That's what you need to figure out. It sounds like a message."

Jemma had been afraid of that.

"Maybe what you did, they're trying to tell you it was wrong."

"But I don't know what to do right."

"You thought about what I said last time?"

"About the séance? Yes, I thought about it. I don't think I'm ready for that. No. I know I'm not ready. I can't . . . I can't talk to them."

"It sounds like they're trying to talk to you," Magdalene said gently.

Jemma spent the remainder of the day in the woods—hiding, she told herself—and when she headed back to the Duchon house, it was past dinner. She wasn't hungry, having shared some stew and bread with Magdalene, so she went straight to her room, relieved to avoid accusing stares from the family.

But missing dinner came with its own punishment, as Jemma discovered before the sun was up the next morning.

Instead of waking to the sounds of chirping birds or Dennis's clippers, she woke to Honorine's booming voice. She sat up in bed, confused at first about where she was or if she was still sleeping and in the midst of a nightmare.

Honorine stood at the foot of the bed, reading from a large book by lamplight. After a moment, Jemma realized her grandmother was holding a Bible. Verses about punishment and adhering to the law rang in Jemma's ears.

"What are you doing?" she called out.

Honorine answered only once she finished a verse. "Miss Barker, you missed dinner last night. You also disappeared before breakfast yesterday."

"I know that. So what?"

"So, when you first came here, I made it clear to you that you would join the family for dinner every night. And I mean every night. That is part of your responsibilities here."

The woman then continued reading in a monotone, describing bad things happening to bad people (and even good ones). Jemma jumped out of bed and slipped into her robe, snatching the sash closed.

She can stand here all day like a lunatic. I don't have to listen.

But when Jemma tried the doorknob, it didn't turn.

"I'm locked in here?" she asked.

"Until I'm finished, yes."

On and on it went, until her grandmother shut the book. Honorine then tapped on the door, and a small click sounded from the other side.

So she had an accomplice just waiting for the signal, Jemma thought, glaring at the older woman.

"Before you go," Honorine said, as if anticipating the very thing Jemma planned to do, "what exactly did you do when you tried to break the curse?"

Jemma eyed the door now that it was unlocked. She could flee the house, the property. She could leave and never return.

But the scorched letters had bothered her. She still didn't know what she'd done wrong, but something had whispered, "Not like this." And if she was going to save the family, and herself, she had to figure out what it was.

Jemma explained in detail how she'd performed the ritual, showing Honorine the book she'd used. She stopped talking, reluctant to reveal everything, but in the end, she admitted to hearing the whisper.

At that, Honorine's eyebrows rose. "You talk to spirits?"

"No, I don't talk to them. Sometimes . . . sometimes I see them."

"But they talk to you."

"Not usually. And I'm not sure that's what I heard. It might have been something else." Jemma's voice dropped, as if embarrassed by the lie.

Honorine's gaze went to the window, and for several moments, silence weighed heavily in the room.

"It's nearly time for breakfast," she said at last. "I expect you to be on time."

Twenty minutes later, Jemma entered the dining room. The walls had been scrubbed clean, but when she took her seat next to Fosette it was clear that the family's memory hadn't washed away. Conversation was minimal and stilted. All of it excluded Jemma. When she asked for the tray of bread, Fosette passed it to her without a word or look before asking Honorine if she could be excused.

She didn't realize how much she'd come to enjoy her cousin's company until it was no longer offered.

For the first time since Jemma's arrival, they were allowed to leave the table early, no doubt to escape the uneasiness in the room. The walls might be clean again, but vestiges lingered, almost as palpable as the smoky odor that seemed always to be present in the house.

IT TOOK SEVERAL days for things to feel normal again, days in which Jemma spent as much time with Magdalene as she could, while making sure to be on time for dinner every evening. They talked in circles about what she could do next, with Magdalene questioning the effectiveness of anything found in a book, while Jemma continued to resist the idea of engaging with ghosts.

"There has to be another way."

Someone tapped on her bedroom door just as Jemma changed into a cotton nightgown, one she'd found in the chifforobe. As she opened the door, cautious happiness washed over her at the sight of Fosette's smiling face. Her cousin entered the room and flopped onto the bed.

"We were scared, you know," she said in her breathy voice, getting right to the point. "About what happened. I told Grandmère that you were only trying to help us. It's not like you were the one who . . . put that horrible word on the wall." Fosette shivered, her eyes darting around the room as if she expected huge black letters to appear there as well. "I'm sorry if I was distant. I don't know if I've ever been so frightened, except for . . ." She shot a look at Jemma, her eyebrows knitted together in worry. And Jemma knew her cousin was referring to her birthday, which had to be the worst day of the year for the family.

"It's all right."

"Do you think you'll be able to help us, to break the curse?"

Jemma hesitated before answering. "I don't know."

Fosette nodded, allowing the silence to stretch, although not in an uncomfortable way. She patted the spot next to her on the bed. When Jemma took it, Fosette laid her head on her shoulder.

"What were your parents like? The ones in Chicago."

A lie waited on Jemma's tongue, ready to spring forth. For some reason, she held it in place before spitting half of it aside.

"They were all right. Mama more than Daddy."

"Was he mean to you?" Fosette lifted her head, but Jemma stared at the floor.

"No. He didn't try to be." *Why was she still making excuses for him?* "He didn't know what to do with me. He did the best he could."

"What about your mother?"

Jemma bit her lip lest the full truth spill out. "She was . . . scared of him. He got angry sometimes. He never hit us, though. Just yelled a lot."

There. Mabel sounded like a saint, while Carl seemed unable to control his temper. Jemma's description didn't make them sound like bad people, did it?

Fosette suddenly turned to the door. "Oh! He's awake already!"

Jemma looked around, hearing nothing. "Who?"

"The baby."

Jemma frowned, straining to listen, but all she heard was a far-off owl hoot. "A baby?"

"He's crying. Don't you hear him?"

Fosette rose from the bed and turned in a full circle, her head angled. Without another word, she rushed from the room. Immediately after, Jemma heard the sound of her cousin's bedroom door clicking shut.

A few minutes later, the unmistakable sound of the usual lullaby reached her ears.

Jemma shrank onto her bed, a chill inching along her bare arms.

ELEVEN

THE NEXT NIGHT, Jemma kicked the covers off and looked at the clock in her darkened bedroom. One fifteen. She hadn't been sleeping well since coming here. Between the heat, the weirdness and the tension, it was a wonder she could sleep at all.

She slipped a robe over her nightgown and pressed her ear to the door before opening it. In the hallway, she glanced both ways before making her way downstairs. Maybe she'd make a cup of coffee. On her way to the kitchen, she saw that the French doors leading to the back garden were standing ajar. Jemma narrowed her eyes in the dimness, just making out a figure moving steadily away from the house.

She moved to the doors, wondering who it was and why it seemed no one could sleep in this house.

It was Laurence again, this time on his own.

Jemma looked toward the kitchen before slipping out after him, the grass tickling her bare feet and ankles. She kept close to the bushes, ready to fall into them should he turn around. But he, at least twenty yards ahead of her, appeared intent on a destination. Where, at this time of night?

She followed him to the carriage house. He glanced around once, Jemma ducking behind a tall magnolia shrub, before he went inside. She couldn't imagine what he'd be doing in there in the middle of the night, the place where Honorine claimed her granddaughter had died. Jemma tiptoed over, telling herself she'd peek in a window and if she didn't see anything she'd leave.

As she drew closer, she noticed a hole in a lower window, as if someone had thrown a rock through it. She stood on her toes, her chin level with the bottom of the frame, and peered inside.

The only things she could see were shadows. At first, everything seemed still, but then she saw what appeared to be figures, grappling. Two of them. Laurence was one, but who was the other?

A low groan drifted across the air, and then Jemma realized what was happening. But who was the other person? There were no women Laurence's age around—or men, for that matter. Was Laurence sneaking out here to meet with someone outside of the family?

The woman whispered, something that sounded dirty, in a very familiar voice.

Jemma frowned, her heartbeat quickening.

No, no, no, that can't be.

But when the woman threw her head back, her mouth wide, a high, ecstatic moan slipping from it, Jemma was able to make out her face as her flushed skin shone in the dimness. Jemma put her hands to her mouth, unable to stop the gasp that rose up, escaping between her fingers.

"Did you hear something?" Fosette asked inside.

Jemma pressed her back to the wall, her eyes moving in all

directions, trying to decide which way she could run without being seen if those two incestuous creatures looked outside.

"It's nothing," Laurence murmured.

"No, I heard something."

The shuffling of feet and the rustling of clothes being put in place reached Jemma's ears. She had to move. She inched her way along the wall toward the back of the building. If they went out the front, they wouldn't see her. Jemma turned the corner, her breath whistling in quiet relief, when Fosette and Laurence banged their way out the back door.

"Oh my God," Fosette cried, her hand clutching the top of her robe at her neck.

Jemma wanted to laugh in their horrified faces. If anyone should be shocked, it should be her.

"It's not what you think," Fosette said, reaching out a hand, which Jemma slapped away.

"Don't touch me!" she shrieked. Words flew through her mind, heavy and insulting, dripping with disgust and scorn, but none of them found their way to her lips. It was just too much. Brother and sister, sneaking out in the middle of the night as if they were lovers. As if they could be.

But what had Honorine told her?

Cousins married cousins, all to keep the family name intact.

A wave of nausea rose in Jemma, nearly choking her. Finally she was able to move, although her first step was unsteady, and she staggered like a drunk. She walked quickly, then picked up the pace, desperate to get away from the two of them. But Fosette caught up to her, grabbed her arm and swung her around to face her.

"Get away from me!" Jemma screamed. "You people are disgusting! I thought it was bad enough that you marry your cousins, but your own brother? Your brother!"

"He's not my brother," Fosette said, her voice hitching. "We're related—he is my cousin, but he's not my brother."

Jemma had already begun turning away, but at that she stopped.

"Another of your family's lies," she spit.

"We're your family, too, don't forget," Fosette shot back, her eyes blazing, the docile creature Jemma was used to nowhere in sight.

"But I'm not fucking my cousin!"

The smirk that marred Fosette's face should have been a warning to Jemma, she realized later. Laurence had caught up to them, his eyes moving between them.

"Did you tell her?" he asked Fosette.

A brittle laugh escaped her as her hands dropped to her sides. The smile she directed to Jemma held no hint of happiness in it.

"If you were fucking Laurence, you'd be the one fucking your brother," Fosette said quietly before sweeping her way toward the house, Laurence following a step behind.

JEMMA BANGED ON Honorine's door, not caring that it was past two in the morning. She was fed up with this family's lies. Fosette and Laurence tried to stop her, but Jemma didn't care if she woke the whole house.

"What the hell are you doing?" Honorine seethed after she opened the door, her teeth clenched. A part of Jemma's mind registered how much smaller the woman looked in her nightclothes, her hair hidden beneath a bonnet, rollers making an impression against silk, instead of it being styled in one of her formidable updos. Fine wrinkles lined her makeup-free face, which appeared even whiter against the dark of her bedroom.

Even so, Jemma almost lost her resolve, despite the swirl of emotions coursing through her. On top of everything else was the anger, but beneath it was mortification. Her face burned when she remembered her many stolen looks at Laurence. The possibility that what Fosette said was true made Jemma want to vomit. She swiped a hand across her mouth, imagining how much worse things would go if she threw up on Honorine's feet.

"I want every one of you downstairs now. We're talking. No one goes to sleep until I get the truth," Jemma ordered. She didn't wait for an answer, simply stomped her way downstairs to the dining room, where she flipped on the light and took her usual seat. She wasn't sure Honorine would do what she'd demanded, but something told Jemma it was likely.

Fosette and Laurence were the first ones there. Jemma leaned away from her cousin as she took her seat next to her, and she glanced at Laurence only once, to find not a trace of embarrassment on his face, before turning to the doorway.

Fosette claimed he was Jemma's brother. But the way the Duchons lied, who knew what was true?

Russell and Simone came next, yawning and complaining, followed by Honorine.

"The least you can do is get us some coffee if you insist on having middle-of-the-night discussions," Simone said to Jemma, who sat with her arms crossed.

"I'm not getting a damn thing," Jemma said.

"Fine, I'll wake up that useless maid." Simone rose, and Jemma stood up at the same time.

"Sit down," she ordered her aunt.

Simone's right eyebrow rose nearly to her hairline, but after emitting a quick snort, she sank back into her seat. Only then did Jemma resume her seat.

"Well," Honorine said, looking at Jemma. "You thought something was important enough to get everyone out of bed at this ridiculous hour. What is it?"

Jemma opened her mouth, but what she'd thought about saying stuck in her throat. She'd planned to have them all settled in their seats and then point at Fosette and Laurence, telling her grandmother about the unnatural act she'd caught them in. But she remembered how the whole family intermarried. Would they even care? Worse, perhaps they already knew.

Instead, she pointed only at Laurence while speaking to Honorine.

"Is he my brother?"

The woman's eyes flicked to Simone briefly before settling on Fosette for a few seconds. Jemma caught Fosette's nearly imperceptible nod.

"He is," Honorine admitted.

Jemma looked at him for a long moment. Although his skin was darker than any of the other Duchons', it wasn't by much. He simply looked like he'd gotten a bit of sun while vacationing on the French Riviera. She searched for anything familiar in him, but nothing, not the shape or color of his eyes, not his ears, lips, chin or nose was like hers.

A wave of nausea rose again. Jemma swallowed what felt like an ocean of shame at the way she'd desired him.

"We have the same mother," she finally said.

"Yes, but not the same father."

Laurence appeared completely unfazed by this. So he'd known all along. And he'd played the part of Simone's son. But why?

"And where is your father?" Jemma asked him.

He shrugged. "Same place as yours. One of the cemeteries."

"Do you remember her? Our mother?"

"I was only two when she died."

"I didn't ask you that. Do you remember her?" Jemma shouted.

"*Mon Dieu*, this girl and her theatrics," Simone muttered.

Jemma turned her attention to her. "You sat there and pretended to be his mother, all of you sitting there, lying to me, about everything. Like it wasn't bad enough that you didn't tell me the real reason you hired me to come down here. Why would you lie to me about Laurence being my cousin?" she asked, unaware until that moment that she'd been crying. "If I had known he was my brother . . ."

"What? What then?" Honorine asked. "What would you have done differently? Did it ever occur to you that we've done what we can to erase the memory of your mother? Simone raised him like a son after Inès died. She may as well be his mother. And we had no intention of telling him, except . . ."

"Except what?"

A pink flush worked its way up Honorine's neck and face.

"When we found out that Laurence and Fosette were sleeping together," Simone said, her hard gaze moving from her daughter back to Jemma, "we felt it was better that they know they weren't coupling with a sibling. Isn't that right, Fosette?" When Fosette didn't reply, her mother went on. "You see, we haven't seen any other person outside of this house—save the parish priest, who only comes once a month—in years. Our acquaintances stopped coming round ages ago. They don't know the extent of the malevolence that's settled on us, but they know something is wrong. What are these young people to do? Of course, my daughter could have chosen to sleep with Dennis, the gardener, which is something my sister would have done, but we like to keep it all in the family, don't we, Maman?"

"Quiet," Honorine hissed.

The one question that had been burning in Jemma rose then,

the one whose answer she suspected but she had to hear anyway. She would know if they lied to her about this, but a part of her wanted them to.

Because the truth was too awful to face.

"But if Laurence is my brother . . . why did you keep him? You said it was my mother's wish that you give me away, but why not him, too? Why wouldn't you keep us together?" Jemma asked.

"Isn't it obvious?" Honorine asked, waving a hand toward him. "He's light enough to fit in with the rest of us, despite Inès lying down with some Black trash. I don't know why she found them so desirable, but she did. Her father and I wanted to marry her off to a distant cousin, but before that happened, she slept with this penniless Black bastard and got in the family way. We shipped her off to Charleston to stay with some relatives, where she had Laurence. By the grace of God, he mostly has our color. The two of them came home and we decided to tell everyone that he belonged to either Russell or Simone, since they were both married. But Inès wouldn't have that. I wanted to toss her out on her slutty behind, but my husband . . . he had such a soft spot for Inès. She was his favorite. Of course, after that, her name was ruined. No one from any respectable family would have anything to do with her. So she spent her nights carousing in the city and turned up pregnant again. And we waited and waited to see what she'd give birth to that time. Your father came round, a great buck of a man, wanting to marry her. Marry her! Into this family! We ran him out of here, threatening to kill him if he ever dared to show his face again. I wanted to send her packing after him, but her father—oh, how he loved that girl. And when you were born, and she cursed us, and we saw your dark eyes and your dark hair, we knew you'd taken after your father. You'd only get darker as you grew up, and you did. You'd never fit in here. You'd never be a true Duchon, with us able to trace our lineage all the way back to the first Duchons who lived here. That's why we gave you away. Because to have to see you every day would only remind us of your mother's great sin. Of lying down with dark-skinned men who we have no connection to."

Jemma pointed a shaky finger at Laurence across the table.

"And he doesn't remind you of what our mother did? The great sin of sleeping with someone who dared to be dark-skinned, as if any of us have any control over that? The sin of sleeping with someone who's not a relative?"

"If Laurence wasn't able to pass as one of us, we'd be reminded of that every day."

TWELVE

IT WAS NOON when Jemma woke the next day. The dried tears caking her face were no surprise. But the shallow bowl of gardenias on the nightstand was, the flowers floating on an inch of water, their fragrance filling the entire room. She tried to sit up, but her head reeled.

Laurence was her brother, not a cousin.

They had the same mother, this Inès who'd brought death and destruction down on all their heads.

Had she known, when she cursed all the Duchons, what she was doing, that she'd cursed her own children in her anger?

And why had she done it? That was the question. Perhaps, Jemma thought, if she started there, with the why of it, she'd get to the solution.

Their mother was dead. And their fathers, too. But Jemma shook her head at the thought. For all she knew, her father was alive, and maybe Laurence's as well. Honorine had lied to her about so much. All the family had, with straight faces and without a hint of guilt.

If it hadn't been for the deaths, Jemma might think the whole thing was a game.

Despite the warm October air suffusing the room, a chill washed over her, goose bumps springing along her arms.

As she slowly rose out of bed, she spotted a covered tray on the bench. Lifting the lid, she found a cold breakfast of croissants, grits, bacon and eggs. She gobbled it all down, including the chilled café au lait.

She peeked out the door before going to the bathroom, and she made quick work of washing up and getting dressed, slipping into her one pair of dungarees. She knotted a scarf around her hair and placed only her identification, her five dollars and the two checks in her pocket, although she couldn't explain why she did that and left her suitcase. She told herself she didn't want to arouse anyone's suspicion. If they asked, she'd say she was going for a walk along the grounds. Was she really going to run, without any clothes except the ones on her back? Was she going to leave her brother, with no explanation or goodbye? She shook her head. She hadn't even known Laurence was her brother before last night. They had no connection, except for the same mother, who sounded as mad as the rest of her family.

Jemma stopped short at the bottom of the stairs. Honorine had just entered the foyer from the dining room.

"You look well rested, despite the night's events."

"Is that what it was to you?" Jemma asked. "Nothing more than a night's events? I guess it's normal around here not to sleep at night but instead to find out that your cousin is actually your brother, that he's having relations with a cousin, that your family gave you away because you're darker than a piece of bread." A laugh that sounded nothing like hers escaped her lips. Wrapped within it was loathing, but also a small slice of satisfaction at knowing something Honorine didn't know.

If her words bothered the other woman, her grandmother didn't show it. "Are you going somewhere? You have work to do."

"I need some air right now."

Without waiting for a response, Jemma walked out the front door, and leaned against it after shutting it behind her. Not wanting a repeat of the last time she'd walked out the front gates, she hurried, not chancing a glance behind her. There was no Dennis working on the front lawn today, no one to stop her in conversation.

She touched the front gates, her eyes closed. She could do this. She could leave. Forever.

We are all you have. One of the few true things Honorine had said.

We owe you the truth, Carl Barker had told her, shattering Jemma's illusion of being his and Mama's natural child.

For the past thirteen years, she'd wondered about her real family, had hungered for them with a greed born out of Daddy's unkindness and Mama's impotence. Friendly faces had swum forward in dreams, dark eyes shining, brown skin glowing. Not once had Jemma dreamed of a family that looked like the Duchons. Of a brother that shared nothing with her besides their mother's blood.

If Laurence wasn't able to pass as one of us, we'd be reminded of that every day.

Of all the things Honorine had said to Jemma since her arrival, that was the most painful. And despite her grandmother's promise to give her what she wanted—her family history, a place—Jemma didn't see how she could stay.

A sound behind her made her turn her head. Her grandmother stood on the porch.

Jemma knew the woman wouldn't give chase, but the sight of

her so near pushed her through the gates. With each tentative step down the lane, farther and farther away from the house, a lightness rose in her, full enough to lift her off her feet.

Glaring back at Honorine, who wore no sign of envy and just the faintest trace of astonishment, Jemma raised her fists to the sky.

"I'm free!" she screamed. "Free!"

And ran.

THE BUS SPIT Jemma out at the edge of the French Quarter.

It was well past lunchtime, but delicious smells wafted everywhere, mixing with the people smells of perfume and perspiration. Riding along that was the scent of the river, strong as a current. Sweet and tangy, musky and marshy.

Jemma stood on the sidewalk for several minutes, greedily taking in the scenery. It was her first day here all over again, except the fashions had slightly changed. More navy blues and grays bobbed about, but the material was still light enough for the summertime climate. People passed by distressed open shutters, many of them in need of a fresh coat of blue or green paint. Ivy trailed down wrought iron railings, drifting from second floor galleries.

The music of horns flowed out of an open doorway, the sax low and sultry, out of place in broad daylight. That song was for evenings spent in dimly lit rooms before a hand pulled the cord under a tasseled lampshade and caressed a waiting body.

It wasn't until a white couple passed her, the man bumping her shoulder and telling her to get off the sidewalk, that Jemma's spell broke.

Ahead of her was a shoeshine stand, the Black owner collecting money from a departing customer. Jemma approached and asked for directions to Tremé.

"Head that way to Rampart, baby, and you'll run right into it."

She started off, then remembered the checks in her pocket. Pulling one out, she asked, "Can you tell me where First Citizens Bank is?"

"It's a few blocks from here, but you can't go in there. It's just for white folks."

"Where can I get a check cashed, then?"

"Try Cajun Mamou's on St. Philip."

Jemma thanked him and followed his directions, wondering what Cajun Mamou's was. She'd been employed by the Duchons for over a month, which meant she was owed over a thousand dollars at this point. She'd agreed to have her future pay deposited into an account at Honorine's bank, and it turned out she couldn't go inside. She frowned, wondering if she even had an account there, if her grandmother was actually paying her. Although Jemma had left the house with no firm plans in place, she had planned to cash her checks and withdraw any additional money from the bank. But with six hundred dollars in hand, she wouldn't have to make an immediate decision on whether to stay or go.

Snatches of conversation alerted her to the change of environment. White faces had been replaced with Black ones.

". . . couldn't cool off nowhere 'cause Schiro closed the pools instead of letting us in. So nobody could swim, colored or white."

"What was you expecting? He was already mad about having to let us in the schools."

Despite the heat, Jemma grew more comfortable. The scenery differed from Chicago's, but the people reminded her of home. A woman rocking on her porch, silver hair arranged into short plaits, smiled as she passed. Lolling on the side of the dirt-packed road was a yellow dog, teats heavy with milk, and a group of babbling schoolchildren swinging book straps swarmed around her, only to melt into a single unit once they were past.

Cajun Mamou's store, painted a jarring shade of purple, was a hodgepodge of voodoo decor and five-and-dime merchandise. The freckle-faced owner, whose red hair was as diverse in texture as Jemma's wilted rag curls, took one look at the checks and dropped them on the rough wooden counter, refusing even to push them back across.

"Can't cash 'em here. Not those," she said, not meeting Jemma's eye.

Jemma raised her voice to be heard over the rusty fan whirring in the window. "They said you cash checks."

The woman shook her head. "Not with that name on 'em. And you ain't gonna find nobody here that's gonna do it, either."

She then called on the next customer, ignoring Jemma completely until she had no choice but to leave. Checks stuffed in her pocket, she weaved her way around tables crowded with crucifixes and rosaries, bowls full of small bones and tiny bags in various rich colors. Next to all that, the matchbooks and packets of Goody's headache powder looked out of place.

Deflation clapped Jemma on both shoulders as she stepped outside. She wasn't six hundred dollars richer, as she'd expected to be. Refusing to accept defeat, she walked until she recognized her surroundings. Glancing down an alley to her right, she spotted a café with a row of dolls in the window.

Lulu's.

She wasn't particularly hungry, but she could sit, get her bearings and maybe figure something out besides returning to that house. Soft chatter and clinking silverware greeted Jemma, so comforting in their ordinariness that tears stung her eyes. She wiped her face as she took a seat at a small table near a window.

"What can I get you, baby?"

She looked up into Lulu's eyes, and before she could wonder if the woman remembered her, Jemma reminded herself that dozens of people passed through the café every day. If she looked familiar to Lulu, it wouldn't be any more so than another customer.

"I remember you," Lulu said, without a hint of disquiet. "You work for the Duchons."

Jemma nodded once at the simple declaration, which only touched on her true relationship with the family, as if with a bony finger.

"You all right? You look like you been through it."

"Had a long walk is all. I could use a cool drink."

"How 'bout some tea with ice?"

When Lulu returned with the glass of tea, jagged ice already smoothing away under the warmth, Jemma ran it across her forehead before taking a sip of the unsweetened beverage.

The woman cocked her head. "I wondered how you was getting along. I don't know a single soul been out to that property in years, not since Celestina. When you came here before and told me you had a job with them, I thought maybe it was a mistake. But Charlie told us he took you all the way out there, talking 'bout somebody had a child."

Jemma didn't know how to respond, but Lulu seemed to be waiting for something from her.

"I'm all right."

"Yeah? 'Cause folks say some strange things about that place." When Jemma didn't take the hint, Lulu went on, placing both hands flat on the table and leaning in. "What they like?"

A straightforward question—with no simple answer, but Lulu didn't appear ready to go until Jemma fed her something.

"They *are* strange." *This is your family you're talking about.* "They keep to themselves."

"That's what I heard, but why? Did they really all grow ugly and deformed?"

"What?" A short laugh bubbled up. "No, they're not ugly at all."

Of course. The Duchons were at the mercy of gossip and lies, unable to appear and defend themselves. As she finished the tea, Jemma's mind cleared away fuzzy cobwebs of stress and heat exhaustion. Lulu had said something . . .

Not since Celestina.

"Who's Celestina?"

"Conjure woman. She went out to the Duchons' long time ago 'cause they had some kind of trouble. When she came back, she wouldn't see nobody for 'bout a week, just shut herself in. We thought she caught what they had. She finally came out, but never said much 'bout what she saw, only that something didn't rest easy in that house."

"Where does she live?" Jemma set a dime on the table, halfway out of her seat, ready to find this Celestina, the only person she was aware of who'd seen her family outside of the parish priest. But at Lulu's next words, she dropped back down.

"St. Louis Cemetery Number Two. She died 'bout ten years back." The woman looked at Jemma closely. "Something's troubling you, baby."

Jemma nearly laughed aloud. *Something,* she wanted to say. *How about everything?*

Glancing around at the other patrons, Jemma noticed how easy most of them appeared. Even Lulu. They didn't have the pinched expression she must wear most of the time.

"I feel strange here. Unwelcome," Jemma said. "Maybe because I'm not from here and not used to how things are done."

"Oh, New Orleans is a different kind of place, *chère,*" Lulu agreed. "Probably got more spirits than live people."

Jemma gave her a sharp glance. "Spirits?"

"This city is full of them." Instead of looking scared at the thought, Lulu smiled.

"You believe in ghosts?"

Lulu gave Jemma an odd look. "Who don't?"

"You ever see any?" Jemma didn't know how Lulu would take the question, but the woman only smiled more widely.

"No, *chère*, I don't see them. But all the same, I know they're around. People draw them, you see. Some more than others. Some got more of a light, and one thing about spirits, they love that light."

"They do?"

Lulu's gaze was keen. "You mighty interested in the dead."

Jemma shrugged in an attempt to appear nonchalant. "I've always been curious about ghosts, why they stay here instead of moving on."

"They got different reasons, I expect. Same as people got different reasons for doing what they do. Some died bad and can't move on. Others don't know they're dead. They keep doing the same thing over and over, maybe even dying over and over, but they don't know they're doing the same thing 'cause they don't have a good sense of time. Most of them don't mean no harm, though. They just want somebody to talk to."

"Talk to?"

"Yeah, just like us. But since most people can't see them, they get lonely. Probably bored. So when somebody comes along who *can* see them, they get excited. They try to get that person's attention any way they can."

As if bringing Lulu's words to life, a boy appeared.

He looked to be about six years old, with short, tightly curled hair hugging his head. He stood next to Lulu, who was clearly unaware of his presence. A small hand slipped around the woman's arm.

Five . . . four . . .

He grinned at Jemma.

No. No, go away!

She jumped up, knocking over her chair, ignoring Lulu's cries, the stares that followed her as she rushed out, the little boy who hadn't moved on. As Jemma staggered down the street, Magdalene's voice rode over the sounds of passing cars, barking dogs and mundane conversations.

It looks like you got something in common with your mama that can maybe help you. Instead of running scared, why not look at it as some kind of gift?

Seeing spirits was no gift. It was a curse. Hadn't Mama and Daddy told her that her entire life?

Jemma stopped, a chill covering her body despite its being slick with sweat. Mama and Daddy weren't her real family. Like the Duchons, she was bound by a death curse, but she was also cursed with seeing things that other people didn't. Yet it was something she shared with her mother. A link.

Laurence was another link, a tie to Inès.

Pressing her forehead against a lamppost, she shut her eyes, remembering that she was nearly broke, two useless pieces of paper in her pocket. She could call Betty, see if her friend would send her money for a bus ticket, although she wouldn't return to Chicago. But it didn't matter where Jemma went—the ghosts would follow.

Running is easy, until it ain't. How many times have you run from something?

All the running in the world wouldn't get her away. For now, there was only one place she could go.

THIRTEEN

ONCE THE FAMILY knew Jemma was not bound to the property like they were, there was much debate about how else she was different.

"Maybe she's not even at risk of dying like the rest of us," Simone said to Honorine at dinner several nights later, talking about Jemma as if she weren't sitting across the table.

"She was here when the curse was set," Honorine replied, her eyes fixed on Jemma, her words directed elsewhere. "All of us who were in the house at the time can die next March."

Jemma didn't care that they talked about her instead of to her. After she'd returned from town, she'd immediately confronted her grandmother about the money.

"You *are* being paid every week," the woman had said. "The funds are being held in trust."

"But I can't go into the bank to get my money!"

Jemma's attention returned to the meal. "Is that what Celestina told you? That only the people who were here when my mother cursed us are liable to die?"

"Who?"

Jemma banged her fists on the table, knocking her salad fork to the floor. "Celestina! The conjure woman who came here before. You don't even remember her name!"

"Can you stop the goddamn histrionics?" Simone snapped.

"Lots of people came through here," Russell said, puffing on a Camel cigarette. "And none of them could help."

"Celestina told us that you could break the curse," Honorine said, her gaze on the table. "It had to be you."

"Look." Simone turned to her mother, waving a hand in Jemma's direction. "We don't even know why she came back here. Why should she have if she'll go right on living next March twelfth?"

Was it enough to believe what the mediums had said, or could Jemma take the chance that she wouldn't die on her next birthday? If she lived past that one, what about the one that followed in seven years? What must it be like to fear the same date every seven years the way her family did?

She met Laurence's eyes across the table. He was just like the rest of them, she thought, remembering his behavior toward Agnes in the library. And yet he was the strongest tie she had to their mother.

Haints can't hurt you, but maybe they can tell you some things you want to know.

She needed to know how to break the curse. That was the only way she'd get out of here and get the money owed to her. The only way she'd truly be free.

Once they'd exhausted the topic of how cursed Jemma might or might not be, they resumed conversation about mundane subjects, as if they were normal people leading normal lives.

". . . integrating the Catholic schools was the biggest mistake," Russell said, his face partly obscured by smoke. "White families are running from St. Augustine's like their hair's on fire. What's going to be left?"

"You know what's going to be left," Simone said, pushing her empty plate out of the way, then lit a cigarette from the end of her brother's.

"You think Negroes being the majority in your church is a bad thing?" Jemma directed this question to her aunt.

"Colored people need religion, probably more than anybody else. But if and when we ever are able to set foot in St. Augustine's again, I'd rather not be surrounded by a bunch of darkies, if it's all the same to you."

"Must you always be so awful?" Fosette drawled.

"It's all right." Jemma turned to her cousin for a brief moment and found her face flushed pink. "I know how this entire family feels about Negroes. You just like to pretend you're not Black."

"Au contraire," Honorine said from her place at the head of the table. "We are a proud colored family."

"And it's not 'colored' anymore. It's 'Negro,' which you'd learn to say if you really were so proud—"

"Why this fascination with color?" Russell asked. "We've been fine all our lives with who we are. Maybe your experience has been different."

"Because I'm so dark, you mean. That's why you gave me away as a baby." Jemma then addressed Honorine. "You only looked for me because you needed something from me. For all you know, the curse won't affect me because Inès was my mother. I don't believe for a minute she meant to curse me like she did you. But we could hold a séance and call her up."

Quiet dropped on the room as all heads turned to her.

"I know you've done it before. Maybe the mediums couldn't help because . . . I don't know why. But I have to try."

"You plan to call up Inès?" Russell asked.

"Yes. You want to know how to break the curse. What better way than to ask the person who placed it?"

"It won't work," Fosette whispered, shaking her head.

As Jemma opened her mouth to ask why not, Simone snapped, "Shut up. Shut the hell up."

"What is it?" Jemma asked her aunt before turning back to her cousin. "Why won't it work?" But Fosette had placed her hands over her ears and shut her eyes.

"Yes, of course we've tried to figure out how to break the curse," Honorine said. "Inès won't answer."

"She might not answer you, for obvious reasons, but I don't see why she wouldn't answer me."

Agnes entered the room and began clearing the serving platters. All of the family tended to treat the woman as if she weren't there, but Russell wouldn't even look at her, even when she slipped his empty plate off the table.

Simone blew out a plume of smoke, her lips curving into an unpleasant smile. "And when are we having this little session to call on the dearly departed Inès?"

"I'll let you know." Jemma stood. "May I be excused?" she asked Honorine.

Without waiting for a reply, she tossed her napkin on her plate, still covered with jambalaya and bread.

She left the room and was nearly at the staircase when a cool hand gripped her wrist. She twisted around to see Simone and snatched herself free.

"What do you want?"

"The séance. You'll do this for Fosette. I don't give a damn about the others, not even myself at this point. I've lost everything but my remaining daughter. If she can be saved, if you can figure out how to save her . . ." The woman's mouth opened, then shut. Jemma was stunned to see her aunt blink back tears. "But forget about calling Inès."

"Why? And why do you all think it won't work?"

Simone's chin lifted, the hard lines of her face back in place. "She took everything from me—do you understand? Everything. My Lucie, my father, my brother. Even my husband. He was a suicide, but she caused it. She won't help you. You'll have to figure out another way." Her aunt glanced back at the parlor, her voice lowered when she spoke to Jemma again. "Fosette adores you and I know you adore her."

Jemma didn't respond, simply let the truth of what Simone said wash over her. She did adore Fosette, despite the strangeness, the initial disgust at her relationship with Laurence. Some of her affection was because of pity, for the life her cousin never got to live. But Simone was right. She did adore the woman.

"And there's your brother. I raised him like a son, even after what my sister did. You'd want to save them, wouldn't you?"

"Why would I believe anything you say? Maybe you're afraid of what my mother will tell me, of what horrible secrets she knows about this family. Is that it?"

Simone took a step back, her mouth widening in a grin. "You goddamn fool. You think you know this family." A harsh laugh escaped. "Go ahead, then. Have your little shindig. Call Inès from the rooftops! I'd love it if you conjured up something, anything! But I know you'll fail, again and again and again."

Coming out of the bathroom at one thirty in the morning, Jemma was startled by Russell walking up the stairs.

"Sorry," he said, the tip of his lit cigarette providing just enough light to make out his features. "I have trouble sleeping sometimes."

Jemma understood that quite well, although she wondered what would keep him up at night. She remembered the absent way he'd looked out the back doors when a ghost had interrupted her phone call with Betty, as if he'd seen it, too. Just as she opened her mouth to question him about it again, a low hum reached their ears. Fosette again, with the lullaby.

At this hour?

Russell didn't even turn his head as he passed his niece's door and shut himself in his bedroom. Jemma turned back to her room but stopped short. She found herself at Fosette's door, her fist raised. Without thinking, she knocked.

The song stopped, as if Jemma's fist had crushed it into silence.

"Fosette?" Jemma whispered.

Soft noises reached through the wood, something that sounded like rustling and then a light thump.

"Fosette? Are you all right?"

"I'm fine, Jemma! Go to sleep. It's late," her cousin called through the door.

Jemma didn't miss the tremble in her voice. But she obeyed, returning to her room and climbing into bed.

A few minutes later, the lullaby started anew.

THE NEXT MORNING, Jemma rooted through the library, looking for a Bible. She needed it for the séance, but she was also sure Magdalene was right about the family keeping records of all their members. Her father's name might be written down there. If she had a name, she might be able to find that side of her family, who had to be more welcoming than the Duchons. But after scanning every book title, she'd found no Bible.

"Any luck?"

Jemma twirled around to find Laurence shutting the glass doors behind him. He hadn't been in here with her since his rude behavior with Agnes, the day the maid kissed her on the lips. Jemma turned back to the shelves.

"With what?" she asked, choosing a book at random without looking at the title.

"With whatever you're trying to find." His voice came from his usual armchair.

Almost against her will, Jemma glanced over at him. As she did, Agnes passed the glass doors on her way to the kitchen. It would have been easier for Jemma to leave, to not confront him, but a spark of anger held her there, as well as a bit of curiosity.

"Why are all of you so awful to Agnes? The last time we were in here, when you knocked the tray out of her hands, you treated her like it was her fault. It was bad enough that she had to clean up your mess. You didn't have to insult her on top of it."

Laurence's eyes met hers, his brows knitted. She fully expected him to make some excuse for his rudeness, perhaps remind her of her own place. What she didn't expect was the way his gaze dropped to his lap and how he crumpled back in the seat. He didn't look like the almost-thirty-year-old that he was. Instead, he reminded her of a young boy, one who'd been hurt many times.

"It's this house," he said in a low voice, looking at the closed doors before bringing his gaze back to Jemma's. "I don't mean to be . . . It's just . . . You didn't grow up here. You have no idea how horrible it's been."

Dennis's words came back to her: *Think on how mad you'd be if you'd been trapped here all these years.*

Laurence went on, his eyes going from one spot in the room to the next, as if Jemma weren't there. "We couldn't go to school, Fosette and me. We had tutors. She didn't get a debutante ball. We've never been anywhere, Jemma. Can you understand that? We've been nowhere besides these four walls and the four corners of this property. When we . . . came of age . . . I didn't want to with her any more than she wanted to with me. We thought we were brother and sister then, but we still couldn't stop ourselves. It was such a relief to find out we weren't siblings." His eyes flicked up at Jemma before dropping again. "I know you think it's not much better with us being cousins, first cousins at that, but when Fosette and I are together, it's one of the only times I'm not thinking about dying. For that brief time, I'm reminded that I'm alive. I feel alive and like I can live forever." He jumped up, the swift move startling Jemma. She shrank back into the shelves as he approached her, stopping close enough for her to feel his body heat. "If we're monsters, we weren't born this way. We were made this way, by our mother. Did you ever think how cruel she was to damn us this way? You and me, innocent children. Fosette and Lucie. We didn't deserve it, even if she thought her mother and father did. So if we're all terrible to Agnes, if we treat everyone else like shit, maybe it's not all our fault. You know?"

He backed off, flopping into his seat, one leg thrown over one of its arms. He hung his head back, staring up at the ceiling before shutting his eyes.

Jemma moved only when the hard edge of the bookshelf began to hurt her. Laurence's words rang and rang through her mind. He was angry, like the rest of the Duchons were angry. And they took their anger out on an easy target. It was wrong, and yet Jemma could begin to understand.

Thunk.

Jemma knew what the sound was before turning her head. The slim gray ledger rested next to her foot on the floor. A part of her imagined kicking it aside, but Lulu's voice sounded in her mind:

They try to get that person's attention any way they can.

She grabbed the book and flipped through it, finding it exactly the same as last time. Incomprehensible.

Jemma looked up to find Laurence staring at her. She waved the book in the air.

"I think this is written in French," she said. "Can you tell me if it is?"

He held out a hand and, after looking at several pages, nodded. "It is. But it's kind of old-fashioned. I can make out some words, but not whole sentences." He continued turning pages, a frown growing on his face.

"What is it?" Jemma asked.

It took a moment for him to answer. He gestured for her to sit on the footstool in front of him before pointing to a page full of names and numbers.

MARY, 13, Negro
PIERRE, 4, mulatto
ANNE, 29, quadroon
SALLIE, 11, octoroon
ADAM, 24, Negro

"This is a bill of sale. These are names and I'm pretty sure these are their ages. In that column are prices."

"For people."

"Yes. This book, whatever it is, belonged to Corentin Duchon, one of our ancestors."

"And he owned slaves."

Laurence's lips twisted. "It appears so."

No words passed for several moments, as they both reflected on this information. Laurence seemed as surprised as Jemma.

"Was he white?" she asked.

Laurence answered slowly. "No. But he looked white."

Like the rest of you hung in the air between them.

"So a Black man who looked white who owned slaves."

Jemma didn't know if it helped to say it out loud or not, but she thought it was better than ignoring the ironic reality of it. At least Laurence had the decency to look embarrassed. And he spoke up before the awkwardness could go on much longer.

"There's something else. There's a page missing, here."

Jemma noted the ragged edge as Laurence ran his finger down it.

"What do you want with this book anyway?" he asked suddenly, slapping it shut, as if the information they'd discovered in it made him angry. Or ashamed.

"I think . . . it might help me." Jemma didn't say why she thought it. She hadn't gone looking for the book as much as it had made its presence known to her. More than once. "There might be more information in there that could help me break the curse."

Laurence's eyebrows rose. He looked at the book more thoughtfully, turning it over in his hands.

"You can't read it, though." He glanced at her. "I can, at least a little. Maybe I could help you."

"You would?"

"Why wouldn't I want to? I want the curse broken just as much as any of us." He grabbed one of the legal pads Jemma had been using, as well as a pencil. "Let's get started, shall we?"

One Sunday a month, Father Louis made the trek to the house and the family gathered in the old chapel. Jemma didn't participate. At Shiloh Missionary Baptist Church in Chicago, the congregation took Communion only on the first Sunday of each month, and there was no wine, only grape juice, and no host, just flat crackers. If the Duchons hadn't been imprisoned on their property, they'd be at St. Augustine Church every week.

There had been a heated discussion about having Jemma attend Mass with the family. Honorine felt Jemma should go. Fosette and Laurence shared that opinion, while Russell didn't care one way or the other. Simone, of course, opposed Jemma's joining them since she hadn't been baptized Catholic.

"But you have been baptized, haven't you?" Honorine had asked her at the dinner during which the discussion took place.

"Yes, in a Baptist church."

"Grandmère," Laurence had said, "she's still family. She should go."

Jemma had glanced at him, wondering if he thought she should be touched by his seeming concern. What no one asked was if she wanted to attend.

She didn't.

So when Simone had gone on her tirade about keeping out those who didn't belong, Jemma didn't argue.

She left them to it and used the following Sunday, while the entire family, plus Agnes and Dennis, attended Mass, to look in Honorine's bedroom for a Bible. Once she saw all of them enter the chapel, knowing they'd be occupied for nearly an hour, she slipped into her grandmother's room, the first time she'd ever been inside it.

Large pink roses danced on pale blue wallpaper that stopped at the creamy wainscoting. A four-poster bed took up the bulk of the space, dark wooden posts contrasting against ivory silk covers. The woman's heavy perfume hung in the air. Several framed photographs decorated one wall, and Jemma found herself drawn to them. Faces of long-ago ancestors stared out at her, the women with their thick hair drawn up in large buns or hidden beneath straw bonnets, the men in stiff morning coats and spats. Jemma searched all of them, desperate for any hint of herself in them despite their uniformly fair skin. Maybe there was a bit of them in her nose, in her eyes. Finding none, she looked for any indication that her mother had been a real person, a part of this family until she'd cut ties with them completely and died. Again, it seemed no sign of Inès existed. There were no family portraits of the current Duchons anywhere.

Jemma moved to the ornate dresser decorated with neatly placed perfume bottles, a comb and hairbrush, powder tins, a couple of lipstick tubes and more framed photographs. One depicted what had to be Honorine's wedding day. A ghost of the woman Jemma knew was there in the impossibly young-looking bride in the picture, her slip of a body beside a handsome groom. Similarities existed in their smiles, the lightness of their eyes evident even in the sepia tones. A photo of the groom, Jemma's grandfather, which must have been taken years later, as maturity had set in but had stolen away none of the handsomeness.

She looked over both nightstands next, finding only a rosary in a shallow dish, an empty pitcher and glass and an old copy of *Little Women*. Jemma peeked out the window, sure that the family would be heading out of the chapel now, but there was only the bare back lawn. Opening the nightstand drawers, she found an aspirin tin, neatly folded handkerchiefs, more rosaries and scattered peppermints. She moved on to the wide dresser, being careful not to disrupt Honorine's brassieres and panties too much, as everything was folded in neat stacks that had to be of Agnes's doing. At the bottom of one drawer, Jemma found a sepia-toned photograph. It wasn't in a frame, its curled edges soft as tissue.

Jemma sat on the floor, the picture drawing her in.

Four children stood in a line, all gazing at the camera with eerily light eyes. Two girls stared back at the photographer, two boys between them, and they were lined up from tallest to shortest, so they must have been arranged by age. They had to be related, with their similar skin tones and eyes. Jemma turned the photograph over, but nothing was written on the back. She peered more closely at their clothes, decades out of fashion, wondering if she was looking at a picture of Laurence and Fosette as young children. The girls wore matching knee-length dresses in a pale color, with wide sashes across the hips. Long sleeves covered their arms, and wide collars finished off the style. The clothes were simple, but something about them whispered of money. Shiny black shoes adorned small feet, and big ribbons tied in bows secured the ends of long braids. The boys, who looked to be about three and five, wore roomy light-colored shirts bunched loosely below the waist with matching belts. Below them were pairs of short knickers and high socks.

Jemma looked back at the girls, the older of whom appeared to be six or seven. The little one was just a toddler, and she held one boy's hand, but her face was mostly hidden by a blur, as if she'd moved right as the shutter was clicked.

They had to be siblings. At the very least, cousins.

The older two looked very familiar, but she couldn't make out the youngest one's face.

Jemma scrabbled along the bottom of the drawer, but found nothing else. How strange that Honorine kept this photograph there while the others were on the walls and portraits graced the stairway.

Four young children in a photo that had to be at least thirty years old. No, closer to fifty.

Two boys and two girls.

Russell. André. Simone. Inès.

These had to be Honorine's children—Jemma's aunt, uncles . . . and mother.

If only there weren't that blur on the little girl's face! Only half of her face was visible, and Jemma stared at it as if she could will the blur to disappear, to get a clear picture of what her mother had looked like, even if she could see her only as a young child. As far as she could find, this was the only likeness of Inès in the house, and not a very good one at that.

With reluctance, Jemma slid the photograph back into its hiding place.

Unlike her room, Honorine's had a narrow closet. Jemma swung open the door and pulled the chain for the light. The smell of old mothballs greeted her, as well as the sight of stacked shoeboxes and a line of dresses hanging on one side, a few men's suits on the other. Jemma stood on tiptoe to see what she could on the high shelves on either side. On one there was a small lockbox, which was probably full of receipts and bills if her experience was any indication, and hatboxes were on Honorine's side.

Voices drifted up from downstairs.

Dammit.

Jemma peeked out the door before leaving. The family was coming in, the priest behind them. They were busy talking, so no one looked up, and Jemma took the opportunity to slip out of the room and quickly make it back to her own.

FOURTEEN

DESPITE LAURENCE'S HELP, Jemma hadn't been able to find out much more to break the curse over the family. Also, the missing ledger page bothered her. Someone had deliberately torn it out, probably to prevent anyone from finding out whatever information was there.

Another secret.

Although the Duchons couldn't leave their property now, at one point they'd had the freedom to go about the city. People knew them and had interacted with them. They had to know something about the family, something that could help Jemma.

She hopped off the bus in Tremé. Laurence had given her not only bus fare but a couple of extra dollars in case she wanted to eat while she was in town. He'd also given her the names and addresses of several families that used to visit them. A couple were in the French Quarter and the rest were in Tremé.

But at each of the homes she went to, her hopes were dashed. The people were friendly until Jemma mentioned the Duchons.

The first home wasn't quite as grand as her family's, but the two-story structure loomed large between the smaller houses on either side. A maid answered the door and hurried away to summon the lady of the house.

Jemma introduced herself, fully expecting to be invited inside. The curt response she received reminded her of her first day in the city.

"I understand you know the Duchons," Jemma said.

The woman sniffed. "Knew them. Can I help you?"

The maid stood well behind her employer, not trying to hide the fact that she was eavesdropping.

"I wanted some information about the family."

"Well, if you work for them, you can get this information yourself."

The door shut in Jemma's face.

As she spent the next couple of hours going from house to house, they diminished in size and impressiveness. But the reactions were the same.

One woman's eyes widened at the mention of the Duchons, and she crossed herself before shutting Jemma out. At one house Jemma assumed someone had phoned ahead, because when she knocked on the door, a man yelled from inside, "If you're here about the Duchons, go away!"

In Tremé now, she found a squat cottage much like its neighbors, in need of a fresh coat of paint. She noted odd symbols carved into the screen door's frame, as well as a few small bundles of dried flowers and herbs stuck there. Behind it, the front door stood open, allowing her a view of the dim interior. She knocked. After several moments of silence, she knocked again.

"Who's out there?" called a man.

"My name is Jemma Barker. I'm looking for Henry Marsbrook."

The man made his careful way to the door. Wavy white hair framed his face; his light brown eyes squinted. Two ragged holes dotted a white T-shirt, and a peeling belt cinched the waist of his chinos.

"I'm Henry. Can I help you?"

"Hello. I work for the Duchon family. I understand you used to work for them."

A small frown creased his forehead. His gaze moved behind Jemma, as if he was looking for someone else.

"I wanted to talk to you. I need some information."

"What kind of information?" His Southern lilt cooled about ten degrees.

Jemma had no answer for him, as she hadn't even considered what to ask. According to Laurence, Henry hadn't worked for the Duchons in at least a decade. As she stood on the other side of the old screen door, failing to find anything to say, the man suddenly pushed it open, waving her inside. She hesitated only a moment before following him down a short hallway. Piles of old books lined both sides.

"You *work* for the Duchons?" he asked, his head turned to the side.

"Yes." That's all she wanted to reveal for now.

He gestured to a square table pushed against a wall before busying himself with a coffee press at the counter. Jemma took the next few silent moments to take in the room, which was as old and cluttered as the rest of the house. Plates and glasses formed an untidy pile in the sink. Another stack of books teetered precariously on a stool next to the stained stove. She hoped he wouldn't offer her a drink, but that's exactly what he did, placing a chipped teacup in front of her.

"Don't worry—it's clean," he said, pouring.

Once both their cups were full, he sat across from her, leaning forward.

"Where are you from?"

Frustration welled up in Jemma. She'd spent the last few hours trying to get someone to tell her anything about the Duchons, having door after door closed in her face. She was here to ask the questions and had no patience for even the smallest of pleasantries.

But looking at the cup in front of her, as well as the mess around her, she figured Henry probably didn't get a lot of company. Maybe he was happy to have someone to talk to. She sipped her coffee and gave him the abbreviated version of events, leaving out all of the weirdness. Seemingly satisfied, he nodded.

"What do you want to know?"

"How well do you know the family?"

"Used to know them fairly well. I tutored the kids for a few years."

"Fosette and Laurence?"

"Yes, that's right—that's their names. I taught them the basics, math and English and a bit of science."

"How old were they then?"

Henry studied the ceiling for a moment.

"Ten, twelve or thirteen, somewhere around there when I started." He shook his head slightly. "Strange family."

"Strange how?"

"Besides the fact they never set a foot off the property? I don't know. I just got a feeling about the place. The young girl was very pretty but skittish, like an alley cat. But at least she talked. The boy hardly ever said anything, only answered if I asked him a direct question. I asked the grandmother once if we could take a field trip just down the road and she screamed holy hell at me, told me under no circumstances was I to take the children even a step outside the front gates. After that, she stood guard over me when we did lessons in the parlor. Oh, she acted like she was just sitting there having her tea or reading, but she was making sure I didn't put a toe out of line. They had a maid, too. Striking woman. But they treated her worse than a dog, even the kids. Always calling her stupid or worse. One time, I saw the grandmother slap her across the face! And the poor woman never said a word, just took it. Each time I went out there, I thought for sure she'd have quit. But every week, she opened that door for me." He paused. "Is she still there?"

Jemma nodded.

Henry cursed under his breath before asking, "What about the children? What are they doing? Did they ever get away?"

"They never left."

He cursed again. "You know, here in town, we'd all heard things about them. Conjure women and psychics going to the house for God knows what. Then, when my cousin Pete told me the story of how our grandfather died there, that was it for me."

"What?" Prickles worked their way along Jemma's skin.

"I thought it was just a family legend, you know, one of those stories the old people pass on. I'd heard it before, when I was growing up. But when I told Pete who I was working for, he asked me how I could do it when our grandfather had died in the house."

"How did he die?"

Henry shrugged. "That's the only part of the story no one knows for sure. We know he was a slave, so his life wasn't worth much to the people who owned him."

Jemma thought of the list of names in the ledger, wishing she could remember them. One of them could be the man Henry was talking about.

"The family said he disappeared one day. Now, even though they didn't care about him as a person, they cared about him as property. If he'd run off, they would've looked for him. Next thing my family knows, someone said he'd died there, but they never gave my grandmother a body. She worked on the next plantation over. When she couldn't bury her husband, she took sick and died not too long after."

"So you never met them?"

"No. My mama was young when they went. After Pete told me that story and I was convinced it really happened, that it wasn't just some family legend, I tried to talk to the grandmother once about the Duchons' history. They had all those big portraits along the stairs. I asked who was who, and oh, was she proud to give me those names. So-and-so was her grandmother, this man was her great-grandfather, on and on. Then I asked if the family had owned slaves and she looked at me like she wanted to kill me. I guess I was feeling kind of reckless that day, on account of them being strange and mean. I told her *our* family history, that my grandfather had died there under mysterious circumstances." Henry paused before raising his eyes to meet Jemma's. In them she saw vestiges of fright, not years old but fresh. "The way Honorine looked at me, I thought I might die the same way he did. Luckily, all she did was fire me. Told me to get the hell off their property and never come back. I was glad to do it, although I felt sorry for the children."

They finished their coffee in silence. The Duchons that Henry described sounded exactly the same.

"I'm sorry about what happened to your grandfather, but thank you for talking to me," Jemma said at the door.

"It's water under the bridge now. I just don't see how you can keep working for those crazy folks."

Jemma had no answer for that, so she turned to the steps, just as Henry called her back.

"I just remembered something else. The smell."

A curious look passed over her face, but she knew what he was talking about. If she'd had any doubt, it was banished when he continued.

"It always smelled like something was burning there."

IT WAS NEARLY ten o'clock when Jemma returned to the Duchons'. The buses had stopped running a couple of hours before, so she'd walked from town, not feeling any pain in her feet or legs because her mind was so busy turning over her conversation with Henry. How had his grandfather died? Where was his body? Why hadn't the family given his body to his wife? Of course, their owners wouldn't have recognized their union as legal, but still. And what did Honorine know?

Jemma was so relieved to finally reach the property that she'd forgotten she'd missed dinner.

Honorine had not.

Jemma knew there was no point in locking herself in her room to escape the punishment, so when she saw the family gathered in the parlor, she joined them, hoping her grandmother would tire before Jemma lost her mind. Honorine stood in front of the cold fireplace, reading in her monotonous tone. Simone shot Jemma a dirty look, as if blaming her for this, although the rest of them could leave the room if they wanted. The chastisement was only for her.

A sudden chill descended, like a hand laid flat on Jemma's arm. As she looked up, it was clear they all felt it. Honorine stopped reading to glance around the room.

"Where's that draft coming from?" Laurence asked.

Right before the spirit appeared, Jemma hoped it was only a breeze, although a part of her knew exactly what it was.

The ghost of a man stood a few feet from Honorine, his baggy shirt hanging off one shoulder, his hair an uneven bush.

Five, four, three . . .

Russell stared directly at the spirit, surprising Jemma and stopping her counting.

"Do you see him?" she asked her uncle, her voice trembling.

"Who?" Fosette looked around, her eyes wide, her hands gripping the arms of her chair.

Russell faced Jemma, shaking his head and rising from his seat. "I don't know what you're talking about."

"You're lying!"

Russell screamed back, "I don't see anything!"

Simone rubbed her arms and peered around, while Laurence approached the fireplace, looking into it as if it were the source of the sudden coolness.

Go away, Jemma thought. Before she could shut her eyes, another spirit appeared, a woman dressed in similar shabby attire as the man. They both looked at her, freezing her in place.

They see me.

The man's mouth was moving, but no sound came from it. The woman gestured, her arms waving in the air. She, too, spoke, but Jemma heard nothing at first.

Then a whispering reached her ears, and she clapped her hands over them. She didn't want to hear anything they said; she didn't want to see their faces.

Something bumped her.

It was Fosette, on the floor, one of her hands at her throat. Jemma looked on in horror as she realized that all the Duchons appeared to be choking. Laurence's hands scrabbled at his throat while Russell tore at his own collar. Simone's nails raked her neck, her mouth open in a soundless scream. Honorine had fallen into a chair, the Bible dropped on the floor, her eyes wild and her fingers ripping the high neck of her dress.

What's happening?

Thick plumes of black smoke poured from their mouths. Each of the family members, save Jemma, sat or stood rooted in place, their jaws wide, as blackness streamed forth and rose to the ceiling. In a flash, the room filled with smoke, and only Jemma could cough or move. The rest of her family seemed frozen and helpless.

Through the thick haze, she saw the spirits. She'd forgotten all about them. They gazed at the smoke with fear in their eyes, and something else as well. A malignant knowing.

"Stop!" she yelled at them, although she didn't know if they could. She didn't know where the smoke had come from, but since it had appeared with their presence, maybe the ghosts were responsible. "Stop it! You're killing them! Please!"

The two spirits gazed at Jemma and, in the next instant, were gone.

Hacking and sobbing broke the silence. Honorine was still seated, but the other family members were sprawled on the floor. One by one, as they realized they were no longer choking, their eyes turned to Jemma, the dissipating of the smoke making it easier to see.

"Who were you talking to?" Honorine asked.

Jemma glanced at Russell, but he faced the floor, his wrists resting loosely on his knees.

"I . . . I saw two people. A man and a woman."

Simone's wild gaze took in the room, the red welts on her neck painfully visible. Fosette clutched Laurence while she wept into his chest.

"There's no one here besides us."

"They were ghosts," Jemma whispered.

Fosette wailed more loudly.

"You wanted them to kill us?" Simone snapped.

"No! I asked them to stop."

"And they listened to you," Honorine said in a flat voice, rising to her feet. "They did your bidding. You talk to them."

"I don't. I mean, I don't want to. I don't want to see them, but what else was I supposed to do? I asked them to stop!" Jemma repeated, unable to believe the blame the family was placing on her. As if she'd caused them to choke, as if she'd brought forth the billowing smoke.

Laurence and Fosette left first, not bothering to glance behind them. Simone and Russell followed, with Honorine sparing Jemma one last look, a look that held just enough fright in it to stay her sharp tongue. The sounds of several bedroom doors shutting reached downstairs.

Alone, Jemma sank to the floor.

The spirits had heard her. Not only that, they'd obeyed her when she'd pleaded with them to stop choking the Duchons. What did it all mean?

Before she could examine that, her gaze fell on the Bible.

Honorine had forgotten to take it in all the chaos.

Greedily, Jemma pulled it to her, glancing at the entranceway to make sure no one was coming back to collect it. No, she'd make sure no one took it from her. She rushed upstairs to her room and locked the door behind her. It was almost midnight now, and the low lamplight made the room as gloomy as the parlor had been. She placed the Bible in the middle of the desk.

Inside the front cover was a small stack of newspaper clippings. Death notices. Jemma read each one, each name ringing a tiny bell in the back of her mind. These were the dead Duchons. Not all of them had died from Inès's curse, as some of the notices went back well before Jemma was born. After she'd gone through the entire stack, she went through them again, more slowly.

There wasn't a notice for her mother.

Jemma flipped through the Bible, thinking maybe it was stuck between other pages. She didn't find it, but she did find a family tree, right in the middle of the book. A careful hand had written in names, most with the surname Duchon. Jemma's finger trailed down the page, bypassing Alexandre, Bridgit, Thierry and Adaline, all with birth dates and dates of death underneath. She slowed when she reached Raymond, Honorine's husband, Jemma's grandfather. There was a birth year and date of death. Four lines fanned out from Honorine and Raymond: Simone, born in 1909; Russell, in 1910; André, born in 1913; and Inès, in 1915.

There was no date of death.

But Inès's name was barely visible beneath black scribbles. Someone had tried to obliterate her name and drawn a line next to it, with another name written in.

Agnes.

FIFTEEN

JEMMA STARED FOR a long time at the maid's name. It couldn't mean what she thought it meant. It wasn't possible. They'd told her Inès was dead.

And maybe, in a way, she was. Dead to them, at least. They'd tried to obliterate her from the family by removing any traces of her. No portraits, no photographs except for the one Jemma had found buried in Honorine's drawer, with a child's face too blurry to make out.

But to make her their maid?

Why didn't she leave? Jemma had seen the horrible way they treated her.

The curse.

When Inès cursed the family, cursed the Duchons, she must also have cursed herself.

Jemma's first thought, upon seeing her mother's name blotted out, seeing "Agnes" written beside it, had been to run straight to Honorine and perhaps shake the woman until she got the truth about everything. But Jemma also wanted to run straight to Agnes—where did the woman even sleep?—and demand the truth. *Are you my mother?* She wanted to embrace her and sob into her neck because she knew it was true.

The Duchons were cursed, in more ways than they thought.

Instead of doing any of that, she put her head down on her desk and wept, heaving sobs that reverberated off the walls, but she didn't care. Let someone knock on the door and either ask if she was all right or tell her to shut up because she was disturbing their sleep. Jemma didn't care anymore.

How had she ever thought she'd want to be part of these people?

Not light enough, not fine featured enough—they'd never accept her. They wanted her only for a job, and then what? If Jemma was actually able to accomplish the monumental task of breaking the curse, what then? She knew, the knowledge a curled-up little knot in the pit of her stomach, trying to hide itself from her conscious mind, the part of her that still wanted to believe they'd love her, but she knew. They'd pay her and thank her and send her on her way, once again cutting ties with her.

The relationship with her adoptive parents sprang to mind. Another family in which she didn't belong.

Mabel Barker, the woman who'd raised her, the woman Jemma had believed was her real mother until the age of fourteen, had told her once that her father had wanted a boy.

And Jemma thought of Magdalene and Dennis carrying her away from the Duchons to save her, and placing her with the Barkers, who'd wanted a baby. How disappointed Carl must have been to discover they were getting a girl.

When the tears finally stopped, Jemma looked at the clock to find it was past three in the morning. The pages beneath her fingers were blurred by tears, and she swiped at them with her hand.

Whether or not she confronted the Duchons—*Your family,* a voice whispered in her mind—she'd have to decide in the morning.

Although Jemma hadn't slept more than two hours, she was the first one awake and moving around later that morning. She snuck downstairs and placed the Bible on the round table in the parlor, wanting whoever it belonged to to find it, to not know what she'd discovered.

That would be her secret, for now. So little, compared with the vast number the Duchons had.

She didn't know how she'd be able to be around the family, to sit at the dinner table and talk to them, knowing what she knew about Agnes, and to pretend that she knew nothing. And why didn't Agnes talk? They said she was mute, but since she was a Duchon, she had to know how to read and write. They weren't illiterate people.

Jemma slipped out the back door, wishing to escape the frostiness from the family, who certainly blamed her for what had happened last night. The first light of day stretched across the back lawn. She had on the same dark dress as the night before, her frizzy hair rejecting any hint of the rag curls she'd been doing since coming down to this swamplike environment. The morning dew licked at the bottoms of her bare feet with soft, cool tongues as she made her way to Magdalene's. Once outside of the woman's home, Jemma hesitated. It was much too early to knock on someone's door, although something told her Magdalene was likely up and probably had been while the moon was still reigning above. She knocked timidly.

"Who's that?" Magdalene called from inside, sounding wide-awake.

"It's Jemma. Can I come in?"

"It's open."

Magdalene was at the table, leaning back in her chair, precariously balanced on its back two legs. She puffed a cheroot, and once she took in Jemma's face, she put the chair flat on the floor.

"What happened?" she asked.

A simple question but without a simple answer. Besides, Jemma was too tired to tell everything. So she asked, in a small voice, "Can I sleep here for a bit?" and before Magdalene had a chance to reply, Jemma slumped forward, just having time to register the speed with which her friend moved to catch her before everything went black.

***

If you're light, you're all right.

If you're brown, stick around.

If you're Black, stay back!

Jemma awoke with the childish chant leaving its prejudiced trail in her mind. She kept her eyes shut to the brightness outside, not wanting to know the time or even the day. She wished for just a moment that if she opened her eyes she'd see the busy streets of Chicago outside the window of her third-floor apartment, nothing but asphalt and concrete and bricks and stone. No more wide back lawns that spoke of genteelness and culture, or grand homes that upon closer inspection hid decay, not just in their moldy cracks but in the people who lived inside as well. She wanted to see people who looked like her, with the same skin color, who might dislike her because she talked too much or was too nosy but never because she was too dark.

Jemma inhaled, the earthy scents of dried sage, old cigar smoke and a rich stew embracing her, making her feel safe enough to open her eyes.

The cabin was empty.

She sat up, only now noticing the lumpiness of Magdalene's mattress, as different from the feather bed in her room at the Duchons' as it could get. Steam rose from a pot on the woodstove. Jemma lifted the lid to find carrots, potatoes, fresh herbs and some meat bubbling away. She filled a bowl with the stew, hoping that the meat was rabbit and not coon, or even possum, as Magdalene was known to eat. Jemma was so hungry that she ate without noticing the scalding of her tongue or the gaminess of the meat. As she scraped the bottom of the bowl, looking to see if any bread was around, Magdalene came in the back door.

"So you do like possum meat, huh?" she asked, a mischievous grin lighting up her face as she took the seat opposite Jemma.

"I guess I do now."

Magdalene waved a hand. "I'm just playing, girl. That was swamp rabbit. There's some bread in the cool larder."

Jemma served herself a second helping, asking if Magdalene wanted anything, but the older woman only lit a cigar and studied the younger woman across from her when she resumed eating.

"You going to tell me what happened to you, what made you come here before the chickens was up and looking like you seen a ghost?"

If Magdalene knew how accurate she was about that, Jemma thought, she might not be so flippant. Or maybe she would.

"That's exactly what happened," she said. She bit off a chunk of bread and sat back in the chair, looking outside at noontime shadows falling from the trees.

Her friend gazed at Jemma with interest.

"At the house. Two different ghosts showed themselves. They tried to speak, but I couldn't hear them clearly."

In fits and starts, she told the rest of the story. How the Duchons had choked. About the thick streams of smoke. How she'd asked the ghosts to stop, and everything had.

But Jemma found that she didn't want to tell Magdalene about Agnes/Inès. How would she react, when she'd believed the woman dead all these years? Not only was Inès alive, but in more ways than one she was a prisoner inside her home. Jemma had barely had time to digest the information herself and had no idea how she could say the words aloud. Besides, she had to talk to Agnes first to be sure.

"I think the spirits were slaves here a long time ago. I . . . I hate that I'm related to those people, the Duchons." Jemma put her hands out and turned them over, palms up. "Their blood is in me and I hate it. But I have a brother there and he's trapped here, like I am, and damn if I don't want to save him."

"That's natural. I guess."

"What do you mean, 'I guess'?"

Magdalene shrugged. "I guess most folk would want to save their family even if they're horrible people. Maybe I'd do the same if I was you. Maybe."

"You think I'm wrong to want that?"

"It don't matter what I think. What matters now is you figuring out how to break that curse and save yourself. I don't care nothing about the rest of them, but I do care about you. Me and Dennis did what we could to save you, so I don't want to see you come to harm now that you're back."

"But I'm not bound."

"But you can die, can't you?"

Jemma set her piece of bread next to her empty bowl on the table.

"Part of the curse keeps that family there," Magdalene continued, pointing in the general direction of the Duchon property.

"The other part kills them off, one by one, every seven years. Ain't that what you told me?"

Jemma nodded.

"I don't know why you ain't bound, but what makes you think you might not die on your next birthday, girl?"

"I thought . . . I thought I was free of all of it."

"You want to take that chance? Sure, leave that house, go into town. Hell, go to the next city over, the next state. But curses got long arms, Emmaline. Them people owe you a birthright, but part of that birthright is the curse your mama put on all of you."

Jemma shut her eyes, not wanting to think of Inès/Agnes.

Was what Magdalene said true? Could she still be under the curse and liable to die, just as any of the other Duchons were, including her brother?

"I know you don't understand, but I do care about Laurence and Fosette. And Honorine promised to give me my history, my place in the family."

"Ain't your brother and cousin just like the rest of them?"

Jemma thought back to the day in the library when he'd bumped Agnes and made her drop the tea tray. She remembered his horrible words to his own mother, his relations with Fosette, his apparent comfort in the family. How Fosette's soft voice gained hard edges when she talked to the maid.

But they were innocent pawns in all of this. None of this was their fault.

"No, they're not. Well, not really. That's my brother and my cousin, Magdalene."

"And that makes them holy."

"No, but I can't help but care about Laurence. We have the same mother. And Fosette has been nothing but kind to me."

Magdalene dropped the cigar on the floor and ground it out

with her boot. "If you think they're going to accept you just because you all share blood, you're wrong."

"Is that what this is about? Them not accepting me?"

"Girl, when are you going to get it? None of them are going to accept you, ever."

"I know that—"

"Do you? You keep talking about them being your family. Do you really think they look at you that way? They look at you like the people who came before them looked at the slaves they owned. Imagine that, Emmaline. Owning your own people! Just because some of them was light enough to damn near pass and the other ones wasn't."

Magdalene's outburst stunned Jemma into silence.

"And now you're so worried about this brother of yours, this cousin. Would they claim you if the three of you walked down the street? Do you think that if you break this curse he's going to show you around, introduce you to people as his sister? What, you think they're going to throw one of their grand parties and trot you out like the long-lost cousin they missed all these years? They going to tell you they love you and accept you, even though you don't fit with them just 'cause you're dark? Or do you think the whole bunch of those crazy high yellow people are going to turn you out the minute you do what they need you to do?"

"I don't understand why you're so angry about—"

Magdalene rose and hit the table so hard that Jemma's empty bowl shook, the spoon clattering against the side. "Damn them! Stop trying so hard to get these people to love you when they ain't capable of loving anyone that don't look just like them."

Jemma rose, too, her hands shaking. "This doesn't affect you in any way, so I can't see why it's got you so upset."

"I hate to see people doing stupid shit just for the sake of family,"

Magdalene said, all the heat in her voice gone. "Sometimes your family ain't worth doing for."

"Maybe not everyone feels that way."

"Then go on and be stupid, girl."

That hurt, but Jemma tried to move past it as a question arose in her mind. "Didn't you tell me to break the curse? Weren't you telling me to figure out how to do it?"

"To save yourself, Emmaline, not them."

"But saving myself means saving them, too. If I break the curse, I free all of us."

"And that's too bad, I say. Your first thought needs to be you, and if they happen to benefit, so be it. But if you can get yourself out of there without being tied to them, that's what you should do. Forget them, forget your brother and worry about you."

"I can't believe you're saying this. I never took you for the vengeful sort."

Magdalene snorted. "Then I guess you don't really know me at all."

SIXTEEN

JEMMA WANDERED THE streets of Tremé unaware of what was going on around her. She didn't see the running children, the lounging cats or the honeybees. The sounds of laughter and sharp curses didn't penetrate her walled mind. It was fully consumed with other things.

Magdalene was angry at her—unfairly, Jemma thought. Her friend's venom seemed misplaced—something she'd work through when she returned to the Duchons', but at the moment Jemma wanted to be as far from the property as she could get.

Once again, the family avoided her. Jemma didn't care much about Simone or Honorine treating her like a pariah, but even Fosette and Laurence looked at her with dread. Her brother hadn't helped her with any translations from the ledger in a week, and Jemma felt as stuck as she ever had, as if she had no chance of breaking the curse.

Before she knew it, she was in a familiar alleyway, and the welcome sight of a collection of dolls in a window drew her inside

Lulu's. The café felt more like a home to her than the grand house where her family lived. Lulu bustled forward.

"What can I get you today, baby?"

Jemma opened her mouth to say *tea with ice* or *a cup of gumbo*, but her true desire intervened: "Something to keep the spirits away."

A frown settled on the other woman's face only briefly before she took Jemma's hand and led her to a small table away from everyone else. Lulu left her there for a few minutes, and returned with a tall glass of tea and put a cool hand to Jemma's cheek, breaking her out of her daze.

"Drink that, now."

Jemma obeyed, and with each swallow, she became more aware of her surroundings. She wanted nothing more than to stay here, to not return to the Duchons'. Maybe she could work in the café with Lulu, sleep in a back room.

But she knew that no matter where she went, the ghosts would follow.

"You feel better now?"

Jemma nodded. Physically, she was all right, but mentally, she wasn't.

"What did you mean when you said 'to keep the spirits away'? They bothering you?"

Lulu's evident concern was so welcoming that Jemma couldn't stop the tears from flowing. She covered her face while the woman tutted and patted her arm.

Yes, the spirits are bothering me, Jemma wanted to shout. *They always have and I don't know what to do. My family hates me, or some of them don't hate me, but I don't think they love me. They just need me. And when they don't need me anymore, what then?*

Jemma didn't realize that Lulu had left once again until the woman was back, pressing something into her hand. A small cloth pouch cinched at the top with a long leather cord rested in Jemma's palm.

"What is this?"

"It's for your protection. You wear it around your neck and them spirits won't bother you no more."

Jemma stared at the nondescript item in wonder. Could it really do what Lulu said? Why hadn't anyone given her something like this before? She squeezed the bag between her fingers, hard and soft items giving way beneath her touch.

"What's inside?" she asked, resisting the urge to open it.

"Some High John root, lavender, things like that. You pray on it, just hold it and ask that the spirits stay away."

Fresh tears sprouted at Lulu's generosity. Jemma embraced the woman, crying and thanking her in equal measure.

LATER THAT NIGHT, Jemma stroked the pouch before tucking it into her nightgown and lying back in bed. Once she'd left Lulu's she'd opened the bag to find a small pile of assorted items inside. She recognized the dried purple buds but nothing else, including what appeared to be a small rock, fluffs of cotton and small leaves. She grasped at a bit of relief, although she didn't feel completely relaxed or safe. She told herself it was because this was a new thing she hadn't gotten used to yet. With time, she'd become accustomed to it, and she'd have to trust the pouch to do its job.

"Protect me from the spirits around this place. Help me to not see them, please."

Jemma didn't know what else to say. After the brief plea, she stroked the pouch as sleepiness began working its way across her body. Right before she fell into dreams, heavy uneasiness pushed the tiredness away.

Her eyes popped open just as the cord tightened around her neck.

The inability to breathe came so quickly that Jemma's mind struggled to understand exactly what was happening. In the next instant her fingers moved to the cord, trying to create a gap, but it was pulled taut.

She fell out of bed, wriggling back and forth. Her foot connected with the nightstand, sending the lamp crashing to the floor. She continued kicking. Black spots appeared before her eyes. With the loss of air, she weakened, her fingers falling away.

Jemma couldn't accept dying here like this, but whatever was choking her had snatched away her voice to plead for her life.

And then just like that, the cord loosened.

Her hands fell by her sides as she fought to remain conscious, gulping for air.

It was Fosette throwing the pouch aside, kneeling over her and calling her name.

"Are you okay? What's happening, Jemma? Oh, what's happening?"

Her cousin cradled her like a baby. Jemma was too weak to resist or reply. She only held on to Fosette and wept.

LATER, AFTER FOSETTE had retrieved a glass of water and Jemma had finished it off despite the stinging in her throat with each swallow, the two of them sat next to each other on the floor, their backs against the bed.

Fosette had saved her from . . . something.

Jemma's eyes fell on the pouch, tossed into a corner.

Not like this, she'd been warned before.

This was another warning. She'd done something wrong, something the spirits didn't like. Trying to ward them off with the pouch hadn't worked. It had almost gotten her killed.

She rubbed her neck, glancing over at her cousin. An apology rested behind Jemma's lips, although she didn't know what she'd be apologizing for. If anything, the family owed her an apology for what they'd done to Inès. The image of her mother's name blacked out in the Bible mixed in with other pictures: the pouch, inert yet seemingly harmful; smoke pouring out of the Duchons' mouths in the dim parlor; "BONES" on the walls.

"Ever since you came here, strange things have been happening," Fosette said in a low voice. "We weren't exactly happy here before you came, but we'd gotten used to how our lives were. We'd accepted things. But the other night, when we thought we were dying . . . and this . . . I don't know anymore, Jemma. Grandmère brought you here to help us, but it seems like you're only making things worse."

Fosette said what Jemma felt, and it stung just as much as she expected.

"Can you really break the curse?" her cousin asked, an edgy urgency in her voice.

Jemma looked at her and answered honestly. "I don't know." After a beat, not wanting Fosette to leave anytime soon, she added, "If you weren't awake, who knows what might have happened to me? I hear you humming sometimes at night. What's that song?"

Her cousin stared for a moment. "I don't know what you're talking about."

Jemma gazed back at her, and before she could say anything further, Fosette wished her a good night and left.

There was no lullaby that night.

JEMMA CRUMPLED THE half-finished letter to Betty and dropped it in the small wastepaper basket beside the desk in her room, where it joined several others.

She hadn't contacted her friend since that interrupted phone call. Before she'd left, she said she'd write often and call when she could. But that was before she'd learned the truth about the family who'd hired her.

So now what could she say in a letter that didn't sound as mad as the people she was related to? Jemma was terrified that the insanity was catching. Certain things ran in families, and lunacy seemed like a fitting condition. She tried to find comfort in her parentage. Although her mother came from a too-closely connected line of family members, she didn't think her real father had. If she could get a name, perhaps she could find his family here.

If she had a name.

If Inès would tell her.

Jemma turned her attention back to the letter.

Dear Betty,

I hope you are well. My job is keeping me very busy here. The family I am working for is all right. Once I am finished tutoring their son, I may return home to Chicago. I miss it very much and I miss you, too.

Jemma read over the few lines, hoping her words wouldn't alert Betty to any distress. She thought about mentioning Marvin—as in, *Please don't tell me anything else about him*—but decided to leave him out. She scribbled a couple more sentences.

It's very different here. Sometimes I feel like
I did before, when I had that trouble.

After debating starting over again, Jemma asked after Betty's family and then closed the letter.

Over the next couple of weeks, the weather changed from warm and sticky, just a shade off high summer, to less warm. She welcomed the break, but looked with longing at the wool jackets hanging in the chifforobe, which would probably remain untouched while she was here.

She went to dinner every evening, to avoid Honorine's punishment. Jemma sat there, next to mad Fosette, across from Laurence, avoiding any eye contact with Simone. Once, she caught herself gripping her dinner knife so hard, she'd almost bent the handle. Only Russell's faintly amused "Good God, girl, are you all right?" brought her out of a disturbing reverie.

And watching Agnes/Inès serve at the table, as if she hadn't once sat here as a member of her family—it was almost too much. More than once, Jemma had to bite back words that would reveal what she knew. She had to hold it all inside for now. When it was time to tell her own little nasty secrets, she'd know.

She didn't feel like she could visit Magdalene, which made everything worse, but her friend had shocked her during her last visit, her disdain for Jemma's need for acceptance evident. If she hated that about Jemma, maybe she hated Jemma as well. So long days seemed even longer, without the distraction of Magdalene's friendship.

One morning, the biscuits she'd eaten at breakfast sitting heavily in her belly, she looked up from the desk by the window to see Dennis cutting the grass across the back lawn. She hadn't seen him in a few weeks, with no explanation from the family as to where he might be. Jemma realized she had no idea where he slept, like Agnes. There were no servants' quarters that she was aware of. A sudden curiosity overcame her, especially because she knew that he'd gone with Magdalene to place Jemma with her adoptive parents.

Why hadn't he mentioned that to her before? And why hadn't he mentioned Magdalene?

Jemma placed the legal pad she'd been scribbling in on the desk and made her way downstairs, glancing in the parlor to see Honorine and Russell playing solitaire. They watched her exit the back door, but bent their heads back to their games once she stepped out.

"Dennis!" Jemma called, raising an arm as he pushed the mower toward her. There was no way he could hear her over the racket the machinery made; she only hoped he could see her. The smells of gasoline and fresh-cut grass mixed with spent gardenias gone brown. The gardener looked up, stopped and shut the mower off, the ensuing silence falling like a soft clap.

"Didn't hear you over Ole Clem here," he said, pulling a soiled rag from his back pocket and dragging it across his forehead, pushing his hat back. "Ain't seen you in a bit."

"I haven't seen you, either. You've been on the grounds?"

"Yeah. But work gets slow round here once the weather turns, so I spend time on a couple other properties close by, but I always come back by nightfall."

"Where do you sleep?" Jemma turned to take in the whole of the back lawn. "I didn't see any quarters or anything for you and Agnes."

"Agnes sleeps in the big house. It's a little room off the kitchen. Most nights, I bed down in the old washhouse." Dennis pointed to a rickety wooden building opposite the carriage house; Jemma couldn't imagine anyone sleeping in it. "But when it's too hot, I just sleep rough, out here under the stars."

Jemma didn't realize that she'd been gazing at the washhouse for several moments without actually seeing it until Dennis cleared his throat.

"You didn't come out here to ask me about where I sleep, though, did you?"

She looked at him, his kind face dotted with sweat, the only truly free person in this whole place.

"Why do you stay?" she asked.

He shrugged. "I got a job and—"

"No." She made him look at her. "Why do you stay? Unlike the rest of them, you can leave, but you choose to stay here. Why?"

His gaze roamed across the ground beneath their feet, his shoulder moving up and down in a half shrug a few times. He didn't seem to want to answer her, but since he didn't outright refuse to, or assuage her with a quick lie, Jemma waited, hoping for the truth.

"I . . . I look out for Agnes."

"Look out for her?"

"She doesn't have anybody, and what with her, you know, her not being able to speak, I try and look out for her. I guess I'd be afraid of what might happen to her if I wasn't here."

"You love her," Jemma breathed, the fact crystallizing in her mind right at that moment by the way Dennis spoke her mother's name.

He shot her a sharp glance but didn't deny it, simply exhaled heavily and wiped his face again.

Did her mother know? Jemma wondered. She'd already asked him some personal questions; she wouldn't embarrass him any further by asking that. Besides, Agnes's knowing or not knowing wasn't important to Jemma. It was enough that Dennis cared about her and stayed on for her sake. Who knew what might have happened to her if he hadn't been around all these years?

"Somebody got to love her, I guess," he said. "Might as well be me."

SEVENTEEN

ONE NOVEMBER MORNING when dusky blue colored the sky and quiet colored the house, Jemma dressed and made her way downstairs before six o'clock. She still didn't know where Agnes slept, where her room off the kitchen could be. Jemma passed through the dining room to the spotless kitchen. She approached the low archway in the far wall and peeked through it before going in. The walk-through larder was neatly organized, although Jemma had never been served any of the sardines or Campbell's soups stacked on the shelves. Bags of flour, sugar and cornmeal rested on other shelves, and Jemma narrowly avoided stepping on a mousetrap not pushed back far enough against a wall. A small door sat at the far end. Jemma could probably walk through without ducking, but Honorine would likely have to lower her head to clear it.

Jemma knocked, and before she could do much more than wonder if this was indeed Agnes's private space and, if it was, if the maid would open up, her mother appeared, smoothing back her hair and tying her apron strings behind her. Her eyebrows rose in a question.

"I didn't want anything," Jemma assured her, her hands up. "I just wondered what was back here."

Agnes shut the door firmly and made her way to the kitchen, leaving Jemma no choice but to follow.

"Do you need help?" she asked as Agnes began grinding coffee beans and setting up the coffee press.

Agnes stopped what she was doing, her gaze resting on Jemma for a moment before she shook her head. She pointed toward the entrance to the dining room, indicating that Jemma should leave.

"It just seems like so much work for one person."

Jemma's hands twisted in front of her. She knew Agnes wanted her to leave, but a part of her kept talking because she wanted the maid to know that she knew.

You're my mother, Jemma imagined herself saying, not asking it as a question but stating it as the fact it was. She'd tell her that she understood what that bizarre kiss was about. It was simply a mother kissing her child.

And what then? Agnes's eyes would fill with tears? They would embrace? Agnes/Inès would be so happy that the truth was out at last that she'd explain to Jemma why the family said she was dead, even if she had to write it all down? Jemma had so many questions she thought she'd never get answers to, but now she could. First and foremost was why Agnes had allowed for Jemma to be given away. Had she wanted to keep her? What had happened? And why hadn't she told her she was her mother?

Agnes waved toward the dining room again and Jemma turned to go, but then stopped. She turned back, meeting her mother's level gaze.

She wanted to say the words, but she also wanted the realization to wash over Agnes on its own. She searched the woman's face for any hint of a resemblance to herself but found nothing. Agnes frowned, her hands falling to her sides, her body growing very still.

And just as Jemma told herself to turn and leave like Agnes wanted, she whispered the words.

"I know."

Agnes shook her head. Jemma took a step toward her, coming close enough to grab her by the shoulders.

"I know you're my mother. You're Inès."

And now Agnes furiously shook her head, her eyes filling with tears, her mouth twisting in a pained grimace.

"It's true, isn't it?" Now Jemma did grab her, and the woman simply stood there, made no effort to push her away. "Just nod. Just let me know I'm right. I found the family tree in the Bible. I saw everything. Laurence is my brother, not my cousin. They kept him because he's light, but did they make you give me away? Is that it? Who's my father?"

Agnes had begun squirming, and she wrestled against Jemma until she let her go.

"Please, just—"

"Agnes, you in there, girl? You got the coffee on—?" Dennis called as he entered through the back kitchen door, stopping when he saw the two women, both with their hands in the air, breaths coming fast and heavy. "Oh, sorry, I . . ." He began to duck out the door.

"Dennis, I know," Jemma said.

He looked at Agnes, who had tears freely streaming down her face, and before Jemma knew what was happening, he took two big steps into the room and grabbed her by the shoulders.

"Who else knows you know?" he whispered, the words fierce

and quick, matching his gaze, moving over her shoulder before going back to her face. He gave her a little shake. "Who else?"

"No . . . no one," Jemma said, struggling to keep her voice level. Why was he so angry? But as he glanced behind her again, she saw the fear on both his and Agnes's faces. He jerked his head to Agnes and she rushed to the kitchen entryway, looking out, Jemma assumed, for any Duchons.

"They told her if she ever told you that she was your mother, they'd kill her and you," Dennis said. "They were scared to death bringing you down here, but they didn't know what else to do. So they threatened her and me, told us we better not say anything to you."

Agnes gestured with her arms.

"How'd you find out?" he asked.

Jemma explained about the Bible.

"You can't let them know," he said, his eyes blazing. He gave her another quick shake, making her teeth clatter. "You got that?"

"Y-yes," Jemma cried, tears now streaming down her face, too. "I won't say anything."

He let go of her. As Jemma rubbed her arms, Agnes gave Dennis a quick embrace before returning to the coffee press. He slipped back outside, and Jemma supposed he'd have to come back for that coffee in a while. She knew Agnes wanted her gone, but she couldn't stop herself from saying one more thing. Moving next to Agnes, trying to ignore the way the woman flinched, she asked, "Could you write this in a letter and explain it to me? What happened? Why you let them take me away? Please? And who's my father?" Jemma's voice was stuffed and broken. "Could you talk before? What happened?"

She wanted to scream that last question over and over. Indeed, what had happened to Inès?

As Jemma turned to leave, Agnes grabbed her wrist. Jemma watched as her mother opened her mouth wide. Where there should have been a tongue there was only a stump, set far back in her mouth. Jemma raised her hands to her face in horror. Agnes pointed up, and as Jemma looked up, she realized the woman was indicating upstairs. Someone upstairs.

"They . . . cut out your tongue?" she asked, amazed that she could get the words out.

Agnes nodded and pointed up again, holding up two fingers.

"Honorine?"

Another nod.

"And . . . Simone?"

Agnes shook her head.

"Russell?"

A nod.

Jemma placed a hand to her temple. A part of her wanted this to be a lie, but she knew it was true. She put nothing past Honorine, but now Russell, too? Genial Russell, who always made the most innocuous conversation at dinner, whose only concern seemed to be whether there would be enough food for seconds, sometimes thirds.

He'd helped his mother cut out his sister's tongue.

"Why did they do this?" Jemma didn't know why she asked this, as if the woman could answer, but now her mother riffled through a nearby drawer and pulled out a piece of paper and half a pencil. She scribbled on the paper and thrust it at Jemma.

So I couldn't curse again

After Jemma read the note, Agnes snatched it back and placed it on a tin plate. She held a lit match to it and both of them watched it go up in flames.

Her family had taken away Agnes's power to curse them again, but by what they'd done to her they'd also removed her ability to uncurse them.

"I'm so sorry," Jemma whispered. "I'm sorry they did this to you."

Had she hated the Duchons before? She hadn't known what hate was, not then. But now she did. This had to be why they didn't want Jemma to know what they'd done to her mother. They would rightly have feared her wrath, perhaps her refusal to help them. She looked at Agnes, standing next to her, her head bowed. Jemma raised a hand and stopped just short of touching her, but Agnes grabbed her hand and brought it to the side of her face, resting Jemma's palm against her cheek. She then placed her other hand on Jemma's cheek and nodded. Agnes let go then, pushed Jemma's hands back to her. Her mother put two of her own fingers together and placed them on Jemma's lips.

"I'll be quiet," Jemma said.

JEMMA STARED OUT of her open bedroom window, a cool breeze wafting in intermittently. She wanted to ask her mother if she knew how to break the curse, but she assumed Inès didn't; she was sure her mother would have done it otherwise, to save Jemma's life, at least, if no one else's.

She'd tried to talk to Inès about the ghosts, but her mother seemed to avoid her. Once, when Jemma didn't come down for breakfast and Inès had to deliver a tray of food, she shook her head, leaving the tray and rushing out of the room as soon as Jemma began asking questions. The same thing happened when she returned to retrieve the tray. So Jemma would get no answers from her.

She must still be afraid, Jemma thought. *Afraid of what her—our—family will do to her.*

The days grew shorter and the nights cooler. Jemma often found Russell and Laurence poring over the giant Sears catalog, and the women of the family admiring the latest fashions in *Vogue.*

"Maman," Fosette said one day during the week before Christmas, "why can't we simply order the clothes and have them delivered? I'm so tired of dressing like it's still 1940."

"And where exactly will we wear these fashionable pieces, *ma chérie*? Around the parlor, to be seen by no one but ourselves? Once that cousin of yours frees us all, we'll have new clothes—we'll have the most beautiful clothes you've ever seen. And we'll go straight to Paris to buy everything we've been denied all these years, too much to carry home. We'll have to send trunks and trunks back here to hold everything we'll buy."

Movement outside the bedroom window drew Jemma's attention.

The lawn was empty, the croquet games suspended for the time being, although the weather was only a trifle cool to Jemma. To the rest of the family, however, fifty-degree mornings were positively frigid. In the day's waning light, she saw a twinkle far behind the lawn, along the edge of the woods. It flashed again.

Jemma slipped into the cardigan hanging on the desk chair. It was nearly dinnertime, but if she got out undetected, no one would know where she'd gone. She was sure Honorine would have some ridiculous punishment in store for her for missing the meal, but some of her old recklessness had come back recently, taking small steps forward as if not sure it was safe.

Magdalene stood along the tree line, a piece of broken mirror in one hand, which she'd held up to the sun to flash.

Jemma paused, glanced at the woman sideways. "You're not mad at me anymore?"

"I never was mad. But maybe I was judging you a little too harsh. I've been known to do that. Living out here alone, I don't talk to a lot of folks. I don't always know how to deal with 'em, I suppose. But I stand by what I said about them." Magdalene lifted her chin toward the Duchon house. "You'd be better off setting yourself off from them."

"What about your family, then? Where are they?"

"All dead and gone."

Jemma wondered about Magdalene's people. Had she had brothers and sisters, parents who adored her and showed it? If she had, that probably explained why she couldn't understand why Jemma wanted to cling to the Duchons so.

"You hungry?" the woman asked Jemma.

Despite it being only an hour before dinnertime, Jemma wasn't, but she followed Magdalene to her cabin and sat at the table.

"My mother isn't dead," she said simply.

Magdalene had been leaning back in her chair, sipping a cup of nettle tea, but at that, the front legs came slamming back to the floor.

"What?" Magdalene jumped up.

"She's not. I talked to her. She didn't want to tell me, but she's alive. They . . . they changed her name, made her the . . . maid." Jemma found it hard to get the words out, stopped as they were by her occasional sobs. When had she started crying? And she hadn't even gotten to the worst of it. "They . . . they cut out her tongue. So that she couldn't talk, so that she couldn't curse them again."

Magdalene was shaking her head, agitation evident in the way she paced the room. "No. No, I saw someone buried the day she died."

"You saw someone buried in the vault?"

"Cut out her tongue? Is that what you said?"

Jemma nodded. The whole conversation was veering wildly, the two of them bouncing around the same as her thoughts. Magdalene slumped down in her chair, a haunted expression underneath ashen skin. As if she'd seen something unspeakable.

"A child died that day. That's who you saw buried. My cousin Lucie."

"Not a child. The body was big, like an adult. And they didn't put it in the vault. I always thought . . . that because of what she did to them, they wanted to bury her quick, to put her in the ground and not in the vault with the rest of the family. The body was wrapped in white, in a shroud. Even from way out here, I could see it was big. It took four of them to carry it."

"Where did they bury it?" *Who?* Jemma's mind screamed. *Who was this person?*

"In the old graveyard. It's way behind the vault, up against the tree line on the other side of the property. Back in the old days, the family buried the slaves there. If it rained heavy and old bones washed up, they didn't have to see it from the big house." Magdalene jumped up again, the heels of her hands pressed over her eyes, and screamed, "Oh my God! What did they do? What did they do?"

After a few moments, with each woman lost in her own private, horrified thoughts, Magdalene knelt next to Jemma, grabbing her hand. "What's she like now? Is she . . . is she all there?"

Jemma wondered how she could answer that. For over twenty-seven years, her mother had lived with her family but was also tormented by them, including her own son. She cooked and cleaned for them and couldn't speak the first word against them. Then she'd had to watch silently as they summoned her daughter to the cursed house with a trick and had been unable to warn Jemma lest the Duchons follow through with their threat to kill both of them. In light of all that, how could Inès possibly be all there?

Jemma brushed her lips with her hand, remembering the day her mother had kissed her. How long had she wanted to see her stolen child, to touch her? Until Jemma had returned to the city and the house in which she was born, her mother likely had no idea what had happened to her.

If Inès hadn't cursed the family, would they have lived together? Could Jemma have grown up with both her parents and her brother?

Magdalene shook her out of her thoughts.

"How is she?"

"As well as you'd expect, I guess. Maybe not as crazy as the rest of them, but I don't know! That house breeds craziness! If I have to stay there until I can figure out how to break the curse, I'll be just as insane as the rest of them."

"Maybe, maybe not."

"What do you mean?"

"You're still scared. If you can get yourself past that, if you can talk to the spirits instead of turning away, you can find out who was buried the day you were born."

Jemma inhaled sharply. Yes, yes, what Magdalene said made so much sense. But having to face the ghosts that she'd spent a lifetime running away from . . .

"I don't know if I can do it."

"You've got to."

EIGHTEEN

INÈS OPENED HER mouth slowly, as if her jaw were on hinges, revealing a black hole and a throbbing stump where her tongue should have been. Jemma turned away, horrified, unable to escape her mother's shrieks.

Jemma awoke in a sweat, her hands clamped over her lips; she was biting back a scream as well as preventing anyone from tearing her own tongue out of her mouth.

Her mind went back to the night before. The body buried on the day Jemma had been born. She had to know who that was, as it had to have something to do with her. Whoever it was, she doubted the Duchons wanted anyone to know they were buried on their property. Otherwise, why bury the body in the old slave cemetery?

Maybe that was something the spirits haunting this place could tell her. When she realized it was after ten and Agnes hadn't brought her any breakfast, as she normally did when Jemma didn't make it downstairs, she went to the kitchen, only to find Russell rummaging in the open refrigerator and Laurence leaning against the counter, a piece of bread in his hand.

"Where's Agnes?" she asked.

Laurence shrugged, while Russell ignored her, so busy with his search.

"Is she sick? Did she make breakfast?"

Russell brought himself out of the Philco, a cold drumstick in one hand. "Do you think I'd be looking for food myself if she had?"

"Where is she?" Jemma's eyes darted toward the short hallway to the outside door, to the small room where her mother slept, and neither of the men seemed interested in answering her question. Both left the kitchen, food in hand and a mess behind them. Jemma checked in Inès's room but didn't find her there. She came back to the kitchen, grabbed a rag from the sink and wiped down the counter and stove. Whoever else had been in here had left crumbs, dirty plates and cups, and sliced ham on the counter. On the stove sat a pot of overcooked rice, a hole dug out of the middle as if someone had eaten right out of the pot. As Jemma scrubbed plates in hot, soapy water, she wondered how her mother did this every day, cleaned up behind such thoughtless people. She had to find her and make sure she was okay. For all Jemma knew, Simone, maybe Honorine, had figured out what they'd been up to recently. Had they punished Inès?

Once the kitchen was clean, Jemma quickly made a ham sandwich and exited through the back door. The morning was cool, just enough for the long-sleeved oxford and dungarees she wore. She found she didn't care about her style anymore. What did it matter? She saw the same people day after day, people who were similarly out of fashion. She couldn't believe it was almost Christmas. If she were back in Chicago, she'd be spending her afternoons downtown, slipping in and out of stores like Marshall Field's and Sears; she'd be wrapped in a thick coat and scarf, boots on her feet, her frosty breath visible every time she talked or laughed, only to have it whipped away by the fierce wind.

She found herself outside of the washhouse where Dennis said he slept sometimes. She looked around the vast yard but didn't see him, so she knocked on the door.

"Dennis?" she called after a moment.

She went inside, calling his name again and getting no answer. It was tidy, just one wide room with a square table in the center. A couple of kerosene lamps sat on it and two straight-backed chairs stood nearby. In the far corner was a mattress with a body on it. Jemma could see right away it wasn't Dennis.

It was a woman.

Jemma turned to leave, ashamed of invading his privacy and an intimate moment with a guest, but she looked at the woman again, just the top of her head visible beneath the covers, her skin pale.

Jemma rushed over, her gasp waking Inès.

Her mother tried to sit up, but Jemma pressed her shoulder to keep her still. Dark purple bloomed around her eye and along her jaw.

"Did Dennis—?" Jemma started, but shook her head. He wouldn't hurt her, and she doubted her mother would be sleeping here if he had. "Who did this to you?" Even as she asked, she knew. It was someone from the big house. But she wanted a name. She wanted a target.

Inès lay back, her eyes open to the ceiling, letting Jemma know she'd get no answer.

"Do you want water or anything?" she asked instead. Her mother looked at her and shook her head, a small smile showing.

She reached out and grabbed one of Jemma's hands, pressing the back of it to her unhurt cheek.

She had to get Inès away from this place, off this property.

"I'm going to figure out how to break the curse," she told her. "We're going to get out of here. You, me and Dennis, if he wants to come with us."

Inès raised her eyebrows, pointing toward the door. Jemma turned, but no one was there. Her mother patted her hand and then turned it over, palm up, patting it again and pointing to herself. Jemma didn't understand. Inès did it again, pointing to the door.

"The house?"

Her mother nodded and held up one finger.

"Someone in the house?"

Another nod. Jemma named Simone and Honorine first, but at Inès's furious head shaking she figured her mother wasn't naming who'd hurt her.

"Laurence? You want Laurence to come with us?"

Inès nodded.

"But the way he talks to you . . . He treats you just as bad as the rest of them."

Her mother put a hand over her heart.

"You love him. Of course you do."

Dennis came in shortly after.

"I had to go into town, do the grocery shopping," he explained, setting a paper bag on the table and pulling out a few items. "But I saved the best for you."

He knelt next to Inès and gave her a beignet, the sweet scent strong and delicious. As she chewed on one side, he examined her bruises. "Got a cold steak to put on that when you're done."

Jemma followed him back to the table. "Who did that to her?"

"She didn't let me know. She never does. What difference does it make anyway? That family—they're all of a piece." He placed half a dozen apples and oranges in a wooden bowl, and set a baguette next to it. Resting his hands flat on the table, he looked hard at Jemma. "Don't get her in no more trouble. It's been a while since they put their hands on her like that. I don't want to see it happen again. It's best you just do what they want you to do and leave everything else alone."

"I can't do that. There's too many questions, too many secrets around this place. The more I know, maybe the more I can help."

"Or maybe the more you don't want to find out. Some things are best left buried."

Jemma shot him a sharp glance—what an odd choice of words, considering what she'd been trying to discover—but Dennis's attention was on the paper bag he neatly folded and set aside.

If you can talk to the spirits instead of turning away, you can find out who was buried the day you were born.

"I'm trying to help her"—Jemma gestured to Inès—"as well as myself. You, too, if I can do it. Then we'd all be able to leave." She couldn't help but wonder whether she'd have a place in Inès's life if it included Dennis.

"If you really want to help her, leave her out of everything. What she knows, she couldn't tell you even if she could talk. You think that family's just going to let her be? Haven't you learned enough about them by now?"

THAT EVENING, JUST as Jemma finished buttoning her nightgown, a knocking sounded against the wall to her left, where the chifforobe sat in the corner. She turned and saw nothing. Her gaze moved between the chifforobe and the door.

Run. Just run.

The knocking grew louder and faster. The closed doors of the chifforobe shook.

Maybe they want to talk to you.

On shaky legs, Jemma took two steps toward the chifforobe, but before she was in arm's reach, the doors flew open, a strong blast of heat rushing across her and flinging her clothes out so hard, they hit her and the floor with a thump. She cried out, backing away. No ghosts were there, but something had pushed a hot wind into her, shoving her back. The doors hung open, and all that she could see by the weak lamplight were the nearly empty shelves, one sweater sleeve dangling over an edge.

A soft knock at the door sent her spinning. She clapped a hand over her mouth just in time to stifle a scream.

The knock came again.

"Who . . . who's there?" Jemma managed to squeak.

"It's Laurence."

She opened the door, her fingers slipping on the knob at first. Could he sense how happy she was to see him after all the trouble she'd caused? Fosette had eventually come around, but Laurence had mostly avoided her. Until now.

"Are you all right?" he asked as soon as he was inside, his brows knitted in concern as he took in the mess on the floor.

She nodded, although she was far from all right. But having someone living and solid in front of her calmed her little by little, even though Laurence only watched her after asking her for a second time if she was okay. Once her breathing was back to normal, she noticed the paper in her brother's hand.

He moved to the desk and laid the paper flat. "I translated a little bit more from the book. At some point there was a fire here that burned the old kitchen. The kitchen that's downstairs now isn't the original."

The blast of heat. Hot like a fire.

She gripped Laurence's arm before telling him what had happened right before he knocked on her door.

"I wasn't all right when you came in. That's why I looked so scared when I opened the door."

Her brother's uneasy gaze traveled the room as if he was afraid he'd see something he didn't want to.

"You think it could be connected?"

Images jumped forward in Jemma's mind, all jostling for first place. "The smoke . . . that came out of your mouths. The smell . . ."

"What smell?"

She stared at him before inhaling deeply. It wasn't nearly as strong as it had been before, unless she'd grown used to it. "The smoke. You don't smell it?"

He shook his head, but she hadn't imagined it.

"Henry mentioned it, too. Your old tutor. I went to see him."

Jemma told Laurence about the visit. Excitement thrummed through her as what felt like puzzle pieces began to fit together. There were many pieces missing, but she was sure they were on the right track.

"The fire has to be related to the strange things that have happened here. Maybe even the curse."

Laurence turned her to face him, his hands gripping her upper arms, his eyes flashing. "You think so? You think we're close to figuring it out?"

Desperate hope lit up his face, but she didn't want to give him false confidence. She chose her next words with care, putting them together the same way someone would reassemble a broken dish.

"I think so. I couldn't do this without your help, so thank you for everything you're doing."

His grip loosened, but he pulled her closer. For a horrifying moment she was afraid he would kiss her, but he only placed his forehead against hers, his eyes shut.

"I'll do anything to help you break this curse and get us the hell out of this place."

NINETEEN

RAIN FELL IN crooked rivulets down the windows one morning. As Jemma entered the library, a cup of coffee in one hand, Inès startled her when she went to close the door behind her. She hadn't known her mother was following her. Inès handed Jemma a letter from Betty, her brows raised.

"It's a friend of mine, in Chicago."

With Jemma not knowing what more to say and Inès seemingly unwilling or unable to give any indication of what she wanted, her mother left the room.

The rain fell harder and thunder rumbled. Lightning flashed at regular intervals. The electricity had gone out, so Jemma burned candles for light so she could complete her research on séances and read Betty's letter:

Dear Jemma,

I'm a little worried about you after your last letter. Are you sure you're all right?

Also, Marvin's other woman lost that baby. When I saw him, he asked about you and he sounded like he missed you.

Have you given any thought to coming back home? You might be able to have something of the life you had before, if you're willing to let the bad stuff go.

Jemma finished the letter, ashamed of her elation over the loss of Marvin's child. But she couldn't go back to that life.

Not yet, anyway.

She had too much unfinished business here.

After dinner, Jemma announced her plan to hold a séance the following night. Fosette did exactly what Jemma expected and began to protest.

"I need information, and I can only get it this way," Jemma explained, her elbows on the table and her hands folded above her plate.

"What kind of information?" Russell asked, the only one of them still eating, on his second helping.

"Information to break the curse and free all of us."

"Well, it's certainly been a long time coming," Simone said, and lit a cigarette. "You sure you don't want to wait until the last week of February? I mean, in case it didn't work, one of us would die and you'd have one less Duchon to deal with." A bitter laugh escaped, along with a cloud of smoke.

"And the sooner I do this, the sooner I'll be out of your lives."

Jemma felt some satisfaction at the way that shut Simone up, although it didn't wipe the disgust from her face.

"We'll meet in the parlor." Briefly turning to Fosette, Jemma went on. "For this to work, it requires all of us to be there. All, Fosette."

"I don't think—" Honorine leaned forward, a warning tone in her voice.

"What, Grandmère? Even you want to leave this place, don't you? To get back to your beloved church, to visit the friends who've all but forgotten about you over the years? How will they feel when they see you on their doorstep? Do you think they'll be happy? Or maybe they'll be afraid, as afraid as they must be now, the way they avoid this place. You can't leave and no one comes, except for Father Louis. Even Charlie, who gave me a ride here when I first arrived, wouldn't come past the gates, wouldn't look back at this place." Jemma's breath was coming fast and hard, although she hadn't moved anything besides her head as she looked at each family member. "Tomorrow night. The parlor. Otherwise, I don't know exactly what's going to happen between now and March twelfth, but on my birthday one of us will definitely die."

THE FOLLOWING NIGHT, the five Duchon family members trailed into the parlor to join Jemma, the women's heads covered with their usual Mass veils, Fosette having given Jemma a spare. Although she was sure no one had discussed what to wear beforehand, all of them showed up in various shades of deep gray or black, including Russell and Laurence, dressed in slate-colored suits as if on their way to a funeral.

As the clock approached eleven, they assembled themselves around the circular table Dennis had brought in from the spare attic room. Small bunches of white taper candles spread a soft glow from the side tables and the center of the round table, where the family Bible rested. Shadows reached from corners and etched themselves in the hollows of the family members' faces, making Jemma wonder if this was a good idea. It wasn't too late to call it off, but with one glance at Simone and the malicious smirk twisting her lips, Jemma forged ahead. She was determined to wipe that expression off her aunt's face.

"Join hands," she commanded. At once, they created a circle, which she warned them not to break until she said it was all right to do so. To Jemma's left, Honorine's cool, papery hand held hers loosely, while Fosette's overly warm fingers gripped hers on the right. From there, it was Laurence, Simone and Russell.

"I'd like to begin with the Lord's Prayer," Jemma said.

Immediately, they all began to recite it in unison. Jemma continued alone with "For thine is the kingdom and the power and the glory, forever" after everyone else had already said "Amen."

A thick silence settled over the room, with Jemma uncomfortably aware of the others' pale eyes fixed on her in the gloom. She took a deep breath and lifted her chin, gazing out over Simone's head to the back of the space, where the heavy brocade drapes were drawn.

Forget Carl and Mabel. Think about Inès and what you share with her, what she gave you.

"If there are any spirits here, I'd like you to make yourself known." The shakiness of her voice brought about another of Simone's stiff smiles.

Silence, broken only by the faint ticking of the grandfather clock in the foyer.

Jemma cleared her throat. "I invite you to make yourself known. If you're here, please give us a sign."

Silence.

As Jemma tried to think of something inviting to say, she became aware of Fosette's increasingly firm grip. She tried to stay focused, but she glanced at her cousin anyway, alarmed to see Fosette appearing paler than usual, her mouth drawn in a grimace, her eyes squeezed shut.

Was she afraid of what might answer?

Jemma took a quick look around the table. Both Russell and Honorine held their eyes closed, but Laurence's eyes moved to various places in the room, even as his head remained still. Simone, not surprisingly, stared at Jemma, barely blinking, her expression seeming to say *Let's get on with this sham.*

She tried again, taking a deep breath and working to keep her voice level. "If there are spirits here, we invite you to make your presence known."

Beneath their clasped hands, the table lifted up a hair and then settled back in place with a firm *thunk*.

Everyone's eyes opened, Fosette letting out a thin moan. Jemma gave her hand a reassuring squeeze, even as her own fingers trembled.

"What is your name, spirit?"

A quick breeze flew through the room, extinguishing all the candles in a wave, lifting the edges of the women's veils as it moved. A sharp scream came from Jemma's right, but before Fosette could make any more exclamations, the candles relighted.

Five . . . four . . .

No, Jemma told herself, her eyes shut. *Don't count them away, not this time. Don't be afraid.*

She opened her eyes. "Can you show yourself?" Fosette's fingers, suddenly cold, began to slip out of her grasp, but Jemma gripped her. She wouldn't let her break the circle, wouldn't allow her to run out, not when she was so close.

From the center of the table, a form began to rise.

I can do this, Jemma thought, even as she heard *I can't do this* at the same time.

All the things the Barkers had told her about ghosts, about her ability to see them, came swarming in as she fought to hold on to Fosette.

Don't look at 'em, Jemma.

Ain't nothing but the devil's work if you look.

Five, four, three . . .

The ghostly figure pulled itself up through the Bible. A man, with woolly hair cropped close to his head, dressed in a tattered shirt open to his navel and with ragged pants that didn't quite reach his ankles. His form rose almost to the ceiling before he floated back down and stood slightly behind Fosette's chair.

A sharp chill accompanied him. The rest of the family didn't seem able to see the ghost—including Russell, whom Jemma studied for several moments—but they clearly felt the coolness in the room.

"What is it?" Fosette wailed.

Jemma jerked her hand without loosening her grip. She wanted to break the circle, but something seemed to clench her fingers around her cousin's. Jemma wanted to let go, wanted to run, but she couldn't.

The spirit lifted a hand slowly, as if it were moving through water, and pointed at each of the Duchons in turn. Fright clawed its way up Jemma's throat. Was she next? He met Jemma's eyes, but placed his hands down at his sides.

"What are you looking at?" Honorine demanded, her face turned in the general direction of the ghost.

"Is something there?" Simone asked, her gaze moving to all four corners of the room. "Why is it so cold? What's there?"

Before Jemma could reply, the spirit's form wavered, and then he was gone.

Relief washed over Jemma, as the family looked at her in

silence. Next to Jemma, Fosette appeared to be in a faint, her eyes half-open. She leaned slightly to one side, her head hanging at a crooked angle.

Just as Jemma's fingers began to loosen and she prepared to tell them that they'd have to try again another time, Honorine spoke up. "Miss Barker, what is your purpose, besides making the room cold?"

The question annoyed Jemma. "I didn't do that." A beat. "I want to try again."

Simone cursed under her breath.

It took several moments for Jemma to regain her focus, gazing at one of the candles on the table, the flicker of the flame hypnotizingly rapid. There was no more breeze in the room, and she didn't know if one of the spirits had caused it or not. As Fosette's lips moved quickly in what Jemma assumed was a prayer, she put forth her own.

I just need you to talk to me. Say anything that can help. I don't know if I can do this again.

Jemma tried to remember what Magdalene had told her about spirits, about talking to them.

Dennis's voice came, too: *Running is easy, until it ain't. How many times have you run from something?*

Too many times to count, but that's what the Barkers had taught her. Run from the spirits; run from the curse of seeing them.

It was no gift to be able to see ghosts.

Without warning, two figures appeared, one behind Russell and the other behind Honorine. Both were women, dressed in similarly ragged clothes. Jemma watched them closely, but neither appeared to be the same woman whom she'd followed out the back door months ago.

How many ghosts were in this place?

The older of the two had hair braided close to her scalp. As her form became more clear, disfigurement on one side of her face became apparent. The younger woman took on more opaqueness as well, and her face appeared melted, the flesh sagging down her cheek and chin, melding into the skin on her neck.

Ask them about the curse. Ask them!

But Jemma shut her eyes, wanting nothing more than to send them away.

Five . . . four . . . three . . .

No. Don't run.

Jemma opened her eyes, to see the older spirit settle her gaze on Honorine before reaching out a hand. The younger spirit took it. Their forms began to grow more transparent.

"What are your names?" Jemma asked quickly, her voice trembling.

"Who's there?" Simone shrieked.

The two women watched Jemma. The younger one opened her mouth to speak, but no sound came out.

Hear them, Jemma. Don't count them away. Don't run. Open yourself to them.

"Jane."

The voice wasn't very clear, but Jemma made out that much.

You have to speak to them. You have to ask them for help.

The thoughts were the opposite of what she'd always done, but she needed the spirits' help. She swallowed several times and licked her lips.

"Hello, Jane," Jemma managed. "Thank you for coming."

"Who's Jane?" Laurence asked.

"Are there any other spirits here? I invite you to show yourself."

The young man reappeared, right as Jane whispered, "It's dark."

"What's your name?" Jemma asked the man.

She couldn't hear him clearly the first few times he spoke, but eventually she heard "Adam."

"Adam," Jemma asked, "is it dark where you are, too?"

"And cold," he replied.

Jemma considered their words. Dark and cold. Where could they be besides in a grave?

"Are you buried here on the property? In the slave cemetery?"

"This is enou—" Honorine hissed, but Jemma snapped at her before she could finish.

"Quiet! Let me hear them speak. Or you'll never be free from this place." She lifted her eyes to Adam's face. "Can you tell me where you are?"

"Under."

"Under what?"

There was no cellar in the house. None of the homes in this region had cellars, what with the area being at sea level.

"What do you mean by 'under'?" Jemma asked, looking at Jane, wondering if she would answer instead.

"The bones," Jane whispered. "So many bones."

Jemma opened her mouth to ask what Jane meant, but within seconds, her form grew more transparent until she disappeared. Jemma turned back to Adam, hoping and praying that he would stay put.

"Adam. What did Jane mean by 'so many bones'?"

At first, he didn't respond, only stared at Honorine. But finally, he croaked out, "We the bones."

As Jemma opened her mouth to ask another question, he blinked out, taking the candlelight with him. Fosette screamed, halfway out of her seat, while Jemma relit the candles.

"Sit back down. This isn't over."

"What's going on, anyway?" Russell asked, leaning forward as if he was about to rise. "For all we know, you're talking to the air."

"You want to die next?" Jemma snapped.

He sat back, and beside her, Fosette did the same, her face ghastly, as if all its beauty could shine only in the light of day.

"We're this close to getting the information I need," Jemma said, resuming her seat and grabbing Fosette's and Honorine's hands. "Now, focus. Please."

Before she could do more than take a couple of breaths, a chill descended on the room. In an instant, the family members were surrounded by more than a dozen spirits, Jane and Adam among them.

"It burns yet, missy," one of the female ghosts hissed.

"So cold, so cold," another spirit moaned.

One said it burned, and another said it was cold. It made no sense.

"What burns?" Jemma asked.

"Stop this!" Honorine shouted.

"What are you afraid of?" Jemma turned her attention to her grandmother.

"Free them," the spirit said. "Set them free."

"The secret is in the blood," another ghost moaned, not looking at anyone in particular. "Free them, free the blood."

A sudden blast of heat blew through the room, but where it came from was unclear. Fosette jumped up, and struggled to free her hand from Jemma's grip.

"Stop it," she begged. "Let me go! I don't know what's going on and I don't want to know!"

"Wait—" Jemma said, although she didn't know why. She wanted this to be over, too.

"Damn your circle!" her cousin screamed. "And damn you!"

Fosette pulled herself back. In Jemma's attempt to maintain her grip, she was yanked out of her seat. Honorine had let go of her other hand, but Jemma and Fosette wrestled. Jemma was vaguely aware that Simone had stood up but made no effort to break them apart. Fosette shrieked and laughed, a horrible, piercing sound that belonged in an asylum, not in a once-grand house with a proud family still inhabiting it. Fosette ran her fingers through her carefully waved hair, dislodging the veil, the strands standing away from her scalp. Even in the dimness, the pink spots high on her cheeks were visible. Jemma didn't think she'd ever seen her look so unhinged.

"Are they here with you? Do they come when you call them?" Fosette went on, her fingers hooked, first tearing at her hair, then pulling at her dress. "What do you see?" Turning to the others, her eyes blazing, she hissed, "Do they tell you things about us? About what we did? What I did?"

"Don't say another word," Honorine whispered.

Questions swirled in Jemma's mind, but she needed to ask the one that she wanted the answer to the most. Not knowing which of the spirits, if any, had the answer, she asked of none in particular, "Who did they bury in the old slave cemetery when I was born?"

Gasps rose from a few members of the family, not surprisingly including Honorine and Simone. They knew. But the ghosts just stared back at Jemma, except for the odd one or two whose attention focused on the rest of the Duchons. She repeated the question, more loudly this time.

Adam looked at her. "Ismael."

A loud, inhuman howl sounded from the doorway, startling everyone around the table. They turned to find Agnes gripping the doorframe—when had she come in?—her mouth a wide O, her eyes wild. Her entire body was a rigid board. And then her knees slowly gave way as she slid to the floor, still howling. The family's attention was rooted on her, confusion marring their faces.

"Who's Ismael?" Jemma asked Adam. "Who is he?"

But it wasn't Adam who answered.

Instead, Simone screamed, "He was your father, damn you! Your father is buried out there on the grounds! Yes, buried the same day you were born!"

"Hush," Honorine seethed.

But her daughter wouldn't be hushed. Her eyes just as wild as those of her sister—the one who continued to howl as she sat on the floor, outside of the circle—Simone stood up, words bursting from her in a rush, as if she'd held them back for twenty-seven years and was finally able to release the floodgates. "My parents had to do it. Inès wouldn't leave that man alone. He actually thought we'd accept him just because your whore of a mother was pregnant with you. They really believed we'd welcome him into the family. And then here you came, with your brown eyes and your tan skin, looking just like him! You'd never fit in with us! Never!"

"Stop it!" Honorine yelled.

"Your mother called him when her labor pains started," Simone continued. "And he came out here to talk to my father, to tell him that he was going to marry Inès, seeking his blessing. Upstairs, my bitch of a sister was moaning and praying, along with the midwife and Maman. And then you were whelped. So much was happening that we missed it when the midwife took you out of here, but she must have known what would've happened to you if she hadn't stolen you away. Because yes, Maman and Papa were going to kill you, just like Papa killed your father, shot him and then buried that common ditch nigger outside."

"Your husband killed my father?" Jemma asked Honorine,

although the answer had already been given to her. The tears were so thick in her eyes that the whole room blurred before her.

Her grandmother, still in her seat, didn't raise her eyes to Jemma. Her gaze skittered across the table in front of her, her mouth hanging slack. After a moment, she seemed to remember where she was, although she merely babbled at first. "We . . . we had to do it. He would never . . . You would never . . . Our legacy. She tried to ruin it. She tried to ruin us! After you were born, as Inès lay there in the bed, I told her that Raymond had sent her man away, that he'd never come back here. She cursed us. 'I curse all the Duchon blood,' she said. 'From this day forth, I bind the family to this house. I bind them forever.'" Honorine met Jemma's gaze. "She actually did that. To her own blood. Not knowing that she was cursing you and Laurence, too. Or maybe she just didn't care. She thought she was going to die, I think. Because she bound herself here just as she cursed the rest of us!" Honorine began to laugh, a high cackle that was even worse than the low howl that still came from Inès.

Jemma turned to look at her mother.

"Is it true, Mama?" she asked. More gasps followed. Jemma turned back to the table, her voice soft. "Yes, I know. She's my mother and you all did this to her, cut out her tongue, made her serve you. You've tortured her and mistreated her. You turned her own son against her. She didn't tell me." A bitter laugh escaped Jemma. "Of course she didn't tell me. How could she? I found out when you left the Bible here that night when you all choked and the smoke poured out of your mouths. I found the family tree. I knew you were horrible people, but murder? Marrying your own cousins just so you could keep having high yellow children? What is wrong with you monsters?"

"Are the ghosts still there? Ask them how to break the curse, you bitch!" Simone shrieked, pulling Jemma's focus from Honorine.

The spirits hadn't moved and didn't seem agitated by anything going on among the living, despite the occasional glares they threw at the family members.

But "Free them," they said. Why on earth would they want Jemma to free the Duchons? And suddenly, Jemma didn't want any of them freed. The people she was related to were vile. She hoped the curse struck them all.

"I'm not doing any such thing," Jemma said, the level tone of her voice surprising her. She didn't have to yell; she knew each of the Duchons heard her clearly. "Because unlike you, I can leave this property. Not fucking any 'shiners, though, just getting out of this rotten house. I could have left months ago. Do you understand? I chose to stay, to help not just you but myself, too."

Jemma wanted to say more, wanted to curse them with her own spell. If her mother could do it, then surely she could do it, too.

Inès's sobs caught her attention. She didn't want her mother to die from the curse, did she? Although it was Inès who'd set everything in motion, though she'd had a justifiable—to Jemma's mind—reason for what she did. As Jemma threw her head back, letting loose with a long wail of her own, she imagined this entire cursed house crumbling down on all of their heads. The last note of her keening died down just as an urgent whispering reached her ears.

Jane knelt next to the prostrate Inès, who appeared almost catatonic. The spirit's mouth was close to Inès's ear, her lips moving rapidly.

Jemma staggered toward Inès and Jane. Dimly, she was aware that the other ghosts were gradually withdrawing into the shadows. Simone was screeching something. Russell was yelling. The sounds came to Jemma as if from behind closed doors. As Jane's form ebbed away, Jemma caught the tail end of the ghost's words: ". . . or you will never be free."

Jemma put a hand on Inès's shoulder and gave her a small shake.

"Mama? Can you hear me?" She sat on the floor and faced her, hip to hip. Not knowing what else to do, not caring that the rest of the family was now rushing out of the parlor, Fosette being supported by Russell, Laurence muttering something about "this voodoo bullshit," Simone being prevented from snatching at Jemma only by Honorine's iron grip.

It was just Jemma and Agnes now. Emmaline and Inès.

Jemma slipped her arms around her mother's back and pulled her close to her. Inès's head lolled, the weight dropping against her daughter's neck. Jemma rocked her back and forth in the gloom, her tears mixing with her mother's, each of them raining a river of pain onto the other as shadows danced with menacing glee around them.

TWENTY

FOR THE NEXT several days after the séance, Jemma slept at Magdalene's, or even in the old washhouse with Dennis and Inès. Her mother went back to the big house to cook and clean, but no longer slept in her room off the kitchen. At first, Jemma had been afraid the Duchons would abuse her, but it seemed an uneasy truce had been struck. From what little Dennis could gather, it appeared the family was afraid of what Inès might do, knowing that her child's father had been murdered in the house while she gave birth and had then been buried on the grounds.

But Inès had no will to do anything more than move robotically between her duties.

"Would you poison them, just slip it into their food?" Jemma had asked as Inès left to prepare breakfast one morning. "They deserve it."

But Inès's eyes were as empty as the rest of her. Jemma's mother was a shell, perhaps had seen the terrible effects of past vengeance and was unwilling to do something so awful ever again.

"Just leave her be," Dennis said, joining Jemma in the doorway, both of them watching Inès walk back to the house where she'd grown up. "She don't have it in her to do anything else to them. They've done enough to each other."

When Jemma told Magdalene what the Duchons had done, that it was her father the woman saw buried the day Jemma was born, instead of cursing the family as she'd done before, she told Jemma to follow her outside of the cabin. There, they gathered chicory flowers and ironweed, dandelions and asters. They walked to the old slave cemetery, slipping between two broken fence posts and making their way to a spot near the back.

"He's got to be right around here," Magdalene said.

They spied a bunch of long-stemmed irises tied in a white bow. So Inès had already been there. They laid their small bouquet next to hers.

"I'm surprised you haven't seen his spirit," Magdalene said, her eyes flicking over the small area full of leaning wooden crosses, their inscriptions long faded under the weight of seasons. "If anyone should rest uneasy around here, it should be him."

"I think they're all resting uneasy. But I don't know why. They talk, but not really clear, like they're talking in riddles."

"You still scared of them?"

"A little," Jemma admitted. "I spent my whole life running from them. That's what my mama—my adoptive mama—taught me. She was terrified that I could see them, so she tried to get me to ignore them, hoping they'd leave me alone. They mostly did, but when I came down here, it's like something woke up. I started seeing them more and more. I'm not as scared as I was, but I don't know if I want to break the curse. If I even could."

"So you're going to stay angry forever, take the risk of dying? What about Inès? What about your brother and Fosette?"

"They're the only ones that make me want to try. But I hate the rest of them like I've never hated anyone or anything in my life."

It took a moment for Jemma to realize that Magdalene hadn't spoken for a while, so lost was Jemma in her own thoughts. The older woman rested against the slanting fence, her arms folded in front of her.

"Maybe . . . maybe things would've turned out different . . . if I could've kept you," Magdalene whispered.

Jemma didn't know what she was talking about, wasn't sure she'd heard correctly. "What?"

"I wanted to keep you, when we took you out the house."

"You? But why?"

A sheepish expression stole over Magdalene's face, looking completely out of place on the normally assured surface. A soft sigh escaped her lips, and when she spoke, the way the words came from her mouth—unsure, hesitant—let Jemma know this was a story the woman had never told before.

"I had a daughter, before you were born. If she had lived, she'd be thirty-two now. But when she was still little, not a crib baby anymore but a little older, she got a fever. Nothing I did worked; nothing the conjure women did worked. You can't imagine how hard it is to sit by, not able to do anything, and just watch a part of you die. And then here you come, a few years later. I knew, as soon as I saw you, the family wasn't going to like it. You were darker than your brother, even as a newborn, and your eyes weren't light like the rest of them. So when your mama said to take you away, my heart filled right up. But in her next breath, she said, 'Take her far from here. Give her to some people who are gonna love her, but get her as far from here as you can.' Well, where was I going to go? My baby's buried here. I couldn't leave. And then Dennis told me he knew some people who wanted a baby, people who were moving north. I argued with him because I wanted you to stay here, even though I'd promised your mama different. In the end, he said I had to give you up. I cussed him, called him all kinds of names. I was so *angry* because I wanted what I wanted, even if it wasn't right. And I guess he was mad right back at me. But there hasn't been a day that's gone by that I don't curse whatever god took my child. For a long time, I was angry at her for leaving me. Ain't that something? Like it was her fault. But you can't tell someone how to grieve or when to stop being angry, can you?"

"No, I guess you can't."

"Just like you can't blame your mama for what she did. She had to be out her mind with grief thinking your father left her, knowing she had to give you up if she wanted you to live. She did the only thing she felt like she could do. And we're all just human. We do plenty of things that don't make a lick of sense—"

Something Magdalene had just said stirred a thought in Jemma. "Wait," she said, holding up a hand, cutting off Magdalene's words. "You said my mother did the only thing she felt she could do." Jemma's mind strained, reaching for something. What was it?

And then it came to her. Honorine's words from the séance—Inès's curse.

I curse all the Duchon blood. From this day forth, I bind the family to this house. I bind them forever.

Nowhere in that was a wish for death, the seven-year cycle the family suffered. Was that really all Inès had said? Was that truly the extent of her curse?

It didn't seem that she put a death curse on them at all.

So why did they die every seven years?

"What is it? What's wrong?" Magdalene asked, grabbing Jemma's wrist.

"I don't think . . . my mother . . . I don't . . . She didn't curse us like they think. She bound us to the house, but she didn't want anyone to die." Jemma looked up, the clear sky a contrast to her chaotic thoughts. "Oh God, what does this mean?" She thought of Inès, of how the family blamed her for everything, of how she'd blamed her.

What if they'd been wrong about her all these years? They'd accused her of something much more awful than she'd tried to do.

Jemma wondered why her mother had never tried to explain that to her family, that although she'd cursed them, she'd never meant for the curse to go so far as to kill them.

To find that out meant staying alive.

Despite her anger toward the Duchons, it seemed whatever she did to help herself and her mother would help the rest of the family, too.

TWENTY-ONE

Since Jemma had blurted out that she knew Inès was her mother, she didn't feel the need to hide her desire to be close to her anymore. After staying out of the house for days, Jemma returned, as did Inès to her small room off the kitchen.

"So, you decided to come back." It was Honorine, standing at the back door as soon as Jemma came inside.

"Only for my mother and my brother. And Fosette. Once the curse breaks for us, unfortunately, it breaks for you, too. But I want to save them."

As much as her grandmother might want her to leave, Jemma knew Honorine wouldn't toss her out. Not when so much was at stake.

Although she'd missed several dinners, Honorine didn't punish her upon her return. Maybe the old woman was as tired of the facade as Jemma was. Or maybe the slight desperation she sensed was getting to the family. After all, she had just under two months now to figure something out to free them all from the curse. Instead of punishment, Honorine doled out indifference. She and all the other Duchons, including Fosette, simply acted as if Jemma weren't there.

Several nights ago, Jemma had asked Russell to pass the bread, only to have her uncle pretend he didn't hear her. The same thing happened when she asked Fosette to pass the rice. If Jemma wanted a dish at the other end of the table, she had to get up from her seat and get it herself. Sometimes Inès passed it to her, but other times it was apparent that her mother's mind was someplace else. Jemma hoped it was a nice place, a cool place full of friendly faces like Dennis's.

Yesterday she'd walked in on Fosette and Laurence in the living room, playing cards in their hands. Jemma stood awkwardly in the doorway before clearing her throat.

"Do you want a third?"

Her cousin had pursed her lips before placing a card on the table and asking Laurence, "Did you hear something?"

Laurence didn't reply, but he didn't look at Jemma, either. His head dropped, so perhaps he had the decency to be ashamed, but he still ignored her, as they all did. She was more cast aside than ever.

This afternoon in the library, she spotted the gray ledger. She swiped the book up, the sound of her family's faint laughter—often little more than brief nervous giggles—drifting in from outside the room.

The sound of approaching footsteps tore her attention away from the book.

Laurence leaned against the doorjamb, his arms crossed, before moving to the settee. He patted the seat next to him. Jemma hesitated for a moment before joining him, her gaze on her lap.

"I don't hate you, you know," he said.

"And why would you? I didn't do anything wrong." She spoke without looking up.

"Sorry they've been . . . we've been . . . ignoring you. After what happened at the séance, we were terrified. You can understand that, can't you?"

Jemma gave no indication that she could.

"When that didn't work, we all felt like nothing would work. Everything just seems hopeless, like bringing you here was a waste of time. And now that you know about Agnes . . ."

At that, she raised her head, warmth spreading all over her face. "You mean Inès? My mother? Our mother?"

He glanced toward the door, as if to make sure no one was listening, then turned back to her. "What do you expect of me? Unlike you, I grew up in this house. This family is all I've ever known. And ever since I was a child, all I've heard is how Inès cursed us, how she's made sure one of us dies every seven years, on your birthday. How else would you expect me to feel about her? It didn't matter that she's my mother, not when everyone else—grandmother, uncle, cousin, aunt—has poisoned me against her."

"She's still your mother!"

Laurence's shoulders dropped, his hands loose between his knees.

"I know. And I know you can't understand what it was like growing up here." He raised his eyes to the ceiling, scanning the room. "To be slapped when I said I had a crush on one of the Gaines girls. That's when we still had visitors. Their mother would bring the girls to play with Fosette. 'Those darkies?' Grandmère said. 'Don't you dare, ever.' To have your . . . our mother act as a servant for almost my whole life, to see everyone else treat her like shit so much that that's what I thought I was supposed to do, too.

And Fosette . . ." He ran his hands down his face. "She's so beautiful and yet so hideous at the same time."

She didn't realize he was crying until the low howl came out of him, awful in its quietness. She sat frozen, unsure whether to comfort him or if she even wanted to.

"I hated her," he sobbed before looking up at her, his eyes red and wild. "I *hated* her. But how can you hate your mother? I used to try . . . and . . . be kind to her. But they . . . Maman, no, Tante Simone . . . she punished me."

Jemma's hands twisted in her lap as Laurence struggled to compose himself before going on.

"I was eight, maybe nine. One night I couldn't sleep. I came downstairs for a glass of water. And I heard talking in the library. Grandmère was telling Tante Simone that Laurence must never know, and I stopped and hid right outside of the room so they wouldn't see me. Grandmère said, 'He has to continue to believe this. Otherwise he'll hate you. He'll hate all of us for what we did to Agnes.' I didn't know then that she was my mother, but I knew something was wrong. The next time I was able to be alone with her, I told her what I'd heard. I asked what they'd done to her." Laurence paused and wiped his face. "And she slapped me. She grabbed me and shook me and slapped me again and again." His shoulders shook as he cried soundlessly. Jemma laid a hand on his arm, as lightly as if she were afraid she'd break him. "She made me hate her. Before that, she'd always been kind to me. But afterward, all of it stopped. And I stopped being nice to her. Even when I found out . . . after Fosette and me . . . By then, I'd been cruel to her for so long that I couldn't stop. None of us could." The next few moments were full of nothing more than Laurence's quiet wails and Jemma's unsure hand patting his arm at random intervals. A part of her wanted to do more, longed to comfort the little boy who'd been severely pushed away by the person who loved him most, while another part held in its own anger.

When he spoke next, no emotion clouded his voice. "All those years, thinking Tante Simone was my mother, that Fosette was my sister. When I found out who she really was, knew that she was the one responsible for none of us being able to leave here, I wanted to kill her. But I still loved her. I wanted her to love me back."

"She does, Laurence."

As he leaned forward and buried his face in his arms, his body trembling, Jemma pictured the child he must have been, traumatized by the woman he didn't know was his mother slapping him for asking an innocent question. Inès had no doubt done it out of fear that the family would think she'd revealed secrets to her son. So she did what she thought she had to—pushed him away, hard.

Jemma raised a hand to her own cheek, the ghost of a long-ago slap stinging there even now. She'd been even younger than Laurence when Mama had smacked her for staring at a spirit in the grocer's. Mama couldn't see spirits, but she could tell when Jemma did.

It had been an old woman, standing by the dried goods, a transparent hand resting on the shelf. She'd smiled at Jemma, who'd been too frightened to move.

Slap.

The smack had brought Jemma out of her frozenness. She'd looked up at Mama through tears, the tip of her adoptive mother's nose touching her own.

"Count them away. Do you hear me?" she'd hissed at Jemma. "Count! You ain't gonna be standing around like some fool. *Get rid of them.*"

The small grocery receded in Jemma's mind until she was aware of her brother's stillness. She moved her hand from her face to his own, hoping to soothe any phantom pain he might yet feel.

IT WAS ANOTHER few days before Jemma found Inès willing to stay put long enough for them to talk. She caught her mother coming out of the washhouse one afternoon.

"Mama."

Inès looked up at Jemma's voice, and if she felt any disappointment that her presence didn't immediately elicit a smile from her mother, she tamped it down. There were more important things to worry about.

"I need your help."

As Inès brushed past her, Jemma grabbed her arm.

"Mama, I need you to help me, in any way you can." Ignoring how the woman shook her head and tried to pull out of her grasp, Jemma went on. "I know you didn't mean to hurt anyone. You didn't curse this family to death, but if you know how that happened, you have to tell me. I don't want to die! And I don't want you to die." Inès yanked herself free and headed toward the house, Jemma close on her heels. "And what about Laurence? He's your child, too. What about him?"

Inès stopped so suddenly, Jemma ran into the back of her. Her mother faced her, a deep frown on her face, but instead of making her look angry, it only made her look frustrated. Her hands waved around in the air, her mouth moving, although she didn't seem to be trying to form words.

"I don't know what you're trying to say."

Her mother's shoulders dropped. Jemma was afraid she'd stop trying to communicate with her altogether.

"At the séance, one of the ghosts whispered something to you. What did she say?"

Inès pulled a notepad and pencil out of her pocket and scribbled, then thrust the note to Jemma.

I didn't hear everything because of all the noise.
It sounded like let go . . .

". . . or you will never be free," Jemma finished.

The words from Betty's letter echoed in her mind.

If you're willing to let the bad stuff go.

Tears sprang forth out of her mother's eyes, but before Jemma could do anything to comfort her, Inès put a hand to her heart and then rubbed the side of Jemma's face. She then pointed to the house and ran her palms back over her head a few times. At Jemma's perplexed expression, she repeated the motion and followed it by patting her head. Jemma threw her hands up, frustrated. Inès pointed to her daughter and then held up two fingers, before making a cradling motion with her arms.

"Laurence and me?"

Inès nodded, smiling, brushing her tears away. She patted her heart again.

And Jemma understood.

Her mother loved both of them. She didn't want either of them hurt. But when she pointed toward the distant cemetery and then ran her hands down the side of her face, Jemma understood that, too. Her mother hadn't forgiven her family for killing Jemma's father. And she might never be able to forgive them.

It would have to be enough for Jemma to forgive.

TWENTY-TWO

DESPITE CLAIMING THE Duchons, Jemma wasn't yet ready to set aside her anger toward them enough for her to act. Only the memory of Laurence broken and sobbing moved her. Only the image of her and him and their mother existing as a happy unit pushed aside the hate.

Her brother continued translating the ledger, but he and Jemma hadn't yet discovered when the fire took place. Both of them still wondered about the missing page.

Unsure what to do next, Jemma wandered the streets of New Orleans one muggy winter morning and found herself in a dim shop full of half-burned candles and beads, shells and bottles full of dark liquids or objects like animal bones. A middle-aged man stood behind the counter, his deep brown eyes following her with mistrust.

"Help you, *chère*?" he finally asked.

Jemma almost told him no, but she did need help, so she blurted out her question before she lost her nerve.

"What do you know about curses?"

He cocked his head, a hint of a smile curving his lips. "What kind of curse?"

"A family curse. A bad one."

"What does it do, this curse?"

"Kills people. Binds them to a place."

"Which one? Kills them or binds them?"

"Both."

He leaned forward on the counter, beckoning Jemma closer. Something about him made her hesitate, but she moved toward him, stopping just out of his reach, as if afraid he would grab her.

"Sounds like a powerful curse."

When she didn't respond, he clapped his hands softly and straightened.

"Breaking a bind isn't hard, but breaking a killing curse . . ." He tutted.

"Is it possible, though?"

"Anything's possible. Tell me more about this curse."

Without mentioning names or her relation to the Duchons, Jemma gave an abbreviated version of events that painted the family as hapless victims of unfortunate circumstances. She admitted to the failed ritual with the water and the salt.

"What do you expect, working from a book with no personal items from the people involved?" he scoffed. "No wonder it didn't work."

He sold Jemma a pair of scissors, several candles and a length of new twine, along with a scrap of paper with instructions and other ingredients scribbled on it.

As Jemma approached the door, paper bag in hand, he cooed, "You come back soon, *chère*."

She wouldn't.

AT DINNER THAT evening, too full of nerves to eat much, Jemma rose from her seat. The family must have sensed something, because they stopped in the midst of what they were doing: chewing, gulping wine, talking. She pulled herself to her full height, gathering courage from Laurence's presence before addressing their grandmother.

"I'm going to break the curse," she said. "Tonight."

Simone didn't retort with a vicious comeback, as Jemma had expected, and Honorine's brow lifted only a fraction of an inch. Where was the emotional display? Jemma excused herself, her lips a rigid line.

Things would be different in the morning, when she'd succeeded.

That night, after the rest of the house was settled, Jemma locked her bedroom door and set about performing the ritual. Through the partly open window, a faraway owl hooted and a cool breeze swept in to tickle her bare arms. Dressed in her white cotton nightgown, she sat on the circular rug. Three candles in candleholders set at regular intervals ringed the border. In front of her was an old photograph of the family stolen from Simone's dresser (although it was dated, everyone who currently lived in the house, except Inès, was pictured). Also in front of her were a note from Inès that she didn't know Jemma had kept, the length of twine, a tin plate containing a scoop of soil from the cemetery, and a small knife she'd grabbed from the kitchen, one she hoped her mother wouldn't miss. Despite the coolness of the air in the room, a thin sheen of sweat stuck to Jemma's skin. She consulted the instructions several times, not wanting to miss a single detail, lest this entire ritual turn into a disaster.

Jemma rolled the family portrait and the note into a small tube, securing it with the twine. She placed the tip of the knife against her palm. Inhaling sharply, she made a quick swipe downward, spilling several drops of blood on top of the tube.

"Stupid," she called herself once she realized she hadn't grabbed a rag to wrap around her hand. Instead, she plucked the scarf off her head and cinched it around her hand, watching as blood immediately bloomed through. Holding both arms straight out in front of her, Jemma repeated from the scribbled instructions:

"What once was bound will come undone; what once was lost will now be won. With each snip, the bonds do break, releasing all for my sake."

Holding the tube over a candle flame, she placed the sharp edge of the knife blade under the string and pulled, the ends falling away into the fire, sizzling and shrinking into blackness. The fire ate into the paper and the photograph, and as the flames licked away, Jemma dropped the dwindling tube into the soil. When it was nothing but ash, when there was no more photo, paper, or twine, she realized she'd been holding her breath. It all flew from her in a big rush.

Looking at the window, she wondered how soon she'd know if she'd been successful. A heaviness touched her eyelids, settled on her shoulders, as if breaking the curse had sapped her strength. She snuffed out the candles and pushed all the tools into one big pile under the desk.

As Jemma climbed into bed and closed her eyes, she thought of nothing but tomorrow.

As soon as Jemma woke up the next morning, she knew something was wrong.

It was the screaming.

Instead of jumping out of bed and running downstairs to see who was carrying on so, to see what tragedy had befallen the family, she pulled the covers up to her neck, warding off the sudden chill that worked its way across her body.

Whatever was going on, she told herself, it had nothing to do with her and what she'd done the night before. Maybe someone saw a rat scurrying across the parlor. Or a bird had swooped down the chimney and was flying around the dining room.

Even as these thoughts tried to take hold in her mind, she knew different.

This was her fault, and soon enough the family would make her pay.

Before she could decide what to do next, footsteps sounded outside the door, then more footsteps, all leading away and growing fainter. Going downstairs.

And still the screaming went on.

Jemma grabbed her robe and slipped it on, wondering how she managed to do so when her arms felt completely unconnected to her body. As she took the few steps to the door, her legs seemed to be jerked by marionette strings. Right before she placed her hand on the knob, a part of her whispered to just stay put, to lock the door and never leave this room. It was safer that way.

The footsteps were coming back now, heavy and quick. How many of the Duchons were pounding upstairs now, fists raised to knock on her door? Or not knock at all, simply barge their way into the room?

And there it was, the furious knocking, a fist banging repeatedly, without break.

"Who . . . who is it?" Jemma called, feeling shrunken.

"Open this door, Jemma. Right now!"

Despite a part of her shrilly screaming that she'd do no such thing, she found herself obeying, to find Honorine in the hallway. Someone must have woken her grandmother, because the woman stood there, with her hair in careful pin curls, a netted bonnet covering her head. She clutched the quilted lapels of her blue silk dressing gown, wrinkling them in her tight fist. With the other hand, she pointed a shaky finger at Jemma.

"Get . . . downstairs . . . now."

Jemma tied her robe sash as she followed Honorine down the stairs, only to find Simone, Fosette and Laurence at the foot, pale and silent, their eyes watching the two women descend. Which of them had been screaming? Jemma couldn't tell. None of their faces were flushed and no chests heaved, hinting at exertion or fright. Just as she wondered where Russell was, she saw him, lying face down in the parlor, his cheek pressed to the rug, his bulging green eyes staring in accusation. A thick line of foam ran from his parted lips. A piece of her mind registered that, unlike the rest of them, he was dressed for the day, in a light suit jacket and slacks.

"Is he . . . dead?" Jemma asked in a small voice. "Oh my God, call a doctor!"

"He's not dead," Honorine snapped from her place next to her. "But whatever you did, whatever you've been doing, this is the result."

Jemma tore her gaze away from her uncle to look at her grandmother. "What are you talking about? I did a spell to break the curse. I didn't do this." She flung a hand out toward the body on the floor.

"Then what do you think did? You think he did it to himself?"

"No, no, no," Jemma said to no one. "I was trying to help. I did a spell to get you out of here. I can't have done this." And yet even as the words escaped, she didn't believe them. "Call a doctor." She spun around to find the others huddled in a knot, their eyes fixed on Russell, their faces mournful, as if he really were dead. "Why are you all just standing there?" And still, they did nothing; they didn't react.

She remembered the spell.

"You can leave now," Jemma said, and was relieved when that seemed to grab their attention. At least their eyes flicked away from Russell and met her own. "I did the breaking. You can leave. We can get him to a doctor. I fixed it, I—"

"Shut up." Simone cut her off, stepping forward. "You did no such thing."

"I did! Just go outside, all the way down the road. You'll see."

"Don't bother," Laurence said to his aunt before turning to Jemma. "Unless you want to end up like him. He tried to go for a walk this morning, thinking we were no longer bound to this house. He wanted to test it out. I don't know how far he got, but at some point he turned back around and staggered inside, falling in the parlor."

Simone's eyes blazed. She snarled, "So not only are we still stuck here, but it seems that if we try and leave, we won't just be turned around and forced back, but we'll be struck down with some illness, too. You didn't solve a damn thing. You only made it worse."

TWENTY-THREE

ONE WEEK LATER, Russell was unchanged. The family had called the doctor out, and he was extremely puzzled.

All of them, Jemma included, were crowded around Russell's bed that morning, where he now slept. During the night, however, loud moans carried through his closed door, down the hallway and all the way downstairs. He didn't wake, simply howled like a hound tracking through the bayou, his eyes screwed tight.

"I'm going to call the hospital, have them send an ambulance out," the doctor said, stuffing his stethoscope back into his black bag.

"No!" Honorine barked. The man looked at her. "We'd prefer that he stay here."

"But, Mrs. Duchon, I don't have the tools . . ."

"I understand, Dr. Abernathy. But my son has to stay here."

"I can't treat him properly here."

He looked at each member of the family in turn, a soft pleading in his eyes, settling on Laurence, as if the only other male family member present could talk some sense into these senseless women. But Laurence, like all the rest, merely looked back at the physician, resoluteness joining the Duchons together. The doctor's mouth set into a thin line as he snatched his bag up and left the room, Honorine padding along quietly behind him.

Jemma left, too, heading for the kitchen. As she passed through the dining room she slowed, the sound of a heated argument between the doctor and her grandmother echoing through the space. He tried to convince Honorine to change her mind. As Jemma stood against the wall, keeping out of sight, she wondered what would happen if the ambulance did come and take Russell away. Would he be able to leave the property then, since he would have no control over going?

"If he dies, it's on your hands," the doctor said.

"I understand."

The front door opened, but apparently the man was going to have the last say. "I would think, after all the other family members you've lost over the years, that your son's life would be more precious to you."

"Good day, Doctor."

Jemma scurried toward the kitchen, running into Inès, who was still cleaning up the breakfast dishes in the dining room. Her mother's eyebrows rose, her gaze flicking upward.

"He's the same," Jemma said. "The doctor wanted to take him to the hospital." Inès nodded once and reached for the creamer pitcher, but Jemma put a hand on her arm. "Could he leave that way, if someone took him off the property? He doesn't have a say in it at this point."

Her mother glanced at her before resuming her task, shrugging her shoulders. Jemma grabbed the coffee pitcher and the butter dish, ignoring Inès's frown and head shake, and followed her into the kitchen. Her mother didn't stop her from plunging her hands into the hot, soapy water of the sink and washing the dishes this time. So as Inès brought in plate after plate, mug after mug, Jemma washed. Once all the dishes were cleared away, her mother stood next to her and dried everything.

"They blame me for what happened to Russell. And maybe it was my fault. But they don't even know what's wrong with him since they won't let him go to the hospital. It could be something else, something that has nothing to do with me." Jemma brought her hands out of the water for a moment, sudsy bubbles breaking across the surface. "I wish . . . I wish I knew what I was doing wrong."

"Probably everything," said a voice behind them.

Mother and daughter turned to see Simone standing by the refrigerator.

"Agnes? Can I get a refill on the coffee?" Simone held up an empty cup, dangling it by the handle.

"You can get it yourself," Jemma said, lifting her chin toward the carafe on the counter. "It's right there."

"But what do you think we have a maid for?"

Before Jemma could stop Inès, she'd already grabbed the coffee and poured it into her sister's cup. Simone didn't bother to say thank you before she left. As her mother brought the empty pitcher to the sink, Jemma noticed the hard lines on her face, the way her lips pulled downward.

"Yeah, I can't stand her, either."

Inès looked at her then, puzzlement stamped on her face. She shook her head shortly before rummaging through a drawer and pulling out a sheet of almost clear paper and a pencil. She scribbled fiercely for a moment before thrusting the note at Jemma.

Simone and I weren't very close growing up,
but it was much worse after Lucie died.
She never forgave me for Lucie, for what I did.

Forgiveness, Jemma thought. This whole family couldn't forgive one another. Just as she couldn't forgive them for everything they had done. Murdering her father. Cutting out her mother's tongue. Giving her away because she was too dark for them. Bringing her here under false pretenses. Holding her at arm's length despite their supposed need for her.

But Jemma knew it wasn't that she couldn't forgive them. She didn't want to. Just as she hadn't wanted to forgive her adoptive father for never accepting her. She'd spent all that money on his funeral to prove to him that she was worthy, but what difference did it make then? He was already dead. But Jemma had thought, *If he's looking down from wherever he is, he can see what I did for him, can see that he should have loved me.*

And her inability to forgive Marvin for getting another woman pregnant, for not stopping her from leaving.

Jemma thought of her friend Betty, Betty who somehow found it easy to forgive others their mistakes, their cruelty, their deceit.

If you can forgive him . . . yes, find it in yourself to forgive him. It's freedom in that, her friend had said.

Freedom.

Freedom in forgiveness.

Set them free, the spirit had said.

Let go or you will never be free.

What if it meant *Set them free by forgiving them*?

Jemma's knees buckled and she sank to the floor, a puff of air leaving her parted lips. Inès wasn't quick enough to prevent her fall, but her mother caught her under the arms right before she hit the floor, softening her landing. Jemma turned to her.

"I think I know how to set us free."

IT WASN'T NEARLY as easy to convince Inès to go along with her as Jemma had thought it would be. Her mother's refusal to immediately hear her out confused her, then angered her. She wanted to remind Inès that it was her curse that had them all stuck here, including herself. But Jemma bit back the words and tried her best to tamp down the negative thoughts. She needed a clear head for what was coming. She needed to act out of love, not anger.

Russell still hadn't woken. The doctor made visits to check on his status and continued to argue with Honorine, but after his third trip out to the house he gave that up. He simply came in, checked the man's vitals, sometimes raked his gaze over any other family members present and then left until the next time.

One cool evening after dinner, during which time Honorine and Simone went straight to Russell's room to sit vigil for him, and Fosette and Laurence went elsewhere (Jemma pushed images of the two of them together from her mind), Jemma caught her mother heading to her small room.

"Can I show you something?" she asked.

Wariness drew Inès's face into a tight ball, but she walked beside Jemma as they made their way across the back lawn, toward the washhouse. Jemma didn't know how her mother would react, but she'd made up her mind that she was doing the right thing. She needed Inès's help to break the curse, and she was afraid she couldn't convince her on her own.

Pointing toward the woods, Jemma asked, "Do you remember who lives back there?" The waning sunlight cast a golden glow over the grass, the sky, their skin. "Someone who thought you were dead, Mama. Someone who deserves to see you."

Inès's arm tensed beneath her daughter's hand before Jemma pushed the door to the washhouse open. In the middle of the room stood Magdalene, looking very much like she had the first time Jemma met her—long braids trailing past the low-slung belt—only this time the woman didn't carry the pistol.

The two older women stared at each other, Inès's hands raised to her mouth, Magdalene's hand on one cocked hip.

"All this time, I thought you were dead, Inès." Magdalene shook her head, eyes heavy with sadness. "Thought you were dead and buried over there." She took a few steps forward and stopped suddenly, displaying an uncharacteristic lack of confidence. "What have they done to you?"

Seemingly deciding that it was safe to get closer, Magdalene approached the frozen Inès until they were within arm's reach of each other. Tears spilled down Magdalene's cheeks as she asked again, "What have they done?"

She reached forward, first with stiff arms, as if she wasn't sure if it was all right that she touch her. But Inès, although she appeared lost for a moment, relented, bent and closed the space between them. Jemma stood by and watched as the women sobbed into each other's shoulders.

WHAT'S YOUR PLAN?" Magdalene asked a short while later, the three of them around the big table. Inès and Jemma sat, while she stood against the counter.

"If Mama is able to forgive, if I'm able to forgive, I think we can break the curse. The spirit said to 'free them.' It said to let go."

Now Magdalene directed her words to Inès. "And can you do

that? Forgive them for everything they did? Not just to you, but to Ismael and Emmaline here?" Without waiting for a nod or a shake of the head, she turned to Jemma. "That's a lot to ask of her. They made her act as a maid to them for almost thirty years. That's thirty years of hate and resentment she's sitting on."

"I know she has more reason than I do to be angry. They've treated her much worse than they have me." She looked at her mother then. "I'm sorry. We're talking about you as if you're not here. Do you want to write something down, tell me if I'm right, wrong, anything?"

At first, Inès didn't react, and Jemma was afraid her mother would close herself off despite her obvious happiness at seeing Magdalene again. After a moment, she jumped up and rifled through several cabinets along the wall before returning with a sheet of paper and a piece of charcoal no longer than a pinkie. She scribbled:

I don't know if I can forgive

"Not even to get out of here?" Jemma asked.

Inès shrugged and waved a limp hand, as if to ask, *Where would I go?*

"But what about Laurence? He hasn't been off the property since he was a little boy. He never even got to go to school. Don't you want to leave? Maybe you and Dennis. We can have a life we didn't get to have before. But I don't think it's going to work if you can't forgive them for what they did."

Inès gazed at the floor. Jemma wanted to give her mother the chance to think about what she asked of her, to contemplate a possible future. Her mother had been just as trapped as the rest of her family for twenty-seven years. If she went into New Orleans, she might not even recognize the city. Jemma suspected a part of the woman wanted to stay at the house, the place that was so familiar to her, even if another part of her hated it.

Inès scribbled something else.

If I do, it's only for you and for Laurence, but I need time

It wasn't a no.

"Of course, Mama, of course."

Jemma didn't have to remind her that time was something they didn't have much of. She left the two women in the washhouse and headed inside the big house, straight to her brother's room.

It's only for you and for Laurence.

He opened the door to Jemma's knock, his hair rumpled.

"We need to talk," she said.

He stepped back, opening the door wide. As she settled into a wingback chair in a corner, she surveyed the space. Pale blue wallpaper and ivory wainscoting lent his bedroom the same formal atmosphere present in the rest of the house, but his felt more comfortable than Honorine's room. On one of his nightstands sat a small framed photograph of two young children, a boy and a girl, both staring somberly at the camera.

"Fosette and me in happier times," he said with a nod to the picture, his sarcasm evident. He sat on the bed and ran a hand through his hair before turning his attention to Jemma. "This must be important for you to come to my room."

"It is. I think there's a way to break the curse, but our mother has to be willing to forgive everyone for what they did. Naturally, it's not easy for her since all of you have been so horrible to her. But she still wants to save us, her children. You have to talk to her, to ask her to forgive. It can't just be me."

Laurence's usual smirk disappeared. He leaned forward, elbows on his knees. "I haven't tried to talk to her in so long. What could I even say?"

"Maybe you can start with an apology."

His eyes flicked upward to meet hers. "Do you really think that will be enough?"

"I don't know. But it's something."

So later that night, after everyone else had retired to bed, Jemma and Laurence slipped downstairs like two children sneaking sweets. He'd begged her to accompany him. He wiped his hands on his slacks half a dozen times as they stood in the kitchen doorway, he telling Jemma he wasn't ready yet.

"We don't have a lot of time."

"I know. Just . . . I feel like she hates me for what I did. I don't even know what to call her. How can she possibly forgive any of us?"

"You might be surprised what people can do if you ask them right."

Their mother remained expressionless while her son fumbled his way through what sounded like a rehearsed speech, stumbling in calling her Agnes and forming his lips over "Ma—" before stopping himself and starting over.

"I've wanted to say something to you for so long, ever since I found out who you were," he whispered. "But it got to the point where I didn't know what to say. They wanted me to hate you. You made me hate you. Now I know that, all these years, you only wanted to protect me. Saying sorry can't undo all that I did—it can't even scratch the surface. But . . . Maman . . . I'll make it up to you in whatever way I can. I promise."

When he finished, his gaze on the floor, there was only the sound of the humming refrigerator.

Jemma reached for her mother's hand. "Mama. You love us. You want to save us. It's not Laurence's fault. He only did what they all did, and what they did was wrong. But to save me and him means forgiving him and all of them. That's the only way. Please."

Inès raised her other hand to Laurence's cheek, as if remembering slapping him there years ago. Tears shone in her eyes.

He placed his hand over hers, leaning in to her touch, while Jemma watched them both, the smallest flicker of hope daring to light inside her.

JEMMA HAD FELT tension in the air from the day she'd arrived, but as her birthday drew closer, it seemed ever greater. Simone's barbs, once infrequent, had increased. Short and sharp, often in French patois.

"Can you pass the soup, please?" Jemma asked Fosette at dinner.

"Careful, daughter, lest you fall into a coma if that *sac à merde* so much as touches you," Simone said, her eyes on Jemma, who didn't bother to ask for a translation.

"Maman," Fosette murmured, pushing the tureen toward Jemma without looking at her.

"What?" Simone snorted, before addressing her niece. "Why are you even here anymore, you useless *garce*? I told you you'd fail, and all you've done is prove me right. Luckily for me, I've already picked out the dress I want to be buried in. I hope the rest of you have done the same."

The family retired early, eager to get into warm beds. Russell's unchanging condition also seemed to have something to do with the strained atmosphere. Without his presence at meals, everything was quieter.

Later, as Jemma was getting ready for bed, Inès came to her room with a note: *I'm ready*

"Tomorrow night? After everyone's in bed?" Jemma asked, and her mother nodded once before heading back downstairs.

The next night, Jemma waited in her room until the stillness outside her door was absolute. In light slippers and a long night-gown and robe she'd found in the chifforobe, she made her way to the kitchen, where Inès waited in similar attire, her hair loose around her shoulders. Her mother handed her a lit white candle, a matching one gripped in her own hand.

The two of them walked across the grass, now cool under the night sky. At first, Inès simply followed Jemma, but when her daughter started toward the chapel, Inès placed a hand on her arm and pointed to the old slave cemetery. Where Jemma's father was buried. With each passing moment, the air grew colder and heavier. They wrapped their arms around themselves for warmth. Right before they stepped inside the leaning wrought iron gate, Inès pulled out two veils, placing one on her head and draping the other over Jemma's.

Inès handed Jemma a note, which her daughter read by candle-light.

"'I, Inès Lily Duchon, forgive my family. I forgive my father, Raymond, for killing my love, Ismael. I forgive my mother, Honorine, for letting it happen. I forgive her and my brother, Russell, for stealing my voice. I forgive my sister, Simone, for her cruelty and her jealousy. I forgive my son, Laurence, for not knowing how to treat me. I forgive myself for the curse I placed on my family, for keeping us prisoner here for all these years. With the power of forgiveness, I free all of us from this land.'"

As Jemma read the words, a steady breeze had increased in intensity until it was now a whipping wind blowing Inès's hair about her head, both of their gowns up around their knees. Fallen leaves smacked them occasionally. They'd tried to shield the candle flames, but the lights had blown out with Jemma's last word.

In the darkness, she spoke again. "I forgive my mother, Inès, for binding the Duchons to this property. I forgive the Duchons for lying to me about who they were and why they brought me here. I forgive them for murdering my father, for sending me away instead of accepting me, for their cruelty and meanness. With the power of forgiveness, I set them free."

The wind whipped into a keening howl. As harsh and cold as it was, Jemma felt a spot of warmth growing inside her. As it grew, the wind gradually lessened, until it was the softest of breezes and then nothing.

Everything was still. The heaviness was gone.

"Did you feel that? Did you feel the warmth?"

Inès nodded, a small smile lighting her lips.

"I think it worked, Mama. I think you all can leave now. You did it. You set them free."

TWENTY-FOUR

THE NEXT WEEK was a flurry of excitement, with the exception of one thing.

Russell was still unconscious.

Despite that, the rest of the family celebrated, as respectfully as they could. Only Honorine seemed cautious.

"Oh, Maman, he'll wake up any day now," Simone said at breakfast. Although the chilly winter air rested heavily on the house, there was a lightness about, an almost springlike feel. "And when he does, we'll all go to Paris together. It makes no sense to go right now anyway. We have so many clothes to buy, so much to catch up on! In September—that's when we'll go. In the meantime, we'll redo the house. How about it? We'll have the old wallpaper stripped and bring this place into this decade. And then, how about we throw a big party? We'll invite the old families who haven't been here in ages. They probably think we've all gone quite insane, but we'll show them." A hard gleam shone out of her eyes. "And Fosette, and Laurence. They'll finally get to meet young people their age—"

"Maman, I'm thirty-four," Fosette murmured. "You can forget about marrying me off."

"Nonsense!" Simone slammed a fist on the table. "You're still beautiful, still desirable. And if none of these common laggards can see that, we'll find you a husband in Paris. Yes, Paris! Oh, you'll be a Parisienne and travel across Europe. That's what we're going to do for at least the next year, travel everywhere. We won't come back to this house until 1964. Maybe later. All we have to do is wait for Russell to wake, and now that the curse is lifted, it has to happen."

"Have you forgotten that it's already been several weeks?" Honorine hissed.

"I don't know how these things work any more than you do, Maman, but I'm telling you, the heaviness has been lifted. I know you feel it just as we all do. Isn't that right, Fosette?"

Her daughter nodded. And indeed, Simone was right about the heaviness. It was as if when the invisible walls that held them inside had broken, so had the suffocating air. The tension the family had felt from being trapped for so long was released. There were more smiles, more laughter, more chatter.

And when Jemma caught a brief whiff of smokiness, she ignored it as a vestige of old things. In the spring, when they aired the house out, that would be gone, too.

It had been strange at first, the way the family had tested the borders. It was obvious they were frightened, unsure if the ties that had bound them had really been cut.

Laurence had been first, walking out of the gates and down the dirt lane, farther and farther, the rest of them crowded on the front porch, watching his diminishing form going far past any place he'd been since the age of two. And Fosette had run next, her arms raised in the air, her mouth open in a soundless scream, until she reached her cousin and he twirled her around and around, finally setting her down and kissing her in the middle of the wide-open space. Simone followed, her steps slow and unsteady at first, but quickening and growing in surety. She passed her daughter and nephew, continued on, her glee evident in the squareness of her shoulders, the upright tilt of her head. For Honorine, it seemed to be enough to see her family free. She didn't set foot off the property until the following morning, when she and the rest of the family, save Inès, Russell and Jemma, took a cab to St. Augustine Church to light candles and pray.

Only Inès hadn't moved off the porch, had simply seen that her curse was indeed broken and had given a smile before going back inside.

But now Jemma, amazed at Simone's utter selfishness, reminded her family that their celebrations were sure to be complicated. She folded her hands over her empty plate, clear of its croissant and scrambled eggs. "What about my mother? You told everyone she was dead. When you throw these big parties, Simone, don't you think there will be questions, especially if she ends up serving them hors d'oeuvres?"

The smile slid off Simone's face to bring back the scowl that was usual whenever Jemma was present. "Your mother chose to stay here. She also chose to continue in her role. I guess she's gotten used to it, so who am I to talk her out of it?"

And it was true. Although the rest of the Duchons had traveled outside of their old boundaries, had gone all the way into New Orleans proper, Inès hadn't changed at all. She was still acting as their maid. Ever since they'd been set free, Jemma had been trying to convince her to leave with her. Now that she'd done what the family had hired her to do, she knew they had no more use for her. They allowed her the time to decide what she would do next. She wasn't so sure she'd return to Chicago, but she had no other destination in mind. What she wanted was for her mother to choose a place. But even Dennis didn't seem motivated to leave. Jemma wasn't going to stay here, but she didn't want to leave her mother far behind, not now that they'd found each other.

Although she knew she shouldn't be hurt, it did sting that the Duchons didn't ask her about going to Paris with them.

Did you really think that would happen? she asked herself sometimes when she lay in bed at night, eyes fixed on the ornate ceiling medallions just visible in the dimness. *You knew nothing would change, not really.*

Jemma had money now, quite a bit of it, with the promised earnings given to her in one lump sum. She and Honorine had taken a cab and visited First Citizens Bank. But no matter how much money her grandmother kept in its vaults, she and Jemma couldn't walk through the front doors. Apparently Honorine had called ahead, so when they knocked at a side entrance door, a young blond woman let them in and ushered them toward a plain office. Presently, the bank president himself arrived to greet them, remarking on the surprise of Honorine's appearance after so many years. If Jemma hadn't known any better, she never would've guessed that her grandmother hadn't set foot in the building in decades. The three of them sat in the small office (clearly not the man's actual office), he and Honorine exchanging pleasantries, which was what happened when someone had many tens of thousands of dollars in the institution.

"I'd like to give Miss Barker here full control of her account," Honorine had said.

"But I'm not staying—" Jemma had started before her grandmother interrupted.

"When you leave, you may do as you wish. Since it appears you'll be here for a little longer while you decide what to do next, this is best."

And Jemma had said no more, simply signed a few papers and accepted the check register the man slid across the desk. Although the four-figure sum was written there in plain black ink, she had trouble believing it was all hers.

Ever since the Duchons had gained their freedom, Simone had continued making grand plans. The pile of fashion magazines on the parlor table grew. Simone, Fosette and Honorine spent many days in town, coming home loaded down with bags and parcels. Still more arrived several times per week, dresses sheathed in clear plastic, small towers of shoeboxes secured with thick ribbons.

"Neither of you has a driver's license," Simone told her daughter and nephew. "We don't even have a car!" She laughed then, a shrill sound edged with unraveling sanity, and within a few days a black 1963 Lincoln Continental was delivered. Jemma came out onto the front lawn on an afternoon in early February to admire it, along with everyone else.

"Who's going to drive it? None of us knows how," Honorine said.

"Dennis will teach us," Simone said, sliding her hand along the driver's side of the sleek car.

"He hasn't driven in years. He always takes the wagon when he goes into town."

"Well, he won't need that old country wagon anymore, and we won't need to call a cab. He'll take us in the car. But we're all going to learn to drive it."

Honorine refused to learn, but Dennis taught Simone, Fosette and Laurence how to maneuver it. Crooked ruts marked the front lawn, and once the three of them passed the test for a driver's permit, they fought over who would use the car. Simone was gone the most often, visiting friends she had from years ago, friends who'd heard rumors about the family and now peppered her with questions. Every night at dinner and every morning at breakfast, she relayed stories about meetings with the Cheneverts, the Elliotts.

"Marcella—you know, Frances's youngest—she was married two years ago and just had the most beautiful little boy. He has a head full of copper curls, and the bluest eyes. Oh! And Edgar. He has four boys now, all with the creamiest skin and the straightest hair. And they asked how you were, Maman, of course, and they asked after Russell." That was when she'd grow quiet, before directing her next words to her sister as she served the meal. "What are we going to tell them about you when they come over?"

"We'll tell them Inès has just returned from Europe," Honorine said.

"More lies?" Jemma snapped.

"Are you still here? When are you going to decide where to go? You've got enough money to take yourself anywhere in the world, so why don't you just leave?" Simone asked.

"Auntie," Laurence said, "I don't see why Jemma has to go at all. We're her family, after all." He paused, only to resume in a soft voice. "Agnes isn't going anywhere."

"And what's your sister going to do here? We don't need her anymore."

"Right," Jemma agreed, her gaze on Simone. "I did my job. Now it's time to hide my dark ass away before your friends come over."

"That's not fair, Jemma," Fosette said.

"Oh, stop. You're no better than your mother, our grandmother. If you were, you never would've been involved with . . . Look, I know where I'm not wanted. I'll be out of your hair as soon as I know where I'm going."

"You could come to Paris with us," Laurence suggested, keeping his gaze forward and not looking in Simone's direction.

"Are you taking my mother, too?"

"Of course not. Inès wouldn't want to come anyway."

"Have you even bothered to ask?"

The silence was its own answer. Jemma wondered why she even tried at this point. Soon she'd be gone from here permanently. She doubted anyone would invite her back, that they'd exchange letters once she settled somewhere. Or maybe Laurence would try to keep in touch, since he seemed to be the only one concerned about where Jemma would go.

Jemma pushed her chair back, having finished breakfast nearly half an hour ago. As she left the dining room, she heard the four of them making plans for a party. She forced herself to ignore the knot in her chest.

Later, after spending the afternoon with Magdalene, who knew all about the Duchons' new freedom and had nothing nice to say about it, Jemma asked herself how she'd been so naïve as to think that breaking the curse would solve all her problems, or even drive the spirits away. As she made her way back to the house, the day's light fading, she stopped short at the sight of Adam standing outside the slave cemetery.

Her heart seemed to stick in her throat. She didn't know why fright gripped her the way it did, a tight hand whose fingers rested at the base of her neck. She wasn't scared anymore, she told herself. She'd worked through all of that. Plus, the ghosts had helped her.

She slowed, then moved toward where he floated, completely still.

He must have a reason for being there, but what could it be? *He's not at rest,* a part of her whispered.

"Adam?" she said, stopping a few feet from him.

"Free them," he said. "You got to free them."

Jemma frowned. "But I did. My mother and I did. We forgave them. They're free to come and go now. We're all free."

"Free them," he repeated, his voice unchanged, and there was distress underneath the words, bristling there. "From under."

"I don't understand." Before she could ask what he meant, his form grew faint. Jemma looked around to see if any more ghosts were there. But there was no Jane, were no others.

An uncharacteristically warm air, which pulled moisture from her forehead, armpits and neck, seemed to disappear with Adam. Once in her bedroom she felt even cooler, the cotton nightgown not nearly enough to keep her warm as she whispered Adam's name in the lamplit room.

No one came.

No one answered.

ALTHOUGH HONORINE HADN'T wanted to have a big party, she acquiesced to Simone, who promised to have just one celebration on a smaller scale, no more than fifty people.

"Once Russell wakes up, and he will wake up, we'll have a huge celebration, invite half the city."

The party was a chance for Simone to show off her new clothes, as well as to parade Fosette and Laurence around in hopes that they'd find marriage partners.

As for Inès, she had made it clear that she had no intention of attending. Jemma was invited, and when she asked how she would be introduced, Honorine said she'd be presented as their family.

"As Inès's daughter."

"And your granddaughter? Really?" Jemma was taken aback, even more so when her grandmother nodded.

The week before the party, set for February twentieth, just before Mardi Gras, Jemma went into town with Fosette, Simone and Honorine. Her cousin had surprised her with the invitation, and after she and her mother had argued over who would use the car that day, it turned into a group trip, Jemma a nervous passenger in the front seat while Fosette drove. It was a strange experience being in the parish proper with the three of them, especially since they stuck to areas that catered to white clientele. As they entered one boutique, a salesclerk looked up.

"You can't bring your girl in here," the woman said to Honorine.

The three Duchons exchanged a glance before Simone continued on inside. When she realized her mother and daughter weren't trailing her, she turned back.

"Come on."

Jemma turned to the door, her face hot.

"Grandmère," Fosette whispered, "Jemma and I will meet you back here in an hour."

Her cousin grabbed Jemma's arm and steered her outside before anyone could protest. As the two of them strolled down the sidewalk, quiet hung awkwardly between them while the regular sounds of New Orleans swirled around their bubble. Jemma wondered if Fosette would say anything. She also wondered what she would have done if her cousin had joined her mother and grandmother back at the shop, leaving Jemma on the street, alone in an unfamiliar neighborhood.

"It's nice without the old guard hanging over us, isn't it?" Fosette finally asked, her arm looped through Jemma's.

"Is that why you left them back at the shop?"

Her cousin stopped. "I didn't want to leave you. My mother certainly would've done it, let them throw you out like you were the help. I'm not like them, Jemma. Can't you see that?"

They ended up at a boutique that catered to Black clientele, and they walked out with several bags. But not before her cousin absolutely embarrassed her by remarking on how nice the "colored" shop was. All the other women in the store stared at Fosette, and at Jemma to a lesser extent, as if trying to ascertain the nature of their relationship. Jemma was relieved to get out of there.

"You should wear the yellow one for the party. That one looked the best on you," Fosette chattered as she drove them home. She had a terrible habit of looking over at Jemma every time she spoke instead of keeping her eyes on the road.

"What are you going to wear?"

"Oh, I don't know. I have about a dozen to choose from. Maybe I'll start the party with one and then change midway through, and then change one more time before it ends." Fosette laughed, her eyes crinkled shut, Jemma grabbing the door handle as the car swerved slightly. "You can help me decide."

It was hard resisting the easy air that enveloped the home, although Honorine reminded everyone constantly that Russell was still comatose. She refused to move him, knowing a white hospital wouldn't accept him and believing a Black hospital couldn't cure him. And while Jemma had taken to helping her mother as much as she could, Inès still refused to give up her role as maid, refused to sleep in the bedroom that had been hers and that Jemma now used, refused to leave the property. Jemma had asked her numerous times to do all these things, but her mother simply shook her head.

Despite that, Jemma found herself looking forward to the party, to seeing new faces around the house. She'd decided to use the occasion to announce her departure, having settled on California as a destination. She didn't know a single person out there, but that was part of the allure. It was far from anything she'd ever known, but close to the ocean, something she'd always loved. She didn't know how, but she'd convince Inès to come with her. And maybe if her mother came, Dennis would follow.

Honorine hired men to come paint the exterior of the house and a team of maids to clean the inside. On the day of the party, a catering service arrived late in the morning.

Jemma went looking for her mother around lunchtime, and saw Inès leaving the washhouse and heading toward the woods as if she was going to visit Magdalene. Or hide out there, more likely. She was rushing after her when Fosette called her from upstairs, needing her help choosing a dress. Jemma looked outside again and saw no trace of her mother, so she went to help her cousin and, in the busyness that followed, forgot about Inès and Dennis and everything that had troubled her.

The party guests began arriving early, before the seven o'clock start time, which Honorine grumbled about. However, she shook off any irritation and played the gracious hostess, which was nothing less than Jemma expected. It was a whirlwind of people, certainly more than the fifty Simone was limited to invite. An hour in, Jemma figured there had to be at least one hundred guests milling in and out of the house, almost all of them similar in color to the Duchons.

When her grandmother introduced her to a couple who could have been cousins of hers, their eyebrows raised at the sight of Jemma, the woman's gaze sliding down Jemma's brown arms, which contrasted deliciously against the creamy yellow gown Fosette had convinced her to wear, a yellow that would have made the rest of them appear as washed-out as jellyfish on a beach.

"Why, I wasn't aware that you had another granddaughter, Honorine," the woman said. "What have you all been doing here, hiding out all these years?"

And with each introduction, it was the same. Surprise—some of it unpleasant, some comical—seemed to be the theme of the night. One guest, whom Jemma mistook for a white man, held Jemma's arm, peppering her with questions.

Where was she from? Why had she only recently come to New Orleans? If she was indeed Inès's child, why had she grown up in Chicago? Where was her father?

Jemma answered everything truthfully, with the small exception of why she'd been in Chicago.

"I had other family there who wanted me to live with them."

And the man's eyes moved over her face, her neck, her arms, taking in her color. He finally nodded, as if he understood. And she wondered if he knew the truth but was too polite to voice it.

The guests' naked curiosity didn't dampen Jemma's mood. Mostly, she watched from a corner (where she was never alone for long) as Fosette made the rounds. It was as if she hadn't been trapped here for almost twenty-eight years, denied new relationships and meeting new people. No, her cousin shone, the years seemingly fallen away as she flitted from one group to another, an agile butterfly. Laurence, too, drew eyes everywhere he went. But Jemma noticed after a while that the initial interest that their guests expressed eventually waned, to be replaced by a cautiousness, a wariness. Once the people had gotten their fill of the gossip, once they'd seen with their own eyes that the Duchons were in fact alive and well, the guests seemed to pull back and away, to whisper among themselves the moment Honorine or Simone excused herself from the group. Young men whose eyes followed Fosette frowned when she wasn't looking. Mothers pulled young women away from Laurence after brief moments of conversation, giving excuses of having an early morning or other obligations.

Pieces of conversation touched Jemma's ears as she passed through the crowd, everything from petty gossip to current events to insults.

"You think Schiro is going to sign that thing, so they'll stop boycotting down there?"

"I told her not to wear that cream dress. What does she think it is, high summer?"

"She's gotten so old. That must be why she hasn't gone anywhere in years."

A group of two men and two women huddled in a corner. Jemma had spoken to one of the men earlier. He gestured to her, and as she joined them, one of the women said, "Haunted. I can feel it. Let's finish these drinks and go."

The man wore an apology on his face as he shrugged, gulped down his martini and left with the others.

As Jemma glanced around, she found more small groups like this, wide and wary eyes taking in the proceedings.

"Maybe *they're* the ghosts and we're in a nightmare," a man said to his laughing companions, all putting on their coats before rushing out the door.

Snatches of conversation grew more troubling.

"You really think the Zulus are better than those niggers marching in the streets? It's embarrassing. They're both an embarrassment. Just wait 'til next week, when they're acting like fools in the parade."

A woman bumped into Jemma and squinted at her.

"Who are you?" she asked, her words slightly slurred.

"Jemma. Honorine's granddaughter."

"Oh yes, the dusky one."

Under the drunken guest's insulting appraisal, Jemma remained stiff.

"You're lucky, though. You escaped all this." The woman waved one arm expansively. "The rot. The decay. The disease."

Before Jemma could respond, the partygoer stumbled away, crashing into someone else and laughing hysterically. Jemma had only a few pockets here and there to wonder after her mother. She was able to spare some gratitude that Inès wasn't expected to work this increasingly rowdy affair. Half a dozen white-jacketed Black men worked the room instead, gliding through with trays of deliciously varied hors d'oeuvres and flutes of champagne.

It wasn't until someone asked after Russell that Jemma overheard Honorine offering her apologies for his absence, "but he's taken ill." This was followed by a series of probing questions, the inquirer completely oblivious to the rudeness. Not finding a moment of silence in which to make her announcement, Jemma decided to head to bed sometime after one in the morning. She'd just tell the family about her plans at breakfast.

When she'd reached the parlor entrance, lying to a guest that she was only going to the bathroom, she turned away from the man and stopped, the last bit of an apology dying on the air.

Russell stood in the doorway.

Her uncle was dressed in the gray silk pajamas Honorine had had him changed into weeks ago, his hair on one side smashed close to his head. His gaze moved around the room. Only the people nearest Russell stopped talking, as they recognized him. One man began to move toward him, a hand out, his mouth forming a greeting.

All of that was interrupted as Russell's face contorted. His clawed fingers rose to his hair and yanked and tore out clumps. As his screams grew louder, the chatter around the room ceased. Everyone turned to look, their mouths falling open at the sight of her uncle, red-faced and shrieking.

Dimly, Jemma was aware of Honorine and Simone pushing their way toward him as most of the guests began stampeding to the front doors. A few continued to stare, as if unable to look away, but eventually they, too, bolted toward the foyer. Sobs and fearful babbling accompanied Russell's ongoing wails.

In the chaos, Jemma didn't know if anyone else heard or understood his words.

"It's not over! They're coming! It's not over! Not over!"

TWENTY-FIVE

BEFORE BREAKFAST THE next morning, after a night of uneasy, broken sleep, Jemma knocked on Russell's bedroom door. Honorine surprised her when she opened it.

"I need to talk to him," Jemma said.

After his awakening and outburst the previous night, and after the partygoers had escaped, Honorine had hustled her son back to his room, ignoring Jemma's pleas to ask him what he'd meant by "It's not over!"

Her grandmother stood aside and let her in.

Russell sat up in bed, looking nothing like the lunatic who'd ruined what was arguably not a great party last night. He appeared a little tired but otherwise fine.

Jemma sat on the side of the king-size bed, the silken covers rustling expensively beneath her.

"You said 'It's not over.' What did you mean by that?"

Russell's gaze dropped to his lap. "I don't remember saying that."

"What do you remember about last night?"

"Nothing. One moment, I was in the dark, and the next, Maman and Simone were helping me into bed."

"You were in the dark? Where? Do you mean when we couldn't wake you?"

He struggled to find words, but Jemma refused to let him squirm his way out of this. He knew more than he was telling. She was determined to get the truth.

"I was in a dark place. I don't know where. It was cold."

It burns yet, one of the ghosts had said at the séance, followed by a confusing contradiction from another: *So cold, so cold.*

"Was anyone with you?"

"No," he answered too quickly.

The doctor then bustled his way in and Jemma was shunted out. She knocked on Fosette's door, and concluded that her cousin was probably still asleep when she didn't receive an answer. It was still very early, but after debating with herself for a moment, she went to Laurence's room. He opened the door immediately when she knocked.

Jemma grabbed his arm. "Russell said something last night. He said, 'It's not over. They're coming.' Did you hear it?"

Laurence shook his head just as an enormous yawn escaped him.

"Something's not right."

"Look, he was in a coma or whatever it was for weeks. He wakes up, sees all the people . . . He was probably scared and confused. Wouldn't you be if something like that happened to you?"

When Laurence said it like that, Jemma wondered whether he was right and she was simply overreacting. After the doctor pronounced Russell healthy, she convinced herself everything was fine and they were all safe. Perhaps she'd been too hard on Russell when she questioned him that morning. More than anything else, Jemma wanted to believe Laurence when he said everything was okay.

With Russell awake and claiming he couldn't remember what had happened to put him in his comatose state, plans to flee New Orleans and head to Europe were renewed. Simone took the lead, as she'd been doing for weeks now, on scheduling shopping trips and organizing the extended vacation. A simple trip to Paris turned into a tour of the European continent, from England to France and Spain, and then perhaps to Germany and Italy.

Even the daily papers didn't hold their usual sway, pictures from a debutante cotillion in the society pages ignored.

"We're going to make up for lost time," Simone said at breakfast.

All they talked about was the party, the guests, how many men had watched Fosette in fascination, how many women had looked at Laurence with naked longing, how Russell had recovered with no ill effects and of course the upcoming trip.

Jemma wondered how the rest of the Duchons hadn't noticed what she had: the shrinking away, the unnerved expressions loosened by liquor. Thinking about Simone, how her aunt's face had worn triumph on it no matter how frightened anyone else appeared, Jemma asked her, "You don't remember how the night ended?"

"With my brother waking up?"

"With him screaming that 'it's not over'? Am I the only one who heard it?"

Jemma looked at each of them, but her questions were quickly dismissed.

"Do you know how much luggage we'd have to pack for such a trip, Simone?" Honorine asked, her attention focused on the bread in her hands before the morsel disappeared behind her small smile. "They won't let us on the plane with all of it."

"We won't pack everything. That's the whole point of this overdue vacation. We're going to buy enough clothes and trinkets and souvenirs and furniture to have to ship it back on its own cargo liner, Maman!"

"But there's Mardi Gras to look forward to first," Russell said.

"You two have never been!" Simone screamed to Fosette and Laurence. "Oh, just you wait!"

The wait wasn't long, as Mardi Gras was the following week. Had Jemma thought the St. Patrick's Day parade in Chicago was a spectacle? She'd never been downtown for it, but she had heard stories of the green river, had seen the pictures of the crowds in the newspaper. Being in the thick of Mardi Gras had to be like that, she first thought, as her family found a tight spot that afforded them a view of the parade. No, St. Patrick's was nothing like this. Men dressed in tight sequined tops and fur-lined skirts threw beads from passing floats. Women in red-and-white-striped clown outfits danced on the sides of the streets. Despite the slight chill, other women marched in skimpy outfits with fringe on short skirts. People covered from head to toe in blue or green or yellow paint smiled down from balconies, their eyes hidden behind masks both beautiful and grotesque. And everywhere, people drank, poured drinks from their cups into their neighbors' mouths or held bottles high above their heads, using their open mouths as targets. The air was perfumed with liquor and smoke and the river, with Avon Persian Wood and Old Spice.

The Duchons were more subdued than Jemma expected, and she imagined that was an aftereffect of the big party. Even Simone wasn't crowing to the sky, simply watching the passing floats and krewes with silent, greedy interest. Jemma realized it was her first time being out in public with them all, save her mother. They'd squeezed themselves into an open spot as if they'd been coming to the parade for years, their mundane scraps of conversation as normal as any other family's.

"You're on my foot."

"That's not me—that's the man in front of you, with the huge hoofers."

Whispered giggles followed, making Jemma smile. This was the closest she'd felt to her family since she'd arrived in town.

A float carrying a Black krewe, white paint around their mouths and eyes, passed by. Feathers and horns adorned their hats, grass skirts their bodies. They grinned and waved, coconut shells sailing through the air to grabbing fingers.

Honorine tutted, hands folded tightly in front of her. Jemma looked for what was coming next, only to see a lone Black woman following the float. She wore a long dark blue dress with a ragged hem, a belt slung low on her hips. She kicked her booted feet up in an offbeat dance while twirling a chain of white beads around one arm.

"Magdalene!" Jemma yelled.

Magdalene stopped at the sound of her name, looking into the crowd. At the sight of Jemma's waving, she ran over. Before Jemma could ask what in the world she was doing in the parade, her friend's gaze stopped on Honorine, whose face held unfriendly recognition.

"Why, if it isn't one of the monkey krewe members putting on a one-woman show," Jemma's grandmother said.

Magdalene laughed. "Look at you, the Great White Twat! Get yourself inside before you tan." She then turned to Jemma. "You coming with me or you staying here with these sticks-in-the-mud?"

The nasty exchange happened so quickly that Jemma didn't have time to react, so when Magdalene put a hand on her arm to steer her away, she froze. Her friend's eyebrows rose as Jemma first looked to her cousin and brother. Before she could say anything, could decide whether to go with someone she cared about or stay with the family she felt a connection with—however new and tenuous—the woman backed away, blending into a passing group of musicians before she disappeared completely.

"How dare she?" Honorine muttered.

"What?" Jemma asked, her face burning with shame as she watched the magic of the day evaporating and felt powerless to stop it. Why had she hesitated when Magdalene reached for her? "How dare *she*? Did you hear what you called her? Why would you say something like that?"

"It's all right, Jemma," Fosette started, grabbing her hand.

"No, Fosette. Not this time." Jemma shook her cousin off and backed away from the group. Matching grimaces marred Fosette's and Laurence's features, while Russell's, Simone's and Honorine's faces could have been carved from stone.

THE NEXT MORNING, Jemma stared down into her half-empty plate, passing time until she could escape and look for Magdalene. Her friend's expression just before she left Jemma standing in place at the parade had danced through her mind all night. In it was the unspoken accusation that Jemma was just like the rest of her family. But she wasn't. Surely Magdalene knew that. As she planned her next move, the scent of smoke rushed into the room.

"Is something burning?" she asked.

All conversation ceased, Simone glaring at her as if she'd just uttered a curse word at the table. Jemma looked at each of them in turn, their bland faces.

"Don't you smell that?" She stood up, dropping her napkin on her chair.

"Smell what?" Russell asked.

"The smoke." But as she looked at them, it was clear they smelled nothing unusual. She headed to the kitchen, where Inès stood at the sink, washing dishes, nearly elbow deep in suds. Jemma looked to the stove, which was off, and then back to her mother, who gazed at her with raised eyebrows. "Mama, is something cooking somewhere? I smell smoke."

Inès shook her head, returning her attention to her task, but in the brief second her mother had met her eye, Jemma sensed the lie. Her mother did smell the smoke and was pretending she didn't. She saw no point in questioning her about it, so she followed the scent to her mother's small sleeping space. She'd been in here only once before and hadn't taken in any of the details then, like the thin gingham curtain next to the bed. It was not an outside wall, so Jemma couldn't imagine what purpose the curtain served. Just as she reached out to move it aside and see what was behind it, a hand slapped her arm.

She turned to find her mother there.

"What's back here?"

Inès shook her head, pulling Jemma away, but she did it without much strength.

"Mama, I know you smell it. Ever since I came here I've smelled smoke in the air, and I think I got used to it. Maybe no one else in the family smells it anymore because they've lived here for so long. But you smell it, too, although you just act like you don't. It's gotten worse these last weeks, and it's strongest in here. Is that why you sleep in the washhouse so much now, because of the smell?"

When Inès said nothing, simply dropped her hand, Jemma leaned forward and snatched the curtain, revealing a small window, just big enough for her to fit through. She glanced back at her mother, whose blank expression revealed nothing, even as Jemma clambered over the bed. Right before she put her face up to the opening, she had an unpleasant vision of skeletal hands reaching through and pulling her inside.

And then she was staring into a black void, a burnt smell stinging her nostrils.

She strained her eyes but couldn't see anything. The next few minutes were a bustle of Jemma running back to the kitchen and rummaging through several drawers before finding a half-burnt taper candle and matches. When she entered the small sleeping room again, Inès had already moved the bed away from the wall, and Jemma scooted into the space between.

She lit the candle and thrust it through the window, the weak light exposing a plain room. It was windowless and slightly smaller than the home's kitchen. And there was nothing in it—no furniture, no forgotten detritus. Against one side wall, a shape jutted out. Years of dirt and grime had built up over a brick fireplace that hadn't been used in a long time. And yet something was burning, because the smell was thick and strong.

Jemma turned back to her mother. "Did you know about this room?"

Inès remained still for several moments, but finally gave a short nod. Before Jemma could say anything else, Honorine appeared. Jemma had the brief but horrifying thought that her grandmother would try to push her through.

"What are you doing here? You just leave the table in the middle of a meal and go wandering around—"

She cut Honorine off. "What is this place?"

"How should I know? I wasn't even aware this room existed."

"And you don't smell the smoke? It's damn near making me choke in here, and you're telling me you can't smell it?"

"That's exactly what I'm telling you. Do you want to join us at the table and finish your meal or not?"

Jemma exited the space, taking several deep breaths and still tasting the smokiness in the back of her throat. Although it was worse in the room she'd just left, it permeated the entire house.

"I don't believe that you can't smell it. Maybe you'd gotten used to it because you'd been trapped here for so long, but since you've all been able to go into the city proper, you have to smell it once you come back inside."

Honorine's pressed lips didn't bother opening with a reply. She simply followed her granddaughter back to the dining room. But Jemma had had enough. She walked through, ignoring the open stares on everyone's faces, and hurried out the back door, hoping that Magdalene was home. Even if she wasn't, Jemma vowed to lose herself in that damp wooded environment full of sweet air.

THE WAY YOU looked at me," Magdalene said. "For a quick flash, it was just like the old lady looking at me."

"I'm sorry." Again, the fear of catching the insanity—the rot that plagued her family, the very grounds on which they lived—clawed at Jemma's insides. She couldn't be like them, and yet she'd been comfortable enough with them at the parade to hesitate when Magdalene had tried to take her away.

The two walked the trails with no destination in mind, until Jemma stopped and faced the older woman.

"Am I really like them?"

Magdalene took her time answering. Jemma was disappointed that her friend didn't immediately dismiss her fears, but then again, she felt she deserved the woman's ambivalence.

"Of course you're not just like them. But sometimes nastiness can rub off. Oh, don't look like that. You'll never be as awful as your grandma, no matter how hard you try. You've been living in that house for months now, and I know how much you wanted to be part of them, even though you can't really. I see it in you, how much you want that, how much it hurts you not to have it. They're your blood, but do they treat you like family, like they love you?" Magdalene took both of Jemma's hands in hers, as if trying to minimize the sting of her words. "When I'm hard on you about family, it's only 'cause I know what it's like. I don't mean the light-skinned thing. My family all looks like me. But my mama didn't like how different I was. If everybody else was going right, I went left. I couldn't stand getting my hair straightened and wearing stockings and gloves and all that. They wanted me to be a lady and I just wanted to be . . . me. So I left my home in Laurel when I was fifteen and bounced around for a while. I worked in a white lady's house until she kicked me out when I cussed at her for talking to me worse than she talked to her dog. I worked in kitchens, washing dishes, and worked on farms, picking oranges. When I got tired of that, I tried to go home. And my mama told me she thought I'd died and as far as she was concerned, I was dead." Magdalene leaned back against a tree, her gaze far away. "When she died, I went back to see her buried, but do you know I didn't feel anything?"

After that, only birdsong, far-off howls and nearby screeching accompanied the soft crunching of grass, dirt and leaves under their bare feet.

In the late afternoon, as Jemma, muddy and tired, made her way toward the house, she looked up to find Laurence walking out the back door, a dark smudge in the center of his forehead. So they'd been to Mass for Ash Wednesday. He leaned against a column, his arms folded.

"Congratulations. You've done it again," he said.

Fatigue made it difficult for Jemma to do much more than glare at him. All she wanted was to get upstairs and clean up before dropping into bed; she was too tired to eat dinner. But her brother seemed to want something from her.

"What are you talking about?" She sighed.

"You managed to piss off Grandmère by leaving the breakfast table and then disappearing for the whole day. If there's one thing she cannot stand, it's rudeness."

"She'd be better off getting mad at people's lies. Oh, never mind. How can she get mad at that when that's all she does?"

Jemma reached for the door, but Laurence put a hand on her arm, stopping her in place. "I know they've been awful to you. And you haven't given them back nearly as much as they deserve." At her curious expression, he went on. "It would drive Tante Simone absolutely insane if you went to Europe with us."

Jemma scoffed, moving toward the door again. "You'll have to give me a better reason to go with you than getting on that bitch's nerves. Why would I want to be stuck on an airplane for hours with this family and then stuck in a hotel or on a train for even more hours? As much as I'd love to visit Europe, I'll do it on my own, now that I have the money to do it."

"Just by yourself?" His scandalized expression amused her.

"I would think that after being trapped in this house for so many years, the first thing you'd want is to escape everyone. Go off on your own, see the city, the state, the world, without your grandmother and aunt and uncle and cousin all stuck to your side."

Laurence looked down at the ground. "It makes sense when you say it, but it's not easy. It's like we have some glue holding us to each other. Fosette can hardly go into town without wanting Grandmère or her maman right there beside her. Even the few times I walked down the lane for no other reason than that I could, I felt . . . strange. Uncomfortable. I'm not used to being on my own."

"I guess you'll adjust eventually. As for me, I'm fine coming and going on my own."

"So you won't reconsider coming with us? Sure, you could go anywhere you wanted now, but would you get the same satisfaction as from seeing how much your very presence annoys someone who doesn't want you to be there?"

"Is that supposed to make me want to go? Feeling hated? I get that here." Jemma looked at the sky, nearly free of clouds, wanting to avoid looking at her brother.

When Jemma examined her feelings for her family, her emotions ranged from heated disdain (for Russell), to pity (for Fosette), to loathing (for her aunt and her grandmother). Only Inès and Laurence prompted any affection at all.

"I'm going to be leaving soon, but maybe . . . we can keep in touch."

"I'd like that." A genuine smile touched his lips, free of his usual smugness. "You better get washed up for dinner."

"I'm really tired. Can you make an excuse for me? Please?"

"After what happened at breakfast? No way our grandmother is going to accept that. Besides, I wanted to talk to you about the ledger. I'm still wondering about that missing page."

After dinner, as much as Jemma would have enjoyed a discussion with her brother, she begged off. She was barely able to keep her eyes open through the meal.

"Tomorrow," she told him at the foot of the stairs.

"Tomorrow," he echoed.

THE NEXT MORNING, Jemma woke feeling as if she rose from the dead. Glancing at the clock, she realized she'd slept right through breakfast.

Faint sounds reached her through the closed door. Voices from downstairs, some high-pitched laughter from Fosette. Yes, there had been so much more laughter lately.

Jemma climbed out of bed and opened the chifforobe. Unlike everyone else, she hadn't bought a trunkful of new clothes, but maybe today she'd go into Tremé and visit a few shops. Just as she was opening the door, a loud noise from outside froze her in place: a car horn and a long screech that assaulted her ears, even over the distance from the street and through the walls. She rushed downstairs as Fosette and Honorine came from the parlor and Simone and Russell hurried in from the dining room, followed closely by Inès. They gathered on the porch. Dennis stood in the middle of the front lawn, a pair of garden shears in one hand. When he looked back at the family standing together outside the front doors, his expression told Jemma everything.

On the other side of the wrought iron gate was a pickup truck carrying a load of cut logs. Or what should have been a load. Two dozen or more littered the road, several having rolled all the way against the fence.

That captured only cursory attention.

It was the car behind the truck that the Duchons stared at, because they recognized it.

The family car, its front connected to the truck's back end. Laurence, in the driver's seat, couldn't have been going that fast, because the hood was only slightly crumpled, not destroyed.

What killed him was the log that had shattered its way through the windshield, straight through his throat, nearly severing his head from his body.

TWENTY-SIX

"GET OUT! GET out! Get out of here, you cursed bitch!"

Jemma was sure Simone would have killed her if it hadn't been for Dennis. Everything after the car accident happened so suddenly and with such fierceness, she had trouble recalling the whole series of events. Flashes of images came to her over the following days and weeks, but in the immediate aftermath of Laurence's death, chaos colored everything.

The entire family rushed out of the gates onto the road in front of the house. The truck's driver, a white Creole, stood outside of his vehicle, too stunned to do more than gape at the ruined car that had rammed him from behind.

Laurence's blood spattered the driver's-side window of the car, obscuring the view.

Jemma was afraid that Fosette's screams would burst all their eardrums. She clapped her hands to the sides of her head while also wanting to shut out the gruesome scene in front of her, but for some reason she found that she couldn't close her eyes, could only stare at the sight. A part of her believed that if she stared long enough, it would change.

Jemma felt more united with the Duchons at that moment than she ever had.

"Call the hospital," Honorine said to no one in particular, her face a bloodless white.

Inès stepped closer to the car holding her firstborn inside.

"I . . . I don't know what happened," the truck driver stammered, kneading his battered hat between dirt-stained fingers. "He just . . . just came outta nowhere. Oh God . . . oh God . . ."

"Someone call the fucking hospital!" Honorine screamed.

"For what, Maman?" Simone yelled, grabbing at her mother's arm with one hand while pointing at Inès with the other. "He's dead! Just like Lucie and Papa and André and Lenore! All of them dead, because of this bitch!" She turned to Jemma. "And this one, still alive, still breathing! You and your mother are the curse! You're the curse! Get off this land! Get off this property! I don't ever want to see your faces again!"

Simone whirled around to Inès, grabbing her shoulders and shaking her. "This is your fault, your fault!"

Jemma broke out of her daze long enough to pull her aunt off her mother. "This isn't her fault! It's not my birthday. Do you hear me? It's not March twelfth!"

If Jemma thought that would break through Simone's violent fit, she was wrong. It seemed only to enrage her aunt more. As Fosette knelt on the dirt lane, her open mouth no longer emitting any sound, an expression of horror frozen on her face, her mother grabbed Jemma by the neck. Vaguely, Jemma was aware that her own mother had moved back to the car, had fallen across the windshield. Honorine stood as still as a statue, while the truck driver continued to babble to no one.

Dennis pulled Simone off Jemma, but it was clearly a struggle for him. Once he'd pried the woman's hands from around her niece's neck, Simone turned and backhanded him across the face.

"Don't you ever touch me again, nigger," she breathed.

Dennis's hand whipped up, but he somehow maintained enough control not to strike her back.

"I should do it," he said in a low voice, Simone eyeing his fist warily. "But I won't. 'Cause of her." He moved over to Inès.

"You disgusting cow," Jemma spit.

She thought her aunt would lunge at her again, but after moving her hair out of her face and licking the sweat from her upper lip, Simone ran back to the house, presumably to call the hospital.

Again Jemma was wrong.

After several moments, everyone's attention turned back to the open front doors of the house as Simone threw all Jemma's clothes and other belongings out onto the porch, before kicking various items down the stairs.

"Out! Out!" she screamed at random intervals.

Dennis put a hand on Jemma's arm, holding her in place. "Don't, Jemma. I'll get your things. I'll call the hospital. You just stay here."

JEMMA WAS GONE by the time the police came to talk to the truck driver and the family. She was gone by the time a doctor came out to the property, along with Father Louis and the coroner. By the time Laurence's crushed body was pulled out of the car and Fosette was heavily sedated in her bed, Jemma was in the back of a cab headed toward the bank that held her money.

It looked like she'd be leaving sooner than she planned.

Dennis had helped rush her away before Simone could get her hands on her again, before Honorine broke out of her frozen spell and decided to do her own damage, either to her or to Inès, or perhaps to both.

"Is my mother going to be all right?" Jemma had asked Dennis as he helped her into a waiting taxi down the street from the Duchon house. "How can I reach you to find out?"

"Just stay in town for a few days. Get a room in Tremé. I'll find you."

Jemma didn't even look out the back window of the cab, and she avoided meeting the driver's eyes in the rearview mirror.

"What happened back there?" the man asked, beginning to accelerate only when he could no longer clearly see the mess behind them.

"Car accident."

"Someone got killed?"

Jemma swallowed a lump in her throat. This was the first time she was able to remember that it was her brother who'd died. Now that Simone's hands weren't around her throat and Fosette's screeching wasn't in her ears, that thought came clear.

Had she thought that she'd be able to fit into that family? Yes, she had, with Inès finally acknowledging her, with the two of them no longer having to hide their relationship. And with Laurence putting forth an olive branch. Jemma wasn't naïve enough to believe she'd be close to all of them (Simone was a lost cause), but she had believed that she could cobble together a small family unit, of her, her mother and her brother.

Oh, Laurence. Jemma put her face in her hands and wept.

In the middle of her crying jag, avoiding the cabbie's gaze, which pressed against her skin like a thick hand, she had the presence of mind to remember the date. Just as she'd told Simone, it wasn't her birthday. Laurence's death was not a result of the curse. So why were they blaming her and Inès?

And yet her brother's death didn't seem all that accidental. Jemma recalled the names of the family members she'd never met, the ones who'd died over the years, most of whose deaths occurred while she grew up in Chicago, blowing out candles on one birthday cake after another.

Laurence's death had the taste of the curse on it.

Once the cabbie stopped in front of First Citizens Bank, Jemma asked him to wait for her.

"I won't be long," she said, leaning in through the open passenger-side window.

"You going in there? How?" The driver nodded toward the bank building.

She didn't answer, simply walked around the side of the building to the same entrance she and Honorine had used not long ago. Jemma knocked several times, each time banging harder and louder. Finally, the same blond woman who'd let them in before opened the door, only enough to stick her head out and demand, "What?"

"I need to come inside and withdraw my money."

The woman's green gaze moved over Jemma, taking in the new dress and shoes, the carefully pressed hair. But even the fashionable clothes must not have been enough.

"You don't have an account here."

"I do. Honorine Duchon is my grandmother. We were here just a few weeks ago, when she gave me control of my account. My name is Jemma Barker."

"Hold on."

The door banged shut in Jemma's face. She stood outside, her hair drooping under the humidity, a line of nervous sweat tickling its slow way down her spine. After fifteen minutes, the blonde ushered her inside, to the same plain office she and Honorine had occupied before. Jemma took the single chair in the otherwise empty space.

The bank president didn't meet her this time, however. Jemma had no idea who the man hovering over her was, as he didn't introduce himself, but after he spoke, she didn't care who he was.

"I'm sorry, but your account has been closed."

"What are you talking about?" Jemma rummaged in her handbag, pulled out her checkbook and opened the register. "I have over seven thousand dollars here. I only pulled out a hundred dollars the one time I was here, and I haven't been back since that day."

"Yes, well, Honorine Duchon called right before you came in. The family, although colored, have long ties to our institution, and on her authority, we closed your account."

Jemma shot up. "Where's my money?"

"As I've already told you, your account—"

The man in front of her was taller and broader, but Jemma was quicker. She snatched open the door and was heading toward the teller counter before he grabbed her and pushed her back inside the room, where, for a few minutes, she heard only her heavy breathing.

She studied his face, looking for the lie, but it wasn't there. He was telling her the truth. Honorine had called while Jemma was sitting in the back of a cab, crying over her dead brother, and had closed her account. She'd withdrawn one hundred dollars the last time she'd been here, to buy a couple of new dresses and shoes, to get her hair done for the first time in six months. Jemma was down to her last ten dollars and there was a cabdriver waiting for her outside.

"What did she do with my money?"

The man didn't answer, simply stood there with his arms folded.

"Fine," she said. "You won't let her walk through the front door, but you'll keep her money here and let her get on the phone and take my money, money that I earned. Fine. Let me out of here."

"You go straight out the way you came in, girl."

Jemma had no intention of doing it, but when he gripped her arm so tightly that she cried out in pain, she had no choice but to be directed by him to the side door, where he shoved her outside.

She looked for the cab and was relieved to see it parked at the curb a block up instead of right by the door. Hoping that the driver wasn't looking in his rearview mirror, Jemma crept along the side of the building, away from the taxi and the fare she couldn't pay (not if she had to find a place to eat or sleep today), and began running once she turned the corner.

She had to stop and ask for directions a couple of times, but Jemma eventually made her way to Tremé. Dennis had gathered her belongings from the Duchons' lawn and stuffed everything he found inside her suitcase, but it was in the trunk of the taxi she'd run from. All Jemma had were the clothes and shoes she was wearing, and her purse.

She was in even worse shape than when she'd gotten off the train last September.

Dennis had told her to get a room somewhere and that he'd find her. After walking for nearly an hour, she found a two-story row house with a sign in the window inviting female boarders. It cost seven dollars a night. The woman who rented the rooms eyed Jemma suspiciously when she came out of her own ground-floor apartment.

"You ain't got no luggage?" she asked Jemma, and blew a thick stream of cigarette smoke out one side of her mouth. "I don't run no fancy place here, girl. Ain't no men allowed."

"My luggage was stolen. I just need to stay the one night. Here, I can pay you in advance."

When she handed over two fives, the woman snatched the bills and stuck them in the top of her bra, which peeked above the lapel of a threadbare robe. She pulled three damp singles out of the same place and pressed them into Jemma's hand.

"Second door on the left up them stairs. The washroom's at the end of the hall."

"You serve meals?"

The woman looked at Jemma like she was crazy. "Where you think you at, the Ritz? You can go right round the corner to Mama Belle's or Sisters. If you just staying the night, be outta here by eleven tomorrow morning." Giving Jemma one last look, she retreated into her apartment and shut the door.

Jemma found her room, which was a far cry from her space at the Duchons'. A twin bed with a metal headboard and footboard sat in front of a narrow window too covered in dust to see outside. The bedcovers not only looked dirty but also held a musty odor that made her gag. Instead of sitting on it, she took a seat in a rattan chair in the corner, kicking off her shoes. Through the closed door and what had to be paper-thin walls, the sounds of the other boarders began to stream in as the day wore on. Loud chatter from a group of women getting off their shifts at a nearby restaurant mixed with barks of laughter and the slamming of doors. For a while, the washroom door opened and closed with regularity, the noise of the flushing toilet and running water constant.

Jemma peeled off her dress and stockings, laying them over the back of the chair. She pulled back the bedcovers only to find the bedsheets in even worse shape, so she lay on top of the blanket, her hands crossed over her stomach, which heaved with sobs until it hurt. Hunger probably made it worse, but she had no appetite.

She'd spent the long day seeing Laurence's face from the previous night, his gentle smile as he told her he'd like for them to stay in touch.

But she couldn't keep that picture in her mind.

Instead, images of the crumpled car, the blood-splattered window and Inès prostrate across the hood all took their turns dancing behind her closed eyelids. Fosette keening on the ground, the pure hatred in Simone's eyes, and through it all, Honorine standing like a sentinel taking it all in.

It's not my birthday, Jemma had screamed at her family.

It's not over, Russell had cried.

Russell was right. This wasn't over. Whatever had tied the death curse to her birthday seemed to be unleashed. And if that was the case, any of the remaining Duchons—including herself—could die at any moment.

As Jemma wondered how Dennis would find her, someone knocked on her door.

"You Jemma in there? It's a man out front looking for you. Name's Dennis."

Jemma wiped her face. "I'm coming," she called, her voice thick and unsteady. She dressed quickly and rushed downstairs, her purse in hand. Dennis waited on the front porch, the single light bulb providing a harsh glare and drawing bugs at the same time.

"What you doing here? I thought you were gonna get a place at one of the hotels."

"Honorine closed my account at the bank and took all my money. This is all I could afford."

"Shit."

"How's my mother?"

"Just like you think she is. Blaming herself. I almost didn't come out 'cause I don't know what she might do, so I got to be quick. You need to come on now."

"You know I can't go back to that house. I can't even be on the grounds. They'll kill me."

Dennis shook his head, his mouth set. "Ain't no way you're going back there. Not if you're coming with us."

"What?"

"Your mama and me are going. I don't know where yet, but she's set on leaving. She wants you to come with us."

The words enveloped Jemma like a soothing balm. Her mother wanted her. She wanted Jemma with her. Although Laurence was gone, they could still be a family: Inès, Emmaline and Dennis. She began to imagine their new home. Would it be in the city or closer to the country?

I curse all the Duchon blood. From this day forth, I bind the family to this house. I bind them forever.

The future Jemma envisioned with her mother began to unravel, the curse working its hooked fingers right through the pretty picture, tearing it in two.

"I can't go, not now. The curse isn't broken, not all of it. I don't think it's tied to my birthday anymore, but I don't know. All I do know is that if I don't break the curse, someone else is going to die. It could be me next. It might even be my mother."

"You sure about that?"

Jemma nodded. "Just get me to Magdalene's. After that, I'll figure out something."

He looked up then, at the bugs battering themselves against the light bulb, the old cobwebs in the corners. "We're leaving tonight."

As difficult as it was to accept, Jemma understood. She didn't blame Inès for wanting to flee, to finally escape all of the abuse and the pain.

"Then let me say goodbye."

TWENTY-SEVEN

I'M SORRY ABOUT your brother, Emmaline," Magdalene said when Jemma entered the cabin. Her friend stood in the corner, cradling an earthenware mug between her hands.

Inès sat at the table, her face blank.

"She still ain't cried," Dennis whispered.

"Mama." Jemma knelt on the floor next to her mother, putting her head in Inès's lap. "I'm sorry. Please don't blame yourself. But I can't go with you. The curse . . . something's still wrong."

Inès didn't react in any way at first, but after several moments, she placed a hand on Jemma's head, reaching through the thick hair to her scalp. She caressed her daughter's skin for a brief moment before gently moving Jemma aside. Inès stood up and pulled Jemma to her feet, embracing her tightly. Jemma cried and shook, but her mother remained still in their hold. At last, Inès stepped back, touching Jemma's face one more time before signaling to Dennis.

He grabbed two satchels from the floor.

"You don't have any idea where you're going?" Jemma asked, the scene blurred before her. She wiped her face, but the tears wouldn't stop.

"She wants to go west."

Dennis and Magdalene shared a tense farewell before he hugged Jemma and moved to the door. Inès pulled an envelope out of her pocket, handing it to Jemma and gesturing to Dennis.

"She knew you were going to stay," he said.

Inès gave her daughter a kiss on the lips and then she and Dennis were gone.

Jemma didn't know how long she sat at the table, staring at her mother's neat cursive on the front of the envelope before ripping it open.

"Emmaline, I'm going to step outside for a spell," Magdalene said, sensing Jemma's desire for privacy. Candlelight glinted off the gun tucked in her belt before she disappeared out the door.

Her mother's slanted, cramped handwriting filled five full pages of onionskin paper.

Dear Emmaline, my only daughter, my last living child,

I am sorry for everything I did that has put you in danger. Losing Laurence showed me how much my actions have cost you and me.

Maybe this will help you understand me a little more, even if you can't forgive right now.

Your father's name was Ismael Richards. You and Laurence had different fathers, and his was married, which was one reason we couldn't be together. Also, he was dark-skinned, and as you know, our family would never have accepted him. My being in trouble was a big scandal. My parents were so embarrassed that they tried to keep me home, not wanting anyone to see my condition. I snuck away when I could to see him, but once his wife found out, he cut things off between us. When Laurence was born, the only reason I was allowed to keep him was because he was born with blue eyes. His skin only darkened a little, but those were days when I held my breath, afraid that he'd turn dark overnight and I'd be forced to give him up.

Then I met Ismael. I knew the family wouldn't accept him, either, because of his color, but I loved him and he loved me. He wanted to marry me even though I already had a child. I wouldn't ever let him come to the house because the family would have been awful to him. But he was so persistent. When I got pregnant with you, he said he was going to marry me no matter what my parents said.

He told me he was coming to talk to my father, your grandfather, Raymond. I was too afraid to tell my parents beforehand. All that morning, I worried myself sick, and I think that's why you came early.

Magdalene came to midwife. I didn't know that while you were being born my father was murdering your father downstairs. Maman told me they'd sent Ismael away, that he wasn't ever coming back for me.

Then Maman was looking at you, not even two minutes old, still connected to me, and saying that you were too dark, that you took after your father, that you were a curse. A curse, she said!

She told Magdalene to take you away before they killed you. And when I looked into Magdalene's eyes, I knew she wanted to take you with her, to raise you as her own, to replace the baby she'd lost. But I made her promise to send you far away from this place so that I'd know you were safe.

I thought I was losing my mind. I cursed our family, not thinking about the consequences. I was so angry that I never thought about what could happen to Laurence or me. And so I thought you were safe, until you showed up on our doorstep, looking so much like your father that I wanted to grab you and hug you to me, but I couldn't let you know who I was.

Of course, you figured some of it out, but I'll have to tell you the rest.

From the time I was a little girl, I could see the spirits that cling to this house. They are many. Maman once told me I could see them because I was born during a big storm, in the fall of 1915.

Some of the ghosts around the house died from illnesses people had back then, the type of sickness that won't kill us today. Others died bad. Those are the ones that used to scare me. I tried to avoid them, but once they knew I saw them and heard them, they wouldn't leave me alone.

And it was the spirits of the slaves that were the most insistent.

Finally, one day I was too tired of fighting, and I listened. They were trapped in the house and they wanted to be free. They came to me for help, but I didn't know what to do. After a while, I got sick of hearing free, free,

free. That's all they could say. I tried to stop listening and I pretended I couldn't see them anymore. They went quiet after that.

But when you were born, as I lay there half-crazed with pain and grief, thinking of what I could possibly do to take revenge on our family, one of those spirits visited me. I opened myself to it, although I didn't know what it wanted. It was only afterward I realized that in exchange for me being able to trap our family here, the spirit had used me as a portal to act on a curse it had wanted to settle on us for decades.

The power to kill.

Our curses intertwined and went up together, and then settled over all of us in the house. That's why one of us dies every seven years.

When you came, I could see the ghosts again. I could hear them whispering. And I knew that you being here had something to do with them and maybe with me. I tried not to think about it because I was afraid of what it might mean. I hoped that things would just go back to how they had been. Because I didn't want to see them.

When you found the room beside my little room, I'd made myself forget it even existed. I'd only seen the window once, when I first began sleeping in that space, back when the family told everyone I was dead and began calling me Agnes. When they made Laurence believe Simone was his mother instead of me. I shut the spirits out again, but I felt their presence in that room. That burning smell never leaves. Every night I slept in that bed, I went to sleep with the scent of smoke in my nostrils, but

I made myself ignore it. I made myself not see and hear so many things.

Something bad happened there, and I think whatever it is, it's why that spirit wants us to die.

Maybe I should have written this letter a long time ago. If so, it's another mistake I made. And while I've made many mistakes in my life, having Laurence and you were not mistakes. Your skin, your hair, your nose are not mistakes. You were created in love, Emmaline. You will always be my beautiful child.

Please forgive me for what I did and what I cannot undo. Forgive me for my cowardice and anger, for cursing without considering the consequences. Maybe if I leave, if I'm gone from that house, you'll be able to soothe the spirits. You'll be able to help them where I failed. For your sake, if not for anyone else's.

Your mother,
Inès

WHEN MAGDALENE ENTERED the cabin hours later, a rabbit carcass dangling from one hand, she found Jemma rereading her mother's letter for the seventh time, tears streaming down her face. The older woman dropped the rabbit on the floor and hugged Jemma where she sat, the younger woman's face pressed against Magdalene's belly. Neither of them spoke until Jemma's sobs eased.

"I should have gone with them. Now I don't know where they are. I might not even be able to break the curse. Why did I stay here? Why didn't she wait?"

Jemma felt Magdalene's warm hand on her shoulder as the

woman knelt beside her chair and grasped the hand in her lap. "Child, think about this. Your mama lost a son yesterday. I know you lost a brother, but trust me—there's no pain worse in this world than losing a child. I know how she feels. Even if the family accepted her back, could she live in that house where he spent his whole life? Could she stand to walk past his room, see his pictures around the place? That boy's smell is still lingering in his bed, in places he sat. No, she couldn't bear it. On top of everything else she went through, yes, even the things she caused, that had to be too much. And I don't know anything about curses or breaking curses or even how Inès's curse worked. I don't even know if you can break it. All I know is, the guilt she carries is too much for her to bear. Her family hates her just as much as she hates them. She was stuck in that house for almost twenty-eight years with the people who murdered your father and cut out her tongue, who told everyone that she was dead. The same people who sent you away because you were too dark for them. The people who made her wait on them hand and foot. But she wanted you to go with her. You hear me? She wanted you."

Jemma knew the woman was talking sense, and yet she couldn't push aside the feeling that she was alone again.

Several days later, Jemma and Magdalene watched as the Duchons put Laurence to rest in the family vault. Father Louis led the somber procession. Neither of them recognized the six pallbearers, however, or the other mourners. Judging by the number of people who attended, it seemed that in the short time the Duchons had been free to mingle with their neighbors and old friends and acquaintances, the family—and probably Laurence most of all—had made quite the impression.

The two women watched from the trees. Even from a distance, Fosette was unmistakable, her bent form shaking throughout, a heavy veil draped all the way to her chest. Jemma scanned the crowd, sure that Inès had to be there. What better time to come back around, when a hat and veil could disguise her? And yet Jemma didn't spot her mother anywhere. She would have recognized the way the woman walked, and seeing no one with that particular gait, she knew Inès was gone for good.

Magdalene and Jemma walked over after midnight, glad for the dark of the new moon. They laid a bouquet of flowers at the door of the vault, Jemma pressing her hands against it and whispering a short prayer and an apology.

The next morning, she realized it was March fourth. In a little over a week, she'd turn twenty-eight. And because the curse on the Duchons wasn't broken, the one the spirit had intertwined with Inès's own, someone in the family would die.

She pulled her mother's letter out of the pocket of her dress, the same dress she'd been wearing for days.

I felt their presence in that room. That burning smell never leaves. Every night I slept in that bed, I went to sleep with the scent of smoke in my nostrils.

Something bad happened there, and I think whatever it is, it's why that spirit wants us to die.

If Jemma was going to help the spirits and save someone in the family from dying—possibly herself—she'd have to go back to the house. She'd have to revisit that dark and haunted space.

She'd have to face the ghosts again.

THE MISSING LEDGER page consumed much of Jemma's thoughts. She welcomed the distraction, because thinking about her mother and her brother only kept the wounds open. Laurence must have found something if he wanted to discuss the ledger with her the day before he died. The translation work he had done could still be in the house. She wanted it (perhaps only to have something of his), which was another reason she'd have to risk going back there.

If the family caught her, they might kill her. Maybe not Fosette, who was probably holding on to her remaining sanity by a shred, but Simone could very well try to finish what she'd started the day Laurence died.

But now that the family was free to come and go as they pleased, they'd be out for Mass on Sunday, two days from now. She didn't know how they might get there, since they didn't have a car anymore. But she knew they'd go.

Early on Sunday morning, Jemma took a wide path around to the front of the property and across the road, down about fifty yards. From her place in a thick wooded grove, she watched as a town car arrived outside the gates and the remaining Duchons—Fosette, Simone, Honorine and Russell—filed inside. As the car moved past her, Jemma sank back behind a tree, although she knew she was already well hidden.

She moved swiftly through the gates and to the back of the house, to the kitchen door, which was always unlocked. Once inside, she listened closely for any sounds, although she couldn't imagine who would be in the house if the four family members were now gone. She passed by her mother's small sleeping room, exactly how it had been the last time she'd seen it, the little pillow at one end and the patchwork quilt spread across neat and flat. Jemma ran her hand over the textured surface before hurrying upstairs.

Entering Laurence's bedroom brought about a sharp ache. His musky cologne hung in the air as if he'd just walked out. She fully expected to turn around and see him leaning casually against the doorjamb, a small smirk on his face.

No, Jemma. He's gone.

She rummaged through drawers and his armoire, finding nothing out of the ordinary, including the translation notes he'd taken. Jemma swiped one of his handkerchiefs, bringing it to her nose and inhaling deeply before stuffing it into her front pocket.

Entering the bedroom where she'd slept for several months, she found it completely devoid of any hint of her. Of course Simone had made sure of that, tossing all of Jemma's belongings outside. Jemma poked around, sure that her aunt had missed something. But it appeared she hadn't. The chifforobe was empty; the desk drawers were clean. Even the bed was stripped.

She left the room and looked down the hallway, at the doors leading to other bedrooms. Maybe someone had found the notes and kept them somewhere. Jemma entered Simone's room and headed straight for the white wooden desk in the corner. She rummaged through its drawers, finding pictures of a little girl who could have been Fosette or perhaps Lucie. There were also pictures of a younger Simone and a man who must have been her late husband. There was a stack of letters tied with a pink ribbon that Jemma didn't have time to look through.

Jemma riffled through Simone's armoire and nightstand and looked under the bed. Nothing.

She went through Russell's and Honorine's rooms next, checking her watch. Mass would be about half over and she hadn't found what she came for. But there was plenty of time, considering that they had to drive from Orleans Parish. Doubting she'd find anything in Fosette's room but determined not to leave until she either found the notes or was certain that they were gone, Jemma entered her cousin's bedroom, done in sickening sweet tones of pale pink and cream, French baroque to the extreme.

Just as she had in the other rooms, she started with the desk before moving to the armoire. It was packed full with new dresses, the smell of unworn fabrics mixing with her cousin's favorite floral perfume. She rummaged through the nightstand. Nothing. A locked trunk sat at the foot of the bed.

"Dammit," Jemma breathed.

On her way out the door, intending to visit the library next, she looked back. She'd found something interesting in her grandmother's dresser drawers months ago. Surely Fosette had something worth hiding if she'd locked the trunk. Jemma swiped a hairpin off the nightstand and stuck one end into the lock, jiggling it back and forth until it clicked.

As soon as Jemma opened the lid, an old, musty scent with a hint of something dark under it wafted out. Right on top was a white crocheted blanket. It wasn't folded neatly, but seemed to have been hastily folded and laid flat. Jemma lifted it carefully, wanting to leave it exactly as it had been when she replaced it, but what she saw beneath the blanket caused her to fall back, dropping the blanket in an untidy heap.

At first, she thought it was a doll—although she couldn't imagine who would have paid for such a hideous toy.

As it dawned on Jemma that she was actually looking at a mummified infant, she bit down on her bottom lip to keep from fainting. She couldn't pass out here, for the family to find her.

The child's papery eyelids weren't fully closed. Jemma had a vision of the narrow slits of blackness suddenly opening to reveal bottomless holes.

She remembered all the times she'd heard Fosette humming a lullaby behind closed doors. How puzzled she'd been—but she'd never imagined this. This had to be Fosette's baby, Fosette and Laurence's. A child who had maybe lived a few hours, but more likely was stillborn. A baby in a dress with an ornate lacy collar and cuffs, the hem tucked in under tiny feet. It had probably been white at one time, but the years and the environment had tarnished it, its sallowness hinting at its age. Her cousin had kept this body here all this time instead of burying it and putting it to rest.

No wonder this house was so haunted.

Simone's words from months ago rose in Jemma's mind: *She was fixed but good, you know.*

The family must have made sure Fosette would have no more children.

Jemma fumbled to put the blanket right. She averted her gaze as she placed it back on top of the mummified child, then slammed the lid shut and lurched out of the room. Before heading downstairs, she worked to steady herself. The last thing she needed was to tumble down the steps and break her neck.

How she managed to make it to the library with the presence of mind to look for notes escaped her. She steadied herself with one hand on a shelf.

Thunk.

The gray ledger.

Jemma snatched it up and fled.

TWENTY-EIGHT

JEMMA LEFT THE house the same way she'd entered, and she ran across the back lawn as if someone was after her, although she knew she had at least half an hour before the Duchons would return from the city. She didn't expect them to visit anyone, as they were still in mourning. She ran straight to the cabin and went into a nearly incoherent ramble about what she'd found in Fosette's trunk.

"Maybe the baby was stillborn. But that family? Who knows? Maybe they killed it. They're insane, all of them, from Honorine all the way down to—" Jemma stopped then, her hands pressed to her chest. "Oh God, what if I'm just as crazy as they all are, just by being related to them? Craziness runs in families. Even if I'm not as far gone as Fosette, I might only have weeks or months before I lose my mind."

She fell heavily into the chair across from Magdalene, wanting, needing, her friend to reassure her, to say anything that would soothe her jitters.

Jemma turned her wrist up, seeing the old jagged scar. Had she really wanted to die at some point not that long ago? She couldn't even fathom her state of mind then. And over Marvin?

Now she wanted to live, desperately. Even though she was penniless and despised by her natural family, even though she'd left everything familiar behind to come here, she wanted to live.

She'd found her real mother. She'd found a friend in Magdalene.

And she was loved by them.

That was enough.

She settled, working to calm her breathing like Mabel Barker had taught her.

Five, four, three, two, one.

"That's good, girl," Magdalene said, reaching forward and grabbing Jemma's hands. "Calm those nerves. We're going to figure this out."

"I don't have much time, if any. And I'll have to go back to the house eventually. I know my work there isn't finished."

"That's not a problem. Whatever you got to face, you ain't going to face alone. But stop that worrying, because it ain't helping."

The two women spent the next day trying to formulate a plan, Jemma grateful for Magdalene's steadying presence.

"You said your mother forgave her family, and you forgave them, too. But now you're not sure if Inès really forgave them."

"Like you said, it would have to be really hard for her."

"Did you ever think that that forgiveness might not be enough? I mean, say you forgave them but you still got some anger in your heart toward someone else. That might be blocking things."

They'd just returned from a walk through the woods. The unseasonable heat and humidity hadn't bothered Magdalene. She was used to it. But Jemma had had enough after an hour. Despite the thick tree canopy and the shade, the bugs bit and stung so much that she couldn't take it anymore. Now she sat on Magdalene's mattress, rubbing a salve over her bare arms and legs while the older woman poked at the branches in the woodstove, tossing in a few sheets of old newspaper.

"Anger toward who?" Jemma asked, her hand paused in the middle of rubbing.

"When you came here, you were mad at that boyfriend of yours, right? For getting that other girl pregnant."

"Yes."

"Weren't you also mad at your daddy? The man who raised you up there in Chicago? Because he never accepted you for who you are?"

"I never really thought about it like that."

"Think about it now, then. All your life, he made you feel like you weren't good enough. Not 'cause of your color. He wasn't like the Duchons. But he wanted a boy and he never got a boy, and he made you suffer 'cause of it."

Jemma set the tin of salve on the floor, her head hanging between her knees. "I don't think this has anything to do with what's going on now, with saving my life."

"Trust me, Emmaline. Everything got to do with everything else. Like they say, no man is an island. And I don't believe in coincidences. Tell me about your daddy, the one who raised you."

It took Jemma a moment to realize how much she'd avoided her true feelings for Carl Barker since arriving here. That wasn't surprising, considering how intoxicated by the Duchons she'd been from the moment she'd met them.

Jemma shrugged, hugging her knees to her chest, keeping her gaze on the cabin floor instead of meeting Magdalene's eyes. "He was a typical daddy, I guess. He only spanked me a couple times that I remember. Mama gave me a few more whippings, but they mostly tried to talk to me first if I did anything wrong. I didn't get in a lot of trouble, though. I was a good kid. But he worked a lot. Sometimes he did double shifts, and then I had to be quiet when I came in from school. It's not hard to be quiet when you're the only child in a house, though."

"What kind of things would he get mad at you about?"

Jemma almost said *I don't remember,* but then she did remember. The memory bloomed like a strange rose.

Daddy had once gotten tickets to an American Giants game, one of the Negro league teams, when she was about eleven years old, right before Jackie Robinson broke the color barrier by playing for the Dodgers. Jemma recalled trailing behind Daddy, a small carton of popcorn in her hand, a baseball cap sitting crookedly atop two stiff pigtails. Mama had insisted that Jemma wear a dress, its clean red plaid pattern a bright contrast to the pristine white collar. But Jemma had had a fit about wearing the Mary Janes Mama had wanted her to wear. The girl had said she wouldn't go anywhere unless she got to wear her peppermint-striped Keds, her "play shoes." Mama had thrown her hands up, complaining about how tomboyish and inappropriate Jemma's outfit was: the baseball cap and old sneakers juxtaposed with the ribboned pigtails and the neat dress.

But Jemma didn't care. She was just happy to have Daddy on her own for a while, even if she didn't know anything about baseball.

So while Daddy tried to interest her in the rules and the players, including one from the opposing team, the Monarchs—"That's Satchel Paige out there, greatest pitcher there ever was; forget about McAfee and them"—Jemma concentrated on her popcorn and adjusting her cap and the boys chasing one another under the bleachers.

A sudden chill next to her made her turn, to find an old man staring back at her while she stared through him.

Jemma's high scream wasn't the worst of it, nor was it her spilling all of her popcorn, fluffy pieces turning black with dust as they hit the ground beneath the bleachers.

It was the warm pee running down her legs as she stood, soaking her white socks and her shoes.

It was having to walk over twenty blocks feeling and smelling the wetness, all while Daddy said nothing, simply held on to her shoulder with stiff fingers that felt like they reached inside her to the bone.

It was hearing the argument later that night, Daddy yelling that Jemma was nothing but trouble, as all girls were.

Mama hadn't been a refuge, either, beaten down as she was by Daddy. So Mama had failed to help Jemma quiet the ghosts that followed the girl and tried to catch her attention, drawn to her child-light like bugs to a bulb.

Both her parents were so busy trying to get her to pretend she didn't see what she clearly saw.

"Turn your face away. Shut your eyes," Mama said. "Ignore them and they'll go away."

"But what if they need—"

"Shut your eyes, Jemma! And don't talk to them! Do you hear me?"

And Daddy: "Knew we never shoulda brought this girl up from there. It ain't nothin' but ghosts down there."

No wonder she was a bundle of nerves by the time she started junior high. Eventually the spirits that clung around the stoop of their third-story walk-up stopped trying to talk to Jemma. The lone little boy, pitiful in his smallness, who wandered the playground across the street no longer waved to her as she passed. Instead, he pressed his back against the fence, his eyes following her down the sidewalk, his arms wrapped around his bent knees. Jemma ignored all of them, just like Mama had taught her. She'd begun to count anytime the anxious feelings started climbing higher and higher into her throat, thickening and spreading, turning her voice into stuttering, breathy hiccups.

Five, four, three, two, one, over and over until she stilled.

Mama was hit by a bus downtown when Jemma was a teenager. One witness said someone pushed Mama into the street, while another one said Mama ran out there on her own, having waited on the corner until the bus was barreling down at forty miles an hour. Either way—whether she did it herself or not—she was gone, and it was just Jemma and Daddy.

Jemma, who still wasn't good enough. And who now had not even the paper-thin barrier of Mama to stand between her and Daddy's discontent.

Once she was eighteen, she moved out, thinking that it would be an escape from all the negativity, the disappointment thick in the air of their apartment. She and Betty lived together for a year, until Betty met some man and moved in with him. Another girl lived with Jemma until Jemma moved in with Marvin. Too ashamed to bring Marvin by to meet Daddy, Jemma told herself she'd do it once she had a ring on her finger. But one year turned into two, and two into three, and no ring.

When Daddy died, Jemma scraped together all her savings to give him a funeral that she hoped proved how much she loved him. It didn't matter that he was dead and wasn't there to see it. She saw.

And yet, although he was gone, she knew it still wasn't good enough to make up for who she was. His displeasure with her had never been just about Jemma's being a girl instead of a boy.

It had been about Jemma not being his own natural child. And he took that out on Mabel and Jemma in big ways and small, breaking his wife underneath it and stripping away any good feelings Jemma had about herself until she was like a defenseless pup, missing any armor in the form of love for herself.

Damn him. Damn him!

She hadn't realized she'd cursed him aloud until she saw Magdalene nodding. "That's right, Emmaline. Get it out. Get it all out. Now, how can you forgive all the Duchons did when you can't forgive your daddy for dying? What about Marvin? You forgive him for what he did? Cry, yell, scream, tear shit up if it makes you feel better, but get these feelings outta you."

And that's what Jemma did for the next half hour. She cried until her stomach ached and her eyes stung from all the tears. She screamed until she was sure she'd ruined her voice for good. She stumbled outside and beat at the trees, kicked up so much dirt that it rained down on her head.

"Be free of him," Magdalene called from the open doorway. "Be free of all of them."

Only when Jemma was sure she'd fall to the ground and pass out unconscious did she finally stop. Dirt covered her from head to toe, wound its gritty way around her lips until she spit out as much as she could. Her dress was a soiled wreck, and aches from various parts of her body made themselves known.

Magdalene helped her inside after Jemma splashed well water over herself, which caused her to drip dirty spots all over the cabin floor. The older woman dismissed the spots with a wave and pressed into Jemma's hands a mug of tepid pine needle tea, a drink she normally would've politely refused, but the liquid soothed her scratched throat.

"Thank you."

"You feel better now, don't you?"

After Jemma drained the mug and set it firmly on the table, she nodded, looking up at her friend from her seat. "It's your turn now."

"What you mean?"

"It's your turn to forgive."

Magdalene scoffed, pushing one braid behind her shoulder to join the other one. "I done forgave everybody who needed forgiving."

"Did you? What about your baby girl? You're still mad at her for leaving."

The older woman shook her head quickly, her lips set in a hard line. "Nuh-uh. Don't do this. You ain't got the right."

Jemma ignored that. "How can you not forgive a child who died? That wasn't her fault, Magdalene! Don't you think that baby would have lived if she could? And be honest. You never forgave my mother for not letting you keep me. Or Dennis for making sure you gave me up. So, you want to talk forgiveness? Then let's talk all of it."

Magdalene rushed toward the door, two large steps getting her there, but Jemma leaped up and grabbed her from behind, pressing herself against the woman and holding her in place. In her arms, her friend was a docile creature, not the gun-toting wild woman who lived in the woods but a timid thing stiff with pain.

"Now you let it out. Tell that baby you forgive her and let her rest in peace. Forgive my mother and Dennis for not giving you what you wanted at the time, but remember, I could never have replaced your daughter. If I'd stayed with you and you raised me, there would have come a time when you resented me for not being her. And I wouldn't have been any better off than I was with the Barkers."

Not until a hot tear splashed on Jemma's arm did she realize that Magdalene was crying.

"I could've been a good mother to you."

"Yes, you could have, but this life wanted something different for the both of us. You gotta let that baby go." The image of the corpse in Fosette's trunk flashed through Jemma's mind. How hard some women clung to their children. "You've been holding on to that anger all these years because that's what keeps her close, you think. But how can she be peaceful when you got your hands around her ankles, not letting her fly free?"

Magdalene shook. Jemma pressed her face into the back of her neck, supporting her, breathing in the tangled scents of earth and pine and tobacco and sweat and root soap.

"She's the only thing I got."

"And she'll always be yours—but let her live in your heart. Just say you forgive her. Let her go."

Finally, after several silent moments, Magdalene inhaled deeply and screamed it out, along with decades of pain. And the two women held and supported each other until Magdalene wiped her face and said, "Now we're going to figure out how to keep you alive."

TWENTY-NINE

LAURENCE HAD STUFFED his notes in the gray ledger. While the book contained information on who lived and worked on the family's plantation, dating back to the 1840s, it also contained drawings and blueprints of the house and other buildings on the property. The author, Corentin Duchon, had also included random musings that read like diary entries.

Apparently there had once been a blacksmith shop located across from the chapel, but it had been torn down in 1858, although there was no mention of why this had been done.

Just as in the family Bible, there were lists of names of people who had been enslaved on the planation. Jemma recognized Adam and Jane among them. She found bills of sale, her heart growing heavy when the names of children were listed, sold alone or with other people who were likely too old to be their parents.

As Jemma read over Laurence's notes, she realized he'd told her nearly everything in them. But there seemed to be something new on one scrap of paper with almost illegible scribbling on it, as if her brother had been in a hurry writing it.

Who died in the fire?

A tiny ache arose as Jemma remembered Laurence telling her about some of his translation work: *At some point there was a fire here that burned the old kitchen.*

According to his last note, it seemed someone had died in that fire.

Jemma studied the blueprints, looking for the small room next to her mother's old sleeping room. At first, there seemed to be nothing. It took her a while to realize that the home that stood today wasn't all the original Duchon home. And while the earliest Duchons had been white, ownership of the house had eventually been transferred to a free Black man: Corentin Duchon. And like his white forebears, Corentin had kept slaves, all of them with the surname Duchon, so it was sometimes difficult to tell who had been enslaved and who had been free.

She returned to Laurence's notes, remembering an odd diary entry that listed the approximate birth dates (or sometimes just ages) of the family's human chattel as well as the dates of their deaths, and the death date was the same for several people: June 14, 1864.

As Jemma sat hunched over on Magdalene's mattress, she ran a finger down that list, the same date next to names like Adam, Jane, Ruth, Marie, Tomas, Thérèse and Suzette. Something must have happened, but what?

Who died in the fire?

Could this be what had happened?

She riffled through more notes.

One translated entry dated December 10, 1860, read:

Arthur's suspicions about an uprising proved correct. It was imperative that I make an example out of one of them to deter any of the slaves from similar leanings in the future. There will be no repeat of German Coast. Arthur suggested that I choose Adam. However, after much thought, I decided on Suzette. What better way to frighten them into submission than to punish a supposed innocent? Had I chosen Adam, I am afraid they would have looked upon him as a martyr. Therefore, it was Suzette who received twenty lashes on the front lawn, as the rest of them stood in a line and watched. With every lash, I hurt like she hurt, but I hoped it would show Élisabeth that I put no slave woman before her, as she has so often accused me of. I warned them that the next one of them to breathe a word about escape or revolt would be lucky to die like John Brown. Hanging is a simple way to die and often quick. Anyone attempting escape or insurrection does not deserve such an easy death.

Another, dated January 18, 1861, read:

I have had another, rather frank, discussion with Arthur about the treatment of the slaves. I feel he resents me, as I am a freeman and he is just one step up from the white trash of his branch of the family. I have caught him looking at me as if he would love to see me in chains myself instead of living in this house with my wife and children. There is little difference in the color of our skin, but there is much difference in ownership when it comes to property. He forgets that if it were not for me, he would be eking out a meager existence in the boggiest part of the swamps. I have allowed him to live here with his own family because he is a distant cousin. I believe that he wishes the branches of our particular family tree had gone another way from our great-grandfather, his in an even less crooked line than my own.

"You find anything interesting?"

At Magdalene's question, Jemma jerked to attention to find her friend standing in front of the woodstove, smoke encircling her head. The door and all the windows were open wide to prevent the cabin from getting even hotter.

"When did you get back?" she asked, pressing a hand to her chest, her heartbeat quick beneath her palm.

"Just now. You were really into something there."

Jemma stood and leaned her butt against the table, her arms folded. "I can't believe I'm related to someone who used to own slaves."

"Every family got skeletons. Besides, a lot of us in this country got white somewhere in our line, like it or not, so we gonna have ancestors who used to own slaves."

"But most of those ancestors weren't Black. That makes it worse somehow, owning your own people."

Magdalene nodded, handing Jemma a small knife and three carrots. "Because of how things were back then, the family might have felt like they had no choice."

Jemma paused chopping carrots. "What do you mean?"

"Girl, you know some people thought it was better to pass and pretend than face a life that was going to be hard. Sure, there was plenty of us who were light enough to pass who didn't, but we got no idea how many of us left the rest of us behind just so they could slip into that world where nobody was calling them 'nigger' and beating them just for being Black. Then you got the slave masters dividing us up and putting names on the ones that looked more like them. Quadroons, a quarter black. Octoroons, one-eighth. Mulatto, half. Or griffe, more Black than white. They wanted an easier life. I ain't say 'better.' I said 'easier.' "

"That's some cowardly shit."

"Hey, I ain't talking about them like I admire them. I'm just saying that's how things was. For some people, like your family, that's how things still are. Think about how much pain somebody got to be in when every time they look in the mirror they hate what they are?"

Jemma had never considered that before.

"You saying I should feel sorry for them?"

Magdalene scoffed. "No. Not if you don't want to. They did a lot of terrible things to you and your mama because of how much they hate themselves, and I doubt they want your sympathy."

"Good, because I don't have any left to give. Forgiving is one thing, but letting people continue to shit on you after they've done it before is something else."

LATER THAT NIGHT, as Magdalene's soft snores indicated the woman's deep slumber, Jemma lay awake, her eyes open to the darkness. Not until she'd moved down here had she discovered just how dark night was. Even in her bedroom at the Duchons', the dark—once the house quieted for the night, when everyone had retired to their own room—had seemed so much more absolute than in Chicago, where streetlights and even the faint light from other apartments and the hallway outside her door had always seeped in. Compared to what she saw now, those nights up north were as bright as noon.

But Jemma had been in Magdalene's cabin long enough to know how to move around without any light. It helped that they occupied only a single room. Jemma rose from the mattress and deftly moved around the table and to the door. She stepped outside, the damp air settling on her bare arms and feet, dressed as she was in one of Magdalene's old cotton shifts. She crept toward the tree line. Although she knew no one in the Duchons' could see her, even if they were awake in the middle of the night, she hung back, her hand loose on a nearby tree, the firm presence steadying her.

She thought of them, sleeping in their beds. How beautiful they'd seemed to her when she'd first arrived! But if Magdalene was right, if they all did hate themselves, Jemma supposed she should feel sorry for them.

They were light enough to pass, if not as white, then as close to it as they could get. But they weren't white and they knew it. Further, they probably hated being so close to something they wanted badly (despite Honorine's insistence on their being "proud" to be "colored") and still falling short. How confusing that existence must be, to be happy to be Black and yet happy that they didn't look it. Like Jemma. Like Dennis. Like Carl and Mabel Barker. Jemma had told herself that growing up with her adoptive parents hadn't been ideal, but it had taken coming here and meeting her real family to show her that there were probably no perfect families anywhere.

A light went on on the second floor. Jemma counted the windows from what she knew was her old bedroom. Fosette must be turning on her lamp at what was maybe two in the morning. She wondered what her cousin was up to. Perhaps she, like Jemma, couldn't sleep. Maybe she was reading or had simply gone to the bathroom.

Or perhaps she was up there opening the trunk at the foot of her bed and pulling out the corpse of an infant who'd been dead for years, cradling it and singing to it.

Jemma shivered, but she remained hidden in the trees, not returning to the cabin and an uneasy sleep until the light in Fosette's room finally went out.

THE NEXT MORNING, thankful to be alive to see another day, Jemma studied the ledger again. As she looked at one blueprint, ready to turn the page because it looked like the ones she'd already studied, she stopped.

Something about this one was different.

She turned back to the previous drawings, flipped back and forth to compare. In the last blueprint the location of the kitchen had changed, although not by much. In the original layout the kitchen had been smaller. In whatever renovation had taken place, the room had been made larger, although there was no indication of the small space where Inès had slept. The room had also been moved to where it was today. On the latest blueprint, Jemma looked for the room beside her mother's but found nothing, although that space had been the kitchen in the old plan. Although it wasn't being used anymore, Jemma found it odd that it wasn't included on the new blueprint. It was as if the room didn't exist.

After she set the book down, it fell open where the page had been torn out. Jemma ran her finger down the uneven edge, her curiosity a greedy—and at this point, mostly unsatisfied—beast.

She pored through receipts, a stack of them dated between 1861 and 1865. It appeared Corentin had sold everything from livestock to people, probably just to survive during wartime. There were no more dated receipts until October 1866, but then he bought instead of sold: several pallets of lumber. She recognized his handwriting in one word, written in English, scribbled across the paper: *kitchen*

This had to be when the kitchen was renovated, but there was no explanation as to why the old one had been closed off. Jemma turned back to the list of death dates. June 14, 1864, was over two years before this lumber purchase. She tapped her finger on the date. The two events were connected; she was sure of it, although she didn't know where this certainty had come from.

Jemma realized that she didn't have to go back to the house to get an answer, though. She needed only to get back on the property.

THAT NIGHT, AFTER Jemma told Magdalene what she had planned, the older woman insisted on accompanying her.

"I don't like the idea of you being out there all by yourself" was all her friend said.

They slipped onto the Duchons' back lawn after all the lights in the house went out. To avoid being seen, they didn't carry a candle or lantern, simply walked along the line of bushes and trees until they were halfway between the woods and the house.

"Adam?" Jemma whispered. "Jane?"

She didn't know if this would work, as the spirits didn't always come when called. Next to her, she sensed Magdalene's presence, felt the rigidity of her friend, held in place by anxiety and fear. But as she moved closer to the house, the soft crunch of grass let her know Magdalene was moving alongside her.

"Adam?" After several moments of hearing nothing except crickets, and trees swaying in a slight breeze, Jemma tried again. "I need your help. I need to know how to set us free. And then I can set you free, too."

Two spirits emerged from the back of the house, from the

kitchen, a man and a woman. Once they'd stopped about five feet in front of Jemma and Magdalene, she recognized Adam and Jane.

"Can you help me?"

Neither responded. Jemma felt uneasy waves coming from Magdalene next to her, but the woman stayed put, although she rubbed her bare arms and glanced around.

"I want to help you—you and the others—so that you're not stuck here. You want to move on, don't you?"

"Move on," Jane repeated.

"What did you mean when you said to 'set them free'? I thought you meant the Duchons, but you didn't, did you? What did that mean, Adam?"

"Cold," Jane moaned.

Jemma wanted to shush her or soothe her. Of the spirits she'd spoken to so far, Jane was the most timid, the one most likely to quickly disappear.

"Set them free," Adam said.

"Who?"

"Them."

Jemma felt her frustration growing, so she tried another tack. "Adam, are you buried over there?" She turned slightly and pointed to the old slave cemetery. "Jane, are you buried there? How did you die? Do you remember?"

She doubted either of them would be able to give her the date they died, but if they did and it was June 14, 1864, she'd know she was on the right path.

"So cold," Jane whispered. "So dark."

Without a word, Adam turned and began walking to the house. Jemma called after him, but he only stopped for a moment, turned to look at her and continued on his way. Jane followed him, looking back at the two women before moving on.

"They want us to follow them," Jemma whispered.

"They who?" Magdalene asked.

Jemma didn't even hear the question. "But they're going back to the house. I can't go in there. What if someone's up and they see me?"

The two ghosts stopped outside of the kitchen window for a moment before disappearing through the wall.

As Jemma debated whether to return to the house where her presence would possibly be met with violence, particularly if she ran into Simone, she noted that the house was dark. If someone was in the kitchen, getting a drink or a midnight snack, a light would be on. She turned to Magdalene, ready to tell her friend that she didn't have to come with her, but the other woman was already moving, so Jemma followed.

The back door was unlocked and emitted a soft squeal that made Jemma stop and listen for any other sounds, like footsteps. Satisfied that none of her family was awake, she and Magdalene slipped inside. Adam and Jane's faint forms waited in the small room where Inès had slept. Adam moved through the curtain, while Jane stayed in place.

"It's a window through there, not a door," Jemma explained. "I'll go in, but you might want to stay here."

"All right," Magdalene agreed quickly. "If anyone comes downstairs . . ."

"Just go back home. I'll find you."

Jemma maneuvered herself through the small opening, landing on the dirt-packed floor. Adam's faint glow provided the barest illumination. He pointed to the floor.

"Free them."

"Who?"

An earsplitting scream tore through the air. Jemma slapped her hands to her ears, sure that the noise would wake the entire house. Though now muffled, other screams rose with the first one. A chorus of voices jabbered incoherently, some in English, others in French. Perspiration bloomed under Jemma's arms. She had to get out of here before the family came downstairs, but when she tried to leave the room, she found her feet stuck.

"Let me go," she panted, turning as much as she could to face Adam.

She could barely hear his repeated "Free them," but it was easy enough to read his lips.

"Please. They can't find me here."

"Free them!"

A rush of heat washed over Jemma, blowing her hair back. She was sure her eyebrows had been singed off. At the same time, something feathery brushed her face, and she instinctively reached up to grab what felt like thick paper. And as dark as the room was, it grew even darker as the thick scent of smoke filled the space, rushing into her mouth and choking her. Jemma coughed, covering her mouth.

The screaming stopped and Jemma was finally able to move. She scrambled out of the window, with Magdalene helping her. There was no sign of Jane, but footsteps pounding downstairs spurred the two women out the door and across the back lawn, neither of them stopping until they reached the cover of the trees.

"What happened in there?" Magdalene asked once they were inside her cabin and they'd caught their breath.

Jemma realized she held a sheet of crumpled paper. Smoothing it out, she asked the other woman to light a lantern, and once she could see, her eyes immediately went to the torn edge. All she could read was the date of the missing ledger page: October 8, 1864.

THIRTY

FINDING THE PAGE wasn't the triumph Jemma needed it to be, as it was written in French. With Laurence dead, she had no one to quickly translate it for her.

"Any of us could die at any time," she wailed to Magdalene. "I don't have time to figure this out."

"Maybe you don't have to. You can ask the spirits. I'm sure they got the answer for you."

"They talk in riddles sometimes."

"Do you really listen to them, though? Or does that scared part keep you from hearing everything they got to say?"

Despite overcoming much of her fear, Jemma knew her friend was right. She didn't allow herself to hear everything the spirits were trying to say. Whoever had torn the page from the ledger did so for a reason. Knowing the Duchons the way Jemma did, she knew it had to be because they had something to hide.

Another secret.

She looked out the window at the dark sky. If she was going to act, it had to be soon.

It had to be now.

"You're right," she said to Magdalene. "I'm going out there and I'm going to listen, really listen."

Jemma slipped outside and headed to the Duchon house, sticking to the bushes along the side of the back lawn. No lights shone from inside, so after she'd fled earlier, the family must have returned to bed. Taking several relieved breaths, she called Adam's name, and was surprised when he appeared at once.

"You gave me the missing ledger page," she said.

He nodded.

"I can't read it. Can you tell me what it says?"

"No. But I can show you."

Ice sliced along Jemma's arms at what he meant. He held out a hand, waiting. Fright wriggled in her chest, but Jemma closed her eyes and imagined it melting away.

Don't be scared. You need the truth.

Jemma reached for his hand, only to feel a hard chill. There was nothing solid there. The cold worked its way up her arm and across her body. It was as if she were enclosed in invisible ice.

"Open," Adam breathed.

Jemma hesitated.

And then obeyed.

SHE STOOD IN the parlor of the Duchon house, but not in 1963, made evident by the freshly painted walls free of cracks, the pristine furnishings and the clothes the man at the desk wore. It was also obvious that he couldn't see Jemma, standing a few feet away.

Jemma looked around for Adam, but for now it was only her and the man. When he raised his head from the book he wrote in, she saw it was Corentin. She'd passed his portrait along the stairway many times.

Adam entered the room, but not the Adam Jemma knew now. This was Adam when he'd been alive, and he, too, seemed unaware of Jemma's presence.

"You wanted to talk to me?" Corentin sat back in the hard chair, fixing Adam with an unfriendly stare.

"Yes, sir. Did you think over what I asked before, about letting me buy my freedom, sir?"

Corentin waved a hand in the air. "I did indeed think it over. And my answer today will be the same as my answer tomorrow and forever. No."

"But, master—don't be angry now, but please—can I speak a little more?"

"Go on." Corentin turned his attention back to the book, which Jemma could now see was the gray ledger.

"I been working on Sundays like you give me permission for. Working as a carpenter for different families, and I been saving that money. It's enough for me to buy my freedom."

"The price has gone up, Adam."

The look of distress on Adam's face reached Jemma through the years.

"Excuse me, master?"

Corentin looked up then, cruelty distorting his pleasant features. "I said the price has gone up. You first asked me about buying your freedom two years ago. Prices have gone up since then. You'll need an additional three hundred dollars."

It might as well be a million, Jemma thought.

"You're dismissed," Corentin said.

Adam crumpled his hat in his hands but didn't move.

"I'll tell," he whispered.

"What?"

"I'll tell everyone what I know. What I heard Mr. Arthur say one time when he was drunk. He's white, but you ain't."

Corentin rose from his seat, blue eyes blazing. "You're trying to blackmail me?"

A jerk in Jemma's middle snatched her from the scene. She had only a second to begin to wonder if she was returning to the present before her feet settled on grass, the Duchon house looming over her in the night.

"You want to tell secrets, do you? You want your freedom? You'll be free, free to burn in hell. After you burn on Earth."

Next to Jemma, Corentin threw a lit lantern into the old kitchen window. Flames erupted and grew within moments, reaching to the ceiling.

Shouts came from inside, just as Jemma screamed.

"Who's in there?" Corentin demanded, his voice quavering. "Who's with Adam?"

Corentin's face blanched as more shrieks reached through the window. It was then that Jemma saw the bar on the outside of the door, trapping whoever was inside.

"Master!"

Jemma reached out her arms, wanting to help the people burning to death. Corentin stood next to her, eyes horrified but mouth and feet set.

She was pulled again, back into the parlor, Corentin scribbling in the ledger. This time she stood behind him. Over his shoulder, she read his latest entry. Although it was written in French, she understood it perfectly.

The kitchen was destroyed in the fire, and there was much damage to the dining room and the parlor, but those rooms were nonetheless salvaged. The slaves who were trapped there all perished, seven in all. All that money lost! All that property destroyed! Adam among them, Adam who threatened to ruin me. So I watched as the heavy beam blocked the slaves' way out, the other exit also sealed. I listened to their screams, which I still hear when I lie in bed at night. I know it is because of where they rest, which is not a rest at all when it is in the same place where they died.

However, I will stop this madness going forward. I am an old man, but my son Nicolas can have a future as one of the gens de couleur libres in this city. Only after I am dead will they know that his father was a coward who lived his life as a white gentleman instead of as the bastard that he was. I will not have my secret hang like a dark cloud over his head for the rest of his life. Whatever the outcome of this cursed war, my son and any descendants who follow after him will live as free colored people. They will not have to masquerade as something they are not, as I have done all these years.

Another jerk into a familiar room.

A young Inès lay in bed, sweaty faced and exhausted. Magdalene sat next to her, cradling a newborn in a blanket.

Honorine approached from her place in the corner, looking down at the baby.

"It's dark."

"Maman, please," Inès panted. "Her name is Emmaline."

"Get rid of it."

As Jemma stood rooted in place, unable to get a glimpse of her newly born self, shouting began between Magdalene and Honorine, between Inès and her mother.

"Your man isn't coming back. We sent him away!" Simone said.

Jemma began to shake, knowing what was coming next.

Adam appeared, as the one who worked with her mother all those years ago.

It was clear that Inès saw him. As he talked to her, a ghoulish smile spread across her face.

"I curse all the Duchon blood. From this day forth, I bind the family to this house. I bind them forever."

As Inès shut her eyes in a seeming faint, Adam disappeared. Hazy outlines shimmering with malevolence appeared around Honorine, Simone, Inès and infant Jemma.

She somehow knew that those same lines were enveloping Russell, Fosette, Laurence and all the other Duchons who lived in the house, tethering them to the property.

Another man appeared, one no one could see except Jemma.

He approached the bed, gazing down at Inès and at the baby in Magdalene's arms. His dark brown skin glowed, his deep eyes shining with love.

"Not you," he whispered to the newborn Jemma. "Not like this."

The shimmering outline around the baby vanished. He moved toward Inès, and Adam reappeared.

"One," Adam said. "You only get one."

And then Jemma's father was gone.

Adam leaned down and whispered to the infant, "Your blood still ties you to death."

Jemma was jerked to the present. Adam hovered next to her.

"Why did my brother die? Was it the curse? Why wasn't it on my birthday?"

"When she broke her curse, she broke the tie between us."

The next thing Jemma knew, she was stumbling into Magdalene's cabin, her face wet with tears, her body shaking.

"I . . . I know what happened. Why the kitchen was moved . . . why they rebuilt. Why I was able to leave here." She looked up at Magdalene, sobbing. "And who I have to free."

THIRTY-ONE

JEMMA AND MAGDALENE talked until the sun came up, both exhausted but too wound up to sleep.

"I'll have to go back to the house and talk to them," Jemma said.

"You think they'll believe you?"

"They probably already know. Or at least Honorine does. I'm sure of that."

Magdalene had cursed quietly when Jemma told her about the visions. "He let those people die and then just . . . left them there. He put a floor over their bodies." The soft light shimmered against her tears.

Jemma barely heard her, lost as she was in her own troubled thoughts.

After all of Honorine's talk about her ancestors being free people of color, it appeared that at least one of them lived his life as a white man. Jemma assumed Corentin's wife—the one who had been jealous of an enslaved woman named Suzette, the same one he had made an example of by whipping—was also white, or at least appeared to be. He stood by and let several people, human beings whom he refused to acknowledge as human beings, burn to death, so terrified was he that one of them would reveal his secret. He viewed that horrible loss not as a loss of lives but as the destruction of his property.

Jemma thought of her mother sleeping in that small space next to that burial room all those years. Had she heard the screams? Had the spirits whispered to her endlessly, begging her to free them, as she tried to rest? Jemma held her head in her hands, gripping her hair, wishing she could stop hearing those screams.

"Whatever else happens to that family, I don't care, but I have to go back and do what Adam asked me to do. I have to set those people free."

Magdalene stopped rocking in place and stared at her. "How you gonna do that? You think they're gonna just let you in?"

"Once I tell them what happened and why they've been cursed all these years, they have to. They don't want any more deaths in that family." Jemma tried not to let her friend's troubled expression raise any doubt in her mind.

Soon, the stream of anxiety finally slipped off their shoulders, leaving a great fatigue behind, and they both fell into an exhausted sleep. They awoke in the early afternoon, and after Jemma warmed up a rabbit stew for lunch, Magdalene told her to sit at the table. As Jemma sat, her friend stood behind her and combed her hair, surprisingly gently. The older woman made careful parts with a wooden comb she said she'd had since before Jemma was born, and she rubbed a finger dabbed with sweet oil along the exposed scalp before braiding each section.

"I ain't combed nobody's hair since my baby girl died. She was so good about sitting still and not making a fuss. Besides just holding her body in my arms and rocking her to sleep, that's what I miss the most. The feel of that soft, thick hair underneath my fingers, the smell of it, the weight of her against my knees. She'd fall asleep most times when I did her hair, just drift off with her thumb in her mouth like a little angel."

"What about your husband? What happened to him?"

A soft laugh escaped Magdalene's lips. "Wasn't no husband, least not a legal one. But me and him, we had something deeper and stronger than a piece of paper. We didn't stand in front of no judge and witnesses, but we were husband and wife. When our baby died, it was like his soul left his body. There was no more light shining out his eyes. When he touched me, it was like being touched by a husk. He was alive, but dead at the same time." Jemma felt Magdalene stop braiding for a moment and shiver. "After a while, I couldn't stand it no more, being touched by a man who had no life inside him, sleeping in the same bed with him. I left. Just got up one morning while he was still sleeping and walked out the door. I ain't stop until I got to these woods and found this old cabin. I cleaned it out, fixed it up and moved in. It was years before I met your family, although they was always out on that back lawn and having parties and coming and going back then. But I kept to myself for a while, just trying to find some peace. And I told myself I did, but that was a lie. I told myself I accepted her dying, but I never did. And when I delivered you and your mama told me to take you before your family killed you, I thought I'd be all right, until she told me to get you far away from here. It was like losing my baby girl all over again."

"You ever wonder what happened to your husband?"

"All the time. But I can't look back at what was."

After braiding Jemma's hair, Magdalene handed her the dress she'd left the Duchons' in; it was freshly washed and line-dried.

"When we go there, you gotta look neat and clean."

"We?"

"You think I'm gonna let you go in that lion's den by yourself?"

Jemma's nerves all but tingled as she and Magdalene walked across the back lawn, stopping at the carriage house, where Jemma swiped a sledgehammer and a shovel. At first, she'd thought about circling around to the front door and ringing the bell, but then she decided to enter by the kitchen. Employing the element of surprise seemed a much better way to start things off. As soon as they passed the small alcove, Jemma stopped in her tracks.

A woman stood at the kitchen counter, her back to them. Her hair was pulled into a low chignon. She wore a black maid's uniform, the white of her apron ties trailing down her backside.

"Mama?" Jemma whispered, ready to run over as soon as Inès turned around.

But when the maid turned, Jemma realized how wrong she'd been. It wasn't her mother at all. It was a woman around Fosette's age and about Jemma's color. Heat flushed across her face. How quickly the Duchons had replaced her mother.

"Who are you?" Jemma and the maid both asked at the same time.

When neither Jemma nor Magdalene answered, the other woman introduced herself as Yvonne, her head cocked and a hand on her hip, clearly waiting for them to repay the courtesy of an introduction.

"I'm Emmaline and this is Magdalene. We have business with the family."

They moved toward the dining room, but the maid blocked their path, her eyes on the tools cradled in Jemma's arms. "Now, wait just a minute. I don't know who you are to come barging in here through the back door like you own the place—"

"Grandmère!" Jemma screamed. "Simone!"

"Girl, what's the matter with you?"

"You might want to run some errands, Yvonne," Magdalene said. "It's about to get ugly."

Jemma had never been so happy to see Honorine, despite the anger etched in every wrinkle of her grandmother's face. Splotches of red bloomed through her cakey makeup, and her lips weren't even visible.

"Yvonne," she said, "go upstairs and find something to do."

Before the maid had taken three steps, Honorine rounded on Jemma, ignoring Magdalene. "What . . . the . . . hell are you doing in this house?"

"Your great-grandfather was Corentin, right? Because he wasn't the proud free person of color you made him out to be, you goddamned liar!" Jemma held up the diary page in her fist. "He was passing as white and . . . No, where's everybody else? They're all going to hear this."

"Who do you think you are to come in here, giving me orders, *pute*? All you've done since you darkened our door—"

Jemma let out a howl that lowered into a cackle. "Darkened your door? How fitting! Yeah, I darkened it, me and this"—she held up an arm—"the darkest thing that ever lived here, I bet, except the people our ancestors owned."

Fosette padded into the kitchen, her hair loose around her shoulders; she was dressed in a black shift. Despite its somber color, it was clearly this season's buy. She didn't look surprised to see Jemma, although her gaze moved questioningly over Magdalene.

"What's she doing here?" she drawled to Honorine.

"I have no idea, but I'm about to call the police and have her removed."

"Yes, please call the police. I want them to come. Because when they get here and I tell them what's buried under the floor of the old kitchen, they're going to be real interested in finding out what happened here."

"What are you talking about?"

Instead of containing its usual imperious tone, her grandmother's voice betrayed a hint of strain. Jemma ignored it. And she wasn't about to be rushed into anything. Moving past Honorine and Fosette, she went out through the dining room and into the foyer until she came to the foot of the stairs. "Simone! Russell! I'm home and I want to talk to you!"

Behind her, she heard Honorine and Fosette muttering in French, with the younger woman saying something that sounded like *"absolument folle."*

"No," Magdalene said. "She ain't crazy, but y'all sure are."

Honorine scoffed. "The town witch. How fitting that you'd be here with Jemma."

Just then, Simone came sweeping downstairs, a magazine in one hand, and Russell strolled over from the library. Yvonne stood next to the telephone table in the foyer, on her face a quizzical expression directed at Honorine. Jemma saw her grandmother give a short shake of her head before gesturing everyone else into the dining room. The family took their usual seats, except for Jemma. She stood at one end of the table, with Magdalene sitting next to her. Honorine glared at her granddaughter from the opposite end.

Jemma held the diary entry up.

"From the first day I came here, I smelled smoke all over the house. I think you all did, too, but you just got used to it over the years. The only person who probably never got used to it was my mother, because she slept next to the room that burned down a hundred years ago. I don't think she was able to get used to it because the spirits that haunt this place wouldn't let her. They didn't want her to forget about them. But she got tired of seeing them and hearing them, because she didn't know how to help them. My parents, the people who raised me, made me ignore the ghosts. They taught me to turn away from them. And then I come here and I have to see them and talk to them. I thought I'd see my mother's spirit, because you monsters told me she was dead. And when that didn't happen because she was actually alive, I tried to talk to the spirits to find out what was wrong here, how I could break the curse that hangs over this house and this family."

Jemma slammed both hands flat on the table, making the others jump. She turned to Russell.

"Tell me the truth, old man. Do you smell smoke?"

His green eyes were round and scared. His mouth worked for a few seconds before he stammered, "N-no, I smell nothing."

"What about you, Fosette?" Jemma turned to her cousin. "You mean to tell me that you don't smell burning flesh? Hmm? None of you?"

"What in hell are you talking about?" Simone barked. "Burning flesh? You're mad."

Jemma ignored her and pointed to Honorine, whose pale fingers, gripping the table, were even whiter than usual. "Your great-grandfather was a freeman of color, except no one knew he was, as you all like to say, colored. He passed as a white man and owned slaves, one of whom had the money to buy his freedom. But your great-grandfather refused, and so this man threatened to reveal his secret, which would have ruined him. So he set the fire to kill the man who threatened him, trapping him in the kitchen in the old part of the house. Other slaves were in the kitchen, too, and Corentin let all of them burn to death instead of trying to free them.

"If the rest of you think they're buried in the old slave cemetery on the grounds, you're wrong. He just packed a new floor on top of their bodies and closed off the old kitchen when he built the new one. But you knew, Grandmère, didn't you? You're the only one who read all the books in the library. You tore the page out of the ledger because you didn't want anyone else to know you—we—are all descended from monsters. You made my mother sleep next to that room for almost twenty-eight years, where seven people probably cried out to her every day and every night, begging to get out of that cold, dark place. She didn't curse us to die like you think she did. It was those spirits who cursed us, who kill one of us every seven years. And if we don't free them, one of us is going to die. But it doesn't have to be on my birthday. It could be at any moment, because the curse is now unpredictable. It went wild when my mother broke what bound you to the house."

Jemma felt an immense satisfaction at the fear staining Simone's face, although all of the others wore the same expression.

"How . . . how are we supposed to free them?" Honorine asked after several moments of silence, her eyes moving over the others at the table as if anyone had an answer. She finally settled her gaze on Jemma. "What can we do?"

"I have some ideas, but before we get to them, if we ever get to them, we're going to do something you people aren't very familiar with, and that's telling the truth. We're going to be real honest here. You know what they say. The truth shall set you free."

THIRTY-TWO

NATURALLY, SIMONE RESISTED Jemma's suggestion. "We don't have time for games, you *connasse.*"

Jemma wagged a finger at her aunt. "And that's why I can't stand you. See that? That's me being honest. Ever since I came here, you've been nasty to me. And why? I didn't do anything to you. If anything, I should've been pissed off at all of you for what you did. And trust me—I was. I was so angry that for a while I didn't want to break the curse. I hoped all of you would just up and die, slow and painful. But then I realized I didn't want to die. I didn't want to be tied up in this cursed family. Hell, I wasn't raised with you. Why should I be punished like you? But no . . ." Jemma shook her head, a cheerless chuckle escaping her lips. "When I first came here, I was . . . enthralled by you. By your beauty. How beautiful you all are! And I wanted to be that and be close to that. I was jealous, yes, and I thought I was jealous of your beauty, but really, I was jealous of how people treated you because of that beauty. I wanted people to stop and stare at me, to fall over themselves just because of how I looked. But that's not going to happen to me, not here. You all think I'm ugly because of my skin, because I look like my father. I'll never be beautiful to you or to the world out there that judges people based on their color. But you know what? I might be ugly. By your standards, I am. But in here?" Jemma tapped her chest with a fist before waving her open hand around the table. "I'm much more beautiful than all of you. You're diseased inside, every last one of you."

Honorine rose from her seat, red splotches on her cheeks. "Enough!"

"No, Grandmère, it's not enough. Because it's time for you to tell your truth. You knew those bodies were buried underneath the floor, didn't you?"

"I knew no such thing."

"Liar! You knew because you're the one who tore that page out of the ledger. You're the only one who read all the books in the library. You knew, but you didn't want the rest of the family to know. You knew those dead slaves didn't rest easy, but you couldn't see them or hear them, so you couldn't fix anything. And that's why you made my mother sleep in that room next to the old kitchen. You wanted to drive her insane. You knew she saw ghosts, and you hoped they'd drive her out of her mind. I bet your new maid, what's-her-name out there—I bet she doesn't sleep there, does she? Where does she sleep, huh?"

"That's not true. Agnes . . ."

"Inès!" Jemma screamed. "Her name is Inès. And my name, the name she gave me before you made her give me away, is Emmaline."

"Amen, girl," Magdalene murmured.

"Corentin lived and died as a white man, but things changed with his son, didn't they? That's when the Duchons became so *proud to be colored*. Even before I got here, you were lying to me. You lied to get me down here and you lied to make me stay. This whole house is built on nothing but lies. But now? We're going to tear it down. We're going to root out all the lies and the betrayal and the hurt." Jemma looked at each of the family members in turn. "Which one of you can see ghosts?"

They wouldn't even look at one another, as if scared Jemma would see the truth in a glance. She turned to Simone.

"I don't think it's you. But I do think you hated my mother all your life because she was more beautiful and because your father loved her best. If you faced that, maybe some of that ugliness you wear would fall away."

Simone's jaw worked. Jemma fully expected her to spit some insult back at her, but when her aunt remained silent, a sheet of red rising slowly up her face, she knew she was right.

Next, she faced Fosette, whose hands were intertwined on the table.

"It's not you. You're too frightened. Besides, you're haunted by your own personal ghosts, right? Like a child you had, and maybe other children you wanted to have, but that's never going to happen. Because they fixed you, didn't they? They made it impossible for you to ever have another child."

Fosette's already white face grew even paler under Jemma's pointed words.

"How do you—?" Honorine started, her eyes fixed on Fosette.

"How do I know this?" Jemma asked, on her face a smile that revealed too many teeth. "Your own daughter told me that Fosette was *fixed*. 'She was fixed but good,' Simone told me months ago. You people have hidden a lot of things, but you can't hide everything. Eventually the truth comes out. So, you? Are you the other one who can see spirits? Did my mother inherit that from you? I don't think so, so that leaves"—Jemma snapped her head to Russell—"you, Uncle."

He wouldn't meet his niece's eyes, simply studied the hands in his lap.

"Russell?" Honorine asked after a short laugh. "He couldn't possibly. He . . ."

"What? And why couldn't he? Because he's only concerned with physical things, like food and wine and other things we can touch and taste? Right—why would you think he could have any connection to anything spiritual?" She turned to Russell. "But when you tried to get away from here, after I tried to break the curse and messed things up instead, they did something to you, didn't they? What did you see? What did they tell you?"

"Leave me alone, girl," he said, his gaze still in his lap.

"You want to die next time? Because that can happen, sooner than you want. It's time to speak the truth."

Russell's eyes met hers then. Unlike the women in the family, he didn't look afraid. "It's true. I can see them, although they don't call to me like they called to Inès. She wanted to help them. They simply flit around me, barely more than shadows." He hugged himself, a lopsided smile playing across his lips. "And you're right. When I tried to get away, they grabbed me. They held me in a dark, cold place for what felt like forever. They whispered to me endlessly, although I couldn't tell if it was day or night. But they never stopped, just kept telling me things about our family, about how they died, about what I did to your mother."

"What did they tell you?"

He didn't answer for several moments, but in the end, perhaps the thought of someone's certain death—maybe his own—loosened his lips. "I know about the bodies."

Honorine gasped, while Simone threw him a sharp, troubled

glance. Fosette didn't move, simply continued to stare at him across the table as if Russell were talking about a new pair of shoes he'd just bought.

"Maybe that's where they kept me," he continued. "In that space where they're trapped." A high-pitched titter escaped him. "It's funny, isn't it? All these years, we've been trapped, but so have they. None of us has been able to leave."

"The bodies of the slaves? They held you?" Simone asked, looking from Russell to Jemma to Honorine. "What's he talking about?"

"The bodies your family has been sleeping on top of for decades, even before any of you were born. The people Corentin owned and the people he allowed to die." Jemma hauled the sledgehammer and the shovel from the floor next to her and slammed them on the table. "The people we're about to set free."

AT FIRST JEMMA had thought she'd have to drag the Duchons into the small room off the kitchen, so she was surprised when they came willingly, Simone bringing up the rear, fear shining out of her eyes.

Magdalene was a calming presence. Jemma was glad her friend had insisted on being there with her, because she'd never felt more anxious. She had no plan, which no one knew besides her. How she wished her mother were here, just to have someone else supporting her.

She knew the Duchons were humoring her only because they wanted to save their own skins. Besides her mother, her brother had been the only family who might have loved Jemma for being Jemma and didn't only need her to do something for them. How different things could be if they were with her now.

But Jemma shook that off.

All her life, she'd looked to other people for acceptance, for love.

She'd thought that if she were only pretty enough, smart enough, or something else enough, they would love her. And all the while, she hadn't loved herself enough. She hadn't realized that what she needed most was herself.

As she stood in front of what used to be her mother's bed, she knew she didn't need Inès, Laurence or Magdalene. She would have appreciated the others' being there, but she was a whole person on her own, capable of doing what she had to do.

"I am enough," she said in a low voice.

And with that, she brought the sledgehammer behind her before swinging it in a wide arc into the wall.

IT HAD BEEN much harder than Jemma expected, breaking through layers of brick. With each swing, she was only vaguely aware of the people behind her, of the controlled chaos. It was as if she were on the other side of the wall, listening to them, from Russell's quizzical muttering to Honorine's occasional snappy question. Not surprisingly, her grandmother had lunged forward and tried to grab her when Jemma first broke into the wall, but someone (Magdalene, most likely) pulled her away. And now no one answered Honorine's questions. Fosette was strangely quiet, and so was Simone. Jemma didn't know what her cousin felt, but her aunt was clearly terrified. The thought spurred her on despite the pain increasing in her forearms and moving up to her shoulders.

"Talk to me," she whispered at one point. "Help me."

Had she expected the spirits—Adam, Jane and the rest—to help her? A part of her mind chided her for the thought.

No, a voice whispered in her mind, a voice that sounded very much like what she imagined her mother would sound like. *This is your work, girl.*

And yet an eagerness pressed against her, letting her know that the spirits were indeed present.

At one point, Magdalene asked if she wanted her to take over. Jemma paused just long enough to tell her friend no, that this was something she had to do on her own. She licked sweat away from her upper lip, ignoring the itchy way it trailed down her face, down her spine. Her muscles ached from her arms to her legs. She laughed once, a high yelp. Why did her legs hurt so much? Why did everything hurt? But still she swung the hammer, until the small window that she'd had to wriggle through before was large enough for her to easily fit through. Just a little more.

When Russell touched her arm, Jemma wondered at first what he wanted. He pulled the hammer out of her slack grasp without a word and took up the job, his clumsy movements indicating a man unused to manual labor.

After a while there was no sound except the heavy thud of the hammer against brick. *Slam. Slam. Slam*, in regular intervals, the sound growing louder and louder, no background voices to cushion it.

The window transformed into a rough doorway.

Jemma peered inside, aware of the rest of the family crowding around her.

The smell of smoke poured out of the old kitchen.

Behind her came the sounds of coughing.

"Magdalene? Can you get me a light? And bring the shovel."

A few moments later, Jemma felt a lantern pressed into her hand. She raised it in front of her, the light shining off the four walls, the rough ceiling and the packed-dirt floor.

"Adam? Jane?"

No answer.

Jemma turned to find Magdalene gazing at her. A hint of

anxiety shone on the older woman's face, but her determination was stronger. She squeezed Jemma's hand.

As Jemma stepped through, she tugged Magdalene with her, and then the two of them peeked out of the hole in the wall. Jemma imagined how she must look in the murky light, covered in brick dust and sweat.

"Are you coming?" she asked her family.

Honorine squared her shoulders before stepping through. The moment she was inside, she turned to Russell, who followed. Fosette came next, and she pulled at her mother to get Simone into the room. The four of them stood to the side, against a wall, as Jemma and Magdalene looked at the fireplace from their spot in the center of the room. They took in the rough stone walls. If Jemma reached an arm up, she could almost touch the low ceiling. And when she looked down at the floor, she jumped, steering Magdalene to the side of the fireplace.

"We were standing on them," she said.

"What now, Emmaline?"

"Hand me the shovel. It's time to get them out."

"You don't think they should have to help?" her friend snapped, raising a chin toward the Duchons.

"Not yet. I don't want the first face they see to look just like the man who let them lie here all these years. Even though I'm family, I don't look like the others."

After Jemma broke through the first few inches of the floor, it became easier. The soil loosened up. Jemma tossed shovelfuls of it over one shoulder, hearing a slushy slap as dirt hit the wall, over and over. Her movements grew frantic. Tears and lines of sweat mixed in trails down her face, but Jemma didn't feel or taste any of it. She was in the grip of some force. She knew that if anyone had tried to stop her or pull the shovel from her hands, she would have fought back. She was covered in dirt, could feel grit on her tongue. More than once, she used a forearm to wipe dirt from her face only to leave more behind.

Although no spirits showed themselves, she felt a presence, calm and eager at the same time. It pressed against her, as if peering over her shoulder with greedy eyes, its bony fingers gripping her upper arm.

"Which one are you?" she huffed, not pausing for a second. "Don't worry. I'm almost there."

"Let me help you, girl," Magdalene said when Jemma had stopped digging because a lightness gripped her head, threatening to send her careening to the floor. That was the only reason she agreed to let her friend take over.

As Magdalene worked her way into the hole, only a foot deep and about three feet wide, Jemma slumped against the fireplace, being overtaken by a weariness so complete that she wanted to lie on her side and sleep for days. But that eagerness thrummed over everything, keeping her awake. She wanted to see them. She had to see them.

Across the room, the Duchons huddled. Russell was also lounging on the floor, seemingly unconcerned about getting any dirtier. But the three women stood in a group, Simone clutching her mother while Fosette stared hard at the enlarging hole, her gray eyes reflecting the lantern light. Her fingers worked themselves into fists and then splayed out at regular intervals.

What Jemma wouldn't have given to have her mother there with her. Where was she? Was she okay? Was Dennis watching over her?

Too tired to move, Jemma simply blew out a hard breath. Maybe, like Magdalene, she'd take up residence in the woods, find her own cabin. The thought curved a half smile on Jemma's lips. Before she'd come down here, she'd never wanted to be anywhere near the woods. She was much more comfortable among concrete and asphalt and brick, weaving her way through bustling crowds, experiencing winters that were actually cold.

She thought of Marvin, too, of his child that was lost, wondered whether he was with the child's mother. Before, she'd often hoped that he'd abandoned that woman, that he'd somehow find Jemma and show up at the door, begging her to come back to Chicago with him. She'd imagined scenarios full of flowers and apologies, of promises and rings. But now she felt nothing when she thought of him.

"What did you say?" Jemma asked. Honorine had murmured something. When she didn't reply, Jemma repeated the question, leaning forward.

"I said, you've destroyed this entire home. And for what? There's nothing there."

"There is something there, which we'll all see soon enough. I destroyed this home? Maybe if our ancestor hadn't built it back up over a pile of bodies I wouldn't have had to. But this house was destroyed long before I got here. You just couldn't see it."

"I'm telling you—"

"Maman," Russell said, startling all of them. "They're there."

Only then did Honorine seem to accept the reason for their being here, from Jemma's tearing down the wall to digging up the floor. All it took was a few words from her son.

"Oh," Magdalene breathed softly, setting the shovel on its end, her hand balanced on the handle. She gazed into the wide hole, only a little deeper than a foot but about four feet wide.

Jemma scrambled forward on her hands and knees, pulling the lantern over and holding it above the hole.

"What is it? What did you find?" Simone asked, shrinking back against the wall, turning her head toward the exit as if readying herself to flee.

Only Russell rose and approached, to stand next to Magdalene and on the opposite side from Jemma. A grim expression colored his face, eerie in the low light coming from the floor.

Jemma made out a bone. As she moved the lantern, the light revealed the length of it, along with another. The bones looked like a leg, bent at the knee. She reached out and touched it, rubbed a finger along its smooth length, the grit of dirt rough beneath her touch. She didn't know who this was, but she knew they weren't alone. They'd continue digging to reveal the rest of this person, as well as the others with whom they'd shared this grave.

"It's one of them," Jemma said, looking toward the family before looking at Magdalene. "From here on, we have to use our hands."

Jemma and Magdalene scooped the dirt, moving more slowly as they got deeper. Without words, they instinctively knew that they didn't want to disturb the bones. They needed to leave them in place and not disrupt them any more than necessary. They deserved that much, at least.

Finally, after what felt like hours, the hole was expanded to almost ten feet across, revealing most of seven skeletons scattered in a compact heap.

A sob escaped Jemma's lips. Knowing that her family was capable of such horror was one thing, but to see the aftermath was another. She was descended from a murderer. Murderers, her mind corrected her.

Her fingers curved over one side of the hole, a steady stream of tears making tracks through the dirt covering her face. She looked up at her family, their forms blurry.

"This is why we're cursed."

THIRTY-THREE

"OH," SIMONE MOANED, leaning forward just the slightest bit before shutting her eyes and pressing back against the wall. "*Mon Dieu.*"

When she made a move to slip out the door, Jemma was on her feet in seconds, grabbing her aunt by the shoulders and shaking her. "Don't you dare do it. You look at them. You look down there." She faced the other family members. "All of you, do it. You too, Grand-mère and Fosette." Turning back to Simone, she dropped her hands, leaving dirty prints all over the woman's pink sleeves. "If I have to face it, you have to face it, too."

A cold hand gripped Jemma. It was Jane's.

"Angry."

"I know. What can we do?"

"Rest. Want to rest."

And then she was gone.

"How many of them are down there?" Russell asked.

"Seven," Jemma answered, joining Magdalene, crouched at the

edge of the hole in the dirt floor, before looking up at him. "We have to get them out of here and buried in a real grave."

"We?" he asked.

Jemma shot up, her fists hard rocks at the end of her arms. "Yes, we, as in all of us. Our ancestor is the reason these people were buried here. Our ancestor let them die and then rebuilt this room over their bodies. It's up to us to set them free. That's the only way to break the curse and save our lives."

Russell, Honorine, Simone and Fosette looked at one another, each with a different expression. Simone still looked terrified, her gaze darting to the grave and the ceiling with regularity. Russell was stony faced, but Jemma thought that he might be the first to bend. Honorine looked troubled and smaller, the imperiousness she wore like a dress nowhere to be seen. And Fosette wore the most curious expression of all—a mix between anger and defeat.

"So if we bury them, we'll be okay?" Russell asked.

Jemma exhaled, wanting nothing more than to clean herself up and climb into a soft bed. But she knew if she did that, she wouldn't wake for days.

"They want to rest. The decent thing to do is to give them a Christian burial."

"Father Louis won't come out here—" Honorine started.

"This has nothing to do with that man or anyone else from your church. This is between family only. We're all going to get our hands dirty and release these people from the hell they've been in for a hundred years. None of you are going to be free until you free the souls our ancestor trapped here. Why do you think you're half-mad and surrounded by rot? So go upstairs and get changed if you need to. Forget about putting on any of that fancy Paris shit you've been buying lately. And get back down here quick. I don't want to have to come looking for any of you."

Honorine opened her mouth to say something, but seemed to think better of it. Simone was the first to go, followed by her daughter, mother and brother.

"You think they're gonna come right back?" Magdalene asked.

"I do." Jemma didn't know where such certainty came from, but it was there.

Magdalene's hand hovered over one of the skeletons. "Down here all this time, under their feet. Good God. No wonder this place is so full of ghosts."

That reminded Jemma of Adam and all the rest. She stood up and dusted off her hands, Magdalene joining her. Looking at her friend, she reasoned that she must look the same, as if they'd been buried and had just climbed out of a grave themselves. A humorless laugh escaped Jemma, and Magdalene reached out to hold on to her arm.

"You all right?"

Jemma nodded, a thickness in her throat. She wasn't going to cry, not yet. Instead, she swallowed the lump and looked around the room.

"Adam? Are you here? Are any of you here? Please answer me if you are. Please. Help me."

She felt Magdalene step closer to her, but to her friend's credit, she didn't look scared. Jemma called out for them a few more times. None of them showed, but her family eventually trickled in, Simone last, dressed in a pair of Capri pants. Jemma shook her head. Honorine was dressed in what had to have been a pair of her late husband's slacks, and Fosette matched her mother in what appeared to be a brand-new pair of Capris. Of course they wouldn't have "work" clothes, she thought, glad that Russell at least owned a pair of jeans, which bunched around his hips. The family looked a sight. In any other circumstances, Jemma probably would have laughed.

Before she could say anything to them or direct them, the ghostly form of Adam suddenly appeared in the middle of the room, hovering over the grave, his face mournful as he looked down into it.

Fosette let out a long moan and grabbed her mother's arm, but neither of them attempted to run.

For the first time, all of the family members could see him.

When Jemma said, "Adam," he raised his head.

"We want to help you and Jane and all the others buried here."

"Free us."

"Yes. We're going to bury you in a real cemetery—"

He shook his head, startling her. Jemma's mouth hung open.

"Well, then how can we free you?" she asked. "What do you want?"

His gaze moved to her family members, huddled together. "Them."

Four pairs of light-colored eyes widened, their gazes skittering from Adam to Jemma as if pleading with her not to let that happen. It was clear they'd heard.

"What do you mean?" Jemma asked, but she already knew.

What the ghost wanted was revenge.

"Adam, you don't want them. That's not the way to be free. Trust me. Is there another way?"

His eyes moved back to Jemma. She found their translucence arresting, although just beneath it she could see the opaqueness.

"Free."

"What about peace?" she asked.

His eyes seemed to lose a bit of their fire. He cocked his head as if waiting for her to continue.

"You don't want to be moved, right?" Jemma asked. "I understand. You've been here for a hundred years. This is your final resting place. You died bad, so you haven't been able to leave, to move on. I'll set you free. All of us will, but it can't be with more death." When he didn't contradict her, she hurried on. "You and Jane and the others will rest here, but we'll do it right. We'll give you the peace you need to move on."

She looked at her family. They shared blood but little else.

The secret is in the blood, one of the spirits had said at the séance.

"Is it us, the family? Do we have to do something for you to give you peace?"

"Freedom. In forgiveness."

She looked at each living person gathered around her before putting her hands out.

"Join hands," Jemma commanded.

Just like they had at the séance, the family members joined in a circle, without anyone raising a question or complaint.

"Each of us has to ask for forgiveness from them," Jemma said. "For what Corentin Duchon did. He's dead, so obviously can't ask for forgiveness himself, but we can do it in his name, we who share his blood. There's freedom in forgiveness. There's peace there, for all of us—not just them, who deserve it way more than we do."

After taking several deep breaths, she continued. "I'll start. Forgive me for what my ancestor Corentin Duchon did to you, not only for taking your life but also for not valuing you as a person."

As soon as she finished speaking, Jane's ghostly form rose from the grave and hovered next to Adam's.

Jemma looked to her right, where Simone gripped her hand. "Go on."

Simone stammered for a few seconds, looking at Jemma with uncertainty, but she eventually began to speak, her husky voice filling the room. "Forgive me . . . for what our ancestor Corentin

Duchon did to you. For not trying to save you. For building this room on top of your bodies. I'm so sorry."

This time it was Marie who appeared.

Fosette spoke next, her voice as high as it had ever been, but even. "Forgive me for what Corentin did to you, for his blood flowing in all of us, for the sins we committed from that madness. Oh God, forgive us. We free you. We free you."

Tomas rose next.

Russell added to the pleas for forgiveness, "I'm so sorry for what I did to Inès."

And then there was Ruth.

Honorine, staring at the ghosts facing the family members, straightened her shoulders and lifted her chin. Jemma eyed her warily, hoping that her grandmother wouldn't choose this moment—a moment when Jemma felt how close they all were to being free of everything this house had done to them—to reassert herself. But she watched her grandmother's shoulders fall, her chest sink a little, as she exhaled heavily.

"Forgive Corentin Duchon for his greed and selfishness, for his inhumanity. His sins invited your wrath on our heads. Forgive us all."

Thérèse rose from the grave to join the five other spirits. But there was one more name, and no more family members were left to speak. As Jemma tried to think of what they could do to raise the last ghost, Magdalene squeezed her hand and cleared her throat, looking around at the Duchons.

"If Inès were here, she couldn't ask for forgiveness the way all of you did. But if she had her voice, she would've been the first to say she was sorry for what happened here." Magdalene fixed her gaze on the spirits. "She tried to help you the best she could. She's not here to speak, but let me speak on her behalf. She was my friend, and I think I speak for her when I ask you to forgive her for not being stronger. Forgive her for being scared and for turning away from you. I wish you all peace and the freedom to leave this place, to move on to a better place, where you're not tied down and suffering. It's time. It's time to move on and be free."

After a moment, Suzette, the last spirit, rose from the grave. To Jemma's eyes, the ghosts looked a little more translucent, although she couldn't be sure if it was because her eyes, and her hopes, were playing tricks on her.

"You're not forgotten," Jemma said. "Adam and Jane. Marie and Tomas. Suzette, Ruth and Thérèse. Say their names."

At her prompting, the rest of the Duchons, and Magdalene, too, spoke each of the spirits' names aloud.

"Again."

They all repeated the names in unison, as the forms grew fainter.

As the sound of the names rose into the air for a third time, the spirits shimmered for just a moment and then all were gone.

And for the first time since she'd arrived months ago, Jemma didn't smell or taste smoke in the air.

Instead, there was the faint scent of gardenias.

It smelled like heaven.

THIRTY-FOUR

When Jemma woke in Magdalene's cabin on her birthday, a few days later, she marveled that she was only twenty-eight years old. After everything that had happened, she felt twice that. As she sat up on the mattress, she knew the weariness would pass once she had time to process it all.

"Happy birthday, Emmaline."

Magdalene leaned against the table, her earthenware mug in one hand.

"Thank you."

"What you going to do today? Walk up to the house, watch them sweat it out 'til midnight?"

Jemma chuckled, rising to her feet. "You think they're still scared?"

"I know they are. Wish I could be a fly on the wall. They're probably sitting around that dining room table, hands flat on top, asking that maid to bring them the runniest soup she can."

Magdalene sipped her chicory, her eyes twinkling over the rim of the cup.

After they all had set the spirits free, Jemma hadn't waited for or expected the Duchons to thank her. She'd been too bone weary to hang around.

"I'll be back after my birthday," she'd told them, heading out with Magdalene. "We have one more thing to do."

Since then, she'd done nothing but sleep and eat the swamp rabbit stew Magdalene pushed on her. When she grew tired of lying in bed, she walked the woods outside, enjoying the sounds of the mosquitoes and birds in a way she never had before. The humidity didn't weigh as heavily on her as it once had.

She told her friend now, "They shouldn't be scared anymore. The curse is broken. For real this time."

"Yeah, but when people been doing the same thing for so long, like shitting bricks on your birthday, it can be hard to stop."

Despite herself, Jemma felt sorry for the quartet at the house.

"You hungry?" Magdalene asked.

Jemma shook her head. "I think I'll go for a walk first, before it gets too hot."

She spent over an hour wandering around the woods, unafraid of getting lost. Magdalene had shown her the trails she'd made over the years, telling Jemma that as long as she kept to the path, she shouldn't run into any danger. Her bare feet crunched over leaves; her hands trailed along tree trunks. Her hair had worked itself out of the neat plaits her friend had fashioned for her. Jemma ran her hands through her thick hair, so unlike the Duchons', something she had so envied when she'd first met them. Just as she'd envied them their skin, their eyes. Had she shared all of that with them, she never would have been sent away. And maybe her mother wouldn't have cursed them.

Her life could have been completely different.

But what kind of life would it have been? One in which she referred to herself as colored, in which she looked down on people who didn't look like her? One in which she'd marry a relative in order to ensure her descendants looked like all the ancestors who came before?

The Duchons hadn't been trapped just by Inès's curse. They'd been trapped by their hatred of what they really were.

To her surprise, when she returned to the cabin a yellow loaf cake sat in the middle of the table, its rich smell filling up the room. Magdalene was banging around in the single cabinet on the wall.

"What's this?" Jemma asked. One side of the cake was browner than the other, but it still looked and smelled delicious.

"It's your birthday. You need a cake." Magdalene came forward with a white taper candle, shrugging. "This the only candle I got."

"Oh, thank you!" Jemma embraced her friend, tears stinging her eyes. She'd never known Magdalene to cook anything besides squirrels, possums and rabbits. She didn't know the woman could bake a cake.

"It's nothing fancy, okay? Best I could do with what I got."

"It's beautiful, Mag."

Magdalene stuck the big candle in the middle of the cake, both of them laughing at the ridiculousness of it, and Jemma made a wish and blew out the high flame. So their breakfast was slices of pound cake still warm from the woodstove.

Afterward, she walked to the edge of the woods, staring at the back of the house. She did wonder what the family was doing, if they were still gripped by the fear that had roosted in every corner and room since the day she was born. A part of her wanted to go there. She'd never spent a birthday with them, after all. But another part reminded her of the last time she'd seen them all, in the dark and dusty room where they'd worked together to free the dead who'd been trapped for ages.

They'd been too wrung out to look like anything besides the haunted. Jemma hadn't expected their undying gratitude, of course. Things were still tender between them, their feelings as fraught and exposed as nerves in a bad tooth. But she'd expected something more than what she'd gotten as Magdalene placed an arm around her shoulders and led her out.

No one had called out after them.

Were they sitting around, sweat running down Honorine's perfectly powdered face, crooked tracks revealing age spots? Had uneasiness dampened Russell's appetite, if that was even possible? Was Simone watching Fosette like a hawk, ensuring that her remaining child was safe?

Jemma knew they had no cause for concern, but like Magdalene said, she was sure her birthday cast a pall over their entire day. And they might not ever forgive her for that.

THE NEXT MORNING, having heard no screaming in the night, and not having been awoken by a frantic banging on the cabin door, Jemma assumed everything was all right at the Duchons'. She awoke to no sign of Magdalene. After washing up and eating a large slice of cake, she headed toward the big house and entered through the kitchen, startling the maid, who was setting bowls and cups on the rolling cart.

"You can't just knock on the front door?" Yvonne asked.

"My family lives here. If you don't want anyone coming in this way, lock the door. Where are they?"

"Mr. Russell is in the dining room, but the ladies haven't come down for breakfast yet."

Jemma lifted the lid on one of the serving dishes, ignoring the woman's tight lips, finding fluffy eggs inside. "Smells good."

She preceded Yvonne into the dining room and plopped into her old chair. Russell looked up from the newspaper.

"Good morning, Uncle Russell."

He shifted in his seat and greeted her, setting his coffee cup down. A look of discomfort distorted his normally handsome face.

"Everything good? Everyone make it through the night?"

He frowned at her lighthearted questions, clearly thinking there was nothing to joke about.

"Oh, come on. You all should be celebrating. No more curse, I'm out of your hair . . ."

"Not quite, are you?" Simone asked from behind her.

Jemma craned her neck to find her aunt, grandmother and cousin filing into the room and taking their seats.

"Good morning to you, Auntie."

Gone was the woman who'd cowered against the wall just a couple of days ago. Back was the woman who'd probably worn pants only a handful of times in her life. It was almost comforting to Jemma to see Simone back to her snippy self.

Yvonne set the breakfast dishes on the table and poured coffee. After she sent a quizzical look to Honorine, the older woman nodded once. The maid went to the kitchen while the family said grace, and she returned with a place setting for Jemma, arranging the plate, fork, knife and spoon in front of her quickly, almost elbowing her in the face.

Silently, they began passing platters and tureens around. At first, Jemma wondered if Fosette would ignore her, but her cousin handed over a platter of sausages while keeping her eyes on her own plate.

Jemma was hungrier than she'd expected. She'd eaten only cake for the past day. And Yvonne's cooking was considerably better than her mother's had been, much as she didn't want to admit it. With the smoky smell no longer hanging over everything, the food tasted better. So Jemma, sure that this would be the last meal she shared with her family, ate almost as much as Russell.

"You promised you'd be back after your birthday," Honorine said to her, pushing aside her plate, half full of food. "What is this about?"

"First, how did you all spend my birthday?"

They exchanged glances.

"No lies now."

Fosette spoke up. "We sat in here for most of the day. We were still . . . scared. Uncle Russell didn't shave, and we only ate broth for breakfast, lunch and dinner. Last night, though, we all moved into the parlor and watched television. *Perry Mason. My Three Sons.* Grandmère listened to the radio. We watched the clock until midnight, didn't we? And when it hit twelve oh one, only then did we know we were all right."

Jemma nodded. "Thank you for being honest."

"Look," Fosette said, turning to Jemma and shocking her with her next words. "I'm sorry. I know that ever since you came, things have been . . . Well, we haven't been kind to you. I'm sorry you were ever sent away, sorry for Tante Inès." Her gaze flicked over to her mother. "Sorry for how my maman treated you."

"Don't apologize on my behalf," Simone hissed.

Fosette ignored her. "But we should apologize. I can't make any of them do it, but I'm sorry."

It was more than Jemma expected. And no, she didn't expect the rest of them to apologize, least of all Simone, but hearing one of them say sorry was surprisingly fulfilling. And if that was all she got, she'd be satisfied with it.

Jemma pushed her plate aside and folded her hands on the table, leaning forward. "The reason I'm still here is because although we put those souls to rest, you can't continue to live on top of their bodies. Something has to be done about that room." When no one protested, she continued. "It needs to be torn down."

"What?" Honorine squawked, but Jemma was already nodding.

"Yes, it has to go."

"If we tear it down, it will affect the structural integrity of this entire house."

"And if you don't tear it down, you'll know you're living on top of a mass grave. After everything that's happened, can you really go on like that?"

Honorine sat back in her seat. Jemma knew that what her grandmother said next would either get the rest of the family on board or have them oppose her yet again. She met her grandmother's level gaze. "Also, if you don't do as I say, *I'll* curse this family."

A silence settled over the room, a river of panic humming beneath it. Honorine's gaze dropped, and when she finally spoke, her voice was little more than a whisper.

"Who on earth is going to tear it down?" Honorine asked.

"I don't know, but I'm sure the yellow pages have plenty of options for you."

She looked at Simone as if daring her aunt to say something, anything, but the smirk that so often rested on the woman's face was gone. In its place was a thoughtfulness Jemma had never seen before. But it was Russell who spoke.

"Maman, she's right. We have to tear it down."

IN THE END, Jemma oversaw the deconstruction a couple of weeks later. The whole family, plus Magdalene, stood off by the croquet pitch as a crew of workmen saw to the demolition. It had taken some persuasion on Honorine's part.

"Madam," the man in charge of the operation had addressed her when they'd come out a few days before, "there's no way we can remove that room clean. Not without bringing down the whole second floor. Now, it's not connected to the second floor, but the roof is attached to the ground level. If we just go in there and tear the walls and roof down, that's going to leave some stone sticking out of the exterior wall. This house is too pretty to have that ugly look on the outside of it."

Like this morning, Jemma had joined the rest of the family when she'd spied the crew from the woods.

"Sir," Honorine replied, "I'm paying you a good deal of money to demolish that room, and I expect to have it done. What the exterior looks like or doesn't look like isn't your concern. You'll do what I'm paying you to do."

The man had looked over at Russell, as if pleading for help from the only other rational person on the grounds, but Jemma's uncle had shrugged and continued smoking his post-breakfast cigarette.

So the crew was now busy tearing down the walls and roof of the old kitchen. Honorine had made it clear that they were to leave the floor alone. The men worked through the day, and when they'd finished, driving off in their work trucks and leaving behind a pile of brick and stone, the exterior of the house was ugly, Jemma had to admit. Instead of a smooth wall, pieces of stone jutted from where the roof had been.

Honorine and Simone stared at the aftermath, tears shining in their eyes.

A square dirt patch was all that remained.

"Call a gardener, Grandmother," Jemma said, staring down at the ground. "Call someone and have them plant flowers here. Roses and tulips. And some daffodils. Let them grow here all the time. This is going to be a place of beauty."

She turned to go back to Magdalene's, her friend falling into step next to her. But Honorine called after her.

"And you? What are you going to do? Where are you going to go?"

"I don't know."

"Come by the day after tomorrow. We have some things to discuss."

Jemma stared at Honorine, searching for something in her grandmother's tight expression, but there was no hint of anything there. So she simply nodded once and walked back to the woods, with Magdalene beside her.

"What are you going to do?" Magdalene asked as soon as they reached the cabin. Instead of going inside, they sat on a log by the well. Jemma turned her head up to the sky, dappled sunlight playing patterns across her face. She leaned back on her hands and closed her eyes.

"I really don't know. I thought about going back home, but there's nothing there for me anymore. No mama, no daddy, no man, no job."

"You thought about staying here?"

Jemma sat up straight and looked at her friend. "Where? You know they don't want me." She lifted a chin toward the Duchons'.

"I don't mean them. I mean just here."

Jemma had thought about staying in New Orleans, although not with Magdalene, in her one-room cabin. The woman had already been more than charitable by letting Jemma share her bed most nights. A part of Magdalene's life had grown on her, though. The quiet of the woods, the sparseness of her home. Back in Chicago, Jemma had often felt that she didn't have enough, although enough of what, she couldn't have said. But being here proved that she didn't need nearly as much as she'd believed she did.

She could easily walk into the parish and find a job teaching, she knew. She could find a room to rent, save her money and eventually buy her own modest place. She might even find a man to love and have children with someday.

And would she visit the Duchons, her family? Would she ride out on Sunday afternoons and have tea with them? Lay flowers on her father's grave?

Even now, despite recent events, when even Simone wasn't sniping at Jemma all the time, she didn't know if it was possible to have a real relationship with them. Sure, they had admitted to a lot of wrongs, but they hadn't changed how they felt about her, about other people who looked like her.

Maybe, though, Jemma thought, if they worked on having a relationship, she might be able to visit them one day without a tightness in her jaw or tension in her shoulders serving as reminders of what they used to be to one another.

Maybe.

"If you do stay," Magdalene said, "I can show you around a little. I don't go into the city much, but I can still show you where it's safe to shop and live."

"I'd like that."

"I like to think that if my baby girl had lived, she would've grown up to be a lot like you." Jemma looked over. Her friend leaned forward, elbows on her spread knees. "I know you used to think you weren't much of anything, but now you see you are. You're a strong woman, Jemma. Inès didn't have that same strength, but I know she was proud of you for it." Magdalene turned to face her. "You going to look for her?"

"I want to, but I don't know where to start."

The other woman nodded. "Yeah, it's a big world out there. But she probably wants you to find her. I think, if you start looking, someday you two will be together again. She had a lot of regrets, but having you and your brother wasn't any of them."

THE NEXT MORNING, Jemma, dressed in her one good dress, fluffed her rag curls in the spotted mirror and sighed at the three different textures: kinky, flattened kinky and somewhat straight. She didn't know why she even bothered anymore. Maybe she'd just let her hair be natural, be like Beneatha in *A Raisin in the Sun* and start wearing African print dresses and getting in touch with her roots. She mussed her hair with her hands and told Magdalene she was going to the house.

The back door was open. Jemma joined the rest of the Duchons in the dining room, where they sat in front of mostly empty breakfast plates.

"Bon matin, Cousine," Fosette said.

"Good morning," Jemma replied, taking her seat and piling what was left of the food on her plate.

The maid cleared the rest of the dishes away after pouring Jemma a cup of coffee and giving her a curt greeting after Jemma said good morning to her.

A long white envelope had appeared in front of Honorine. "I assume we won't be seeing much of you after this. Will you stay in New Orleans?"

"No. I thought about it, and I don't have a place here. It doesn't feel like home to me, and I'm not sure it ever would." She chewed a piece of baguette, wondering if she should tell them about her plans. "Wherever I end up, the first thing I want to do is to find my mother."

Honorine nodded, as if she expected it. "If you find her . . ."

"You want me to tell her you're sorry?"

"I want you to tell her that she will always be a Duchon."

Jemma stopped chewing. "What does that mean?" When her grandmother didn't answer, she put her fork down. "That's it? 'You're still a Duchon'? No apology at all? Look, I don't need one. You all aren't into that, clearly. But after what you put her through, for the reasons you put her through it, I would think that at the very least a tiny 'I'm sorry' is called for."

"Inès will understand" was all Honorine said.

Jemma fell back in her seat, the bread a rock in her stomach, sinking in a bitter sea of coffee.

She took a look around the table, not wanting to see all their faces but needing to all the same. This was her last time in this house, she knew. So she wanted to remember it for those times in the future when she might try to convince herself these past months with them had all been an extended nightmare, with just a few bright spots to break up the horror.

Honorine pushed the envelope forward. Jemma's full name was written on it in an elegant cursive hand.

"You were hired for a job, which you have done," her grandmother said. "Inside are your earnings, via cashier's check. You may cash it at First Citizens Bank if you wish. I have already called and instructed them to assist you, as your account is open again."

Jemma stared at the envelope, not reaching for it. All the money that she'd briefly held just a few short weeks ago was inside it, allowing her to do just about anything she wanted, to go almost anywhere she wanted to go. Maybe even allow her to hire someone to find Inès.

She took it and held it in her lap.

Just as she wondered if, or how, she should thank her

grandmother for giving her what was rightfully hers, Honorine said, "We thank you for your services."

Jemma looked up at her before turning to each of her family members in turn. Russell's sheepish gaze. Simone's stony face. Fosette's blank stare.

Thank you for your services. As if Jemma were another hired hand, like Dennis had been, like the workmen who'd demolished the old kitchen, like Yvonne.

Like her mother had been.

She had helped free her family, but she could see that these remaining four would probably always be trapped in their way of thinking. Even though they could now leave this crumbling house, their minds were still rotten. Although Fosette was the youngest and had the greatest chance to change, Jemma knew her cousin wouldn't. She imagined Fosette wandering the rooms and the hallways in ten, twenty years' time, her beauty even brittler. There would be no husband, no children.

A small part of Jemma took pity on them all.

She rose from her seat, sticking her hand out to her grandmother. "This is goodbye, then." And Honorine shook her hand as if they were employer and employee, which was how their relationship had started, after all. Jemma went around the table and repeated the action with the others, except Fosette, who rose out of her seat as she approached. Jemma stiffened, hoping and also not hoping for a hug from her cousin. And then she was wrapped in a quick embrace, Fosette whispering in her ear, "Laurence did love you, you know," and then it was over, Fosette back in her seat.

Jemma took them all in one last time, their upturned faces, their eyes not so much standing out as blending into their skin.

This was her family.

She walked out through the kitchen and stopped by the plot of land where Adam and six others were buried. Honorine had done what Jemma had told her to do. Instead of being a dirt patch, it was now covered with new sod, grass sprouting throughout. A line of lush pink rose bushes flanked the wall. Left alone, they'd grow tall enough to hide the unsightly stone parts sticking out. In front of the roses sat yellow daffodils and blue hyacinths. Bordering the patch were white tulips.

Jemma reached down and pulled one of the tulip stems free before taking one last look at the back of the house.

She made her way to the old slave cemetery and stopped by her father's grave. She knelt and laid the tulip on top of it.

"Thank you for saving me, Daddy. I won't be back here, but I'm carrying you with me. I wish you an eternity of peace."

THIRTY-FIVE

SEVERAL DAYS LATER, toward the end of March 1963, as protestors marched down the same streets floats had traveled weeks before, Magdalene helped Jemma pack several outfits inside a new suitcase. She'd spent the past couple of days buying clothes for the spring—although the shops here didn't stock the heavier jackets and sweaters she was used to—as well as a new handbag and shoes. Jemma had also paid a visit to Henry Marsbrook and told him about the bodies at the Duchons'. He reassured her that his grandfather had died at least a decade before the fire at the Duchon home and that he'd accepted he might never know the truth of what happened to his ancestor.

"How am I supposed to get in touch with you, to let you know where I am and how I'm doing? And to see how you are?" Jemma asked Magdalene, folding Inès's quilt on top of her clothes and fastening the straps holding her belongings inside. She gave everything a once-over before snapping the case shut.

"You send it to the post office with my name on it, I'll get it,"

Magdalene replied from her place at the counter. Her arms were folded across her chest, a small crease on her forehead.

Jemma straightened up and faced her friend. Magdalene felt more like family than any of the relatives she'd met here.

"You sure about this?" the woman asked. Jemma assumed Magdalene's doubt was the cause of her frown. "They could be anywhere."

Jemma nodded. "I have to try at least. My mother didn't want to leave here, not really, but I think . . . after being trapped here for so long and going through all she went through, when she was finally able to leave, she took the chance to do it. My brother is dead. She lost her oldest child. I can't judge her for her actions because of that. She wants a relationship with me. It just can't be here. There's too many bad memories for her to want to stay here."

Magdalene nodded, but she didn't look happy or relieved. Just resigned to what Jemma felt compelled to do.

"Besides, I have enough money to hire a private investigator, at least to get a head start on where they might have gone. After that . . ." Jemma shrugged. She had nothing to tell Magdalene about what she'd do after that because she still wasn't sure where she'd go. "If I come back here, it'll only be for you."

For the third time since Jemma had met her, Magdalene cried.

Then, after her friend had asked Jemma, several times, if she had everything and Jemma had assured her, several times, that she did, they hugged. Jemma cut it short, not wanting to cry any more than she already had, afraid that if she continued to cling to the other woman she might not leave.

"I ain't saying goodbye," Magdalene said, leaning against the doorframe as Jemma stood in front of the cabin, taking in the image for the last time. "I'm saying, ''Til next time.' "

" 'Til next time, then."

Jemma hoisted the suitcase in one hand and made her way

along the tree line until she was on the far side of the Duchon property. As she passed the house, she wondered whether any of her family might be staring out a window and watching her solitary trek.

Instead of wearing her new dress shoes, she wore canvas sneakers for the walk ahead, white shoes that would surely be dusty by the time she made it to the bus stop. Her head was covered with a blue scarf knotted below her chin, the best way she could camouflage a head of hair that needed a good, hard press. That would have to wait. She'd decided not to linger in New Orleans. She was headed for the train station. Once she got there, she'd decide where to go.

The bus spit Jemma out at a little past noon. Remembering that there would be no dining car for her, at least until she got out of this region of the country, she looked around for a place to eat.

Maybe she'd gotten used to the heat, because it didn't seem nearly as oppressive as it had when she'd arrived in New Orleans six months ago.

Jemma figured she'd gotten used to a lot of things.

As she settled herself in a café, she took a moment to get her bearings. Dennis's voice drifted through her mind: *Running is easy, until it ain't. How many times have you run from something?*

But now she was running toward something. Not leaving something behind, but stepping into her future, whatever it held.

The waitress slid a plate of fried chicken and mashed potatoes in front of Jemma, along with a glass of water. Jemma had grown tired of shrimp etouffee, baguettes, white rice, oysters and all the other small rotation of meals she'd eaten at the Duchons. Fried chicken sounded deliciously exotic.

Loud laughter made her turn her head just as she cut into the breast. A young couple sat at a round table to her right. The man wiped at his eyes with a handkerchief, a wide smile on his face.

He reminded Jemma of her brother.

She turned back to her food, not as hungry now as she had been just a few short moments ago. Still, she remembered that it might be a while before she had the chance to eat again, so she made herself enjoy the crispy greasiness of the chicken and the buttery fluffiness of the potatoes. When the waitress stopped by to ask how she was doing, Jemma asked for a cup of chicory.

She left a sizable tip before leaving for the train station. Unlike last year, she wore a dress appropriate for the climate, a plaid number with a roomy skirt and short sleeves. Her hands were bare, but she did have a cardigan draped over her shoulders.

At the train station, she bought a map and sat on a bench to study it. People swarmed around her, people alone and people with families. Jemma's gaze roamed over the map of the United States, instantly ruling out anywhere south of the Mason-Dixon Line. Still, Chicago was too full of ghosts, those of people and those that clouded her mind. She didn't want to step back into those memories, at least not yet.

Her gaze moved west. She wanted to go somewhere where she'd see no COLORED signs hanging in train cars or over water fountains. No nice bathrooms set aside for white people while her people had to use rundown shacks, if they had anything to use at all.

She'd thought of California once, land of beaches and sunshine. A balm to soothe all that needed soothing.

So Jemma bought a ticket to Los Angeles, giddy with the spontaneity of it.

"That train don't leave until eight o'clock tomorrow mornin'," the clerk said, his blue eyes big and round behind a pair of horn-rimmed glasses.

"Oh," Jemma said, surprised by the flicker of disappointment that arose in her. She'd have to wait overnight. And while she had plenty of money for a room, she didn't want to leave the station.

Her suitcase at her head, she slept on a bench, feeling stiff and achy but still excited for what lay ahead. She rested on top of her handbag; it was uncomfortable, but she had forty dollars in cash inside it, plus a cashier's check made out to herself, which she'd gotten from the bank when she closed her account.

The Jim Crow car, of course, wasn't a sleeper. The next morning, she crowded into the train with other passengers, most of whom looked like her, while a couple reminded her of the Duchons. She tried not to stare or feel too much pity for them.

After a long, hot couple of days, the COLORED signs were removed and Jemma upgraded to a sleeper car in New Mexico, enjoying the rest of her journey in comfort.

It was on her last night on the train, as she lay awake, watching the countryside zip past under the slowly darkening sky, that she saw something flicker out of the corner of her eye. Jemma looked, to see a young girl materialize in the aisle, her hair in two plaits with ribbons on the ends; she was wearing a white dress with a wide sash at the waist, the color striking a pleasing contrast to her deep brown skin.

Instead of counting to herself and focusing on her breathing, Jemma, resting her chin on her two fists, gazed down at the girl. The girl gazed solemnly up at her.

"How did you die?" Jemma asked.

The girl didn't answer right away, but eventually she spoke in a clear voice. Jemma knew that the spirit didn't speak more distinctly than the ones at the Duchons'. She hadn't been able to hear them clearly at first because she hadn't wanted to.

"Got runned over on the tracks."

"I'm sorry."

The girl shrugged. For the rest of her trip, the girl stayed put, even as the Pullman porters walked through her on their way up and down the train. Jemma asked her some questions. Sometimes she answered; other times she didn't.

It seemed that even spirits didn't want to answer everything. Or maybe they couldn't.

"Los Angeles, California, next stop! Next stop, Los Angeles!" a porter called in a loud voice.

Jemma gathered her belongings. Looking out the window, she saw nothing but blue skies.

Before she left the car, Jemma made sure everyone else was gone, then turned to the girl.

"What's your name?"

"Dottie."

"Nice to meet you, Dottie. I'm Emmaline Duchon."

Acknowledgments

First and foremost, thank you, God, for the gift of writing.

Thank you, Mom and Dad, for your constant support, love and guidance.

To Asia, Kenneth and Christopher, thank you for giving me the gift of being your mom (same to my bonus kids, Stephen and Sean!).

To all the family whose support and love has never wavered: every single one of the Robersons, Kims and Sandeens, the Perrys, Macks and other extended family members. David, thank you for never saying "You can't."

Thank you to Jim McCarthy at Dystel, Goderich & Bourret, agent extraordinaire and all-around awesome human being.

Thank you to my brilliant editor, Anne Sowards, who helped me take a messy manuscript and turn it into an actual book. Thank you to Berkley for the Open Submission Program, which got my manuscript into Anne's hands to begin with. More thanks to the Berkley team, including the copy editors and designers, who transformed some typed words on a lot of pages into something beautiful.

And a huge round of thanks goes to the following people I'm blessed to know:

Yas, you the real MVP, my ride-or-die, my sister-friend. You've listened and advised, commiserated and consoled. And through it all, made me laugh and laugh. Connecting with you was like finding a priceless treasure.

Alaysia, who's always down to chat, brainstorm, give feedback, and is everything a good friend should be.

Jess M., who believed when I didn't. You heard this germ of an idea and told me that this was the one. And guess what, Sis: you were right. Your encouragement and support are invaluable. You are an absolute jewel, and I couldn't be prouder to call you a friend.

Esteban, a fantastic cheerleader and wonderful supporter. What if, indeed. Keep shining, bright star.

Julia, who did it first. Thanks for listening, praying, virtual hand-holding and wisdom sharing.

Leah, who truly understands friendship. Rock on, Metaphysical Soul Sister.

Tanya, for the reconnection and the laughter, the lunches and the dinners. Shalom, girlfriend.

Kawana, for all the meals, the laughs, the listening.

For Gerrie, Bharat, and Jolie—you are all amazing writers, and I'm so honored to know you.

There are a lot of other people who've inspired and helped me, too many to list here. Just know that I'm incredibly thankful to have you in my life.

And to the reader, I'm very grateful you're here.